THE PRODUCER

Aaron

ERIKA VANZIN

Want to get more FREE from Erika?

Sign up for the author's New Releases mailing list and get the first ten chapter of "Backstage." You will periodically receive free short stories and unique chapters.

Click here to get started:
https://www.erikavanzin.com/newsletter.html

To my mother.

CHAPTER 1
Aaron

The chairs in the meeting room are uncomfortable, especially if you sit there for eight hours straight. It is difficult to work in the fast-paced Hollywood world. To do it with back pain that torments you for days doesn't make it easier. *I must remember to tell Tracy to add office renovation to the budget.*

"We can add a supernatural element." Jacob Lautner's voice brings my attention back to the fifteen people in front of me.

The emergency meeting I called last night is not going as I expected. When my father stormed into my office and slammed the paper with the audience ratings of the last episode of *Sweet River* on my desk, the lowest in the history of the broadcaster, I had no choice but to summon everyone this morning.

My father threatened if I didn't shut down the show, he might reconsider my position as head of the streaming project. Considering that he is the owner of the largest and oldest broadcasting company in the United States and he thinks the streaming division is a whim I'm obsessed with, I believe him.

It's always like this with him. He wants me to sit on the throne of his empire once he retires, as he did with my grandfather, but he never gives me the reins of anything. My every decision is subject to his opinion. If my idea doesn't suit him, he forces his hand to direct my project where he wants.

This continuous power struggle has been going on since I was twenty, and I began to follow him in his work. I'm thirty-six now, but nothing's changed. He still treats me like that inexperienced kid who can't make decisions. If I didn't love this job madly, I think I would have punched him and left by now. Indeed, if I changed companies, I would undoubtedly occupy a better position than the one I'm in now.

My father keeps me here as a producer, even though we are all aware this is not what I am. I am the head of an entire division, not a simple producer of the shows we air, but this is my father's way of holding me in the palm of his hand. He wants me to be conscious I am nobody compared to him.

"We could introduce a shapeshifter or vampires. Or fairies. Teenagers are crazy about fairies right now," Jacob continues with his ideas.

One of the young interns can't hold back a half-laugh that he badly disguises with a cough. Jacob Lautner is one of the decisions my father forced me to make. He's one of the old-school screenwriters he likes so much and forced me to hire as head of writers when I needed funds to start the *Sweet River* show. He doesn't have the faintest idea of what it means to write for the new generations, and the historic low ratings are a clear example of this.

"*Sweet River* is an old-school teen drama. We chose a very specific path, dealing with topics such as drugs and alcoholism among teenagers, taking a position on the matter. You want to put vampires in it? Are you kidding me?" Sarah Weber, one of the producers of the series, snarls.

I'm glad to have her on board with this project because, in moments like these, I would fire on the spot another of my employees who without a doubt does not know how to do this job. I always respect her ability to impose herself on decisions in an industry like Hollywood, where women are often considered only beautiful faces.

"Not to mention that our flagship show, *Hunters of Shadows*, is based on the supernatural, and you'd be going to compete with it," I say.

They all turn to me with wide, terrified eyes. We've been sitting here for eight hours trying to find a solution to save a beautiful show with important themes that's sinking faster than the Titanic. It's a project close to my heart, and I would like to see it come to a second season.

"It was just an idea," Jacob mutters.

The truth is he has no valuable suggestions on what to do. I turn to the guy struggling to hold back laughter and nail him to the chair with one glance. His hazel eyes are huge and terrified.

"You. You don't think the supernatural is a good suggestion. Do you have any ideas about the show?" I ask him amid the surreal silence in the room.

"He's an intern! What could he suggest?" says Jacob, raising his voice, upset.

I turn to him, and every protest dies on his lips at once. I'm known in this company as *The Butcher*. I have fired people for much less. I don't care if my father worships him. If this show shuts down, he will find himself out of work.

I glance back at the intern who, in the meantime, has paled even more. "I want your sincere opinion. No bullshit. There are no right or wrong answers. You've been here since the beginning of production. In your opinion, what does it take to make a change in this show?"

He gazes around disoriented and then focuses on the notebook in front of him. I wonder if something is written on it or if he is trying to come up with some ideas on the fly.

"In my opinion, the protagonist's girlfriend should kiss his best friend. Or rather, the best friend should follow the momentum and kiss her." His voice trembles, but it is loud enough to hear his words clearly.

"She's a good girl, a goody-two-shoes. It's entirely out of character," says Jacob, outraged.

I turn to the head of the writers, and I glare at him. He clenches his jaw, but I notice he would like to insult me in every language. I hope he chokes on those insults. It would save me a lot of headaches.

"Explain yourself," I order the intern.

"She is too perfect. She's boring. She is the one who is adored by her boyfriend's parents. They see them practically married with a family, but she is also the one who always goes to save his best friend whenever he makes a mess. So far, she's done it because she wants to avoid upsetting her boyfriend, but what if it were not so?"

I lean back in my chair and cross my arms. It's the first time since we got here that we're going in a direction that could turn the show around.

"Go ahead," Sarah urges him to continue.

"When they are all three together, they have fun, are in harmony, and experience a deep bond. But what if the friend feels something more toward his best friend's girlfriend and guilt strangles him? It could be a drunken kiss when she goes to bail him out of jail after yet another fight. But it must upset her. It must shatter all her certainties, make her less *flawless*," he adds more decisively.

Sarah turns to me with a smile on her face.

"His alcoholism problems could be related to the abusive family and the guilt of being in love with his best friend's girlfriend. After all, the couple is the only real family he's got, and his betrayal would ruin it irreparably," she adds, following the intern's train of thought.

The weight I've had in my chest all day lifts. I stand and put on the jacket I took off hours ago when I realized it wouldn't be a quick meeting.

"Keep working on this idea. I want the episodes written by this weekend," I order Jacob, who is smoking with anger. "Hire the kid and make sure he has a say," I tell Sarah as I walk to the door.

"Of course, boss." She winks and nods.

I leave the conference room tired, and when I finally arrive in the parking lot and get in the car, I allow myself to untie my tie's knot.

***

The club's sauna is almost empty right now. The large circular room can accommodate about twenty people, but only four familiar faces are sitting sweating with me. Raphael Wyden, who is running for a senator seat. Harrison Bates, an Oscar-winning Hollywood actor worshipped by hordes of screaming fans and, damn him, hasn't starred in one of my productions yet. Leonard Walton, a billionaire who founded so many companies in his twenties I lost count. And then there is Sady, the tatted chef whose real name is still unknown to the public, but since he opened *The Jail*, the most famous restaurant in LA, he's rose to stardom. Eyes closed, towels tied at our waists, no one speaks, but everyone is attentive to who enters and leaves this place.

For all intents and purposes, the Hunting Club of Los Angeles is a hunting club. One of those places registered as a sports association that unleashes the ire of environmentalists, more than anything in a city like this, where respect for the environment and animals is almost a cult. The thing I like most about this place is that none of us has ever picked up a rifle or any weapon in our entire lives—that I know of anyway. We are not hunters. It's the perfect cover for a private all-male club where only the richest and most influential can be a part of by invitation.

No one approaches this place, thinking it is a den of bloody cavemen. Because of this, it is perfect for establishing relationships with people who value the discretion of conversations. And if someone shows up to sign up for a hunting trip, we decline with a polite "we'll let you know."

Sweat drips down my face, and I finally begin to relax when the door opens, letting some light filter through an otherwise dim place. The sound of heels stepping firmly on the floor makes me open my eyes. Only when she is in front of me, do I realize the figure I'm struggling to recognize is Tracy, and she is halfway between furious and bored. Her long hair descends on a shoulder in a low braid, softening her face a little.

"What the hell is she doing in here?" Raphael, sitting a few feet away, gives voice to the thoughts of all those present.

"Tracy, what are you doing here? And above all, how the hell did you get in?" There is a counter along the entrance of this place with a person checking everyone twenty-four hours a day, seven days a week.

My assistant doesn't even sweat about my tone.

"I told the mannequin at reception that they were towing your cars, and he immediately rushed out to check," she explains with such naturalness that it makes me smile.

I chose her precisely because nothing stops her. If I ask her to bring me the moon, she asks me when I need it. A counter and a polite little boy certainly doesn't scare her.

"Can we have some privacy?" one of the men complains, annoyed.

Tracy turns to him slowly, like a predator before the attack. "Sweetheart, don't worry. I'm a lesbian. Your virtue is safe with me."

I smile at her uninterested attitude and stand to walk out. Outside, I scan around to find a private place where we can talk since I only wear a towel. The problem is that this place is not designed for women. Everywhere you turn, half-naked men are coming out of the pool, sweaty after being in the gym, or high at the bar counter of the club. There is a reason why women are not allowed: men here can allow themselves to relax without having to maintain the appearance being a public figure requires of us.

"Don't worry about finding a place to talk. It's fine here."

"Can you explain what you're doing here? Couldn't you send me an email?" If she came all the way from the office to Beverly Hills in the middle of late afternoon traffic, it must be something urgent.

"It's Dakota," she sighs.

My stomach writhes in a nervous spasm. Dakota Anderson is Hollywood's rising star and the leading actress in our most successful show, *Hunters of Shadows,* where she plays the part of a supernatural hunter trying to save the world from demons and vampires. She is also a thorn in my side.

"Please, not again. Not when I'm sweaty and with a towel tied at my waist," I implore her as I lean against the wall behind me.

Tracy lifts a corner of her mouth, unable to hold back a smile. She is aware of how much it bothers me to be caught off guard when I can't hide behind my tailored suit and the cold expression of *The Butcher.*

"The whole PR office is waiting for you at the studios. The paparazzi caught her drunk again at a pool party this afternoon with tits half out. It's all over the gossip sites." She gives me the news with the funeral tone of a doctor who announces the patient's death to the family.

Dakota is a brilliant leading woman, one of the best of her generation. She is twenty-three, young and wild, and loved by the public, who almost idolizes her, but has a considerable problem with alcohol. And the newspapers have a field day with something like this.

"Can you see her nipples?" Something like that could force me to shut down the show and fire her.

In the golden world of Hollywood, you can kill someone by driving drunk and walk away with it, but if you show a nipple in public, your career is over.

"No, but I think it's the least of your problems at this point."

She glances at me, trying to weigh my reaction.

I inhale deeply and try to calm the desire to go and pick up the girl and shake her until she starts to act like an adult.

"Give me time to shower, and I'll see you there." I shake my head and walk down the corridor.

"Hurry up. They are on the warpath." The pity smile on her face makes me understand how critical the situation is.

* * *

When I enter the office, I find Tracy, four PRs, and two assistants. Their faces are so severe that it really looks like someone died. They don't say anything, they just turn the laptop sitting in front of them toward me, and a video of Dakota, drunk and unstable on her feet, appears in front of me.

She wears a red micro-bikini that stands out like an eyesore against her pale skin and blond hair holding a bottle of vodka. She comes across the screen as she is taking a sip and, despite seeing a mile away she is wasted, she is sexy to die for. Too sexy for a young audience like the one that follows the show.

I slump on the chair in front of the desk and lean on the backrest. We had this conversation so many times that I have no more words to describe the situation.

"How pressing is it?" I ask when no one dares to talk.

It is Sharon who nails me on the spot with her gaze. "Enough to think about firing her and doing a recasting."

I wouldn't be surprised if she punched me.

"She is the show's protagonist with a renewed fourth season! We might as well shut down the production. It's ridiculous to replace the protagonist after the pilot. After three seasons, it's suicide," I burst out, raising my voice.

Sharon sits at the desk in front of me. Her long legs wrapped in a pair of elegant pants are within reach to kick me in the face. I think this time, she could do it for real. Her colleagues seem to be holding their breath while Tracy approaches my chair, perhaps ready to intervene if the situation should degenerate.

"Aaron, the girl is out of control. You knew taking an inexperienced kid on board for such an important project was risky, but you wanted her anyway. It's time to cut her off," Sharon tells me more calmly than her eyes let shine through.

When we did the casting, we opened it to the public. We sifted through hundreds of girls and when the choice was between two, a famous star and Dakota, the casting director asked for my opinion.

Dakota was perfect in every respect, but it was also her first experience in Hollywood. The risk of her being unprofessional was high, mostly because she was only twenty. She turned out to be a smart girl, able to learn and manage her work perfectly. Her only problem is she can't keep her private life separate from her professional. The excesses and the wild parties are on all the front pages of the newspapers.

"Where the hell was the assistant we hired to live with her? We pay a person to stick to her all day to keep her out of trouble. Where the hell was she this afternoon?" I cling to anything to avoid making the decision that I already know will blow up the entire show.

We all turn to Tracy, whose face tells me she would rather swallow a live toad than give me the news.

"She resigned a few days ago. She found a better job than babysitting. I can't blame her, she's a great production assistant, and she can't take care of Dakota her entire life."

"Awesome," I whisper as I rub my hand across my face.

"Aaron, we can try to turn the news in our favor, but we can't think of going on like this. If she doesn't put her wits together, she'll become a problem to the show and the company. You must consider replacing her or having the writers write her exit from the show." Sharon's voice is calm but resolute.

I look up at her. "The exit of the protagonist of the show? She is twenty-three. Why do they continue torturing her with it?"

"Because people are tired of seeing Hollywood stars get drunk and high causing a scene and getting away with it every time. So they focus on those who are repeat offenders. It's not that others don't do it. It's that they know how to hide it better. It seems her mission to get caught in these situations." Sharon points out what I already know.

I'm not an idiot, just that sometimes I wish the paparazzi would forget about her.

"A recasting could be the solution. We have a list of actresses that could replace her." The trembling voice of one of the PRs, whose name I do not remember, makes me stare at him.

His face is hopeful, and he has a folder full of photos of actresses who could replace her.

"You're fired."

"But…" he tries to object.

"Instead of doing your PR job, you're doing the casting director's job. Since you don't know the difference, lift your ass off that stool and get out of this room."

Pale as a rag, he walks out of the door, closing it behind him without making a noise.

I glare back at Sharon. "I'm not joking about his dismissal."

"And I'm not joking about firing Dakota," she counters.

"What if we made one last attempt by sending her to live with someone who could keep an eye on her?" Tracy proposes, trying to mitigate the situation that is becoming increasingly tense.

I turn to her, trying to figure out if she is serious or just trying to throw a hook for a compromise. Forcing Dakota to live with the assistant did not solve our problems. It mitigated them but didn't solve them.

"And who do you have in mind?" I ask when I see a half-smile on her face.

"You."

The silence that falls into the room lasts an eternity. I'm waiting for her to tell me she is joking, but her lips remain sealed.

"Have you gone crazy?" I burst out when no one admits this is the worst idea ever proposed.

Tracy rolls her eyes, as she usually does with her insolent attitude that I like when it is aimed at someone else, but it makes me lose my temper when it is turned to me.

"Before you freak out, try to think about it. In six months, the third season will be over, there will be a long pause where she disappears for some exotic vacation, and we hope the newspapers will no longer cry scandal when she comes back. In the meantime, she stays with you. You are the boss of her boss's boss, she will be intimidated, and she will hold back. Impose rules and you will see that she will not be able to say no to you. She is smart. She recognizes that you hold the power to ruin her career. If she flies below the radar for six months, they will forget her wild days. At the end of the day, this is Hollywood, nothing last more than a few weeks, not even marriages last so long here." Her enthusiastic tone irritates me.

"What if someone discovers it? They will assume I'm sleeping with her. Don't you think it's a bit inappropriate?" I ask incredulously.

Tracy looks at Sharon who thinks about it.

"We ask her to keep it quiet. She is the only one who can spill the beans. Everyone around you has already signed a non-disclosure agreement to work with you. Nobody enters and exits your house without signing it. It's six months, you can keep it quiet for six months."

"But what if this comes out?" I insist.

"We will work on a reasonable justification for that. We will be prepared if it happens," Sharon adds.

I think about it, and I can't shake the feeling this is a bad, bad idea.

"No. I'm used to my home, to my spaces. I don't want to share them with a twenty-three-year-old. It's not a frat house!" Although from a certain point of view, she is right. When I met Dakota in person, she always treated me with great respect and seemed intimidated by my presence. Surely if I order her to do something, she'd do it.

"You are a cynical and antisocial thirty-six-year-old who hates people," Tracy replies.

"That's not true! I'm all day among people. I just need peace when I get home. I want to walk around in my underwear without feeling compelled to cover myself because someone lives under the same roof." I cling to any excuse because I know this might be the last resort not to make more drastic decisions. We really need this show and the money it brings into our division.

"Do you often walk around the house in your underwear?" She raises an eyebrow in defiance because she knows me well enough to know that I don't even leave my room without being dressed.

"You live in such a huge mansion. There is a reasonable possibility that you will never run into her. And then, it does you good to have some company. When was the last time you conversed with someone for the sheer pleasure of doing so?"

"I speak every day with dozens of people!"

"I'm not talking about your job or the club where you take refuge with other hermits. I'm talking about a real outing with someone you don't give orders to or contract a deal," she says, emphasizing my inability to cultivate a social life.

"I'm a man busy managing millions of dollars. I don't have time to go out and waste time on completely irrelevant activities."

"Put it this way, if she doesn't come to live with you, you'll deal with the loss of millions of dollars shutting down the show." She throws her final punch, leaving me with no argument to counter.

Do I really go so far as to babysit a young woman? From a certain point of view, Tracy is right, because closing our most crucial show means giving a win to my father, who sees me as an amateur. I'm not used to throwing in the towel, especially when the show is a success, and giving it up because of a person who can't control herself is ridiculous.

On the one hand, she is an intelligent, attentive, scrupulous professional like most consummate actresses. On the other hand, when she leaves the set, she turns into another person. I want to understand what drives her to behave this way.

"Okay. Six months and then I want her out of my house."

CHAPTER 2
Dakota

The headache hammering my brain is unbearable, but the rancid taste in my mouth is the worst part after I called an Uber from the party at Lionel's house this afternoon. I didn't even want to go to that pool party, but people from the studio invited me, and I didn't want to play the part of the haughty actress. If I keep turning down their invitations, I will look like someone who doesn't stoop to hang out with those who work with her day and night on set. I felt almost compelled, and in the end, I gave in, knowing that I would feel embarrassed if I didn't.

I shouldn't have to start with Jelly shots or continue with tequila and drinking vodka from the bottle to try to relax. But at the time, it seemed like a good idea to get rid of the taste of nervous anxiety on my lips. And then I felt euphoric, invincible, and sexy. Everyone was smiling at me, and there weren't those awkward conversations that crowd my social life when I'm sober.

The cold surface under my cheek forces me to open my eyes and I recognize the toilet bowl in my bathroom on which I am resting my face. I remember running in here to vomit, but I don't remember falling asleep.

"What a crap," my hoarse voice resonates between the bathroom walls, so low that I can hardly recognize it.

"Yes, I would say it just sucks."

I turn my head toward the door and find Tracy, the big boss's assistant, studying me with a disgusted look on her face and her arms crossed at her chest. If it weren't for the fact her presence here means trouble, I would be annoyed by how she is judging me, as if she's never had a social life.

"What the hell are you doing here? And how did you get in?" I ask her, trying to get up despite my head spinning, my stomach twisting, and my legs almost collapsing underneath me.

"Ady left the keys in the office when she resigned and emptied her room," she tells me without moving a muscle to help me stand. Not that I need her help, but she could at least make sure I don't end up lying on the ground like a sack of potatoes instead of standing there looking at me as if I were a worm trying to crawl out of the mud.

I look into the mirror, and the view appearing in front of me is almost gruesome. I'm pale enough to look dead, and my eyes are injected with blood. But the thing that makes me shudder is the sight of my red bikini. I got dressed before I got home, right? Or did I leave Lionel's house with only this on?

The thought escapes my mind as soon as Tracy's words make their way into my foggy brain.

"Ady left? When? Why?" The questions come out one after another, but the woman's face doesn't reveal an answer.

I never put up with Ady, not so much because she was a bad person but because she lived in this house just to keep an eye on me. Like a babysitter for a little girl who doesn't know how to take care of herself. The studio forced me to take her in as my mother hen because of my inexperience here in Hollywood, and you could see a mile away she hated me. But in a way, I had become accustomed to her cumbersome presence.

Tracy watches me as I try to figure out what the hell is going on. Her pity smile makes me angry, as few things can do, but I remain silent. This woman scares me.

"She was tired of being the babysitter to a problematic toddler. A few days ago, she resigned and came to take away her stuff, but you didn't even notice it, did you? Too busy getting drunk to realize that half of the apartment is empty. However, I don't blame her. She was wasted being the babysitter of an actress with a diva complex."

Her words stab straight into my chest. I have never been a diva, and my private life has never interfered with my work. What I do in my spare time should not interest anyone but me. The problem is that everyone seems obsessed with my private life, especially the paparazzi, who can't wait to find some outrageous photos to go viral. I didn't notice Ady had left because I was too busy working on set sixteen hours per day.

"How serious is the situation?" If she is here, the photos are at least embarrassing, if not worse.

"Enough to think about firing you."

I snap my attention toward her, and the dizziness almost makes me end up on the floor. My heart pumps into my chest, but I'm not sure if it's because of the alcohol or the news she just dropped. Did she come here to fire me? Now I can explain the presence of Aaron Steel's assistant. I am sure that the sense of nausea that grips my stomach is not only because of the alcohol. I love this job, and the very thought of being fired is enough to make me vomit.

"They haven't kicked you out." The terror must be evident on my face because her tone becomes almost sweet. "But consider this as the last warning. The next bullshit stunt, you're out."

I nod and inhale thoroughly. The mixture of relief and nausea that overlaps in my stomach is enough to make me cling to the sink to not end up lying on the floor.

"Take a shower and pack a bag for tonight. Tomorrow someone will come and get your stuff to take it to your new accommodation," she orders, and, once again, I find myself confused.

"New accommodation? I have a lease for this apartment until the end of the year," I say, stunned by the news she is dumping on me.

"That will be taken care of by the studio. Until you finish filming the third season in six months, you'll live in Aaron Steel's house," she announces, as if she were offering me a vacation in a maximum-security prison.

I feel the blood leaving my face.

"I beg your pardon?"

She smiles at me. "You got it right. You will live with the big boss. He'll take care of you when you vomit lying drunk in his bathroom."

The anger that grows inside me is violent.

"You decided my life without saying anything to me? What if I don't want to go to live with *The Butcher*? Has it never occurred to you that I might have something to say about this agreement?"

Tracy looks at me with a half-smile, perhaps because of the

nickname I used for her boss, then shakes her head.

"Of course, we thought about your opinion. In fact, you have two choices: live with him and act like an adult or be fired. You royally messed up, and we found a way to save your ass. We thought you would prefer the first solution."

I am so furious that I have no words to retort.

"Are you blackmailing me?" My voice comes out shrill and petulant like a toddler throwing a tantrum, and I immediately regret my lack of control. I'm not like that. I don't get caught up in my emotions and react over the top.

Tracy nails me with a stern look.

"We're giving you the chance to save your career because you're incapable of making mature decisions. You are free to leave whenever you want, you are not under arrest, but this involves losing your job. No one forces you to do anything, let alone live with someone you don't want, but every decision has consequences, and, trust me, you have screwed up all the second chances you got until now with this stunt."

Her words make me feel small and inadequate. I know I've been wrong many times, know I ended up on the front pages of the magazines for my lack of willpower, but that doesn't mean her words hurt any less. Because it's true. They have given me many chances to act like an adult, but I constantly let them down.

Every time I come home drunk, I promise myself that it will be the last, that next time I will not give in to the temptation to "loosen up a little." Then Serena convinces me to go out, or she comes with me to the parties like today, and I find myself in front of her exuberance, her ability to converse with everyone without appearing like an idiot, and I feel inadequate. If a shot helps to loosen my tongue it's not the end of the world, but afterward, I find myself wasted without even realizing it.

"Take a shower. You stink," she adds before leaving the room and disappearing down the hallway.

I look in the mirror again, and my cheeks flare with shame. I am wasted, pale like a rag, and my hair is plastered with what looks like vomit. I slip into the shower and let the water wash away the dirt, but nothing can take away the scorching humiliation that has fallen on me. Thinking about the shame my mother will endure reading those magazines makes my new living arrangements looks like a fair punishment.

***

When Tracy told me to pack a bag for tonight, I didn't immediately realize she meant to take me to the man with my future in his hands right away. She didn't even leave me time to dry my hair or eat something to absorb the alcohol I ingested during the afternoon. The winding road that takes me to the most famous hills in the world with the villas and their wealthy inhabitants doesn't help to keep my stomach worn out by vodka and nervousness at bay. When I get out of the car, it is almost a liberation to be able to put my feet on the ground.

I stare at the villa in front of me. I've often seen pictures of this place in architectural magazines as one of the trendiest homes of the last decade, but those photos don't do justice to this beauty. The angular lines of reinforced concrete and stained glass disappear, merging with the hill on which it is built. It gives you the impression that the earth has given birth to this appendix that integrates with the arid soil surrounding it. Its flowerbeds are dotted with shrubs that appear to have survived centuries of drought and heat in a city like Los Angeles.

It is a house that gives me the idea of solidity and robustness, almost a modern fortress suitable for hosting *The Butcher*. It suits the personality of its owner, a man so powerful, he has set the terms among the sharks ruling Hollywood.

"It could have been worse" A knowing smile appears on Tracy's lips.

The woman doesn't wait for my answer but strides toward the front door pulling out a bunch of keys from her bag. Through the heavy glass that separates us from the inside, I can see the open plan of the living room overlooking the windows, the pool, and the view of downtown. It's baffling how only a few people in this city of millions can enjoy a breathtaking view like this.

The house we enter is bright, made of white marble floors and matching color furniture overlooking a modern open kitchen with three sets of sliding doors that take you onto the pool and the garden. I look up at the ceiling and the glass railing of the stairs leading to the gallery upstairs, where I glimpse some paintings I recognize from the art textbooks I studied in high school. I'm not an expert on whether they're authentic, but they don't seem like those dollar prints found in museum souvenir shops.

"Here she is. Now the problem is yours." Tracy's voice brings me back to reality, and when I look down, I notice the imposing figure of Aaron Steel leaning against the marble counter of the immaculate kitchen. Dressed in his dark gray suit that seems sewn on him, he looks even more intimidating than the few times I met him in the corridors of the studios.

His gray eyes rest on my face. His impassive expression doesn't let any emotion shine through. I am so confused by his look that he may be about to scold me, spank me, or even choke me and bury my corpse in the garden and I wouldn't realize what is happening.

"Thank you, Tracy. You can go," he dismisses her with his authoritarian tone without taking his eyes from my face.

I sense the assistant moving next to me, and I hear the ticking of her heels on the white marble walking away until it disappears behind the front door, but I can't look away from the man in front of me.

Aaron Steel exudes power, authority, and dominance. When he chains you to his gaze, the only thing you can do is breathe, making as little noise as possible. I feel my legs tremble, my hands clutch in a painful grip around the handle of the bag that holds my clothes, and my stomach tightens in a grip I don't like. To say that I am nervous is an understatement. When I followed Tracy up here, I knew it would be an embarrassing encounter, but I didn't realize how much. How can I share a house with a man who makes me tremble simply by looking at me?

"The rules as long as you live in this house are very simple: no parties, no hangovers, no loud music. If you spill something, you clean it. I don't want to find your stuff tossed around. The rooms you are granted are your bedroom with the en suite bathroom, the living area–excluding my office–and the pool. A driver of mine will take you to the set every morning and pick you up to take you here in the evening. If you stay out in the evening, I demand to be warned. I'm not waiting for you until morning to turn the alarm back on, so come back at a decent time, or don't come back at all. If you have any particular food preferences, leave a list on the counter, and I'll let the house-keeper know to buy it. Do you understand?"

His voice is so authoritarian that it makes this whole ac-commodation look like a beautiful prison in Hollywood Hills. The anger that boils inside me in front of the arrogance he uses to rattle off his rules makes me forget that he is my boss. In-deed, he is the boss of my boss. He's so high up the food chain I look like a goldfish by comparison. This, however, doesn't dampen my fury. On the contrary, it feeds it.

"Am I allowed the one hour outside, or do I only get forced labor?" I blurt out without restraint. My voice comes out firm-er than I expected, and the question seems to catch him by surprise. I feel my cheeks going up in flames. This is my boss, I shouldn't say everything that crosses my mind out loud, but I'm not famous for handling my conversations well.

His eyebrows barely rise; it is the only reaction I can pull from him, but it is enough for me to understand that he is not used to someone who speaks her mind.

"Let's make one thing clear right away. This is my house. You are my guest. These are the rules. If they don't suit you, you can always leave." His tone is threatening, and when he approaches with his imposing body, the anger almost disap-pears, giving way to shyness. Almost.

I look up at him and nail him in place. "I'm here because your show shuts down without me, and we both know it's your best show. I'm not a stupid little girl who destroys your house, and I demand the same respect you ask from me." Maybe this time, I crossed the line.

I hold my breath, sure the stretched silence is because he will fire me. While I have always been awkward in talking to my peers, growing up in an adults-only home has forged me from a young age to deal with people way older than me. In fact, I'm more comfortable standing up to my boss than flirting with the cute guy at a party. With Aaron, I know how to handle the situation. Maybe I'm a bit too straightforward, but at least he is someone I can reason with.

"I'll show you your room." It is his only reaction after an extenuating silence, and I watch him as he walks away with his regal bearing toward the massive staircase that leads upstairs.

I sigh in relief when he shows me a room with a queen size bed in light tones and a window overlooking the pool instead of kicking me out of the house.

***

It's been two hours since I locked myself in my room and hung the few things I took with me in the empty walk-in closet. No noise comes from outside. There is no one in the garden or pool, and I wonder if there is anyone in this house. The silence is so oppressive it makes me almost melancholy. At least in the apartment where I lived since this afternoon, traffic noise kept me company in the evenings when I was locked up at home reading.

Alcohol is giving me some peace, and the hangover is almost gone. The problem is that now hunger is making my stomach grumble. I wonder if *Mr. I-make-the-rules* even set up the alarm at the refrigerator. I open the door slowly, making no noise, and peek down the dark hallway, almost expecting to find him in front of me with his gray suit wrapping him like a glove and a gun in his hand to ensure I'm not going anywhere. But the house seems deserted, and I wonder if he went out. The more I think about this situation, the stranger I find that someone like Aaron Steel decided to babysit me for six months. I feel a little guilty. I haven't seen the photos yet, but they must be awful to push him into considering such a drastic solution.

I retrace the steps to the kitchen and open the fridge, searching for something to eat. I have no idea if there is anything for me, but he can't think of keeping me in this cage without feeding me. I find a plate of fruit cut into pieces and grab it without a second thought, then open the kitchen cabinets until I find a glass and pour myself some orange juice. I look at the counter in the dim light and feel the melancholy making its way into my chest without being able to stop it. This house may be a palace, but it's as cold as one of those you see in the magazines. No one really lives here.

I grab the plate and the glass and walk out on the patio, sitting on one of the deck chairs around the pool, illuminated by the lights strategically placed in the water. I grab my phone, and for the first time, I find myself scrolling through the photos that portray me wasted by another pool just a few hours ago. They are photos that do not represent me, yet that is me, immortalized in one of the worst moments of my existence and shared so that the whole world can have an opinion about me.

I grab one of the strawberries on the plate, put it to my lips, accentuating the pout that mother nature has gifted me, and look straight into the camera lens of the phone as I have been doing for years. By now, I know every pose, every angle that enhances my strengths and hides my flaws. I show off my innocent but at the same time flirty look that makes me look sexy but never gross. I practiced it for months until it became natural, and I didn't need to be in front of a mirror to strike the flawless pose. I have the complete feel of every single muscle of my face, the proper inclination of the head, and how much to open my lips memorized. If you want to work in Hollywood, this is what is required of you: perfection and an image to project to the public.

I just need one shot, the suitable filters, and the perfect caption under the photo, *Do I really look drunk? #fakenews,* to give my version of the facts on my Instagram profile. There will undoubtedly be videos to deny this photo but not saying anything, passively accepting the crusade against me makes me angry. I built this career sweating every day on set. I will not allow junk magazines to sink it.

Not even five minutes have passed since my post, and the sliding door of the living room opens with a dull thud when it slams into the jamb. Aaron's imposing figure appears to probe every inch of the pool until he finds me lying on one of the deck chairs. He is as furious as I have ever seen him, light years from the impassive mask he is used to wearing.

He wears a black tank top, gray sweatpants, and sneakers. He is sweaty, clearly just out of a gym or back from a run. The dark curls are messy on his head as if he had just passed his fingers through it. If I thought that dressed in an elegant suit he was sexy to die for, seeing his sweaty muscles and the light fabric of the tank top stuck to his sculpted body makes me breathless. I haven't seen a more handsome man in my life. Not even the actors around me every day can compete with this vision.

I look at him, embarrassed, as he furiously approaches and tears my phone from my hand.

"Hey! Can't I even have my phone? Will you send me to bed without dinner?" I complain, annoyed. Gone is my drooling over him.

Aaron lowers himself just enough to look me straight in the eyes.

"Photos and videos show you were drunk this afternoon, but the PRs managed to turn the story around to mitigate the consequences. Do you know what your post means? That frustrates the work of six people who tried to save your ass," he hisses so angrily that every protest dies on my lips.

I didn't know that anyone had already solved the problem. I was so angry with the paparazzi that I didn't check the other news. I feel guilty because I should have checked more carefully instead of focusing on the pictures. I'm so tired of all this attention surrounding me, I completely forgot that if I'm here it's because an entire team is working overtime to fix my mistakes. I wasn't raised to take for granted what other people do for me, and I feel the embarrassment heat my cheeks.

"If you want, I'll delete it," I whisper when he gets up to go back inside with my phone in his hand.

"It's too late. It has already been reposted by gossip sites. You have a bounty on your head, Dakota. Do you really want to ruin your career by behaving like a rebellious teenager?" he asks before turning around without even waiting for my answer.

I look at his back, illuminated by the pool's lights, and I notice black drawings covering the skin on his shoulders. A tattoo. I can't identify the shape, but it's clearly ink. I pause to study this man until he disappears into the living room, perfect in appearance but hiding secrets under the starched shirts and ties that suffocate him. A man who clearly loves his space and doesn't want to share it but who takes me into his house after my umpteenth bullshit. He is composed and impassive in public but almost animalistic when he gets angry in private. A living contradiction that leaves me disoriented.

CHAPTER 3
Aaron

I watch my father sitting in the armchair in front of my desk. Impeccable in his tailored suit, dark hair like mine, same ice-gray shade of eye color. We are so physically similar that it almost annoys me. Because about everything else, we are at opposite poles. He is one of those old-fashioned entrepreneurs who love to feast on the carcass of the weak to gain more and more power. Nothing and no one is as essential as his empire, not even his sons. You only have to look at how he cut out my brother Evan when he decided to follow his passion for music instead of slipping into the murky waters of the family business to understand how much he loves us.

It takes a tremendous effort to keep my face bored while he scrutinizes me with his reproachful look. He walked in here without even knocking, interrupting a call for which he didn't even have the decency to apologize. I will not give in to asking him why he felt the need to enter here like fury.

"Have you read the newspapers recently?"

His voice is calm and composed, his posture relaxed, and his expression completely impassive. But he is my father. I have worked with him since I was twenty and have flanked him at every event since I was ten. I've learned to decipher his every little gesture, and the way he's touching the bezel of his watch with rhythmic movements shows me he's furious. He is ready to strike at the jugular, prepared to kill, but I am his son. I know very well how to defend myself. I've seen him too many times bring people to their knees until they cry.

"The Los Angeles Times this morning." I was trying to distract my mind from the gossip news with something else entirely, but I don't tell him that. And I will not give in to the temptation to ask him why. I know where this conversation is going, and I don't need to serve him the controversy over a silver platter.

"Did your rising star show her tits there, too? Or does she reserve that honor only for low-level magazines?"

I knew this conversation was about Dakota, and the fact that she brought his attention to her makes my skin crawl. I don't want him to approach her for any reason. I don't even want her to be on his radar. I know how he is used to treating people who work for him, who unfortunately fall under his clutches, and I don't want him to ruin her, too.

"I didn't know you read gossip newspapers. Maybe it's time to retire if you have all this time to devote to that garbage." I can't resist the temptation to taunt him.

Aaron Steel Sr. doesn't like to talk about retirement, and I know that very well. He will die in the corridors of this broadcasting company rather than leave the command to someone else, including me, at least not while he can still run it. But this is the only way to make him drop the mask and react. In fact, his gaze becomes glacial, one that nips your legs if you are not used to it. He's given me that look of disgust since I was a child when I was still unable to understand that the fault was not mine, that my father would never be proud of me, no matter how good I was. I have years of scars to act as armor against this look.

"Don't make me lose patience because I can just snap my fingers and shut down this streaming toy of yours. Remember that even if you are my son, you are not essential to this company."

His words hit me in the chest, making me bleed once again, but I don't give it to him to see. For him, the streaming project I have been carrying out for years is just a whim I don't want to give up. He doesn't see the potential, doesn't see where our competitors are aiming, and doesn't understand that if he doesn't rebrand the company's image, his empire will collapse like a sand castle at high tide.

He is so arrogant he thinks I am incapable, suitable only to carry out a project that develops only on the internet because I cannot compete with the "real world." He doesn't realize the whole universe is moving on the web and what has become obsolete and unrealistic is precisely what our grandfather built.

"No, you won't. Because this *toy*, as you call it, wins awards like Emmys and carries millions of dollars to your pockets that you won't give up. I know that you have done your homework and know exactly how much this division brings you. You have calculated it to the last penny. Do you want to shut it down? Be my guest, but you'll have to explain it to the rest of the investors because they'll end up with lighter pockets at the end of the business year." My tone is calm, I have not even moved from the position on the armchair that I have maintained since he entered here, but the anger that boils inside me burns my stomach and chest to such an extent I struggle to breathe.

He's caught off guard because he knows I'm right but didn't expect my reaction. He doesn't consider me up to the role, but he knows this project has brought money to the company's coffers.

"Put your employees in line, or I swear I'll replace you at lightning speed. You are not so irreplaceable, Aaron." The poison with which he spits his words digs into my chest, making it a little less alive, a little more rotten. The fact that he feels the need to reiterate the concept that I am not indispensable is yet another confirmation that his esteem for me is non-existent. The only reason I'm still here is that he will never give this company to anyone outside the family, and I'm the only son he has left after kicking my brother out.

"I already solved the problem days ago." I should not provoke him, but it is too strong a temptation when I see his reaction. "The fact that you only noticed it now is embarrassing."

He stands up, puts his hands on the desk, and gets so close that I feel his warm breath on my face. His nostrils dilate, driven by a fury I rarely see on him.

"Another single bullshit from your rising star, and I swear I make her cry until she wants to quit Hollywood. A single bullshit, and I'll ruin her," he hisses before getting up and leaving the room.

His words dig into my chest like a disease that cannot be cured. I know he is capable of doing it. I have seen countless employees come out of his offices in tears, men or women there was no difference, but every time I tried to do something to cut his disgusting habit, I found only a wall of fear in front of his victims. I have no idea what he does to them, what he says to terrify them like that, but I've never been able to find something useful to help them stop him. The mere thought that he can do such a thing to a young woman like Dakota makes my skin crawl. She may be difficult to handle, but no one deserves to end up in the filthy hands of this man.

"I'll bring you a new suit, but it's better if you wash your hands before putting it on. I doubt that the laundry will be able to save that disaster." Tracy's voice brings me back to reality.

I am so angry with my father that I didn't even notice that she entered my office. I look down at my pants where a blue ink stain contrasts with the gray of the fabric. In my hand, the pen I gripped so hard it broke. Only my father makes me reach certain levels of anger that I can't handle my emotions.

***

After parking in the garage, I turn off the car and observe for a few moments the bluish color of the ink that I couldn't remove from under my nails. The anger that boils inside me is a bit diminished, but it's left me tired. Every fight with my father tests me not only emotionally but physically. This one drained me so much that I hesitated when it came time to decide whether to go to the club and relax in the sauna or go home.

I grab my jacket from the passenger seat, get out of the car, and walk to the entrance that takes me into the house. I check the messages from this afternoon, and when I get to the one from the driver who tells me that he drove Dakota home two hours ago, I freeze. Where do I find her if, in the meantime, she decided to go out again to get drunk with her friends? For the umpteenth time, I find myself cursing the moment I decided to give this crazy idea a chance.

What makes me hesitate the most before opening this damn door is that I'm not sure what I want to find behind it. The empty house, with my silent and uncontaminated spaces, is tempting. I'm not used to sharing my home with anyone. I didn't even want cleaning staff living within these walls because I don't feel like meeting anyone when I get home in the evening. However, my father's words echo in my head and the idea Dakota is out photographed by the paparazzi, given his threats, makes my skin crawl.

I inhale deeply, open the door through the laundry space, and walk down the corridor that leads me to the living room and kitchen. I immediately notice the door to the patio open. Dakota's sunny laugh comes as a wave of relief I didn't know I needed. I didn't want to drive around the clubs in Los Angeles looking for a drunk girl who doesn't want to be found.

I put my jacket on one of the stools on the counter, untie my tie and place it next to it, then allow myself to unfasten the first two buttons of the shirt, inhaling deeply and enjoying the freedom to relax here at home. I roll my shirt sleeves to my elbow and approach the fridge, grabbing a water bottle. I'm about to close it again, but I stop, grab a second one, and head to the pool to take one to Dakota. It's not my ideal accommodation to have someone living under my own roof, but I'm also not an asshole who makes her feel unwanted.

I look out the door, and the anger I had managed to contain explodes in my chest like a bomb. She is there, sitting on one of the deck chairs squeezed inside that damn red bikini that leaves nothing to the imagination. Her long and pale legs stretched out on the dark pillows are an invitation to put a hand over them, and that is precisely what the guy who cleans the pool is doing.

He has a hand on her knee and is telling her something funny because I've never seen her smile so radiantly. He is showing off all his muscles; the body of a fit twenty-year-old with blue eyes and blond hair lightened even more by the sun. He looks like one of those Abercrombie models, blatantly flirting with her. From how she doesn't hint at moving that damn hand and how she blinks her long eyelashes, it seems that she doesn't mind his attention.

Before I even think about what I'm doing, I reach them with long strides, and when my imposing size catches their attention, the guy moves away from her, stands up, and straightens his back, looking at me guiltily. If it weren't for the fact that I spent years managing my emotions in public, I would have already pushed him to the ground and punched him a couple of times on that perfect face, just to remind him who is in charge in this house.

"You're fired," I say calmly.

"What?" he stammers, stunned.

"Aaron!" Dakota snaps, but I don't move my gaze away from his.

"I pay you to clean the pool, not to bother my guests," I continue with the same coldness in my voice.

"I'm sorry… I swear it won't happen again," he stammers as he tries to scrape together his shirt and the few things he brought with him.

If it weren't for the anger boiling inside me, I would almost feel pity for him. Almost.

"It will not happen again because you will no longer set foot in this house. Leave the keys on the kitchen counter."

The boy doesn't even answer. He walks with his head down the few feet to the door behind which he disappears.

"He wasn't bothering me," Dakota protests.

I finally look at her and find her sulky, with her arms crossed just below her breasts, pushing them up so much that they almost get out of those tiny triangles covering her.

"He was bothering me," I reply with the same coldness.

I watch her for a few seconds, and I can't blame the guy. Dakota has a girl-next-door beauty that makes you breathless. Blue eyes, blond hair, a slender and long-limbed physique but with breasts full enough to make you lose your head. In his place, at his age, I would have tried my luck too with a young woman like her.

"He had finished his job. We were just chatting," she snaps, standing up and following me into the house.

All my desire to relax slips away completely.

"I pay him to clean the pool and leave once he's done his job. Not to stay here to have the time of his life at my expense."

An incredulous huff from her makes me spin. I find her looking at me as if I have gone crazy, her mouth wide open and her eyebrows raised.

"What do you want to do now? Spank me and send me to bed without dinner?" she challenges me.

The image of her lying on my lap with her butt up is a forbidden fantasy in which no man should linger if he doesn't want to go crazy with desire. It takes a few seconds longer than it should to drive that thought out of my mind.

"Listen to me, kid. This is my home. I don't want a bunch

of guys coming and going day and night, got it? Not to mention that I want to be free to walk around the house without running into unsolicited sex scenes." The mere thought of seeing her fucking with someone in this place makes me nervous.

The bewilderment painted on her face before turning into anger is so evident that it surprises me.

"Who do you think I am? We were just talking. I wasn't getting fucked by the pool," she shouts.

"Really? Because if I didn't stop him, his hand on your knee would soon be elsewhere." I cross my arms, challenging her.

I was a teenager, and I know how excited males can be in these situations. Within five minutes, she would have found herself with her legs apart, without a bikini, and with the filthy hands of that boy inside her to make her come. He certainly wouldn't have had time to get to her room.

"Are you serious? Do you really think I would have allowed him to put his hands in my panties just because he has two fawn eyes and muscles?"

"Considering how you were looking at those muscles, I'm pretty sure the answer is yes."

She snorts, stunned, as if I really hadn't caught her drooling over the pool guy not even five minutes ago.

"I bet this rule doesn't apply to you. You can bring as many women as you want into the house, right?" Her crusade to try to have the last word is almost sweet.

Surely Tracy was wrong when she said she is afraid of me. She's certainly a young woman who can speak for herself, even if I'm the big boss. And that's precisely why I stay here to argue with her because she has a fire inside that I didn't expect, and I've found myself having one of the most passionate conversations of the whole day.

"It's exactly how it works since it's my home. And now go and put something on. I'm cooking dinner." I don't want to point out that no woman has ever come here, whether to fuck or sleep. None of them ever caught my attention enough to decide to show them how I live, much less have to prepare breakfast for them in the morning.

She looks at me for a few moments, parts her lips perhaps to tell me something but then thinks again, shakes her head, and starts at a brisk pace upstairs. I lean on the counter and inhale deeply, closing my eyes. I didn't want to make a scene, but when I saw her lying on that deck chair with that guy's hand on her knee, all the anger I tried to suppress during the day rose to the surface, exploding into an argument that, on my side, is immature. I could have just told her not to fuck around the house but to do it in her room.

When she returns to the kitchen, she has changed. She wears a blue summer dress that makes her eye color stand out. She seems a bit uncomfortable, unsure whether or not to sit at the counter where I am cooking for both of us, and I can understand. I wasn't sure she would come down again after what I told her.

I fix my eyes on the chicken breasts in front of me, avoiding crossing her gaze when she finally decides to sit on one of the stools. I can instill fear in a room full of adults with just a couple of sentences, but I don't know where to start a conversation with her. I have no idea what we have in common, and my outburst doesn't help create a pleasant atmosphere.

"You know how to cook." Hers is an observation, but I find

surprise in her eyes when I look at her face.

"I'm thirty-six years old. This is one of the basic skills to survive as an adult." I raise an eyebrow, unable to understand where all this novelty is from.

She rolls her eyes, and I'm more and more convinced that if Tracy thinks I can intimidate her with my job position, she's very wrong.

"I thought you rich people had someone to help you with every little thing." The way *you rich people* slips from her tongue makes me think she doesn't come from a wealthy family. She hasn't been in this place for long and, perhaps, has not yet let herself be led astray by the Hollywood luxury. After all, many would consider her paycheck a "rich man's" salary.

"We rich people work too much to have a routine to make it easy to find dinner ready when we get home, and I don't like to have staff walking around." I go back to look at the stir-fry vegetables in the pan next to the chicken breasts.

"That was more than clear," she mumbles quietly, and I can't hide a smile.

Dinner is a very long embarrassing silence where you can only hear the sound of cutlery on the plates. It's so frustrating that I take a deep breath and turn to her at the umpteenth clink of the knife on the plate.

"Okay, listen, we have to live in this house for six months. Can we behave like civilized people?"

She watches me, squinting and studying me for a few seconds as she chews and swallows.

"I'm not the one who came in ranting and firing her employees. I was having a *civil* conversation." She raises an eyebrow as if to challenge me to contradict her.

A corner of my mouth lifts up in a half-smile. She is not entirely wrong.

"Okay, let's start over with a decent conversation," I say, trying to build a minimum relationship to survive these months without going crazy.

"Okay."

"What do you like to do when you're not on set, or you're not out getting drunk with your friends?" I can't resist the temptation to taunt her, maybe because I like to see her roll her eyes as she's doing right now.

I have always admired those who don't let my position stop them. I am used to people bowing down to please me every day or who are so intimidated by my presence that they disappear into the corridors blending with the wallpaper. The fact that she has no problem telling me what she thinks is a breath of fresh air.

"Read. If I don't have to be on set the next day, I often stay up all night to finish a book."

"Really?"

"Are you amazed because I read? Do you think I'm the cliché of the blond dumb actress?" She's not offended, but she seems to want to test me.

"No, I wasn't surprised you read, but because you stay up all night doing it. It takes dedication for such a thing. I would fall asleep after a few pages," I admit.

She shrugs. "Maybe because you didn't find the right book. I can guarantee you that if a novel gets you, you get to the end and don't even notice it."

"What genre do you like?"

"Romance novels, mainly. Dark romance, fantasy, romantic

comedies. Everything that has to do with love." She surprises me with a smile.

"You are twenty-three years old. Wouldn't it be better to *experience* love instead of reading it?"

She shakes her head and smiles. "This afternoon, you ruined my chance to 'experience love.'" She nails me with an accusatory look. "And then, do you see the people out there? It's not easy to find someone who appreciates you for who you are and not just to get something out of you, especially if you're an actress."

I study her for a few moments, and then I nod. In a way, I understand it because I find myself in the same position. When you start making a name for yourself, you never know why people approach you, whether because they are genuinely interested in knowing you or getting something.

"Actually, you got a point," I admit.

"Is that why you're still single, or is it because you like to have sex with more than one woman? Isn't monogamy for you?" she asks with a smug smile on her lips.

Her question is so direct and flippant that I burst out laughing after a moment of confused silence.

"You remember that I am your boss, right? Indeed, the boss of your boss's boss…whatever, I am the one who gives you a living, right?" I tease her, pleasantly amused by the spontaneity of this conversation.

"Of course, I know that, but apparently, you use this excuse not to answer. It's you who asked for a civil conversation." She winks at me.

She winked at me! This unapologetic twenty-three-year-old I should intimidate, just winked at me. I shake my head bewildered and smile.

"No, I don't like to fuck left and right, but this job doesn't leave me much free time to cultivate relationships."

And then I had my chance and missed it, but that's not something she needs to know.

"What the hell do you do with all the money, the million-dollar paintings, and a mega-mansion in the Hollywood Hills if you can't enjoy life?" Her question is as simple as it is complicated to answer. Lately, I've been wondering about it too, and I haven't found an answer yet.

"You know what? Why don't you help me clear the table, and then we go to the bookstore to spend some of the millions that come out of my pockets? You can buy as many novels as you want," I blurt out before my brain can even process the proposal I'm making.

How the hell did it occur to me to invite her to the bookstore to avoid giving her a direct answer to a question she asked me? The surprise is as much mine as it's hers since she looks at me with wide eyes. I must seem crazy to her. I'm almost about to retract the offer when she anticipates me.

"Are you serious? You'll pay? Can I really buy all the novels I want?" She seems to light up at the proposal, and I know it will cost me a fortune.

"Yes, as long as it doesn't take a lifetime to choose because tomorrow morning I have an appointment at dawn, and I would like to sleep a few hours." I realize I'm speaking like my father when he scolded us. When we were young, my brother and I would come home late and thought about nothing but having fun. Since when did I switch to the side of the grumpy old man?

"You are going to change, won't you? Don't make me look like the one who goes out with the… the… the middle-aged man with Chino's, please."

"You were going to say old, weren't you?" I tease.

She shrugs and shows off two innocent doe eyes. "It's not my fault if you dress like an old mummy."

When I told her to start having a civil conversation, I meant something more like talking about the weather or if she likes her job or her commitments for the week, not this bickering in which she has no filter between brain and mouth. Neither do I, since I just invited her to the bookstore to buy books. I must say, however, it is the first time since this afternoon that I don't think back on the conversation with my father, and it makes me so happy that the idea of going to the bookstore with her tastes almost pleasant.

***

When I told her that she could buy anything she wanted, I thought she was buying a couple of books, but when we walked in and I watched her pull out a mile-long list, I realized that mine was just an optimistic hope. She put a cart in my hand, not a basket, an actual cart like those used in grocery stores, and I've been following her for half an hour between the shelves while she picks up book after book.

"How do you get such a long list of books to read?" I ask her. If I find five or six interesting books to read in a year, it's a miracle.

She glances at me, furrowing her eyebrow in concentration. I have never seen anyone so busy searching for books.

"BookTok. When you enter that spiral, you don't come out alive. Every day, some new release teases me, and I add to the list."

She turns to me and notices my bewildered expression. Her face softens into a smile, the one you have in front of a puppy who can't juggle in the bowl of kibble.

"You don't know what I'm talking about, do you?"

"No," I admit laughing.

"They are bloggers who do book reviews. It's a vast community, and every day there is some new book everyone is talking about. You start by buying the book, find out that you like it, and add all the ones they suggest to you. For an author, getting to these bloggers means stepping from anonymity to the bestseller lists, whether it's the *New York Times*, the *Wall Street Journal*, or *USA Today*. The power of word of mouth on that social network is enormous, so much so that it changes your life."

She speaks of it with such conviction and competence that I stop, enchanted looking at her. For one of my age, TikTok is just a social of stupid challenges that send you to the emergency room. Still, it is evident that the target consumer, the one for whom this social network was invented, uses it entirely differently. Today I thought my father was old because he never understood the potential of streaming. I realize that Dakota believes the same thing about me. I don't understand the potential of a social network that substantially impacts the purchasing habits of my company's target audience: teenagers or kids barely older.

"Would you like to explain to me, one day of these, how it works? I'm interested in that."

She shrugs and nods. "Okay, but it's not difficult. Do you already have an account?"

I raise an eyebrow to ask her if it is a serious question.

"Sorry, I forgot you're old. If you give me your phone, I'll set up an account so you don't mess it up."

"I'm thirty-six. I'm not so old that I need your help with my cell phone," I protest.

It is her turn to look at me with the expression that asks if I am serious and it makes me smile.

"Are you going to stop me, or do we go on all evening putting books in the cart?" she finally asks.

I look at her, perplexed. "Are you done?"

"I was done with the first box set of books I put in the cart, but I wanted to see when you would flip out and stop me. Apparently, I underestimated your stamina and the depth of your wallet," she admits with a smug smile.

"You mean I'm pushing this cart for nothing?"

"I just wanted the special edition of this series. The rest is extra," she admits. "By the way, you should option this fantasy series for a movie or a TV show. It's the one everyone is talking about right now," she adds.

"Are you stealing my job?" A smile appears on my lips.

"No, but if you don't know which books teenagers read, how do you make a successful TV show?"

She's right. How can I think about maintaining and growing my audience if I don't know what they like at their age?

"Okay, *Miss I-know-everything*, I'll take a look, but now let's go to the checkout. This cart is getting heavy to push."

She looks at me with wide eyes.

"Do you really want to buy me all these books? I just wanted to piss you off for firing Caleb."

"Who?"

"The pool guy." She glances at me in disappointment at not knowing the name of my employees.

Just hearing his name, I feel anger boiling inside. "I don't want to go through all the shelves in reverse to put the books back in place, so consider yourself lucky."

"Okay, boss." She smiles smugly as she looks at the loot in the cart.

"I'd tell you not to call me that, but technically, I'm your boss," I reason out loud.

She winks at me, turns around, and strides toward the till.

I watch her as she walks away, and I find myself disoriented in front of one of the most surreal evenings of my life. Not so much because of the frankness of a young woman who treats me as a person and not a mythological entity to be venerated or feared, but because, for the first time in my life, I spent an evening as an average person, not like Aaron Steel, *The Butcher*.

CHAPTER 4
Dakota

"Cut!" the director shouts, and I can barely put my feet on the mattress that one of the assistants places beneath me fast enough to help me with the security ropes.

"We take a break, then repeat the scene. Dakota, go fix your makeup, then come back here. It was fine, but you must push yourself a little more with your legs to accentuate the jump and open your arms wider. You have to look like an angel flying into that building," he continues as he approaches with a smile.

"Reset!" his assistant shouts, and everyone goes back into action to set up the scene for the next take.

I can barely nod to him, sweat runs from my forehead, and my breath chokes in my throat. I've always wanted to do my own stunts on set, at least those not dangerous enough to require professionals. Still, running with heels, squeezed inside a pair of leather pants, with a heavy tunic fastened at the waist by a leather belt, is not the easiest thing to do, especially inside a building that today has reached hellish temperatures.

"You were good." Roland smiles. He is the assistant who helps me get in and out of the safety harnesses they put on me to jump from one fake building to another twenty feet high.

"Thank you. I must improve the jump, though, or I'll have to repeat this scene endlessly, and I don't know if I can do it. These boots are killing me." I try to smile at him, but after eight hours inside this costume, trying to run, breathe, and act without looking like a cat hit by a car, I think it came out more like a grimace.

"You'll see that the next one will be fine," he reassures me as he accompanies me off the set and to the trailer where Sarah will have to do the miracle of making me presentable again. "Listen, I was wondering… would you like to get a drink with me tonight? There is a new place where you can build your own cocktail. They told me it's fun," he continues hesitantly.

Roland is a guy that the studio has assigned me for a few months to help me manage the equipment used during stunts. He's about my age, cute, and has sweet green eyes, but, in all honesty, I see him more as a brother than a possible guy to date. We talk mainly about work, and we exchange a few jokes. He helps me stitch up the cuts I have on my feet after hours in these boots on the set. I could never date someone who saw and smelled my feet after twelve hours inside this leather trap.

"Thank you for asking, but tomorrow morning I must be here again at six, and I need to rest." I decline the invitation with a bit of embarrassment since it is the umpteenth time that I've said no. I should be clear and tell him that I only see him as a friend, but I'm afraid the working relationship will become unbearable, and I don't want to look like the diva who requires the change of the assistant on the set. Although the situation is getting harder and harder to ignore.

"Of course, of course, I understand. I don't want to prevent you from sleeping," he stammers hastily as, step by step, he walks away and disappears among the production trailers.

"Roland still hitting on you?" Serena's mocking voice makes me turn around.

"What are you doing here?"

"I dropped your name at the entrance, and the doors opened magically." Her mischievous smile annoys me.

I don't like it when she uses my name to get into places she shouldn't be. I work here while she spends her day eating for free from the trucks of the different studios and fucking extras in the hidden corners of the parking lots. I open the door of the makeup trailer, and when Sarah notices Serena climbing in behind me, her smile dies on her lips. She can't stay in here. If she gets hurt or breaks something, the insurance doesn't pay because she is not one of the employees, and we'll all end up neck-deep in trouble. But the makeup artist will never make a scene by kicking her out because she fears I may complain to the studio and get her fired.

"You know you shouldn't be in here, don't you? If they catch you, you'll get all of us in trouble." I try to make Serena understand that she should leave the set, but the stern expression on her face kills the words in my throat.

"If you hadn't stolen my starring role, I would have let you do whatever you want on this set. I probably would have found you a job as a co-star or something," she reminds me harshly, awakening my guilt.

Serena and I met when we were both in the queue for the auditions for *Hunters of Shadows* for Sabry's role, the protagonist. We spent hours under the scorching Los Angeles sun waiting for our turn. She never had a callback, while I, audition after audition, got the part. She has never resented me. In fact, she has become my friend, but I can't help but feel guilty that I am succeeding while she continues to audition but never gets a part.

I look at the mirror and see Sarah imperceptibly roll her eyes. "You know I tried to ask, but the casting was closed," I admit as I open the zippers on my boots and pull out my swollen feet.

I notice right away the bloodstain on the heel and toe of one of my socks. The patches I wore this morning didn't stop the wounds from reopening after a week of stunts, almost making me cry. From the corner of my eye, I notice Sarah open a small fridge behind her and pull out an ice pack which she gives to me.

"Thank you." I smile at her and place the cold wrap on my battered feet, breathing a sigh of relief when the pain begins to subside.

"Anyway…" The smile returns to Serena's lips, and I am glad she has dropped a topic that always puts me in a bad mood. "I went to your house and found it empty. Where did you end up? You change houses, and you don't tell me any-thing?" she asks with a bit of irritation in her voice.

The sense of guilt returns, overwhelming my chest. It's been fifteen days since I moved in with Aaron, and although we chat daily, I never told her anything. I don't know why I didn't, maybe because I was afraid she would invite herself to his home and ask him for a job, embarrassing me in front of him.

It is strange the relationship I have with my boss. Although he intimidates me, most of the time, I tell him what I think without filters. After that first conversation, where nervousness led me to babble about what was going through my head without thinking, I noticed that he seemed almost relieved by my frankness. I don't believe many people tell him to his face what they think, and the fact that he let me speak freely without scolding me or, worse, firing me led me to relax so much that sometimes I forget he is the big boss. Not that I've seen him much during these last few weeks, as we're both busy with work.

"I had to change accommodation," I vaguely reply although I know she will not give up until I confess the truth.

"Really? Where do you live?" The smile that appears on her face is halfway between curious and impatient.

"On the hills, but it's something temporary. In six months, I'll be back in my old apartment. There was a problem with the…pipes." I'm an actress, I literally live repeating fake stories other people write, yet I can't lie even if it was the only way to save my life. I'm hopeless.

I play with my belt buckle, wishing I could be swallowed up at this very moment. Sarah behind me is making a titanic effort not to interfere in the conversation. Usually, when it's me and her alone, we spend time in a friendly conversation that we've had for over three years. The tension that you breathe when Serena is here with us is something that I have never been able to mitigate.

"Really? A problem with the pipes leads you to ask Aaron Steel for hospitality?" she asks with a smile on her face that I can't read.

My heart hammers in my chest, and when I cross Sarah's eyes through the mirror, I find them as big as saucers. Apart from Tracy and the PR office, no one knows about this accommodation, and I prefer it to remain so, to avoid uncomfortable rumors about why I ended up under the same roof as the big boss.

"How do you know?" I blurt out.

"Because I followed you off the set when I found your house empty. Imagine my surprise when my best friend didn't tell me she lived in the boss's house." There's a pain in her eyes, and I wonder if it was the right choice to keep it hidden from her.

Of course, Serena is impulsive, always over the top, but she is not stupid. Maybe if I had asked her to keep the secret, she would have understood and done it in the name of our friendship. In this way, I didn't give her a choice. I didn't trust her. What kind of friend am I if I can't even trust her?

"Sorry. I was embarrassed and didn't know how to tell you." I tell her a half-lie.

Serena surprises me with a hug. "It doesn't matter, don't worry. I forgive you, as long as you let me use that pool when your boss is not there just once."

If Aaron isn't at home, he doesn't know if I've invited a friend, right? "Okay."

She kisses me on the cheek and stands up. "Now I'm going because Roland will need to be comforted after you dumped him for the millionth time."

At the same speed she appeared, she also disappears and the air seems almost lighter now that it's just Sarah and me.

"You know you got this part because you're a better actress than her, don't you? You didn't steal anything from her," Sarah tells me as she continues to dab my forehead to redo the makeup that sweat has ruined.

I look down at my battered feet because I don't know how to answer. Maybe she's right, but maybe Serena just flunked that audition and she's better than me. The fact that she decided to be my friend, the only one I've had since I moved here, despite everything, doesn't mitigate my guilt. In fact, seeing her struggle every day with auditions that fail one after the other makes me feel like a bad friend.

***

When the driver opens the door, I leave the car and rest my bare feet on the hot concrete. When I finally took off my boots after filming, I tried to put my regular shoes back on, but my feet were so swollen and sore that I couldn't fit them in. I wave goodbye to the driver and offer a half-smile, and head toward the front door, trying to avoid stepping on the white marble with the bloody part of my foot. I limp upstairs until I close the bedroom door behind me and collapse on the bed. The only thing I dream of right now is a shower and a good night's sleep until five tomorrow morning. It shouldn't be difficult as the darkness and silence of this house is more like a grave when Aaron isn't here. I wonder if that man lives under this roof or if this house is just a façade for his image.

The vibration of my cell phone pulls an exasperated moan from my throat. I would like to pretend not to have heard it, but if it is my mother and I don't respond right away, she overwhelms me with phone calls.

Serena: I'm at your house. Let me in, so I can use your pool! I know Aaron is still in the office. I have my sources.

I let out an exasperated sigh. I guess it's no coincidence that she showed up not even five minutes after I entered the house. She was waiting for me, and this attitude bothers me a bit.

Dakota: I want to go to sleep. Tomorrow morning I have to get up at five, can we do this another time?

Maybe she feels pity for me and decides to go home.

Serena: If you don't open immediately, I will ring the bell until five tomorrow morning. You have time when you're old to sleep.

I grab the pillow and let out an exasperated scream, then get up, put my battered feet into a pair of flip-flops and use the app that controls the doorbell cameras to open the main gate as I go down to the front entrance. When I open the door, my surprise soon turns into horror when I see about thirty people behind Serena. Some with crates of beer in hand, others with bottles of wine, most of them already drunk.

My friend makes her way into the house, and when I grab her wrist to make her turn, we are pushed by the people who make their way into the living room, laughing, joking, and admiring the mansion. They are all about our age, but I don't know any of them. When I go out with her, it's usually just the two of us. I had no idea she had so many friends. Some of them glimpse the pool, open the doors to the patio, and with a run, throw themselves into the water, splashing everywhere. The horror painted on my face must be evident because my friend bursts out laughing.

"You can't stay here. If Aaron comes back, he'll kill me."

The anger I feel inside is so intense it makes me tremble. How can she think I would agree with such a thing? And to think today I felt guilty for not telling her I lived here.

"Relax. Aaron is not here, and we'll leave before he gets home. We'll just use the pool for a little bit." Her bored attitude makes me simmer with anger.

"You don't understand. I don't want you in here. It's a matter of respect for the person who hosts me and doesn't want people in the house," I shout indignantly and immediately regret it when I see the grim expression transform her face.

"Of course, because Aaron deserves respect. While I, your best friend for the last three years, even though you stole my job, don't deserve anything, do I? Since when have you become so snobbish that you prefer powerful people to friends who have been next to you since you were nobody? Just because you've become famous and have a verified profile on Instagram, you think you're better than us." The pain that shines through her words strikes me in the chest.

I haven't forgotten about her, only she can't understand that I can't do certain things anymore. Aaron is my boss, not a friend or roommate. He is the one who holds my future, and I can lose my job. The same job I stole from her.

"It's not like that, but you're getting me into trouble." My voice comes out with little conviction. "Aaron wouldn't understand."

"Wouldn't understand what? That we are just having fun? Or maybe we're not up to his majesty Aaron Steel and his faithful kiss-ass Dakota. Are we too gross for your standards?"

Yes, that's precisely why. Aaron and his tailored pants, ties with the perfect knot, and million-dollar paintings would not understand. They are disrespectful kids infesting his pool, stepping on the white marble of his living room with muddy shoes, and draining his reserve of fine spirits by drinking straight from the bottles. The contrast between Aaron's class and the vulgarity of the people here is so jarring it makes my skin crawl, and for the first time in my life, I feel embarrassed because of the friendships I have chosen. But I can't tell her this because she's my only friend in the viper den that is Hollywood.

"No! Aaron would not understand because he is an old dude who doesn't know how to have fun. Have you seen him? He looks like a mummy inside those tailored clothes. It's a miracle he doesn't sleep in a sarcophagus." Every word that comes from my lips disgusts me because I don't mean them, but the smile that returns on my friend's lips makes me feel better.

"Serena, are you coming? Apparently, Dakota has forgotten how to have fun." Roland's voice makes me turn toward him.

I am surprised to see him here, and, above all, I am surprised not to find his usual sweet smile on his lips. He seems almost disgusted by my presence, and how he looks at me makes me uncomfortable. It contrasts sharply with the shy and awkward guy who has been following me on the set like a shadow for a few months now. I watch them as they move away and join their friends in the pool, and the distress growing inside me makes me tremble. How the hell do I get rid of them? Do I make a scene? Considering they are already drunk, I don't know how much I will be able to make myself heard.

I approach the pool, terrified of what I might find there, and when I find myself in front of reality, I realize that it is much worse than what I had feared. Bottles of beer are scattered on the patio and concrete around the pool. One of the deck chairs is turned upside down, and the pillows are partly soaked in the water. One of the umbrellas lies on the blue bottom of the pool, but the worst thing is that one of the guys has lowered his pants and is urinating in the water. Here, in front of everyone, while the people who are swimming scream and avoid his trajectory.

Only ten minutes have passed. The knot that tightens my throat is so big that, although I would like to shout at everyone to get out of here and go home, nothing comes out of my lips. I remain petrified, staring at the horror unfolding before my eyes without being able to do anything. A powerful voice behind me, however, attracts everyone's attention.

I turn just in time to see the fury behind the calm mask that is Aaron himself. I follow his slow pace as he approaches the pool and observes the disaster that has become his home. I feel so small I'm sure I could disappear between the cracks of the wood on the patio. Or at least that's what I hope because if I thought I saw Aaron furious the night I moved here or when he fired the pool guy, I was very wrong.

"Everyone out. And I advise you to run fast because I have already called the police." His tone is calm, but no one is breathing.

They are all wide-eyed, and the laughter that accompanied them until a minute ago is just a distant memory. It takes just a fraction of time to process his words with their foggy brains to unleash a stampede leaving the house. Something I couldn't achieve. Aaron is impassive, at least until Roland passes by him, and then he grabs his arm to stop him. Roland's eyes are as wide as I've ever seen them. Green irises seem to want to escape from their orbits.

"You're one of the show's production assistants, aren't you?" He asked it as a question, but I know Aaron knows exactly who Roland is. Maybe he doesn't know his name, but in the few interactions I've had with him, I understood that he is never unprepared and never leaves anything to chance.

"Yes, I…" Roland stutters.

"You're fired."

The words are like a lash on Roland's face. He physically stumbles a bit, even though Aaron is gripping his arm.

"But…" he tries to counter, but the coldness on Aaron's face freezes him on the spot. I can't breathe either.

"Don't even show up on set tomorrow morning," he says before releasing Roland's arm and letting him go.

Roland throws me a furious look but reaches Serena, who is waiting for him at the door, and then disappears inside the house.

Aaron's eyes move from the bottles scattered in the pool to my face, and my cheeks blaze with shame.

"Go to your room." The disappointment that exudes from his words almost hurts.

For some stupid reason, the fact that I betrayed his trust gives me a sense of guilt I didn't think I could feel for a person I have known for just over a few weeks.

"Aaron, I…" My voice trembles under his glacial gaze.

"I said, go to your room," he repeats in a less calm tone than before.

"Let me at least explain…"

He shoots toward me with a movement so unexpected I wince, almost for fear that he may hit me. He doesn't, but the fury on his face once he drops the mask leaves me with a mixture of fear and humiliation. He no longer has to pretend now. There is no audience to project the image of the iceman, it's just him and me, and the disgust that exudes from his person makes me feel small.

He is so close that I can smell his expensive aftershave, observe the texture of his shirt, and notice the small wrinkles around his eyes that make him look like the mature man he is, far from the kids who were here in the pool until a few minutes ago. He is furious, and knowing I am the cause of this fury makes me feel insignificant. Not because I am afraid of him, but because I betrayed the trust of the person who gave me a second chance by opening the doors of his house.

"I don't want your explanations. I want to see you disappear from here. Go. To. Your. Room," he hisses with such fervor that his hands clenched in fists along his hips tremble.

I look down, and with humiliation in my chest, I start upstairs until I lock myself in my room. The pool lights filtering through the window are a sad reminder of the wrong I did tonight.

I look out the window, hidden by the curtains, and watch Aaron by the pool. He'd taken off his jacket and tie, rolled his shirt sleeves to his elbows, and removed the deck chair's cushions from the water. I watch as he grabs one of the bottles, then a second. He looks around, and there are so many that he will have to bend over for a long time to collect them all. He angrily throws one of the bottles and it shatters on the wall that divides the pool from the garden, then sits on one of the deck chairs and puts his hands in his hair. He seems defeated, and for the first time, I see Aaron not as *The Butcher* but as a man whose private life has just been violated, and guilt makes me slump defeated onto the bed.

The phone buzzes in my hands, and when I thought my evening couldn't get worse, I realize it's just the beginning of my nightmare. The video where I call Aaron an old mummy went viral, and the TMZ website reposted the news focusing on just one question: Why does the rising Hollywood star live in the producer's house?

CHAPTER 5
Aaron

I stare at the computer in front of me as Tracy rattles off the appointments that have piled up this morning after Dakota's video went viral. The PR office is on the warpath and wants to fire her, and I no longer know how to contain and justify her behavior.

"Aaron! Are you listening to me?" Tracy's resolute voice calls me back to reality.

I look at her and find her frowning. I must resolve this situation before the newspapers turn it into a shitshow.

"Have I aged so much that I am considered a museum piece?"

The features of my assistant soften, and the shadow of a smile appears on her lips.

"Is this what bothers you the most about this whole story? That a girl sees you as a mummy?"

I shrug and think about it for a few seconds.

"It's not a matter of personal pride. I'm confident in my physical appearance to not be intimidated by her words."

Tracy smiles and shakes her head. "Never let the great Aaron Steel become humble."

"It's not a question of humility. I know how I look. I see myself in the mirror, take care of my physical appearance, and have no problem admitting it. What bothers me about that video is that she's part of the target audience to which the streaming division aims, and she sees me as old. I always thought my father was obsolete for this job... What if I have become one myself and haven't noticed it?" I express the doubt that has tormented me since last night.

Tracy thinks about it for a few moments and then smiles.

"Your shows are not old. They hit the target you want. In fact, she is adored by folks her age and younger. What makes you doubt?"

"The fact that I don't know her world. I don't know where the kids nowadays meet to chat, their social networks... I am not present where my target audience is gathered, and this makes me lose sight of what they like and the trends of the moment," I admit with concern.

She shrugs and shakes his head.

"Hire someone young to help you keep up or ask her to explain it to you, but don't sign up for social media as one of those creepy middle-aged dudes sneaking into teen chats." She makes a disgusted face that makes me smile.

"I'm too old for TikTok, am I?" I tease.

"I swear if I see a single video of you flexing your muscles without a shirt on winking in front of a camera, I quit."

I smile, amused, and look back at the computer in front of me, watching the number of emails go up by the minute.

"Now, do we want to focus on the real problem of that video? The rumors that circulate describe her as your lover, and the denial will not be enough to silence them. You have to give a reasonable explanation for the fact that she lives in your house. You must work with Sharon, she is prepared for this, but you have to put your face out there. You can't just rely on a press release."

I don't have time to answer when the office door opens wide and my father enters as if he owns the place. He technically does, but still.

"Get out," he orders to Tracy, who, in response, looks at me in a silent question.

"Get your ass out of that chair and get out of this office if you don't want me to kick your ass so hard you end up in the parking lot," he orders.

Bile rises in my throat, but I don't need to say anything to defend her because Tracy gets up, approaches my father without batting an eye, and looks him straight in the eyes.

"You just try to put a finger on me, and I swear I will take your flaccid balls and close them between the jamb and the door of this office," she hisses before turning around and leaving the office without giving him a second look.

The fury that paints my father's face is something that makes me almost physically enjoy this moment. That's why I hired Tracy. Because she doesn't let herself be intimidated by those who try to crush her.

"Fire her," my father orders me as soon as the door closes.

"I won't even think about it," I answer with arrogance, basking for a few more seconds in the victory of my assistant.

"You'll do exactly what I tell you, or I swear you'll find yourself in the middle of a street."

My father's threats stopped scaring me a long time ago. Now they just make my anger rise, but I have learned to control it.

"Why did you feel the need to interrupt my meeting? I don't have time to waste with you." Even though I know he's here for that video, I get straight to the point.

"I believe you have no time to waste, given the mess you've made fucking this girl." He looks like a rabid dog.

The mere fact that he's insinuating I slept with Dakota annoys me, but I can't get angry with him. Everyone thinks so, and denying it to my father is not one of my main problems right now.

"That's all? Have you come here to scold me because of who I take to bed?" I pretend to be bored by his insinuations.

"I am here because I am the first to close an eye on the affairs, but I don't slam them on all the front pages of the newspapers. Are you too stupid to do it? The two golden rules in this industry are simple: be discreet, and use a condom. You are thirty-six, holy Christ, have you learned nothing at all?"

My father's vulgarity disgusts me. He has always been a person who treats people like scum, and I will never get used to it. I would do anything to see him pay for the suffering he causes.

"Have you finished your preaching, or do you want me to waste more time? My private life is none of your business." I want him out of this office.

"Teach the girl to stay in her place, or I swear I'll do it, and you won't like it," he hisses before leaving, slamming the door behind him.

A few moments later, Tracy's head peeps in, and I beckon her to enter.

"What a ray of sunshine, your father."

I throw her a look that would be reproachful, but makes her laugh instead.

"Thank heaven that you and Evan grew up with nannies who instilled some decent value in you. That man is Satan himself."

"You don't need to remind me." I rub a hand across my face, trying to drive away the bitterness my father's meeting left in my mouth.

"Aaron, you have a meeting with the PRs," she continues seriously.

I inhale deeply before I get up and tell her to follow me. "Do you have Dakota's filming schedule? I need her with us. At least she'll know what we are feeding to the press."

"I'll see what I can do," she tells me before disappearing. I already know that the director will be pissed, but Dakota will be present in the office for this meeting.

Not even fifteen minutes later, Dakota enters, accompanied by Tracy, still dressed in her stage costume. She is serious but doesn't seem particularly worried.

"Okay, let's get straight to the point," Sharon begins as Dakota sits next to me. "The problems that have arisen with that video are two. The fact that you live together and that you clearly make fun of him. While for the second problem, the thing has been quietly resolved with some jokes and some meme circulating on the internet, the fact that you live together has made the press cry scandal."

I inhale thoroughly. Being the object of online jokes is not pleasant, but at least it is something I can manage while ignoring the virtual idiots.

"Sorry for the story of the mummy. I didn't want to," Dakota mumbles with her gaze resting on her hands in her lap.

I look at the tunic she has on. It appears very heavy. She is dying of heat buried by all those layers of costume.

"Didn't want to? Really? Because you seemed very convincing." I would like to reproach her, but I can't because the truth is that she has done nothing wrong but leverage my insecurities.

She turns to me with a firm look.

"Look, Serena cornered me, okay? If the video of the entire conversation had circulated, you would also have seen the part where she insinuated that I had become a snob who gives up friends to play the precious princess with her big boss. What should I tell her? That I am ashamed to go out with her because she is vulgar and boisterous? She is the only friend I have. I would have said anything to keep her. So I told her that you are a mummy because confessing to her that I much prefer your class and the chats I have with you to her bullshit didn't seem nice." She blurts this out all in one breath and takes me by surprise. "I didn't want to put you in the middle of a stupid girl's fight when you have an empire to run." She gestures with her hands, pointing to the room. My kingdom.

Did she really try to protect me? Her reaction is almost… sweet. I look at Tracy and Sharon and see that they are trying to hide their smiles. I think it's the first time someone has bothered to do something nice for me when they're not forced by their job description.

"Okay, you clarified this point," Sharon continues. "But what remains is the fact that you threw a party while you live in his house and we asked you to keep it quiet. We have to justify this so as not to make you look like his lover."

"Oh no. I didn't organize anything at all," she snaps in disgust.

"There were thirty drunk people in my pool," I remark incredulously, raising my voice a little. She cannot deny the evidence.

She turns to me, and the furious look I find takes me back. "If you had let me explain, *Mr. Go-to-your-room*, I would have told you last night that I had just come home, and that Serena showed up at your house with thirty drunk people that I couldn't stop. When she didn't find me at my old apartment, she followed me from the set to your home. I never told her where I lived. Ask your driver when he took me back last night, and you will understand that I had no desire to throw a party." She lowers to unfasten her boots, and when she takes them off, I am surprised to find white socks stained with blood. "Because my feet are torn up after twelve hours of shooting, and I have only a few hours to rest before starting again. Trust me, I have no desire to party by the pool."

I am so stunned by her confession that I feel like a complete idiot. I assumed she was the one who behaved like the irresponsible girl I always painted in my head, but maybe this time, I'm wrong. And why the hell didn't she tell the costume department that those boots are killing her?

"Okay, we understand your position. It doesn't change the fact that that video was released by one of the participants and that we have to silence the newspapers," Sharon continues, exasperated by the continuous interruptions.

"By the way, do you know who released the video?" I ask when I realize that I don't have this information.

Dakota rolls her eyes and snorts. I suspect she has the answer.

"The only one who witnessed the conversation was Roland.

After you fired him, he probably wanted revenge and put the video online, I suppose," she explains as if we were perfect idiots. And perhaps we are since we have not come to the most obvious conclusions.

"Did you fire Roland?" Tracy blurts out. She had taken the kid to heart after I had her do a check on all the people who work on set with Dakota. Considering that she lives under my roof, I wanted to ensure the people she hangs out with aren't crazy freaks.

Next to me, Dakota exhales indignantly. "Not only him. Also, the pool guy. Two guys showed a modicum of interest in me, and *Mr. Caveman* fired them." She looks incredulous at me. "I don't know. Do you want me to become old like you, a spinster, and with a house full of cats?"

I am so stunned by her reaction that I don't even have the words to answer when she gets up and grabs the boots she has taken off from the ground. "Now, if you will excuse me, I'm returning to the set. I have already missed my entire lunch break to give you some information you would already have if he had let me explain last night. Have a nice day."

I watch her limp out with boots in her hand and close the door behind her as if we were not worthy of her time. We are all three stunned by the impudence of this young woman, dumbfounded by her frank way of speaking that borders on insolence. It is Tracy who breaks the silence with a wild laugh.

"I swear it's the most epic scene I've ever witnessed," she says in fits and starts. "Please don't fire her. It's too good to see how you can't hold your own with her." I cast a bored look at her, but I actually struggle to hide a smile.

Dakota reminds me a lot of me, cocky and brazen at her age.

"She's aware you're her boss, isn't she?" Sharon asks with a smile on her face, and I can't help but imitate her expression.

"More than aware, I would say. She just doesn't care." I laugh, throwing my head back.

"Coming back to us. There could be a solution that could silence the rumors of your relationship, and that could make you look like the hero," says Sharon warily, and her hesitation makes me straighten in my chair. She knows I don't like when they paint me as someone I'm not. Cold, calculating, I can accept. Hero makes me turn up my nose.

"We can say that there is a person obsessed with Dakota and that, as a temporary solution, the production has decided it's better if she remains in your house. We can say there are security guards and cameras that can keep her safe. In six months, we will say that the emergency has settled down and that she can return to live as a free woman," she explains.

"This is all you've come up with in fifteen days?" I ask dumbfounded.

Sharon doesn't bat an eye at my remark. "This is a big scandal. The only way to divert attention from it is by creating a bigger one. Making bland excuses will only make us look like we are trying to cover some sordid affair."

I think about it a bit, and I'm not convinced. This story has taken on epic proportions when we could simply go back to the accommodations we had before, making Dakota understand that the next time she messes up, she is fired.

"Doesn't that sound a bit exaggerated? Is it so unthinkable to find her another place to live and try to let the rumors die? I'm not comfortable with all these lies we are spreading around," I try to convince her. After all, having had the opportunity to live under the same roof, Dakota doesn't seem to be a vapid girl throwing a tantrum.

"And how do you explain the past fifteen days? She will look like your lover, and while you will look like the alpha male who nailed a young and sexy girl, she will pass for the one who has opened her legs to make her way into this show. She will be branded for life while you come out with a few pats on the back." Tracy's voice is firm in a reproach that I deserve.

What she says is true. No one will give Dakota credit in this industry, no matter how good she is at her job. The gossip will continue to follow her at every future project, even if we spend hours on official press releases. If there is no valid explanation for this story, our denials will remain only beautiful words that no one really believes.

"You know you put me in an uncomfortable situation with this idea, don't you? From the beginning, making her come to live with me." Mine is not a reproach, just a simple observation.

Sharon nods and looks down. "I know, but we are prepared for this and we can make her look like the victim. We will make it appear more convincing by placing a couple of security guys in front of the gate at your place. They will keep away the paparazzi, too."

I appreciate her honesty as I stand and button my jacket again.

"I'm going to talk to Dakota. I'll leave it to you to manage the press. Or do you need my face on video?"

Sharon beckons me to go.

"We will make a press release. It should be enough to divert attention. If your intervention is necessary, we will let you know."

When I arrive on set, Dakota is engaged in the shooting of a chase that has her jumping from a fake building to slip into a window a few feet away. It is a stunt that is not particularly risky but still requires precision, exercise, and preparation beyond simple acting. She performs it perfectly, running on those heels that hurt her as if she didn't even have them on. Knowing how her feet are bleeding, my esteem for her, and her professionalism, grows.

When the director stops the action and realizes I'm nearby, he shows off one of those fake smiles he reserves for me every time I see him. I have never seen a person try with so much determination to please me. If I told him now to kneel in front of me and wag his tail, I am sure he would.

"Aaron, what a pleasure to see you!" He puts his hand on my arm, and this already bothers me.

My stern look doesn't seem to annoy him at all.

"Things are going wonderfully. Do you want to stop for a few minutes to watch what we are doing? We're about to shoot some juicy scenes." He waggles his eyebrows conspiratorially.

I have no idea what he means by *juicy*, but I don't want to stay here to discover it.

"Thank you for the invitation, but I just came by to talk to Dakota."

I spot people around us starting to notice my presence. Maybe it wasn't a good idea to come in person to talk to her, fueling the gossip.

"Of course, of course. Dakota, honey, come here. Mr. Steel wants to talk to you," he shouts to make himself heard. By now, not only is Dakota informed of my presence, but so are the people busy arranging the lights on the other side of the set.

When she reaches me, I notice that she is embarrassed by the curious glances the technicians and dozens of other people who work here throw at her.

"Did you really have to come to the set?" she grumbles in a low voice while looking at her toes.

I can't help but try to hide a smile. She is entirely different from the proud and determined young woman who stands up to me in every conversation.

"Sorry, I realize I made a mistake coming down, but now I'm here, I might as well talk about it," I admit.

She pretends to be shocked, leaning a hand on her chest. "*Mr. I-am-perfect* just admitted he was wrong?" she teases.

I raise an eyebrow and bite my cheek to not smile again. I have a reputation to maintain, for Pete's sake!

"It won't happen again, believe me." I pull an amused smile from her. "I came to tell you that, if you agree, we'll send out an official press release explaining that you came to live in my house because of a crazy stalker who threatens you. We can pretend you're safe by having guards and cameras inside the residence."

I study her as she frowns and looks at me as if I were a perfect idiot.

"Literally less than twenty-four hours ago, thirty strangers entered your house destroying the pool because I opened the gate with an app on my phone. You don't have security guards in your house. And shouldn't I have gone to the police instead of asking my boss to be a hero?" she asks, puzzled.

She's right, this explanation is full of holes, but I count on

Sharon's skill to direct the conversation elsewhere and confuse the gossip magazines until the story deflates.

"They will not verify these details. They will focus on the crazy stalker. We will make you look like the victim, and no one will ask questions." I downplay it, but I see that she is hesitant.

She shakes her head. "Okay, if you say it works, I trust you. You are the genius of these things. I'll follow your lead. At least now I have a slightly more credible lie than the broken plumbing to give to Serena."

I furrow my brows and study her. "Did you really tell your friend something like that? You know there are people paid to repair certain damages, don't you? There is no need to wipe out a neighborhood and rebuild when a light bulb burns out." I tease her a little for her naivety.

It amazes me how she holds conversations much more maturely than her age and stands up to people who, on paper, have more authority than her, but then gets lost when making excuses with her peers.

She rolls her eyes and crosses her arms to her chest. "She caught me off guard. I wasn't ready!"

I shake my head and smile before letting her return to her job and call Sharon to give her the green light. Walking out of the set, I notice one of the trailers where they keep all the stage costumes for the show. I knock on the door and wait for someone to come. When the girl with green hair and eyebrow piercing opens the door, her eyes almost jump out of her sockets.

"Mr. Steel! Is there a problem? Can I help you?" she almost stammers.

I smile, trying to reassure her, and this seems to surprise

her more than my presence here. Do I instill so much fear in people that I upset them when I smile?

"No problem. When Dakota comes back to change, I just wanted to ask if you can take a look at her boots. I noticed that she has wounds on her feet, and I was wondering if you can do something to make her more comfortable," I explain as tactfully as possible without making it appear as an order, even though my instinct is shouting at me to fire her for not having checked herself.

"Really? She has been using them for months. She never told me they hurt her!" she says, outraged, and I can only read honesty on her face. Not that it justifies her lack of attention to her job, but at least it's not total indifference.

"I don't think she told anyone. I just noticed the blood stains when she removed them," I explain and realize how absurd I sound. When does a producer ever notice the feet of the actresses who work for him?

"I will definitely check as soon as she comes back. Thank you for pointing it out to me," she replies, embarrassed.

I smile at her and she seems disoriented again. As I leave, I give her a wave of my hand, a gesture that sends her into complete confusion. For Pete's sake, I am not a bloodthirsty tyrant.

***

The dinner with the investors was filled with a bunch of jokes about the fact that I have "young meat" around the house at my disposal. Apparently, all straight males over forty believe I have fucked Dakota on every surface of my house. It was challenging not to punch them at the umpteenth joke or how they addressed women like they were a piece of meat.

I put the keys on the entrance table, enter the study on the ground floor where I keep my whiskey collection, and pour two fingers of Glenmorangie Signet into a glass. I lay my eyes on the box containing the fifty-four-year-old Singleton and sigh of relief, thinking back to last night. The kids could drain a forty-five thousand dollar collectible bottle and not be able to discern it from the Jack Daniels they find at the pub. I close the alcohol cabinet and, without turning on the lights, go upstairs to finally take off my tie.

There is no noise, no lights on, not even filtering from under the door of Dakota's room. I wonder if she went out because, even though it is past midnight, she doesn't work tomorrow and would have every right to go out with her friends and have fun.

I enter my bedroom and put my tie on the bed with my jacket. Unfastening the shirt's buttons, I open the door that leads onto the terrace overlooking the pool. I sit on one of the armchairs and relax, sipping the whiskey while watching the city lights in the distance. I will never tire of this view. I chose to build here just to enjoy this show every night, to feel like I have the world at my feet.

The phone buzzes in my pocket and when I pull it out, I notice the Instagram notification I set on Dakota's profile. If I have to keep an eye on her, her social media accounts will give me an immediate preview of her life. The post is a close-up of her face, taken in dim light, with those innocent eyes and sulky lips that make her the forbidden dream of every man on this earth. She is breathtakingly beautiful.

The caption below the photo is one of those approved by

Sharon. She insinuates an outing with friends, but I recognize those pillows behind her. I look down at the pool and find her in her red bikini, focused on the same view I'm enjoying. She's put a bag of what looks like the frozen peas I asked the housekeeper to buy last week on her feet.

She's twenty-three years old. It's Friday night. She should be out having fun instead of pretending with her fans. I sip from my whiskey and watch her looking at the phone, maybe hoping someone will call her. I don't know. She is one of the rising stars of Hollywood, adored by millions of young people like her; yet, she is here alone, with a melancholy look and signs of fatigue from her work on her feet. I wonder if she has any friends to hang out with, apart from Serena, who always seems to get her into trouble? Los Angeles can be beautiful but also cruel. It can make you live big dreams but at the same time make you die of loneliness.

I sip from my whiskey and lean out, resting my elbows on my knees watching as she stands and approaches the pool stairs, slowly slipping into the water and savoring every moment. She dives. I follow her as she swims to the other side of the edge and re-emerges with her eyes closed and lips parted to catch her breath. She puts her hands in her hair to remove the water, letting me glimpse the curves of her breasts behind that bikini that adheres to them like a second skin. I am hypnotized by her movements, her pale skin, and the pout of her lips.

I should get up from here and go back to my room instead of watching her every little movement like one of those crappy pigs I was having dinner with. She's barely twenty-three. Yet, I can't move, not even when she opens her eyes and notices me sitting here in the armchair, undressing her with my eyes without any shame. And it wouldn't be Dakota if she didn't surprise me even now, staring back at me. She reciprocates my attention with such intensity that she ignites every single cell in my body, awakening an erection I should not feel for a woman thirteen years younger than me and my employee.

CHAPTER 6

Dakota

"I really don't need to be escorted into Starbucks. No one is going to attack me unless I steal their coffee, but I swear I don't plan to do so," I beg Gaspard, the middle-aged driver that Aaron has assigned me for my every move, even to get coffee after following me step by step during all my exercises at the gym. I was terrified he would also want to get into the shower.

When I tried to object, Aaron pointed out that I shouldn't go out alone if I'm under threat from a madman. The story of the stalker seems to have taken hold after the PRs released the statement two days ago. Only Hollywood can believe that a crazy person is on the loose rather than a hot affair between a producer and an actress.

"Mr. Steel ordered me to accompany you…" He is embarrassed, trying to justify himself for something his boss has imposed on him.

I inhale deeply and beckon him to follow me. "Then let us not give *The Butcher* a way to use his ax on your head, too. I don't want you fired."

I can see him barely holding back a smile as he keeps the

door open for me to enter the cafe.

"Do you want a coffee?" I ask since he will have to be my lady-in-waiting.

"No, thank you for the offer." He smiles.

"Did he also order you not to drink?" I raise a questioning eyebrow.

Gaspard chuckles. "No, I'm trying to quit because of stomach problems."

"Okay. I thought he has a say in your diet as well. Knowing him, I wouldn't be surprised if he checked how many breaks you take to go to the bathroom," I mumble before ordering my caramel Frappuccino.

The smile that appears on the driver's lips intrigues me. I have no idea how many years he has been working for Aaron, but from how I have seen them interact, it makes me think he wasn't hired recently.

"Mr. Steel has his own way of organizing his life," Gaspard announces cryptically.

"That's for sure. Never let someone propose an alternative solution to him." I say it as a joke, but it is the truth. With Aaron, you either do it his way, or you don't do it at all.

The driver smiles and looks down. I observe him and wait for him to contradict me because it is more than clear he doesn't have the same opinion. I urge him to continue when I see he doesn't add anything else.

"Sometimes it's hard to understand why Mr. Steel behaves like this, but you should understand it most of all."

I watch him curiously as I sip from my Frappuccino and approach the car.

"Should it be some wise suggestion? A life lesson? I don't

understand, really."

He shakes his head and smiles. "I would never dare to lecture you, but I think the two of you have a very similar life. When someone asks you to do something, do you ever ask yourself if this person's interest is to do you good or to take advantage of your position as a famous actress?" he asks before closing the door and walking to the driver's seat.

With a sentence, in his cryptic way, Gaspard allows me to shed light on an aspect of Aaron that I hadn't considered. In my small way, I have to be very careful about the people around me. I don't have many friends I trust, and I suppose it's the same for Aaron, only in a much bigger sense. To have reached his level of power in Hollywood means that he has made many friends and enemies on the way. It is not always easy to discern who is one and who is the other. For this reason, perhaps it is easier for him to manage every aspect of the lives of the people surrounding him, to have complete control of what happens around him.

***

Today is one of those rare Mondays when I don't have to work. After taking me home, I told Gaspard to go for a ride, go home, or whatever he does when he's not forced to babysit me. Aaron is in his office, meaning I can enjoy this immense glorious mansion. Too bad that in all this ultra-modern space, there is not much to do apart from basking on the deck chairs near the pool.

I'm in the middle of one of the hottest chapters of my latest novel when I'm distracted by the ringing of my cell phone. When I see who's calling, all the excitement for the sexiest scene I've ever read fades at lightning speed. I take a deep breath and answer the call.

"Hello, Mom." My tone is almost funeral.

Not that I have a terrible relationship with my mother, but since I moved to Los Angeles to be an actress, not a single minute goes by without her reminding me what a big mistake I'm making.

"Are you Aaron Steel's lover?" she snaps with her scolding tone that makes me go back to when I was five years old.

"I'm fine, thank you, and you? Nothing striking has happened since the last time we talked, but thank you for asking," I reply in an acid tone, knowing that it makes her angry.

The day that was supposed to be one of total relaxation is becoming one of those where I swim for two hours to get rid of the nerves.

"Stop being a little girl and answer the question," she scolds.

"No, Mom. I'm not Aaron Steel's lover. I am surprised you are completely calm about the crazy stalker since, apparently, your sources of information are gossip magazines," I answer, annoyed.

I hear her sigh and take a break, perhaps to calm down, since she is making a scene that she also knows to be ridiculous. I've never been a person who sleeps around, and she knows very well that I would never carelessly slip into Aaron's bed. It doesn't matter how sexy he is.

"I know the stalker story is not true. Otherwise, you would have told me. You are not someone who takes such a threat lightly."

"But am I one who slips lightly into the bed of a man I barely know?"

"I don't know, you tell me. Do you live in his house, or is that a story invented by the newspapers?" she replies.

Guilt makes room in my chest. I never told her I came to live here because then I would have to explain about my umpteenth appearance in the newspapers wasted, and I'm not proud of that part of my life.

"I don't sleep with him," I repeat.

"But you live in his house." Hers is not a question. She knows very well that when I avoid answering her questions, it is because she is right.

"Does it make any difference where I live?"

"When it's at *that* man's house, it makes all the difference in the world."

The guilt soon turns into a subtle vein of anger that has consumed me since I was twelve and we started having this conversation.

"Did you finally decide to explain to me why you hate him so much? Because if that's not the case, then we can end this conversation here," I answer acidly.

I hear her sigh again. "Mel…"

"Don't call me that. My name is Dakota. We've had this conversation before." I know my frustration is turning me into a real bitch, but I've been waiting for an explanation from her for eleven years.

Eleven years in which the subject of Aaron Steel has been taboo, and I am tired of hearing her excuses for not talking about him.

"Dakota, please come home. It's not too late to go to college and find a real job," she implores.

And like every time I bring up the subject of Aaron Steel,

my mother diverts the conversation, making me feel guilty for choosing to be an actress instead of becoming something she considers more. To have thrown away my excellent grades and scholarships for prestigious universities to pursue a dream that she cannot understand.

"Have a good day, Mom," I mumble before ending the call.

Every conversation with her reminds me how much of a disappointment I am, and I feel the weight of my every decision.

***

I'm still annoyed by my mother's call when the doorbell app sends me a notification. Serena's blond hair peeps out in front of the camera. The temptation to pretend not to be home is strong, but the tired smile and the certainty that she will remain glued to that gate for the rest of the day makes me give in. Five minutes later, she is sitting next to me on the deck chair.

"Bad day?" I ask her when she doesn't flood me with her usual chatter.

She shrugs and stares at the city of her dreams that, in her case, are turning into nightmares.

"I flunked another audition," she murmurs without looking at me.

I feel sorry for her. I don't know what it's like to try and try again to break through in an industry that doesn't give you any chance because I was damn lucky. I arrived in Los Angeles with big dreams, showed up at the first casting open to the public, and got the leading part. I believe that no one has had a life as simple as mine, and I feel guilty when I see her fail at every audition. It must be frustrating, but the truth is that I have no idea how it feels, and I don't know how to help her.

"I'm sorry," I whisper, not knowing what else to say.

She turns and offers me a tired smile.

"I'll do fine next time." She doesn't seem convinced.

"Do you need money to pay the rent?"

She looks down and blushes. I know it's embarrassing for her to ask for help because she can't make it to the end of the month. That's why I feel always so conflicted when she visits me on set and I don't push her away. Because the trucks that offer food to production sometimes are the only decent meal she manages to have during the day. She shouldn't be there, but she also should be able to afford to eat every day.

"I will find something. Don't worry." She forces another smile, but I see how discouraged she is.

I grab my phone and transfer the amount she needs to her account as I have done many other times. I live in a mega villa with a pool. It costs me nothing to help her when she needs it.

"Sorry for inviting all those people the other night." She finally looks up at me.

I study her for a few moments. She really regrets having done it.

"I was a little jealous of where you live and wanted to come and see for myself. I told Roland…who then told some of his friends…who told some other friends, and in the end, things got out of hand. I didn't want to get you into trouble."

I shrug and smile. "Don't worry. Aaron instills fear, barks, but doesn't bite."

A mischievous smile appears on her face. "You mean he didn't put you on his lap to spank you?"

The implications of her tone are far from chaste, and I blush.

"Serena!" I reproach.

She bursts out laughing, and I with her.

"Don't tell me you've never dreamed of putting your hands on that hot body," she teases.

The embarrassment becomes more and more evident because I must admit that when I found him staring at me from the balcony of his room the other night, I caught fire. I've had several guys, and it was also quite pleasant to go to bed with some of them, but nobody's looked at me with such intensity that I almost came.

"I might have imagined him while using BoB," I admit with a bit of shame.

Serena laughs even louder. "Are you serious? Do you use a vibrator when you have him in flesh behind the door literally next to yours?"

I push her until she gets up and lies on the deck chair next to mine.

"It's not like I can walk into his room and slip into his bed," I protest.

"Why not?" Her question is genuinely curious.

"Have you seen the models he usually dates? I can't be so femme fatale. I am… Awkward. I blather about romance novels. He can't find me attractive," I confess.

"Do you really tell him about the porn you read?" she teases.

"I don't read porn. They're novels with a plot!"

"Yes, of course. Have you ever found a man who makes you come as described in those books?"

To tell the truth, the only one that made me experience decent orgasms is BoB, the boyfriend on battery I keep in my bedside drawer.

"Exactly as I thought. Hold this, take a sip, and forget the mediocre fucks you've had." She pulls out a bottle of Jack Daniels from her bag and all the lightness of this moment slips away.

"Serena, I don't…" I hesitate instead of grabbing the bottle as I usually do.

My friend rolls her eyes and pushes it into my hands.

"We don't have to get drunk, and it's just you and me in this house. No press, no witnesses. What harm can it do to take a sip of this stuff? It relaxes you and brings back your smile. Don't believe I didn't notice your serious face when I arrived. Have you talked to your mother?"

I look down, and I don't need to say anything. She's witnessed enough phone calls home to understand when my conversation with her puts me in a bad mood.

"Just a sip. I don't get drunk." I accept her offer and let a sip of the liquid that burns my throat descend into my practically empty stomach, apart from this morning's Frappuccino.

"Just a sip." She winks at me as she grabs the bottle and drinks a generous amount.

Two hours later, we are both in her car with two of her friends, with light heads and a smile on our faces. Serena is sitting in the front, next to Sean… or Dean, I don't remember, with her head out the window singing at the top of her lungs the songs that play on the radio. Next to me, in the back seat, Sean or Dean, is telling me something about one of the auditions he flunked because he arrived drunk and vomited in front of the casting director.

I laugh when he laughs, and I make a surprised face when he makes a surprised face, but I'm not really following what he is saying. My head is elsewhere. It travels between the guilt of succumbing to the temptation to go out and the sense of freedom that alcohol causes me. I'm not drunk, but I'm tipsy enough not to be held back by my inhibitions, by the sense of duty that tells me to behave like an adult.

I manage to have a decent conversation with the guy next to me, and he doesn't think I'm a perfect idiot. We speak like two ordinary people, and I don't babble my usual nonsensical reasoning about the current book I'm reading. It's been over fifteen minutes, and he's not looking at me like I'm a pathetic geek. And he's not gone yet! It's a record by my standards. It usually takes me five minutes to ruin the conversation.

We arrive at Mystique, one of the clubs where my fame allows us to enter without being carded, considering Serena is still twenty. We approach one of the bouncers of the VIP area, who, as soon as he sees us, shows off a huge smile and lowers himself to unhook the red velvet cord from the golden ring that opens the doors to an evening of entertainment.

"Thank you," I whisper, smiling before kissing his cheek covered with a well-groomed dark beard. It's lovely how a drop of alcohol makes me feel invincible and sexy.

"It's a pleasure, honey." He reciprocates my smile.

When we enter, the room's dim light makes me feel immediately at home. The neon lights that surround the bar are the only source of lighting for the club, and perhaps this is why it is often frequented by famous people. When you sit at one of the tables, the shade guarantees the little privacy you need to spend the night unbothered.

A waitress comes to pick up our orders, and I leave her my credit card to open a tab for the evening. Next to me on the sofa, Serena has her hands stuck in the flap of Sean's jeans, while he explores her tonsils with a kiss that has far too much tongue for my taste. I grimace, disgusted by the scene, and I turn toward the blond, Dean, next to me, who has a mischievous smile on his lips.

He gets closer to tell me something, but the loud music prevents me from understanding even one word. I think it's a question because he is waiting for me to say something, but I have no idea what to answer, so I simply smile, and he seems to light up and get even closer. Far too close for my taste. I am happy when the waitress comes to our table with the tray of cocktails we ordered. At least Serena has been forced to detach herself from the guy who seems to want to devour her.

My friend's hair is tangled, her lipstick is smeared, and her makeup drips from her eyes making her look a bit vacuous. I think she's drunk, and seeing her like this makes me sad. It's not a nice view, and I can't help but wonder if I look like that too… vapid.

I grab the glass with the colored liquid and sip some, washing away with its sweet taste all the doubts that assail me. Serena laughs and plays with her phone. Next to me, Dean gets closer and closer and tells me about things I can't understand. The music is loud, the lights are low, and I feel like I'm wrapped in a cocoon where I feel safe. I don't know how much time has passed, but when Dean's hand starts stroking my knee, I realize he's too close. I get up, and my head spins a little.

"I'm going to the bathroom," I shout to be heard by Serena.

Step by step, I arrive at the corridor where I know I will find the bathrooms. I've been here so many times that I could get anywhere with my eyes closed. The black walls and lack of lighting make this hallway darker than the rest of the venue, but luckily I know it well enough to know where I am. The music is much less deafening here, and when I lean against the wall, I can inhale deeply and focus on what surrounds me. I don't have to go to the bathroom, but I don't want Dean's hands on me either.

"Here you are. Do you want me to accompany you?" Dean's voice has the same effect as scratching nails on a blackboard.

"No, thank you, I can do it myself." I smile at him, but I would like to scream when he rests his hands on my hips and lowers his face next to my ear.

"Are you sure? Because I swear I can keep you entertained," he whispers, and when I try to push him away, his grip becomes firm.

"I'm sure. I'm not interested," I say confidently, even if the words come out slightly slurred because of the alcohol.

"Come on, don't play hard to get. We can just have fun," he repeats and presses his chest against mine. My back is pressed against the wall, and I struggle to push him away.

"Hands off." A deep voice that I have learned to recognize makes my head turn.

Next to us, the imposing figure of Aaron covers that little bit of light that filters through the room.

Dean either doesn't immediately realize what is happening or pretends not to have heard because he doesn't hint at giving up. My eyes, however, are glued to the figure of my boss, who appears furious.

"I said hands off," he repeats with more anger than before, and Dean finally understands and turns to him.

"Listen, man, we are busy here. Go fuck yourself?" His bored voice is annoying.

"I said. Hands. Off," Aaron repeats, taking a step in our direction and staring at Dean with a murderous look.

The guy finally leaves my hips and faces Aaron, crossing his arms.

"And who are you? Her father?" he asks amusedly.

I look at Aaron's face, an impassive mask of coldness. The only hint of his fury is a tiny flicker of his jaw muscle when clenching his teeth.

"I'm the one who tears off your fingers, one at a time. When I'm done with those, I tear your whole hands off, and when I'm done with those, I'll rip off your arms. If you dare to touch her again, I swear I'll tear you to pieces so small that they will need a microscope to identify you."

His threat is so glacial that a shiver runs down my spine. I'm not sure if it's fear or excitement. No one has ever defended me with such determination that I'm sure he could kill this guy with his bare hands.

Dean finally listens to the survival instinct that is shouting at him to run as fast as he can and murmurs, "Psycho," toward Aaron as he scoots by to leave.

A wave of excitement hits me when Aaron's gaze passes from Dean's back to me. His eyes exude anger, possession, and maybe even a little lust when his gaze runs over my body, covered only by a top that leaves my belly uncovered and a skirt so short it barely covers my butt. A flash of what I could only read as jealousy runs through his gaze before he's able to compose himself. It's only a fraction of a second but just enough to set me on fire.

This afternoon's conversation with Serena comes to mind, along with the sensations I felt reaching orgasm, imagining that instead of BoB, there were his expert fingers moving inside me. The excitement rising inside is something I struggle to contain, and the alcohol doesn't help curb my hormones that seem to awaken only with his presence.

Aaron approaches, entering my breathing space, making me hold my breath. His aftershave fills my nostrils and makes my head spin. He rests his hands on the wall behind me, on either side of my face, and lowers himself until he reaches my height and nails me with his gaze. It would be enough for him to touch me to make me come here on the spot.

"You're drunk." It's not a question.

"A bit"

His nostrils flare with fury. Knowing that I trigger these reactions in him makes me feel euphoric.

"And you would have let that scum fuck you in a corridor where everyone can see you?" His tone is low, icy, which reaches my belly and turns my bowels upside down.

I raise one hand and rest it on his face, feeling his muscles tense under my fingers as his eyes become the color of the storm and his breathing becomes shorter.

"Not him, but maybe someone else…" I slide my fingers over his perfect skin until I get to his lips. They are soft. I didn't expect them to be this smooth. They are the lips of someone who cares about his appearance.

Aaron is a living paradox. Pure virility, but at the same time, his attention to his image borders on the manic.

"Dakota, you don't know with who you're playing." His voice is hoarse, as if he were making a titanic effort to restrain himself.

"Really? Maybe I know, and I decided to taste the forbidden fruit." Alcohol makes me bold and uninhibited, like the models accompanying him during events and who probably warm his bed during the after-party. I feel sexy and able to seduce a powerful man like him.

I slide my hand down his neck, resting my fingers on his jugular, and pause to appreciate the blood pumping crazily in his veins, the only sign of an uproar that storms inside him, but he doesn't let shine on his face. I slip down to the collar of his immaculate shirt, drifting behind his neck, until I stroke the hair on his nape, enjoying the silkiness. His gaze catches fire without ever leaving mine.

I glide my fingers down the edges of his shirt again, and the desire to pull it off him tears me up inside. I get to the knot of his tie, grab it, and pull to bring him closer. He doesn't move an inch. His arms are planted firmly on the wall on which I am leaning. With a little push, I detach myself from the wall and cling to the expensive fabric of his tie to get closer to his face, brushing his cheek with my nose. I deeply inhale his intense scent, closing my eyes and letting his heat invade me. I feel his warm breath on the skin of my neck and naked shoulder. It's a feeling that sends an adrenaline rush down my body, bringing every single cell to life.

Aaron sets me on fire with his mere presence, intoxicates me with his perfume, and makes my knees give with his beauty. I bring my lips closer to his ear and barely touch his skin, anticipating the moment when my tongue will taste every inch of his body.

With a sudden gesture, Aaron detaches himself from the wall, grabs me from under the butt, and carries me upside down on his shoulder, making me scream.

"What are you doing? Put me down!" I demand, dumbfounded when he walks down the corridor and opens the emergency door next to the bathrooms.

The fresh evening air hits my legs and butt, and I realize that I am practically naked while Aaron carries me with long strides along the parking lot at the back of the club.

"Put me down! I'm going to be sick," I beg, but he doesn't seem to hear me.

We arrive next to his SUV. He opens the door with one hand and puts me down on the passenger seat with the other. The small bag with the phone I carry on my shoulder slides until it slips between me and the seat, sticking on my bare thigh. The movement is so sudden that my stomach gives up. I bend forward and throw up on the mat of my boss's luxurious car.

I notice him close his eyes, inhale deeply, and swear under his breath.

"I told you that I was going to be sick, but you went on like a caveman," I mumble, looking inside my handbag for a tissue to clean my mouth.

He firmly moves my legs to the side, pulls the filthy carpet from under my feet, and puts it in one of the garbage bins leaning against the club wall. When he returns, he gives me a handkerchief, not one of those cheap paper tissue, but one made of fabric with his initials embroidered in one corner. Only Aaron can have such a thing in his pocket and use it to clean vomit.

I watch him as he goes around the car and gets in without

saying a word. The trip home is full of silence, and the embarrassment makes me curl up in my seat. I study him from the corner of my eye. His hands clasp the wheel so tight that his knuckles turn white, the only indication that he is furious. His profile is impassive as always. He's handsome enough to take your breath away and entirely out of my league. Why the hell did I make a fool of myself jumping him?

When we arrive in front of the house, he lets me out of the car and drags me by the arm toward the entrance.

"Slow down. These shoes are killing me," I complain.

He stops, looks at the impossibly high heels I'm wearing, then takes me in his arms like a gentleman this time, and takes me into the house. I tie my arms around his neck for support, look at his face a breath away from mine, and get lost in that square jaw and perfect features.

He walks up the stairs without ever putting me down, effortlessly, as if I didn't weigh anything, then gently places me on the bed. As soon as I put my head on the pillow, I close my eyes and enjoy the soft sheets. In a state of semi-unconsciousness, I realize that he is taking off my shoes and a lament of pain escapes from my lips when he pulls them off. I hear him murmur something incomprehensible and then feel a slight burning in my feet. It lasts very little and gives way to a pleasant feeling of freshness.

***

I open my eyes and realize that the sun is already high. My head explodes, and when I finally focus on my surroundings, I realize I am in my room. On the bedside table is a glass of water and two pills of analgesics. For a split second, I wonder who put them there, then Aaron comes to mind, how he dragged me out of the Mystique and put me to bed. I also remember how I made myself a fool trying to seduce him and then vomiting in his car. How the heck did he find me?

"Shit! Shit! Shit!" I cover my face with my hands, trying to hide the embarrassment, even though I'm alone in the room.

I sit down and rub my sweaty hands over the clothing I wore last night. At least he didn't undress me once he dumped me in bed. I notice, however, that I wear a pair of black cotton socks, too big to be mine. I take them off, perplexed by such a singular choice by my boss. When they fall on the floor, I realize there is white ointment now clotted around the wounds on my feet. After weeks of torture, they seem almost healed. Did he put a healing cream on my feet? A smile tugs on my lips for the sweet gesture, but it's promptly replaced by a frown when I think about how wasted I was last night.

"I hit on him!" I cringe when the image of how I clung to his tie comes to my mind.

I grab my phone from the bag on the floor and I notice three things: I'm utterly late for work, there's a message from the production assistant telling me to get well soon, and I have a credit card balance of one thousand two hundred dollars on the card I left at the venue.

"Shit! Shit! Shit!" I open the door wide and run down the stairs to the kitchen to put something in my stomach before taking a shower.

I've never been late for work, not a single time. I have always been on time and professional, even on those days when cycle cramps make me almost bend in two from the pain. I arrive at the kitchen and stop on the spot when I see Aaron leaning against the marble counter, sipping coffee. It's ten in the morning. He should have been at the studio hours ago. Instead, he looks at me sternly, dressed in a pair of Chinos and a white shirt. He is even barefoot.

"I called the producer of your show this morning and said that last night at dinner, we ate something that gave us food poisoning. Shooting will resume tomorrow," he announces with such seriousness that it seems almost a funeral announcement.

"Thank you... I..." The words die in my throat because what can you say to your boss who just lied to the whole production team to cover your mistake?

He approaches, gives me a cup of steaming coffee, and studies me for a long moment.

"I have no idea why you insist on going out with that girl, but this is the first and last time I do something like this to save your ass. At the next bullshit, you're fired." His tone is so low that it vibrates in my bowels. He's not joking.

"She's the only friend I have... she's the only one who doesn't try to stab me in the back," I whisper, more to myself than to him.

Aaron stops, looks at me for a few moments, then barely shakes his head.

"Are you sure about that? Because I discovered from her Instagram stories you were drunk in that club. If you consider her your only friend, I'm sorry to give you the news so brutally, but you're alone under the hot Hollywood sun," he says before leaving and locking himself in his office.

I sit at the kitchen counter, look at my phone, and at the one thousand two hundred dollar charge from the Mystique. I had time to drink only one cocktail. How did they spend one thousand two hundred dollars in one night?

Aaron's words dig a hole in me I can't fill. Still, the thing that most devastates me about this whole story is seeing the disappointed expression on the face of the only man who, despite everything, continues to give me second chances.

CHAPTER 7
Aaron

Karthik, the head of the accounting department of the streaming division, has been rattling off numbers and budgets for hours at our monthly meeting. Usually, I would ask about every single number, every budget overrun, and every penny lost or earned. It's my job, I want to be aware of how my company is doing, and I want to know if we are in deep trouble so that we can make any drastic decisions in time before sinking.

This is not the case today. The whole week was unlike any other because the image of Dakota in that club, with a top and a skirt that left nothing to the imagination, occupies my mind twenty-four hours a day. The way she touched my lips, how she stuck her thin fingers through my hair, how she approached sensually, and how her nose touched my skin, fueled my erection until it was about to explode. I've never had so much trouble holding back in front of a woman in public.

The only thing that stopped me was the fact that she was drunk. When I sleep with a woman, I want her uninhibited, consenting, and above all, completely controlling her mind and memories. But if she had been sober, I would have dragged her into one of the small closets and fucked her until she shouted my name loud enough to hear it over the deafening music of that place. To hell with her age, to hell with the fact that I am her boss and in a position of power. I would have blown up my entire career just to sink between her thighs and enjoy an orgasm that would have given relief to the solid rock erection inside my pants.

She was excited, attracted to me, and entirely out of control. The thought alone makes me so confused that I don't even know where to start convincing myself that thinking about her is a bad idea. I always thought she found me vaguely interesting but not the forbidden fruit in which to sink her teeth and damn her soul. I'm old. She's always considered me old. Pleasant to the eye, perhaps, but still ancient in comparison to her.

I am the living cliché of the thirty-six-year-old infatuated with the twenty-three-year-old. I've always thought that old men alongside girls in their mid-twenties were ridiculous, and here I am pumping my ego because a young woman made a move on me.

"Aaron," Karthik's firm voice makes me look at him.

"Pardon, what were you saying?" I ask, trying to get my wits together when he caught me daydreaming about a woman I can't have.

"Your phone has been ringing for several minutes," he tells me, embarrassed.

I realize only at this moment that the phone in front of me is lit with a notification that I hope never to see in my life.

"Holy shit."

"Problems?" he asks, raising a perplexed eyebrow.

"It's the fire alarm in my house."

The news makes him scramble for his phone.

"I'll call nine-one-one."

I wrinkle my forehead as I scroll through the alarm system app and realize it's just the kitchen.

"No, don't worry. Surely someone from the security company went to check. Possibly they have already called for help."

What puzzles me is that it's just that room. If it were a full house fire, the security system would have isolated the upstairs rooms that contain the most expensive artwork. And then I am reminded of the message from my driver who drove Dakota home an hour ago, and anger rises from my stomach. She's probably smoking in my house with that friend of hers that I can't stand. Maybe weed, given her predilection for illicit substances.

"Do you want to go home to check? We are almost finished."

"Something I should be aware of?" I ask, just to be sure.

He smiles and shakes his head as he closes his laptop. I think he wants to go home to his family, too.

"No. Nothing relevant. We tackled the tricky part at the beginning, and there are no particular variations from last month on what is left."

I sigh in relief and get up with him to walk out of the office. When I get in the car and slip into Los Angeles's slow traffic, I curse my decision not to hire another driver when I let Gaspard drive that infuriating woman around. The one who is now soaking my house with the smell of Marijuana.

"Are you going to move? It's green!" I'm glued to the horn earning a nice middle finger from the guy in front of me who shows no sign of moving his car despite the clear road.

Finally, an hour later, I cross the threshold of my house, stomp like fury toward the kitchen, and I am disoriented by the chaos in front of me. It looks as if a bomb exploded in here. There are dirty pots everywhere, remnants of vegetables on the white marble counter and on the floor, and Alexa repeating a recipe for a filet mignon that no one listens to.

"What the hell…?" The words stick in my throat when Dakota dumps the pot she was scrubbing inside the sink with a deafening noise. I startled her.

When she turns, her hair is gathered in a messy bun over her head, her eyes are red, and I think there is broccoli stuck to her T-shirt with the print of some cartoon. She looks so innocent and fragile that the only feeling in my chest is tenderness.

"I wanted to make you dinner to apologize for vomiting in your car, but it caught fire when I poured the Cognac into the pan with the steak. And while I was looking for a fire extinguisher in this damn house the size of a mall, the vegetables in the oven started to turn black. So I panicked and tried to pull it out but got burned, dropped the baking dish which broke on the floor, and I made a mess." She sobs, trying to explain why the kitchen looks like a battlefield.

The only reaction that comes from my chest is a laugh which I can't control. I thought she was here smoking a joint with those degenerate friends of hers, and she was panicking in search of a fire extinguisher. The relief that opens in my chest is so great that with two huge strides, I reach her, take her by the arm, and draw her to my chest for a hug. She clings to my waist, her hands still wet and the sobs shaking her.

"I'm dirtying your shirt with broccoli," she complains between hiccups as I stroke her head to calm her down.

She was afraid to set my kitchen on fire, and I feel a little guilty. I'm so strict and jealous of my space that she probably thought I'd be barking at her.

"Don't think about the shirt. I'll wash it, and it will come back as new," I whisper as I hold her tight.

"I ruined your pots… and the furniture is blackened where the fire has almost burned them."

"The furniture can be cleaned, and the pots replaced," I whisper as she continues to sob.

"I was terrified. When I saw the flames, I was terrified," she whispers.

And that's what I thought. She's not crying because of the mess but because she really thought she'd set the house on fire. And to think that, like a perfect asshole, I immediately thought about the art upstairs when instead she was the one who could have gotten hurt.

"I know, but now it's all over. Nothing irreparable happened," I try to console her. "How about you go upstairs and take a shower while I clean the kitchen? I'll order a pizza in the meantime."

"So, let me get this straight. I didn't prepare dinner, so you are starving. I set your kitchen on fire, but you'll clean the mess I made and also pay for the pizza? I don't know how you can run a production company. You suck in negotiations," she mumbles while I free her, and she tries to remove the broccoli stuck to my white shirt, making a much bigger stain than the one already there.

I burst out laughing. Her lack of filter between brain and mouth is so ridiculous that it only makes me laugh.

"Go upstairs before I change my mind."

She doesn't let me repeat it twice, and I watch her, amused, as she runs up the stairs. But when I look at the disaster in front of me, the smile dies on my lips.

**

I am just putting the pizza and silverware on the table when Dakota comes downstairs and frowns as she watches me.

"Ok, I accepted many of your rich man quirks, but the pizza on the plates with cutlery… No. Just no," she snaps when she reaches the table.

I look at her with a raised eyebrow. She is very wrong if she thinks I will eat pizza from the box.

"You are still wearing your suit. Go change, and I'll prepare dinner."

"I see your fear has died down and given way to the flippant teenager," I provoke.

She's nothing like a teenager, tucked into a pair of blue shorts and a top of the same color as her naked belly. She is beautiful enough to take your breath away with her wet hair that descends down her back.

She beckons me with one hand to go upstairs to change, and I can't help but smile and shake my head. Either I accept her like this, or I will choke her.

When I finally go down to the living room, I can't find her, so I venture a look toward the pool and find her there, sitting on the deck chair with the pizza box between her legs, sipping a soda.

"Don't even think about it. I don't eat pizza with my hands," I tell her when she sees me coming and starts separating the slices with her thin fingers.

"Can you stop acting like an old man and start relaxing?"

There it is again, her definition for me that I missed.

I sit astride the deck chair in front of her and watch her pick up a slice of pizza and put it in her mouth, savoring it with her eyes closed. A drop of grease slips from the side of her lips and, with all the ease of her twenties, cleans it with the back of her hand. I don't think I ever made such a gesture even when I was five, but my childhood was not exactly like that of my peers.

I grab a slice from the cardboard box and bite in despite my body's almost physical protest.

"See? It wasn't that difficult," she tells me with a full mouth and then smiles, nodding at the sweatpants I'm wearing. "So you don't just have elegant clothes. You also have something like us mere mortals in the closet."

"It's not that I'm an alien. Every now and then, I enjoy a little rest and do it with something comfortable," I object.

She raises an eyebrow to call my bullshit.

"Really? When have you had a moment of rest since I came to live here?"

"Tonight?" I admit with a half-smile. It's not that I have many opportunities to wear these clothes.

"As I thought." She smiles at me.

The silence lasts for a few minutes. It is not one of the embarrassing ones. In fact, it is almost relaxing. When I open a can of soda I took from the fridge, I'm almost tempted to go back to get a glass of wine, but then I change my mind. Drinking before her and telling her that she should not get drunk sounds a bit hypocritical.

"Why did you decide to save my career?" she asks me out of the blue.

I observe her for a few seconds and try to decipher the expressions that cover her face. Worry, embarrassment, and maybe even a little humiliation, but at the same time, curiosity.

"Money," I answer without too many words.

I notice her surprise. Perhaps she tried to give an answer to this question herself, so I explain it to her.

"*Hunters of Shadows* is the most important show in the broadcaster's streaming division. The sponsors are breathing down our necks because of your out-of-control behavior, but at the moment, they have not yet come to close their wallets. I had two choices, get you on track and continue with a show that keeps the whole company afloat or decide to fire you and, in fact, shut down the show before even shooting the fourth season. I have chosen the money I need to continue the streaming project." I am brutally sincere with her. She is not dumb. She is far from it. Coating the pill or belittling the problem is not helpful to either of us.

She looks down, clearly ashamed of the situation. She is young. She made a mistake, and she will learn from it.

"I'm sorry. I don't do it on purpose to end up in the newspapers... I mean, I don't do it because I want to be a diva. I wanted you to know," she whispers, and I can feel all the guilt that permeates her words.

"May I know why you get drunk when you go out and know you're going to make the front pages of the newspapers? You are not stupid. After the first time, you should have learned." I'm sincerely intrigued by this behavior which seems completely unusual compared to her personality.

She looks up and blushes.

"Alcohol helps me relax enough so that I'm not a total disaster when I have to interact with people."

I dwell on her words, but I cannot understand them. "Are you shy? Is that you can't talk to someone?"

"Not exactly. When I go out with someone, who knows my job, they always expect me to have something super interesting to say. When they realize that, in reality, my life is not as exciting as everyone thinks, they lose interest in me very soon and find someone else to chat with. I've gotten to the point where I get performance anxiety when I have to go out because I already know I have to be the funny, sexy girl with a sparkling personality; otherwise, my conversations with people last five minutes. Alcohol helps me overcome my initial nervousness. The problem is that it also erases my sense of limitation, and I don't notice when I go from relaxed to completely drunk," she admits.

"You're an actress. Your job is to interact with people. How can you be anxious about dealing with normal conversations?" I ask incredulously.

"Being an actress is easy. You learn the lines, you act, you become someone else. You play the part of the independent, sarcastic one, the person who always has a joke for every situation. When I go out with someone, they expect me to be exactly like that, but in reality, I am the one who fails to be brilliant when I answer their questions. Have you ever thought of the perfect joke in response to someone, hours after you had that conversation when it's too late? It happens to me every time, and alcohol helps me not to feel the pressure of having to impress someone. When I drink, I become the person with the perfect response at the perfect time."

It is challenging to imagine her inability to communicate with people because I have never seen this side of Dakota. In fact, it is the exact opposite, and I wonder what her true personality is.

"You've never had this problem with me. You always answer me without ever missing a beat."

She smiles and shakes her head, blushing.

"I know, but with you, it's different. I don't have to impress you. You see me as potentially interesting. Or rather, you find me interesting if I'm a good actress, and that I know I am. It's something I can work on and prepare for. With you, I have to be professional at work, which I can do because I can prepare in time. It's not something I have to improvise. I can talk with you about topics that really interest me, that I am passionate about, of which I know even the slightest nuance. You don't expect me to be like the character I become on set. And it is easier because you answer me with just as many interesting facts, and it isn't difficult to keep a conversation alive for hours. When you find yourself in front of a guy who just wants to slip into your panties, it's hard to find a topic of conversation that interests him and keeps his focus on anything other than my tits squeezed into a bikini."

Somehow I understand. I often have to change four or five topics to get the conversation to flow, especially in Hollywood, where nobody is himself in public. But I have years of experience on my back that have taught me to juggle these situations and a father who has beaten me to the point of branding this skill all the way into my DNA.

"And then there's Serena, who doesn't help. She is exuberant, always comfortable in every situation, and drags me into parties that sometimes are a little too out of my comfort zone."

"Why do you keep going out with that girl? It's clear that when you're with her, you lose control."

She shrugs and shakes her head as she swallows another bite of pizza.

"She is the only one who has remained close to me these three years, despite everything. I have noticed that people in this industry often approach me to get something. An audition, a good word with the casting director, with the director… They pretend to be my friends until they understand that my opinion in Hollywood is worth nothing and I can't give them what they want. I know that Serena is not perfect and often plays on my insecurities, but sometimes a friend like her is better than being alone."

I look at her for a long moment and realize how lonely she is. This industry tends to isolate you and let you flounder alone in shark-infested waters. I tried it, but at least I always had my brother. We have never been particularly close, but I know for a fact that if I need a word of comfort or even just to clarify my ideas, his opinion is always sincere, and his help comes without ulterior motives. I can't help but wonder how deep her loneliness is if she feels the need to fill the void with fake friendships and alcohol.

"Don't you have brothers or sisters?"

She shakes her head and smiles a melancholy smile.

"My father died when I was seven years old, and my mother never remarried."

"I'm sorry."

"Don't be. It happened long ago, and my mother never let me lack the affection I needed growing up."

I'm glad she at least had a parent to support her.

"Does she live far away?"

"Idaho."

"What does she think about you living alone in a city like Los Angeles?"

The question pulls a kind of amused grunt from her.

"If it were her, she would make me go home instantly and continue my studies."

Her reaction intrigues me. "Isn't she happy about your career?"

She shrugs and cleans her mouth again with the back of her hand, a gesture that I find particularly sexy and distracts me for a few moments.

"When I took two years off after high school to perfect my acting skills, found a job to have money to move here, and then came to Los Angeles, she thought I would never be able to break through. She hoped I would soon give up and use the full scholarships for college I was able to nail. But I was lucky, I immediately got the part at my first audition and blew up all her dreams." She laughs, amused.

"Don't say you were lucky. You're a good actress. You got this part because you deserved it, and you beat hundreds of other girls who showed up," I tell her, and I see her blush with shyness.

"If Aiden Rodriguez hadn't given up the part because of a conflict with the filming schedule of her other movie, I wouldn't be here now." She smiles half-heartedly.

I furrow my brows and study her to see if she is serious or fishing for compliments.

"It didn't go that way," I tell her, drawing her attention.

"When the casting director had to choose between the two of you, he called me for the final decision. You were definitely better than her and more suited to the part, but you had no experience, and it was too big a risk to bet on a stranger. Sending Rodriguez home and finding ourselves with an unprofessional actress who blows up the production schedule was a risk to be taken with due precautions. When I saw the videos of your auditions, I had no doubt that you were perfect for the part. I preferred to risk a recasting after the first few episodes rather than let you go. It never happened that a casting director left the last word to me for the final decision."

She widens her eyes in surprise.

"Really?" She almost seems to doubt my words. "She told everyone that she had to give up the part because she had a contract for another movie and couldn't be on two sets at the same time."

I smile at her naivety.

"Of course, she said something like that. She certainly couldn't say she lost the part to a complete stranger from Idaho!"

She bursts out laughing, amused, and I see her relieved for the first time since I set foot in this house tonight.

The phone vibrates in my pocket, and when I pull it out, I don't have time to see the preview of the message. Dakota has already taken it and placed it on the deck chair next to ours.

I raise an eyebrow in a silent scolding.

"Tonight, you are here to relax, remember?"

"What if it's something important?"

She raises an eyebrow as if to say, *don't bullshit me.*

"It took you an hour to get home when you thought the house was on fire. What's more important than that?"

"You know, sooner or later, that tongue of yours will get you into trouble, right?" I can't hide the fun in my voice.

"Do you want to play the boss card now? You're in sweat-pants and a T-shirt!" she teases.

"You're incredible," I whisper in front of her frankness.

"When was the last time you enjoyed this pool to relax?" she asks.

I wrinkle my forehead and think about it for a few moments.

"Never. This is the first time I've used this pool for the sheer pleasure of doing it and not for some party for the big shots," I admit, a little ashamed.

I find her staring at me with her mouth and eyes wide open.

"Are you serious?"

"I'm always too busy," I try to justify myself as she gets up and reaches out her hand.

I hesitate for a moment before grabbing it and getting up to follow her without understanding what she wants to do until a moment before she pushes me into the water, fully dressed, and follows me with a bomb dive. I re-emerge and spit out a puff of water.

"You've gone completely crazy," I complain, passing my hands through my hair, trying to get it out of my eyes.

She rolls her eyes. "It's a pool, Aaron, not a pot of hot oil."

"I'm fully dressed," I point out.

"I repeat, it's a swimming pool. It's full of water. Your clothes will dry."

"Do you always have an answer ready for everything?"

"I would like that! Do you know how much easier my life would be?"

I turn toward her and find her staring at my chest, more

specifically the muscles she can glimpse under the white fabric of the shirt glued to my skin. I knew the hours spent in the gym sweating like a twenty-year-old would not be wasted. She bites her lip, and when she looks up at me and realizes that I caught her staring, she looks down and blushes. It is that mixture of sexy and sweet that my body seems to appreciate so much that awakens the erection in my pants. I'm happy to be immersed in the water so she can't see it.

When she looks up at me again, the embarrassment has disappeared, and the moment she swims toward me, I feel vulnerable. When she is one step away from me, she grabs my arm and makes me turn, giving her my back.

"You have a tattoo," she whispers as her fingers slide down the dark lines under my shirt, sending a shiver down my spine.

"It's a phoenix," I whisper. Not many people know that I have it, even though it is as big as my whole back.

"Why a phoenix?" she asks, clinging to my shoulders and swimming around me to see my face. Her hands rest on my shoulders, and mine slide to her hips.

"To remind me that you can be reborn from your ashes, again and again." Every time my father crushes me until some of my dreams die, I am reborn, stronger than before.

She looks at me for a long moment, her thin fingers lightly caressing the skin on my neck. I'm not even sure she's aware she's doing that. I think she wants to ask me more about the ink under my skin but decides not to. I thank her silently for this because I don't know if I would be able to explain and make myself vulnerable in front of her.

I pause to observe her lips, the drops of water that stop on her cupid's bow. I stare at her as she bites her lower lip, and my fingers tighten around her hips as I struggle to resist the desire to kiss her.

Her breathing becomes labored as she approaches slowly, reducing the distance between us. My phone vibrates again on the deck chair a few feet away, like an alarm bell waking me up. I detach myself from her and swim to the edge, pushing myself out of the water and grabbing the phone where Dakota threw it a few minutes ago. I read the messages without understanding them because all my reasoning is completely clouded by the erection that presses against my pants. I hear Dakota swimming to where I am and getting out of the water to sit in front of me. I'm so turned on that I don't dare look her in the eye.

CHAPTER 8
Dakota

The thing I like most about Aaron's house is that, despite it being June and the heat of Los Angeles being unbearable, by the pool, there is always a light breeze that gives you relief. Lying on the deck chair under the umbrella and sipping strictly non-alcoholic fruit cocktails is an excellent way to spend my morning relaxing, especially if there is one of the fantasy books I love to keep me company.

I look up at the kitchen window where Aaron is focused on reading the newspaper while sipping one of his smoothies with cabbage leaves and other ingredients, all too healthy for my taste. He tried to get me to taste one, saying they are rich in antioxidants that are good for my skin, but I couldn't swallow it. The muddy texture and bitter taste were so horrible that I spat it all into the sink under Aaron's bewildered gaze. In response, I teased him a bit by telling him that those things help him more because he is old, and, as expected, he left the room pretending to be offended.

I study the way his sweaty tank top adheres to his body after hours spent in the gym this morning, the sweatpants that hug his perfect butt, and the dark lines of the phoenix emerging on his shoulders. He's sexy to die for. I have always considered him a man with charisma, pleasing to the eye, but always too distant to be considered distinct from the public figure he represents.

Living together, however, I've seen aspects of him that the public doesn't have the opportunity to admire, and I must say that they are sexier than an elegant suit sewn on him. It's sexy how his hair curls on his forehead after a shower, how his lips become sulky while he's cooking, and how he looks at me as I tell him something while he is focused on the pan.

It's sexy his way of speaking, reasoning, and making adult chat, allowing me to express an opinion on something that is not frivolous, such as politics or economics. He was pleasantly surprised when I told him I had opened an investment account to put money for my future with the first check I received. We have spent hours discussing the best ways to make the most of my investments to ensure a retirement paycheck that is adequate to one's standard of living.

It's official, I have a huge, gigantic, stratospheric crush on my boss.

I still have my eyes resting on him when I see him get up in fury, reach me with great strides, and grab me by the arm to get me up from the deck chair. For a moment, I blush, almost frightened that he may have read my indecent thoughts about him and wants to kick me out of the house.

"You must go to your room and don't come out until I tell you, okay?" he orders, putting everything I left scattered next to me on the deck chair in my hands and rearranging the pillows to make it appear unused.

I open my mouth to ask him what the hell is going on, but he nails me with a look.

"I'll explain later, but now you have to run upstairs."

His tone is so resolute that every protest dies on my lips, and I find myself running up the stairs with my arms full of my stuff. I don't have time to close the bedroom door behind me when I hear his father's voice thundering from downstairs, and I stop my run. That man always gives me chills. I drop my stuff on the floor and crawl to the glass parapet overlooking the living room below, lying on the ground on the precious carpet that tickles my naked stomach. I'm lucky that its bristles are so soft that they almost look like a cashmere sweater.

"I told you to fire that bitch of your assistant, and you didn't do it!" I hear him shout. I can only see Aaron's bored face and his father's back from this position.

"I don't fire one of my best employees just because she threatens to chop off your balls. I hired her precisely because she is not intimidated by the bullshit you pour on her." Aaron raises his voice a little, the only sign that this conversation is making him angry.

It is strange how I learned to read the small signs of his rigid posture and the intonation of his voice so that I understand when he is uncomfortable. He is angry, but there is something more, something that stops him from clenching his fists or putting his hands in his pockets to hide his white knuckles. He seems almost paralyzed, and the realization causes an icy shiver down my back. Aaron never lets himself be intimidated by anything.

"When I tell you to do something, you do it, you understand?" his father rants.

"And did you show up to my house for the first time in your life just to tell me I have to fire Tracy because she threatened to take your balls? You must be attached to your testicles to feel threatened by her words." I believe his intention is to ridicule his father, but an inclination in his voice makes him appear insecure.

His father gets closer, and although Aaron doesn't move, he slightly widens his eyes and appears surprised. I don't think he's used to such an attitude on his father's part, and if I'm honest, I've never seen Aaron Steel Sr. lose control in this way. Of course, I have only seen him in public, I don't know if this is typical behavior between them. From how Aaron seems caught off guard, I think he's at least as surprised as I am.

"I came here because the girl still lives with you. Only gossip magazines can believe the absurd story that there is a crazy stalker. I know you fuck her. Do you want to get stuck with her for the rest of your life? I hope at least you have the decency to use a condom and not get her pregnant. I don't want you to waste money you can put in the family business for a child born by mistake," he hisses.

I am so shocked by his words that, for a moment, I don't realize they are addressed to me. I'm too focused on looking at the mask of fury that covers Aaron's face.

"If you think you're coming into my house to use your filthy mouth to insult one of my employees, you haven't understood anything from life. I shouldn't even be here to respond to your disgusting insinuations, but one thing I want to be very clear, I don't sleep with Dakota, and I don't allow anyone to talk about her in this way," Aaron hisses with a fury that could incinerate his father.

His father bursts into a laughter so wicked that the blood freezes in my veins.

"Who do you think you are dealing with? With the newbies you surround yourself with? There is no reason to keep her within these walls. You will never convince me that you've never fucked her." He chuckles, amused, before pulling a sheet of paper out of his pants pocket. "Keep this. It's a prescription for the pill that a friend of mine prescribed. Put it in her breakfast every morning without her noticing, so at least you won't have a bastard around the house in nine months."

I am so stunned by his proposal and insinuations that I am amazed to watch as Aaron grabs his father's tie and draws him a few inches from his face. I can't see his father's face, but he doesn't seem to react to the physicality of that response.

"Get out of my house, and if you dare to come back, I swear I'll break your legs. If you approach Dakota, you are a dead man," he hisses.

It's the second time I've heard Aaron intimidate someone who somehow threatens me. While this situation makes my skin crawl, Aaron's low, furious voice melts my lower abdomen into a pool of lava that sends every cell in my body into fibrillation. I should be terrified by this whole situation, but since he looked at me in the pool the other night as if he wanted to devour my lips, I can't help but find his Alpha male attitude sexy to die for.

When Aaron finally lets him go, his father fixes his tie and turns around with a creepy smile.

"When the novelty is over, and you want to get rid of her, don't ask for my help," he says before walking out of my sight.

Aaron remains impassive, and when I hear the front door close, I see him lean against the back of the sofa and emit a deep sigh while looking at his bare feet. He seems almost entirely defeated by the meeting.

"You can come down. He's gone." His voice comes calm but clear upstairs.

He looks up toward me as I stand and walk down the stairs until I reach him.

"How are you?" he asks, glancing at me furtively.

"I'm fine, but how are you? It wasn't a pleasant conversation."

He looks into my eyes, caught off guard by my question, as if no one's ever cared about his feelings. Living together for the last few months, I've realized that his life is quite lonely. I don't know if he has women warming his bed outside this house, but since I've been here, I've never seen him take someone to bed, much less stay long enough to have breakfast together.

He shrugs and looks down. "He's my father. I'm used to it."

"I didn't ask you if you're used to it. I asked you how you are."

His gaze snaps up to mine with a mixture of surprise and, perhaps, relief. A half-smile appears on his lips. "In a few minutes, I will be better. I just have to try to calm the anger I feel."

I nod and accept his answer without insisting. If there's one thing I've realized about him, it's that he's used to managing his feelings on his own and at his own pace.

"You know he's a filthy pig and nothing he said about you is the truth or something I think, don't you?" His question is cautious as if to test my reaction to what I just witnessed.

I nod and smile at him. "As disgusting as those words were, I know they are not true."

"Are you okay?" he insists.

"Words that have no foundation in truth cannot hurt me. I know we don't sleep together, and I'm also aware that I don't open my legs with everyone. The words of a lousy man don't make me feel like I am worth less just because he is in a position of power even if they disgust me."

"You were supposed to stay in your room as I told you," he mumbles, realizing only now that I didn't listen to him.

I roll my eyes and snort. "It's not that I couldn't hear what you were saying. You were shouting."

Aaron extends a hand and grabs my shoulder to make me turn entirely toward him.

"That's not why I told you to disappear. I don't want him to set his eyes on you, ever. You have to stay away from him, got it? I don't want you to ever be alone with him. Don't open the door if he comes back here and I'm not at home."

I am surprised by the apprehension that shines through his gaze. Of course, his father has a mania for power that equals that of a psychotic dictator, but Aaron seems almost concerned for my physical safety.

"Aaron, I've been working in this city for three years. Trust me, I have already dealt with filthy pigs and am not so easily impressionable. I know how to look after myself." I try to reassure him, but his forehead wrinkles in an expression that shakes my confidence.

"Don't underestimate him. I'm not joking or even exaggerating the situation to scare you. That man is dangerous, and you have to promise me that if you find yourself for some reason alone with him, the first thing you do is leave, even if he threatens to fire you. You don't have to listen to what he says, got it? He has the ability to get into your head and ruin you if you are not careful. Promise me." His speech is so heartfelt that it enters my chest and remains there.

"I promise you, Aaron. And thank you for defending me."

I stretch my arms over his shoulders and squeeze them behind his neck, adhering to his figure with a hug. He is hesitant, perhaps because he didn't expect my gesture, but then his arms find my body, and the squeeze makes me almost short of breath. It's a firm hug. His hands stretch out wide on my back, and his fingers touch my skin with a delicacy that contrasts with the powerful size of this man. Being enclosed in his arms is like being wrapped in an armor that protects you but at the same time warms and pampers you.

It's one of those hugs that slips deep down inside and makes your stomach tremble like you read about in books. There is no desire to fondle my butt as happens with guys my age, but somehow this contact is more intimate, profound, and turns on every cell of my body as if it were immersed in flammable liquid.

When we separate after a time that seems endless and, at the same time, too short, Aaron pauses for a few moments to scrutinize my face, eyes, and lips in particular.

"Excuse me," he whispers, pushing me slightly to pass in order to lock himself inside his office, leaving me with an irresistible desire to wrap my arms around his perfect body once again.

***

Aaron stays locked up in his office all day while I take refuge in my room, unsure what to do. That hug had more meaning than any other gesture between us, and now I wonder if there will be any embarrassment when he leaves that room.

My stomach begins to grumble, and, tired of overthinking what will happen when I set foot outside this bedroom, I decide it's time to find out. I find him busy with something inside the fridge when I get to the kitchen. He took a shower. His hair is still wet while the gray sweatpants adhere perfectly to his butt. The white shirt that wraps around his shoulders is so tight that it could explode around the muscles that he usually hides under his shirts.

He smiles at me when he notices I am behind him. "You're home. I thought you had gone out with your friend. I didn't hear you wandering around here all day."

I sigh in relief when I realize the hug didn't create all that tension I was afraid of and every doubt was just in my head.

"I didn't want to go out with Serena. She is with some guy she met at an audition, and she is already drunk from the messages she's sending me," I admit with embarrassment since my social life is the same as a ninety-year-old lady.

Aaron pauses to study me for a few moments before pulling out the ingredients he needs from the fridge. He places a pack of vegetables on the counter and then rests his hands on the white marble, pausing to look at my face.

"Don't you miss having a normal life? Going out with friends and everything else?"

I shrug and help him put the cheese cubes he has already finished cutting into a bowl. I don't know how to explain to him that in high school, I was the most introverted in my class, and I wasn't invited to parties. I have always preferred the chess club to cheerleaders, and I wasn't very popular.

"I didn't have a great social life even before I moved. I'm

not a hermit, but I often prefer to read a book rather than deal with people," I admit, pulling a smile from him.

"Do you like the books *I* gave you?"

"I love them. There's the fantasy series that's driving me crazy. I'm five books into it, and it's exceeding all my expectations. You should really opt it for a TV series. A film would not be enough to do it justice."

He looks at me with a smile on his lips that he struggles to hold. I know that this is not my job, but I feel satisfaction in suggesting something to him that, in my opinion, is worth studying more thoroughly.

"You know what? Why don't you lend me the first book, and tonight we can sit on the couch reading? Maybe you're right, and I can stay glued to the pages all night."

It's my turn to study him for a few moments.

"How come a successful man like you doesn't have anything to do on a Saturday night?"

"It's the first time in months I don't have a dinner or a business meeting on the weekend, and I enjoy my home. Do I look like a loser?" He chuckles.

"No, it just seems strange to me. I can tell you don't lack charm nor women drooling all over you. It wouldn't be strange if you had someone claiming your presence on a Saturday night for something not work-related."

Aaron stops seasoning the salad and turns completely, devoting his full attention to me. His gaze nails me on the spot, making me a little embarrassed.

"Is this your way of asking me if I'm single?" he asks with a half-amused grin on his lips.

"No, that's clearly your business. But you have a list of

models constantly circling around you like sharks…" What the hell do I want to know, exactly? If I can hit on him? On what planet could someone like Aaron even consider someone like me?

"For work, sure. I have been photographed with many models on the different red carpets. It's something our publicists organize. Advertising for both."

I cross my arms and raise an eyebrow. Since he is in the mood for confessions, I see nothing wrong with taking advantage of it.

"Don't tell me you've never taken any of them to bed. I'm not a naïve girl. I see how some of them strip you naked with their eyes, and the same goes for you. That attraction cannot be faked, not even for work." I challenge him to contradict me.

He bursts out laughing and shakes his head.

"I never said it didn't happen, just that it was always something occasional, nothing that ever made it through the night."

"Well, that is more realistic," I laugh, and he joins me.

The conversation quickly slips into a less personal but no less pleasant topic. Aaron loves to explain to me how the world of film production works. When I ask him to explain what could hypothetically happen if he were to opt for the series I like, he launches into a detailed description of the whole production process of a film. I could spend hours listening to him tell me something he's passionate about.

***

When Aaron said he would read next to me on the couch, he wasn't kidding. After dinner, he went to his studio to get a pair of glasses and got comfortable next to me with the first book in the fantasy series I'm reading. If I thought he couldn't be sexier, I was wrong. With his thick black frames and the concentration on his face, he is a vision that overshadows even the spicy scenes of the book I have in my hands. Several times I've found myself staring at him, losing the thread of my reading.

"Holy Christ," I hear him mumble for the umpteenth time.

I lower the book and watch him widen his eyes as he reads. I drag myself over the couch until I lean on his shoulder and peek at how far he has come. It's past four in the morning, and he has never stopped reading.

"Chapter twenty-seven. Yes, that really deserves a Holy Christ." I laugh, amused by the bewilderment on his face.

He puts the book on his legs using a receipt as a bookmark and looks at me with wide eyes.

"This is porn! Do they really publish such explicit things? I mean, I've read my good dose of novels with sex inside, but usually, they were not so…graphic in their descriptions. It's porn with people with pointed ears," he blurts out.

"That's the best part. You can live the fantasies of a perfect lover when you have to settle for reality." I shrug.

Aaron looks at me for a few moments, frowning.

"It's not like there's nothing written here that you can't do in the bedroom, just that it's very explicit. I didn't expect it."

It's my turn to look at him, frowning.

"You can't be serious. Certain things are clearly fantasies. You can't find a man who really does those things."

He wrinkles his forehead even more and sits straight.

"For example?" Curiosity exudes from him.

"Like, I don't know, a man who likes to have oral sex. To a woman, I mean, not to receive it. In these books, it always seems that a man has nothing on his mind but to stick his head between your legs and make you enjoy it. Such men exist only in books." As I proceed with my explanation, his eyes get bigger and bigger.

"You have never received oral sex? Like never? Are you a virgin?" he asks in disbelief.

It's the first time we've had such a straightforward conversation about sex, and the image that materializes in my mind of Aaron's head between my thighs makes me quiver on the couch. This thought, mixed with the sex scenes I've been reading for hours, almost makes me feel physical pleasure. I tighten my thighs, searching for that orgasm that has been mounting for hours.

"No, I'm not a virgin, but I've never found any guy who went beyond a quick fondle down there and immediately got to the point. I thought it was something that sucks, that's all," I admit with a bit of embarrassment considering my inexperience, thinking of the models he takes to bed and who certainly know how to make a man lose his mind.

"What kind of savages did you date?" he asks me, scandalized.

I shrug and show off a half-embarrassed smile. "Guys who it's a miracle if they change their Star Wars T-shirt every three weeks, and who can't make a woman orgasm even if you give them an instruction manual."

The total silence that follows is almost funny because of his scandalized expression. Too bad we are talking about my inexperience between the sheets.

"You have never experienced an orgasm in your life?"

"Not given by a man, no. But with BoB, I have no problem."

"Who the hell is Bob?"

"My Boyfriend on Batteries, the vibrator." I laugh when he opens his mouth, amused.

"You really have to find a man who knows how to make you enjoy sex. I thought mine was a generation of idiots, but yours isn't joking either."

I shrug and lean further on his shoulder.

"Maybe I should find someone older who knows how to wear a suit and tie without looking like an idiot," I whisper as his eyes catch fire and linger on my lips. "Do you have any friends to introduce me to?" I ask him in a tone that is, perhaps, a little too coy.

In a quick gesture that makes me squeak, Aaron reaches out his arm and pulls me to himself, making me sit on his lap. His eyes become the color of a stormy sky like that night at the club when he came to save me from the guy who put his hands on me.

He gets closer to my face, and I feel his warm breath on my neck. "Don't provoke me, Dakota," he whispers, unleashing a storm inside my body. "This time, you're sober and might discover a part of me you don't know."

I catch my breath and stare at his face and lips without even trying to move away or put a minimum of distance between us. It would be enough for me to lean forward and kiss him, a single tiny movement and our evening would change radically, but I am so paralyzed by this gesture that I don't move. Sitting on his legs, the intimacy is such that a lament of protest escapes my lips when he opens his book and goes back to reading because suddenly I would like him to teach me all the indecent things written between those pages.

CHAPTER 9
Aaron

"I went out last night and robbed a bank."

Tracy's voice comes to me as background noise that I can't turn off. The image of Dakota sitting on my legs as we read is imprinted on my brain. How the hell did it occur to me to act like a caveman?

"Then I went to the movies and strangled a couple of people because I was bothered by the noise they made chewing popcorn."

Tracy keeps talking, and I can't help but think of Dakota's slender body pressed against mine. That little moan that came out of her lips when I opened the book and started reading again as if it were a protest. Did she want something different? Did she want me to lay her down on that couch and let her experience how a real man makes his woman come? The problem is that she is not *my* woman. She's a girl I took in so she doesn't mess up again. I am so close to becoming her most significant trouble myself. But it's hard to resist those lips, that smart, impertinent brain that stands up to me.

"Then I went into a church and performed a satanic ritual by setting fire to the altar."

"Yes, that's fine," I answer automatically.

Tracy reaches out and closes the laptop I've been staring at since she arrived. I look at her and find her with her arms crossed and exasperation on her face.

"You didn't hear a single word of what I said, did you?"

I can't lie to her. My thoughts have distracted me so much that denying it like a kid caught in the act is ridiculous.

"I'm a little distracted today," I admit with a bit of embarrassment.

Tracy's face softens, and she looks at me for a few moments as if she were studying an animal at the zoo.

"You've been for a while. Not just today. What's been distracting you? Maybe a blond walking around your house with tiny bikinis that makes the blood go to your head?" She raises an eyebrow challenging me to deny it.

I have no argument. Since Dakota came into my house, I have even changed my habits. I haven't been to the club for almost two months, when before they saw me at least two nights a week. The truth is that I often can't wait to get home so I can spend some time with her. At first, it was an unpremeditated gesture, dictated by my concern that she would get into trouble. Now, it is an obsession.

"Trust me. My blood doesn't follow that path. It remains much, much lower than my head," I admit with a sigh as I look up at the ceiling, unwilling to see the sly smile that appears on her face.

"I didn't take you as someone who likes young women who are all about shopping and selfies." She laughs, amused, and her comment annoys me a bit.

"The problem is that Dakota is the exact opposite of frivolity." My serious tone dampens the smile on her face, and she watches me, focused. "When she came to live with me, I was convinced she was one of the many actresses who think more about their celebrity status than everything else. I couldn't be further from reality."

"Are you surprised that she's not vapid?"

"I was hoping she would be. It would have been easier. Instead, I talk to her about politics and economics, and I love how she gets angry about certain topics that fascinate her. Even just talking about romance novels becomes the best experience I've ever had. She's intelligent, and I can't resist a beautiful brain."

Tracy tilts her head and studies me. I've always had very open conversations with her, even about my private life, but we never got to talk about women. Not because there was no will, but because there wasn't anyone worth spending more than five minutes thinking about.

"Is it vital for her to stay and live with you? She doesn't get into trouble anymore. Maybe she understands that she has to calm down."

I inhale deeply and hold my breath. A single conversation was enough for Dakota to understand the situation and stop behaving like a rebellious teenager, but the mere thought of her leaving my home annoys me. To go home in the evening and not find her sitting by the pool reading is inconceivable.

"No, but I don't want her to leave," I admit sincerely. Tracy is the only one who can understand the battle I am carrying to not give in to the temptation to fulfill my fantasies.

"Did you sleep with her?"

"No, but it's becoming increasingly difficult to hide my

clear attraction for her. The other night we were reading on the couch, and I pulled her on my lap, you know? It's not normal behavior." I rub a hand across my face trying to drive away the frustration I feel inside.

"And you didn't do anything about it? I mean, no kiss, no fondling, nothing?" She furrows her eyebrow in a puzzled expression.

"No, that's the point."

"And her? Did she react in some way to that?"

I shrug and shake my head. "I had the impression that she expected a move from me, but when she saw that I wasn't going down that road, she snuggled up on my chest and kept reading."

It was the most intimate moment I've ever had with a woman—more than sex, more than a kiss.

Tracy shakes her head and seems to think about it. The best part of talking to her is that she doesn't get carried away by the feelings or judgments she carries inside. She analyzes the situation and tries to come up with a sensible suggestion.

"Why don't you make a move on her? I mean, she is young, but she is of age and, from how you talk about her, she isn't influenced by the producer's charm. It is not something forced or seedy if she sleeps with you. She is more than consenting." Her question is not a reproach. She almost seems to want to understand the motivations that make me stay away from her.

"It's complicated."

"Because you live together? The accommodation is temporary. Six months then everyone goes their own way."

"It's not that."

"So, what's the problem?"

"I don't know."

"Maybe you should first find out why she differs from the other women you surround yourself with. It has never been a problem for you to sleep with someone and then continue with your life."

Maybe that's the point. I am afraid that if I taste the forbidden fruit even once, in the end, I will no longer be able to do without it. But I'm not ready to confess it out loud yet.

"How the hell did we end up talking about my sex life? We were discussing the author of the fantasy books that Dakota suggested to me."

Tracy pauses to study me for a few moments, perhaps surprised by my sudden change of subject.

"Because after I told you about the bank robbery, the murders, and the exorcism, I realized you weren't listening to a single word of what I was telling you."

"Touché"

"However, we were saying that this woman—if she is a woman and not the pen name of a creepy old man—has no contacts. She is an indie author. She has several social networks, including Instagram, TikTok, a Facebook page, and a group, but no way to contact her," she explains.

"No email, private messages, nothing?" I ask, perplexed.

"No, she disabled the option to contact her directly."

"Why the hell doesn't she want to be contacted? From how Dakota speaks of it, she is the author phenomenon of the year. Doesn't she want to live her moment of glory?" This author is a puzzle I can't figure out.

Tracy turns her laptop to a website with a list of one-star reviews.

"Maybe because she wants to keep her mental health from going insane? Some of these reviews have nothing to do with the book's quality. They are just plain insults to the fact that she killed the most popular character in the series, thus destroying the most beloved couple. If I were her and I received such messages privately, I too would remove any possibility of contacting me."

I take a look at the reviews and realize she's right. There are even phrases in which they wish her the worst suffering. How the hell can you wish a person an illness because she made the editorial choice to kill one of the characters? Usually, I don't deal with reviews of our shows or films. There is an office that deals with precisely this. I only get the summary if viewers like or dislike our choices. I am almost in pain for those poor interns who have to sift through all this wickedness to give me the finished result.

"How the hell can you not understand that a book is fiction? These reviews are unheard of nastiness against a real person with feelings. It's chilling what they write." I'm stunned by yet another comment that makes my skin crawl.

Tracy shrugs and shakes her head. "The Internet is a den of frustrated people who feel powerful behind a keyboard. But look at her numbers. She has almost one hundred thousand followers on TikTok and about fifty thousand on Instagram. These are huge for an independent author."

I must admit that her social media management is masterful. Behind this name is someone who knows how to do marketing, how to take care of a brand, and who has managed to build a loyal reader's following that has brought her to the top of the rankings. She is not someone who has had luck with a book and found herself at the top of the charts by chance. There is hard work behind this product.

"I know. The problem is that we have no way to contact her." I lean on my chair and stare at the computer.

Tracy gets up and catches my eye. "Give me a few days to investigate more deeply. I'll see if I can find out something more. Do you think these books are worth all this work?"

I nod decisively. "I think it's an excellent product that fits perfectly on the small screen. Dakota thought of a movie for every book, but there's so much material you can adapt it to a TV show."

"Dakota suggested it to you, eh?" She shows off a smug smile.

"I told you she is a smart person with which you can talk about serious things."

"She sounds like quite the keeper." She winks at me before going out and leaving me with an idiotic grin on my face.

Dakota is not a woman you take to bed once and forget about. She is the complete package, one that includes getting up in the morning and having breakfast together. That's why constantly thinking about her is the worst decision I've ever made.

***

I put my jacket on the armchair in the living room and take off my tie. I see Dakota by the pool sitting on the deck chair through the window. In front of her is a tray with something to eat and a basket of bread. On the low table next to her, she has a can of soda and an ice bucket with a bottle of wine and a glass.

Until a few months ago, I would have thought it was for her, that she was getting drunk by the pool, but now I know that is the "table" she prepared for our dinner, that the wine is for me. I walk out with a smile on my face and notice she has her nose stuck in the book. It isn't until I'm close enough that I notice the sobs.

My heart pumps into my chest when I am on my knees next to her, worried as never before. "What's going on? Why are you crying?"

She is so desperate that the sobs shake her violently. Who the hell did this to her? The mere thought that someone has hurt her so much that she is almost sick makes my blood boil.

"Who did this to you? Tell me, and I swear that when I'm done with him, even his mother won't be able to recognize him," I hiss as I grab her by the shoulders and force her to look at me.

"You can't. He's dead, you know? He's dead, and you can't do anything to bring him back," she desperately cries as she shows me the book.

Her heart is so broken that I would like to bring this guy back to life and kill him myself for making her cry like this.

"Who died, Dakota? A friend of yours?" It breaks my heart to see her like this.

She shakes her head and rests the book on the pillow. "No, Drake! Drake is dead. After seven books, he died, you know? I can't live with this news," she blathers, and I breathe a sigh of relief.

He's just a fictional character. He's just a fictional character, and I wish he were real, so I could beat him until nothing is left. All because he made her cry. I sit on the deck chair behind her and cradle her to my chest until she snuggles up and clings to my shirt. I squeeze her tightly and sink my nose into her hair, inhaling deeply and getting lost in her sweet scent. I kiss her on the head and cradle her until the sobs go away.

"I know it's stupid," her voice is a whisper, "but I feel awful, as if a friend of mine has died. I know he's just a fictional character, but to me, it's like he's real."

"It's not stupid. You spent seven books living and struggling with him. Your feelings are no less real just because they are directed toward a character who doesn't exist in everyday life," I whisper as I hold her in my arms.

"Don't you think I'm a stupid little girl?" she asks me uncertainly, her nose clogged with all the tears she has shed.

"I think the author has succeeded in what I try to do every day: to involve the reader to the point of making them live the emotions as if they were true."

"Do you try to make people cry? You're cruel!" She bursts into half a laugh.

I smile and hold her closer to me, losing myself in the shape and warmth of her body. She is so perfect in my arms I never want to let her go.

"I could not live off my work if I didn't arouse emotions in the viewer. This leads the person to continue watching a show, episode after episode. Whether it's joy, anger, grief, or lust, no TV show would survive if it didn't elicit emotions. No one wants a boring life without jolts, even if it is the fictitious one of a book or a movie."

"So you don't think it's stupid?"

I grab her chin and force her to look me in the eye.

"I have many adjectives to describe you. Intelligent and fascinating are just the first ones that come to mind, but stupid is not really in my vocabulary when it comes to you," I confess.

I get lost in those blue eyes swollen with tears, her little red nose, her lips bent in a suffering grimace. She is beautiful enough to take your breath away, even when crying. These are the emotions I was talking about, aren't they? Those that make life appear less dull. The ones that make your heart pump in your chest and turn off your brain from any rational reasoning. The ones that put you on autopilot and let instinct guide you to what you want.

My instinct tells me to kiss her. Hold her in my arms and sink my tongue into her mouth until she forgets all the tears, the suffering, and the death of a character who made her suffer. Yet, the part of me that holds me back is stronger than even my instinct. I clench my arms around her, place my lips on her forehead, and let my rational part take over again.

CHAPTER 10

Dakota

I observe Serena wandering around the Venice Beach skatepark like a woman studying her surroundings for her next conquest. There are several people out with their skateboards. Mostly males of our age and younger. My friend looks at the shirtless ones as if she's feasting on their abs. Some of them have noticed us behind the barrier, dressed like we have never seen a skateboard.

I lower the front of my cap over my eyes and put on my sunglasses. I don't want them to recognize me and start chatting, as often happens when I'm out with her. I agreed to go out with Serena because the idea of staying at home all Saturday with Aaron was embarrassing. After he found me crying the other night and held me close to him until I calmed down, it became hard to hide that I'm attracted to him. We've crossed that fine line that divides the working relationship from something friendlier so many times I don't even know where the border is anymore.

I think he suspects I like him since I was not drunk this time when I threw my arms around his neck and rested my head on his shoulder, inhaling his perfume like my life depended on it.

I felt him stiffen when I touched his skin with my lips, but he squeezed even tighter immediately after.

This dance between us, where the attraction is so evident that it can be felt, but neither of us dares to take a step, is exhausting. I know that if we cross that line, it would be impossible to go back, which is why neither of us dares to take that step first. I needed a day away from him to think lucidly again.

"The blond one is mine," Serena mumbles with a mischievous smile on her lips.

I was so lost in thinking about Aaron that I didn't notice that two guys are getting closer to us. The blond is shirtless and has sculpted abs, surfer vibes, and a cheeky smile. The other boy, with curly dark hair, seems a little more shy and thinner than his friend, wearing a Super Mario shirt, and seems embarrassed when his friend leans on the railing opposite us.

"I saw that you were interested in my abs, so I thought I'd bring them here so you can also touch them, not just admire them." He shows off a smile so mischievous that it becomes arrogant. Serena doesn't seem to notice and reaches out a finger, sliding it down the guy's skin without ever taking her eyes off his.

The scene is so cringy that I can't help but look away, annoyed. I glance at the blond's friend, who lowers his embarrassed gaze like he wants to disappear instantly rather than be here watching them.

"I'm glad you did because I wanted to find out if they were as inviting up close," Serena meows.

I inhale deeply and bite my tongue so as not to comment on this scene. Most of the time, she is a funny girl who pulls me out of my shell and makes me try things I would never have the courage to do, but there are certain moments when her being over the top goes from being cute to being vulgar. This is one of those.

"So, am I to your liking?"

"You are better than I expected," she whispers conspiratorially.

The image of Aaron, of his sculpted physique, appears in my mind in a flash, and I can't help but notice the contrast between the class of the man I live with and this guy. Are all the boys my age so irritating? My face must be disgusted because when I look at his curly friend, he shrugs with a grimace that says, "I know he is an idiot. We can't do anything about it." His expression is so embarrassed that I smile.

My reaction seems to attract Serena's attention, who takes it as my interest in the other guy.

"We were going to eat something at the restaurant over there. Would you like to join us?" she asks, pointing at one of the restaurants whose terrace overlooks the walk that divides it from the beach.

I am glad she didn't propose going to Nobu in Malibu. It wouldn't be the first time she suggested something out of her reach and for which I'd have to cover the expense.

"You go ahead. We'll come in a bit."

The boy's smile is so radiant that it begins to annoy me. Serena turns around, winking, and grabs my hand, leaving them there.

"You don't even know their names. Are you sure you want to invite them to lunch?" I ask when we are far enough away that I don't make myself heard.

"With abs like that, I don't need to know his name. And

then, you smiled at his friend, don't tell me you don't like him." She throws me a cocky look that irritates me.

"No, he's definitely not my type," I burst out, irritated by the turn of the day.

Serena rolls her eyes and dismisses me with a wave of her hand.

"Of course, because you now live with Aaron and you don't lower yourself to date guys your age. They're all kids to you, aren't they?" she asks condescendingly.

I furrow my brows and nail her with my gaze. "What the hell does my living with Aaron have to do with all of this? I didn't say he's a kid, just that he's not my type."

"Why? Do you fuck Aaron? Is that why you don't give him a chance?"

I stop a few steps from the restaurant and grab her by the arm until she turns.

"I don't fuck Aaron, got it? I never did and never will."

"How can you expect me to believe you? You have been living with him for months. You see him half-naked, walking around the house. Don't tell me you've never taken a ride on *that* merry-go-round," she spits annoyed, and it makes me angry.

"No! I've never done that."

"Is he a boxer or a briefs kind of guy?" she continues, making me want to punch her.

"Serena, stop."

"Wait, I bet he's a pig dirty-talking in bed. They say his father is a lousy man. I bet the apple didn't fall very far from the tree."

The mere thought of comparing Aaron to his father makes

me shudder. The scene from a few weeks ago when he came to his house, the words that came out of those lips, are still imprinted on my mind, and I don't want anyone to compare Aaron to that man. Not even as a joke.

"Serena, that's enough!" My voice is still, and my gaze nails her on the spot because I see she's surprised by my reaction.

She shrugs dismissively, turns around, and walks the few steps that divide us from the restaurant. The boy who welcomes us smiles at her.

"We would like a table for four." She has a friendly expression, but her voice is stern.

"Do you have a reservation?"

"No."

The waiter looks at his iPad and then shakes his head.

"The next free table is in an hour. Is it a problem for you to wait?" he asks with a smile but the bored vibes of someone who has to endure all day the complaints of those who arrive here without a reservation.

"Of course, it's a problem. I see very well an empty table from here," Serena points out.

The guy inhales deeply while I would like to take her by the arm and drag her away. Unfortunately, I know that if I do it, she will make a scene worse than this.

"That's for a person who has booked a reservation." He smiles at her, but his tone reveals what he thinks: "You're an idiot, but I can't tell you to your face; otherwise, they'll fire me."

"Listen, Serena, if you don't want to wait, let's go to another place," I whisper in her ear loud enough to make myself heard by her and the guy who would like us to disappear from his view.

She doesn't even turn to look at me but continues with her complaint.

"Do you have any idea who she is, or are you such a loser that you don't even watch TV?" she asks him arrogantly, crossing her arms.

"Serena, please, let's go." The embarrassment that her arrogance causes me makes me almost run away, leaving her here alone. Every time it's the same story.

People at the tables next to us begin to look in our direction. The guy who would like to slap my friend looks at me, and I see the exact moment he recognizes me. The irritation becomes visible on his face, and I already know what his following words will be.

"This way," he pronounces with gritted teeth, and I am mortified.

He thinks I'm yet another celebrity who uses her status to get what she wants. Just a post on my Instagram where I speak badly of the restaurant, and immediately their business loses clients. It becomes a place where celebrities don't bother to come. That's why I hate when Serena uses my name this way. They don't give us the table because it's been freed up but because they feel obliged. They think I'm going to give bad publicity to the place.

"Look, if you don't have a table, it's really not a problem to wait. I don't want to steal someone's spot," I tell the guy.

"No problem. This table is free," he tells me with another fake smile.

"Don't apologize to him. It's his job to find a place for us," Serena says, sitting in front of me and raising her hand to call the waitress.

I would like to answer her, but the two guys we met at the skatepark come to sit next to us among the protests of the guy at the entrance. When he sees them taking a seat at our table, he shakes his head angrily, and I am more ashamed. I will definitely never come back to this place again.

The waitress comes to pick up our orders, and when she asks for the IDs for the alcohol they are ordering, Serena pulls out her fake one. The other two guys don't look much older than her, and from how nervous the curly guy is, I suspect their cards are as legitimate as my friend's.

"For me, only sparkling water, thank you." I smile at the waitress, who seems relieved that at least one of the four of us will not get her fired.

"Of course, you're the party pooper. Couldn't you order a cocktail like the rest of us?" Serena's tone is so disgusting that it gets on my nerves.

"It's noon. Isn't it a bit early to get drunk?" I bite out angrily.

The blond bursts out laughing while Serena rolls her eyes. I look out over the ocean in the distance, and my brain shuts off any conversation at our table. Almost two hours pass, and Serena and her two friends indulge in ordering the most expensive things and leaving them half-eaten on the plate because no one can eat all of this without getting sick. All this waste bothers me, but I don't say anything simply to avoid making it worse. I hope they choke on the dessert they just ordered.

"At my three, we jump the railing and run," the blond suggests, attracting my attention.

They are all looking at me in expectation. Only the curly guy seems embarrassed.

"Excuse me?" I ask, stunned by his proposal.

"I don't know about you, but I don't have the money to pay for all this stuff. Before the dessert arrives, we skip the railing and scoot. We will already be far away when they realize that we are gone," he explains, and I feel the blood flowing from my face.

"You sat at a restaurant without having the money to pay?" I ask incredulously.

Serena bursts into a half-sarcastic laugh. "You are the only one loaded with money. Normal people don't have the money you have."

"And it's okay to steal from the people who live with this work?" I ask.

"God, you're boring. You're nicer when you're drunk." She raises a bored eyebrow.

I don't have time to answer that as the blond takes Serena by the arm and drags her over the balustrade, followed immediately by the curly guy. It all happens so fast that I'm still speechless when the waitress arrives.

She looks at me with compassion, immediately understanding what happened. "I suppose I'll have to bring the bill to you."

I nod, looking down and feeling my cheeks go up in flames. I don't think I've ever felt so embarrassed. "Yes, thank you."

I look up and see Serena and the blond sneering in my direction while the curly guy looks at his shoes. I shake my head in disbelief, and when the exorbitant bill arrives, I leave a generous tip to the staff.

***

It's late afternoon when I enter the house. I had to take a long walk alone to simmer the anger I had in me. Tossing my glasses and cap on the kitchen counter, I breathe a sigh of relief. For the first time, after three years of moving to this city, I have the vague impression that I almost feel at home.

I peek out the window and contemplate Aaron's statuesque physique as he swims in the pool. He really has nothing to envy about the twenty-year-old blond I met today. In addition to good looks, he has class to sell. I enjoy the view for a few more moments before opening the sliding door and heading toward the pool.

"My presence in this house has really ruined you if you're using the pool for pure pleasure."

My voice makes him stop halfway and turn toward me. The smile on his face as soon as he looks at me is priceless.

"I may have discovered that I like to enjoy my home," he admits, and there's a streak of serenity in his voice that I have never noticed before.

He seems to be happy to spend Saturday afternoon basking here in the sun, something that until I moved here did not happen. It seemed uninhabited at first, this house.

"I'm happy to have brought something positive into your life." I approach the edge of the pool as he reaches me.

He puts his hands on the concrete and pushes himself up to get out, but I push him back into the water. He looks at me with a half-amused smile that soon turns into a look of lust when I grab the hem of my dress and lift it above my head to pull it off. I drop it on the floor next to my sandals and sit by the pool edge before gliding into the water wearing only my underwear.

Aaron's gaze never leaves mine as I approach him and rest my hands on his shoulders. His fingers squeeze my hips, and when he speaks to me, his voice is hoarse, charged with a desire he cannot hide. Our bodies are so close that I just need to breathe a little deeper to touch his chest with my breasts.

"How was your day? Did you have fun?" His gaze slips from my eyes to my lips, and then struggles to climb back up when I answer.

"It was a disaster, but it's definitely getting better." I smile and close the distance between us.

To hell with hesitation. If I have to live another three months in this house, either we do something because of the tension that has been created between us, or I explode.

"Really? And why this improvement?" His mischievous smile makes me tremble right in my belly. He has never been one to throw these kinds of smiles toward me.

"The view from this house is much better," I whisper, taking in his chest, shoulders, neck, and jaw with muscles darting before my gaze rises to his lips.

"Yes, I have no doubt about that." His gaze becomes fiery when my tongue touches my lips to moisten them.

His arms slide to wrap around my waist and hold me against his body. I stick my fingers in his hair and enjoy his expression as he closes his eyes and his lips open, enjoying the pleasure I give him. When he opens his eyes again, I am breathless. I was wrong if I thought I had seen the passion that this man can hold within himself.

His stormy gray eyes set fire to parts of me that no one has ever been able to light, much less with a simple glance. His hand runs up my back and caresses my shoulder, my neck, and my cheek until he lingers with his fingers on my lips.

He seems mesmerized by his fingers sliding on my skin, appreciating its delicacy. I let my tongue slide over his thumb, and when I wrap it between my lips and tease him, all his control slips away.

His hand moves to my butt, grabbing and squeezing it into a vise that almost makes me groan. My legs wrap around his hips, and his hand pushes me against his erection, making me sigh.

His lips take the place of his fingers, and when his tongue sinks into my mouth searching for mine, the moan coming out of my throat is almost heartbreaking. One hand clasped on my butt, the other stuck in my hair in a firm grip, the explosion that this kiss causes in my stomach is devastating. No one has ever kissed me with the voracity of a hungry man in front of a banquet, branded me to the deepest, or possessed me in the most animalistic sense of the term with a single kiss.

The guys I dated always used kisses as a premise to get to something more, a means to achieve their goal. Aaron is kissing me as if he wants to brand me, possess mc, make me his. The way he sinks his fingers in my hair, his tongue fighting with mine to subjugate it, his fingers digging into the flesh of my thigh almost to the point of hurting me, makes me feel like his woman. The one he dedicates his unconditional attention to, the one that he makes come with all the experience of his thirty-six years. For this reason, when he detaches himself from me panting and rests his forehead on mine, it's as if the sun has gone out and the world is freezing.

"Maybe it's better if we order dinner," he whispers before putting me down, stepping back, and putting distance between us. I am so shaken it takes me a while to understand his words.

No! I don't want to order dinner. I want him to take me here, right now, in this pool. But the resoluteness in his gaze leaves no room for any reply, and my heart stops in my chest. I got a taste of the fire Aaron can light and, at the same time, the ice that can freeze any feeling that warms your chest.

I kissed her and then left her at the pool to order dinner. What man behaves so immaturely? I've never run away from what I felt, even when I was eighteen, yet I found myself over-whelmed by that kiss. If I hadn't stopped, I would have fucked her in that pool, without a condom, completely ignoring all my responsibilities as an adult. Because Dakota makes me lose my mind. Is this how men feel when they fall in love with younger women? Powerful and entirely overwhelmed by their emotions?

"Aaron, you're still staring at the screen." Tracy's voice calls me to reality.

"Sorry, I'm not in here with my head," I admit.

"I understood it the third time I repeated your appointments for today." She looks at me, worried.

She probably feels like she's been taking care of a toddler the last few weeks as I've lived in this limbo where Dakota enters my thoughts without warning and stays there until I strive to move my thinking elsewhere. Whereas before it was easy for me to focus on my work, now I have to make twice the effort to keep even the simplest things going. I need to find a way to find my balance.

"I kissed her," I admit when it is evident that we won't get out of this if I don't pull out of my chest what I feel.

She doesn't seem surprised by my confession, and I raise an eyebrow inviting her to tell me what she thinks. I chose this woman to be by my side at work because she has no problem telling me what's on her mind. In an environment where everyone kisses my ass, it's refreshing to have someone around who isn't afraid of you.

"You are not someone who just kisses. Not at thirty-six, at least." Her observation reinforces what I already know.

"There was nothing else."

"I know. Otherwise, you wouldn't have flinched from telling me you fucked her. That's what puzzles me. Did you fall in love with her?" Hers is not an accusation but a simple curiosity to understand the full picture. With her clinical problem solving, she is the one who manages to put my ideas into perspective.

"In love, no, but that kiss did not leave me indifferent. When I am with her, I become possessive in a completely irrational way. When I found her crying because one of the characters in a book had died, I wanted that man to become a real person so I could punch him. What sick mind thinks such a thing?" I confess in a low voice, embarrassment crawling in my chest.

Tracy smiles and shakes her head. "So you're human, too. I almost thought that you kept your heart in a glass jar on the nightstand," she teases, but before I can answer the door to my office opens and my father enters with a smug smile that freezes the blood in my veins.

When he has that expression, it means that the person he is aiming it at is already dead. In this case, his victim is me. He slams a piece of paper onto my desk I can't decipher, at least until I start reading.

"Do you know who Dakota is? Do the names Isabella Anderson and Robert Chapman tell you anything?" he asks smugly when he sees the blood flowing from my face.

I look at the sheet in silence, my heart pumping in my chest at an unsteady pace, as if one side of it wants to stop while the other keeps running away from my ribcage. I'm so dazed I don't even know what I want: to know the truth or burn this paper before the words written on it change my life forever.

"How?" I keep staring at the paper, unable to read it. The names resonate in my chest like the echo of ghosts that I wanted to forget sixteen years ago.

"She is the daughter of Isabella and Robert," he hisses in a tone that sounds like a victory hymn.

And so it is. My father won, he managed to revive the only memory that still makes my chest bleed, and he used it to crush me. It's such surreal news that my body almost doesn't seem to react. My hands feel numb, and the piece of paper between my fingers seems to become incorporeal.

"It's not possible. The name of the kid is Melanie Chapman." My voice comes out trembling, underlining my defeat. The smile widens even more on my father's face, given my weakness.

"She changed her name, like most people who work in this industry." His disdain toward me is so great that I look down, unable to withstand his judgment.

He doesn't even bother to close the door behind him when he leaves victorious. I look up at Tracy and find her worried gaze on me. I almost miss my breath. How did I go from talking about the kiss with Dakota to being thrown under a train by such news? I believed that nothing could hurt me anymore. I built so many layers of indifference on myself over the years that I thought I had become immune to the suffering. It only took a girl thirteen years younger to take down every single wall I had built. Feeling so vulnerable makes me uncomfortable.

"I need to go and talk to Dakota," I announce in a whisper.

"I'll cancel your appointments for the afternoon."

Finding Dakota with the other actors on their lunch break isn't hard when I arrive on the set. Sitting at one of the tables in the parking lot, she is laughing with the others at some joke. I pause to observe her, to grasp similarities that have escaped me so far. She has nothing of Isabella's dark hair and eyes, but I recognize Robert's colors from the pictures Isabella shoved in my face sixteen years ago. A pang widens in my chest when her eyes rise to mine and widen slightly.

"Can I talk to you privately?" I ask her when I approach.

People at the table greet me and cast curious glances in our direction, but my attention is all on the woman in front of me. A woman I thought I was beginning to know but about whom I really know nothing. A sense of betrayal creeps into my chest like an illness that grows little by little, tearing my life apart.

"Yes, of course." She gets up and beckons me to follow her to her trailer.

I hold the sheet with the truth about her identity until I crumple it. When we close the door behind us, the anger I have inside is almost uncontainable. The only thing I can do is stretch the piece of paper out in front of her and stay with my eyes glued to her face absorbing every reaction. Confusion, realization, surprise, and shame alternate on her perfect face, and the ice that spreads in my stomach freezes my every emotion. I don't need to ask her if she knew who I was before she showed up in this city. I read the answer clearly on her face.

"Did you approach me for money? A career? What?" My hiss is so glacial that I take her by surprise, nailing her to the sofa where she sits.

She looks up at me, and I find in her gaze a mixture of fear and regret that makes me boil with anger. How could she use me like this? How did she lie so well that she slipped under my skin and stayed there like a fucking tattoo?

"I…" Words die on her lips.

"You what? Was it all your plan to get something out of me?" I raise my voice and see her hesitate. For a moment, I would like to hold her in my arms and tell her everything will be fine, but then I remember how she betrayed me.

"I just wanted to know you…" The words leave her lips in a whisper, but it is as if she has shouted them.

Of all the answers I would have expected, this one hadn't even crossed my mind. The sincerity with which she said it contrasts with the lies she told me so stridently that I need to get out of here. I came for answers, but I'm not brave enough to listen. I don't know what will come from those lips I kissed, from that tongue I savored until I wanted more. She is the daughter of a man who died in front of my eyes. I cannot sit here and listen to what she has to say without knowing if what I am listening to is the truth.

I leave the trailer, hear her calling my name but don't stop until I get to my car and leave the parking lot.

***

I drive for hours without a destination, following the slow Los Angeles traffic, thinking back to every conversation I had with Dakota. I retrace every expression on her face in search of some signal that could trigger the alarm and point me to some lies. I can't find a single one, not even the semblance of a half-truth. It's as if two people live together in my head: Dakota, the actress who makes me lose my mind, and Melanie, the little girl I've never seen. I wonder how I didn't realize they were the same person. Maybe because I never saw Melanie, I just knew she existed like an abstract entity.

When I stop in front of the valet parking of the Club, I get out of the car without overthinking and go straight for the cigar room on the second floor. Raphael and Harrison are seated on leather armchairs, a glass of golden liquor in one hand, a cigar in the other.

There are only the two of them and a couple of other members playing pool on the other side of the room, out of earshot. When they raise their eyes on me, they stop midsentence, furrowing their brows. My face is probably giving away my mood because they don't even try to make some joke about me going MIA for months from this place.

"Do you want to talk about it?" Harrison pierces me with his deep blue eyes.

"I want to forget about it" My tone is so resolute no one tries to force me to explain what is going on.

Raphael puts down his glass, places the cigar between his lips, and reaches out over the armrest to grab the bottle of whiskey and pour two fingers into a glass before giving it to me.

I accept it without a word and start to sip, not giving in to the temptation to throw my head back and empty the glass. I want to numb the feeling in my chest, not get wasted and let my mind roam free over what I just discovered.

"So, are you going to ask her out or what?" Raphael asks Harrison, resuming the conversation they were having before I interrupted them.

In this moment, I'm grateful for this place. The men who populate this club are good at giving advice if you need some because they have the same complicated life you have, but at the same time, they understand when you need time to be upset in a place where you can be yourself.

"I don't know, man. Have you seen her messy divorce all over the gossip magazine? I like her enough to consider it, but honestly, I don't need to be dragged into that kind of feud." Harrison leans his head on the backrest messing up his perfectly styled blond hair.

"Who are we bitching about this time?" asks Leonard, sitting in the armchair next to me.

I was so focused on licking my wounds I hadn't noticed him entering the room.

"Mia Sawyer," Harrison fills him in.

Leonard pours a glass of whiskey and picks up a cigar from the wooden box on the coffee table. "Christ. Her husband is a piece of shit. I feel bad for her."

"Ex-husband," Harrison points out.

Leonard smirks at him, then shifts his eyes to me and notices my gloomy face. He says nothing but looks at Raphael who just shakes his head to stop him from asking. I silently thank him for that.

"Are you going down that road?" He focuses his attention back to Harrison and just like that the night flows around me with a conversation I don't even hear because the thoughts in my head are louder than their voices.

I lower my eyes and stare at the golden liquid in my glass, surrounded by the familiar chatter of this place. I stare at it for a long time and think about how my life has crumbled in on itself because of a kiss and a piece of paper.

CHAPTER 12
Dakota

It's four in the morning when the door opens, and Aaron's slow pace resonates on the white marble. The room is dim. Only the pool lights illuminate enough to see his defeated expression and the untied tie. I waited up for him for hours, hoping to be able to explain and receive answers in turn. At one point, I thought he wouldn't come home.

"Aaron." I take him by surprise. He hadn't seen me here curled up on the couch.

"What are you still doing awake?" His tone doesn't seem to be worried I am not sleeping, maybe he just wanted to slip into his room without meeting me, and this thought hurts.

The image of his betrayed expression today comes back to my mind, awakening that sense of guilt that grips my chest. I never thought of asking him for money or favors, I honestly just wanted to know him, and when I ended up living with him, I thought that maybe it was the only way to really know him. I never thought that, for him, learning the identity of my parents was like seeing a ghost.

"Don't you think it's time to talk?" I ask tiredly.

He pauses for a few moments to scrutinize my face and his

expression turns from exhausted to angry. I have no idea why he is furious with me. What difference does it make who my parents are?

"Do you really want to talk now? Didn't you have to do that when you decided to work for me three years ago?" he asks furiously as he approaches the couch I'm sitting on.

I get up and nail my eyes to his. The anger that mounts inside me only asks to be freed.

"Why should I? Explain to me why my parents are so important. What difference does it make to know who my parents are?" I shout, and he looks at me as if I have gone crazy.

"Are you serious? Can you tell me what you want from me? Money? A career? Or do you just want to fuck up my life and bury my future? Do you want revenge?" His questions leave me stunned.

I can't understand why everyone gets angry when I bring up this topic that, apparently, concerns me personally, given everyone's reaction.

"I just want to know you!"

"Why? Why, Dakota, do you want to know me? Why now!" He doesn't seem to have a clue about why I may have approached him, which makes me confused.

"Because you are a ghost who has populated my life since I was twelve!" I blurt out and see the confusion on his face.

I take a deep breath and try to put the bridles to the feelings that rattle in my chest.

"When I was twelve, I was rummaging in the attic looking for Christmas decorations, and I found a box with the checks that my mother cashed in my name. Your name was on those checks, one every month from after my father's funeral. I searched online for who you were and found out that you were a famous Hollywood producer. When I asked my mother for explanations, she scolded me because I poked my nose into something I shouldn't have and sent me to my room."

I take a deep breath when I see him sitting on the couch, defeated by my words. "For years, I tried to uncover anything useful, but she always closed the discussion. For a while, I thought you were my real father or somehow related to me even if the age difference was way too slim to make sense, until one day, I bought one of those online paternity test kits and used my paternal grandfather's DNA to confirm that the grave my mother cried over was really my father's. Discovering, however, that I have no blood connection with you has confused me because I cannot understand why one of the most powerful men in this city has been contributing for sixteen years to a million-dollar investment fund in my name." I sit next to him, keeping enough distance to allow me to reason without being intoxicated by his scent.

He shakes his head and looks down at his feet, fingers crossed in front of him in a grip so tight I fear he will break them. He seems defeated, as if all that anger that kept him standing has abandoned him.

"Your mother didn't tell you anything?" The hesitation in his voice makes me angry.

"No, Aaron. You can't keep this secret like her. You have influenced my entire existence. I deserve an explanation," I say, and the suffering painted on his face takes my breath away.

He inhales deeply, and the more seconds pass, the more I am unsure if I want to know anything about this story. I don't know if I can endure years of secrets that, given his face, are not pleasant.

"Your father died in my arms."

His whisper comes to me like a stab in the heart. The ice that expands in my chest is so cold that it freezes my throat and mouth, making it impossible to pronounce the thousands of questions I have in my head.

"I had just started to work for my father and he tasked me to find a company to repair the roof of one of the studios. I found someone that used a third-party company where your father worked. Five days in, I was checking on them during my lunch break and I saw your father slip from the roof and get stuck halfway in the scaffolding." He pauses, perhaps to remember those moments.

Tears begin to rise in my eyes. I don't know if I want to know about my father's last breath.

"When I reached him I tried to alleviate the pressure on his neck, supporting his body weight until the firefighters came, but when they managed to take him down it was too late. Fifteen days later, your mother showed up at our door, shouting and crying because the insurance found a loophole in the papers and they weren't going to pay. I was already wrecked from what happened, seeing her like that was a stab in my chest," he continues, and my heart sinks into my stomach.

"Did you know about the insurance?" The question leaves my lips before I can stop it.

Aaron looks up at me, asking silently if I really think he could do something like that on purpose. His eyes are veiled with tears.

"No. It was not even our insurance, it was your father's company who messed up. But she threatened to sue us and my father went berserk. He told me that if she sued us I was going to pay everything from my pocket. But I was just starting, I had nothing to pay for that. So I did the only thing that came to my mind: I convinced your mother to not sue us and that I would send you a check out of my pay every month to help her out with the expenses of raising a child alone. But Isabella never forgave me for that."

The air comes out of my lungs in a whoosh, and I struggle to breathe again. I always thought that my mother was hiding some sordid affair involving Aaron's family, I never thought for an instant this could be the truth about that day. She always told me my father died in an accident during one of his many out of state work trips, but I never really asked what happened because the topic upset her so much, she still has difficulty holding back her tears. I always thought it was a car accident.

"I felt so guilty for not being able to save him, I started to build layer upon layer of armor and not getting involved with people working for me. But I lived my all life thinking about Melanie Chapman, the little girl I never met but always remained on my conscience."

He never looks up at me, even when he says my real name. Tears run down my face, partly because it makes me melancholy to hear about my father, partly because of the pain that permeates Aaron's voice. I remember that when I thought he was my father or even my brother, I felt anger toward him because he had abandoned my mother and me. I felt orphaned a second time. I never thought that Aaron could be the one hurting for my father's death. The truth I have been looking for for so many years is a truth I now wish I had never heard. This is why my mother never wanted to talk to me about him because she would open the wound of that day that changed our lives forever. Not just our family, but Aaron's too.

I reach out my hand and grab his, squeezing it tightly, and when he looks up at me, the discomfort I read inside him is deep, sincere, bleeding.

"I'm sorry. I'm sorry for what you went through. I'm sorry for how I entered your life…but I'm not sorry my father wasn't alone when he died," I whisper slowly.

Aaron extends a hand and wipes away the tears that wet my face with his fingers. "Don't be sorry for me. You are the one who paid the higher price growing up without a father."

"It was not your fault. Any of it. You shouldn't be feeling guilty for an accident you had no control or responsibility over." The words hurt me as I pronounce them and my heart is breaking for him.

"No. I should have dug deeper with the insurance company or at least forced my father to pay what was yours since the beginning." He smiles at me sadly. "What hurt me the most was the betrayal your mother felt toward me when I told her she should have dropped the idea of the suit. I promised her I'd help her find a way and I betrayed her."

His admission tears my chest even more. I betrayed his trust, though not entirely voluntarily. I didn't know what was behind our story, but that doesn't mean it hurts any less.

"Why did you come here, Dakota… or should I call you Melanie?" His voice is tired.

I shake my head and look him straight in the eye. I want him to understand how sincere I am right now.

"My name is Dakota. Melanie Dakota Chapman. I took my mother's last name when I decided to be an actress. Dakota Anderson is more endearing than Melanie Chapman, at least that's what my agent said."

"Did you decide to do it for me? Did you decide to be an actress to sneak into my life?"

I shake my head again, and the terror that he can't understand my actions creeps into my chest. I don't want any doubt that my intentions toward him were ever in bad faith.

"I'm not here because I want something from you or to ruin you, Aaron. I really just want to know you," I tell him with more conviction. "When I was fifteen, I thought one way to do that might be to get to Hollywood. Understanding what surrounds you is a bit like getting to know you, so I studied to become an actress. But the more I went down that path, the more I realized I like this job. I didn't plan to be hired for one of your productions or to come and live with you, but when it happened, I realized it was my chance to get to know the man who somehow influenced my life. I didn't expect to feel attracted to you, but it happened, and I don't know how to turn off these feelings."

My confession seems to soften his features. Maybe he believes my words and I hope so with all my heart.

"What does Isabella think of this path you've chosen?" His question is sincere. He seems curious more than angry.

"She thinks I'm crazy about giving up both Yale and Brown scholarships. She thought it was just a whim, that I would never breakthrough, that I would eventually get my head on straight and come back home. When I got the part, she was scared because she realized I would never return."

"You gave up two prestigious universities to get to know me?" he asks incredulously. It almost seems that he considers it impossible that someone is really interested in him as a person and not in his money, and the idea alone makes my heart bleed for him. I don't know how he can live surrounded by people who always want something from him.

"No. I gave up two prestigious universities because I like this job. Until the last year of high school, everyone considered my desire to act just a hobby, something I enjoyed. When they asked me what major I would choose, I felt uncomfortable because I never really thought about what I might like as a career." I reach out my hand and stroke his cheek.

His gaze rests on mine as he tilts his head and leans on my fingers, craving contact. There are millions of emotions that pass through his face, but what stands out is uncertainty.

"Is it so hard to trust me?" I whisper as I continue to slide my fingers down his cheek.

"It's hard to trust anyone," he admits.

"So why am I still in this house, Aaron? Why didn't you tell me to leave when you saw that I was no longer drunk? Why didn't you kick me out today when you discovered the truth?"

He lays his hand on mine and holds it tightly against his cheek as if he is afraid I may run away.

"Because the very thought of coming home and finding it empty again is an idea I can't even contemplate. Since you came to live here, this house is alive and no longer looks like a huge block of concrete." He gets up from the couch and gently kisses my head before turning around and disappearing upstairs.

I watch him climb the stairs slowly, looking tired, and, despite his words detonating in my chest with an injection of hope, I understand that this is not the time to press him further. Aaron needs to face the demon that has been waving in his chest for sixteen years, and I can do nothing to help him except give him time.

I came to Los Angeles to meet the man who sleeps a few steps from me. I looked for answers to questions I have been asking myself since I was a little girl. I wasn't ready, though, to discover the infinity of facets that Aaron wears on himself. I wasn't prepared to recognize the masks he wears to protect a heart that has been bleeding. And I wasn't ready to have feelings for each of those masks.

CHAPTER 13
Aaron

If they had told me that I would spend a sleepless night pining for a twenty-three-year-old girl who didn't even sleep in my bed, I would have locked them up in an asylum. For this reason, when I walk down the stairs to have breakfast and see her leaning against the kitchen cabinet, I almost turn around to leave. The conversation we had last night is still fresh in my mind, and I can't make peace with my feelings.

I can't crave the daughter of the man that died in my arms and the woman I betrayed. Yet, after she clarified her position and explained why she is here, I can't find the strength to stay away from her, because it is the first time I've found myself in front of a person who is sincerely interested in me as a human being, without ulterior motives, without asking me for something. She just wants to know me, and that's precisely what I've always looked for in a woman but never found.

"Do you want coffee?" she asks with a hoarse voice.

I don't think she slept much either from the dark circles surrounding her eyes. I approach, grab the cup she hands me, and try not to dwell too much on those lips I kissed once and would like to savor again.

"Thank you."

The silence created between us is embarrassing, and thinking of living with this tension makes me want to leave this house and never come back. Dakota is right, I no longer have any reason to keep her here in this house, yet the mere thought of coming back and not finding her here makes me feel uncomfortable. They are two mixed feelings I struggle to contain in my chest. I've gotten used to her presence, her books almost everywhere, her silences while reading, and her pout of concentration while cooking. It's strange how I established the routine of a couple with a woman I don't even sleep with.

"So from now on, is this what it will be like between us? No words apart from a few sentences when we need something?" she whispers, looking at me.

If there's one thing she has never had a problem with, it's telling me to my face how things are from the first moment we met. She is correct. There has never been this tension between us.

"No, but I have yet to recover from our conversation. I find it difficult to talk about frivolous topics when I still can't wrap my brain around the information I've received."

She turns and studies me. "Is my family so important? I am a person, Aaron, regardless of who my parents are. I'm the woman you kissed in that pool. I haven't changed."

Her frankness makes me uncomfortable because she comes straight to those feelings that I'm not ready to face. She is right to say that she is her own person, an adult with a life independent from her parents, but it is I who cannot separate her from them. What happened that day profoundly affected my life. She is the reason for the guilt I tried to bury years ago, which has resurfaced, making me waver. They are the reason why I don't let people in, even those who have known me for years. There is always that feeling that I'm going to mess up their lives so badly they will literally die in my arms.

When Dakota came to live in this house, she made room in my life without me even noticing, earning that piece of heart that I deny to many. I felt betrayed and vulnerable when I found out whose daughter she was. I thought she was here to make things even. The rational part of me knows that it was not an intentional way to get back at me. I believe her explanations and realize that she is just looking for answers. But that part of me that was hurt many years ago raised that wall again, the one she had managed to break down.

She rests her hands on my hips and leans her forehead on my chest. It's a sweet gesture that makes me want to squeeze my arms around her slender body and I feel that wall creaking a little, the discomfort making its way into my chest.

"Is it really so impossible to think of me as a woman and not as someone's daughter?" she whispers, almost like a prayer.

I stick my fingers in her hair, enjoying the desire that clouds my mind. It would be easier to turn off the rational part that tells me to leave. I could get lost worshipping every inch of her body, making her come like never before, and teaching her what pleasure really is. It would all be so simple, turning off my brain and letting instinct take over. But I'm not that kind of man. I don't let my rational part lose control of my life.

I lower my head and inhale the sweet scent of her hair before touching her forehead with my lips.

"Don't ask me to think of you that way. Don't ask me, please," I whisper before turning around and leaving her confused at the kitchen counter.

I leave my home, once again, questioning my life choices.

***

When I call Tracy, asking to cancel all my appointments for today, I'm not surprised to find out that she has already done it. After my father left the office yesterday, a glance was enough for her to understand that the news shook me deeply. I chose her as an assistant because she can understand on the fly when I need time to put my head in order and start again. It doesn't happen often, but when my father manages to get me on my knees, I need someone to help me take the time to get up.

I enter the club's sauna and sit down, closing my eyes and enjoying the solitude of this place mid-morning. Being a businessman's club, it's hard to find someone who doesn't work during the day. That's why I'm surprised to hear the door open a few minutes later. I open my eyes and notice the sculpted physique of the future senator of California. Raphael Wyden, at just thirty-five, is running to be one of the youngest senators to rise to the Olympus of U.S. politics. When he recognizes me, he shows off a mischievous smile that he uses only behind the closed doors of his private life.

"In a completely empty sauna for twenty people, do you really feel the need to sit so close to me?" I make fun of him when he takes his place close enough that our thighs, covered with a towel, touch.

"Forgive me. After seeing you sulking all night, I thought you were crying in the bathroom like a teenager. I thought I was hallucinating when I opened that door." The grin he shows off is almost manic.

I have a pretty good idea how he's managed to deceive everyone and crush every political competitor that got in his way. This man is a wolf disguised as a lamb and has been feasting undisturbed in his flock for years. That's why we wanted him in this club.

"Do you often daydream of me? You can say goodbye to your campaign if someone hears about it."

The laughter that resonates between this place's warm, damp walls is sincere. It comes from his chest.

"I see that the girl has managed to drain you but not suck all the humor out of your old bones."

I raise an eyebrow and study him for a few moments. "I didn't take you as someone who reads gossip newspapers."

He intertwines his fingers on his knees and closes his eyes.

"It's my job to know what's going on in the lives of the most influential people I deal with. If I come to find out information through gossip newspapers, why not use them?"

Here he is, the cold calculator that emerges sinuous like a snake ready to devour its victim. Sometimes I'm happy to be on his side and not an opponent. With him, you never stop learning. He always knows how to juggle even the most unexpected resources. That's why he's perfect for politics.

"Because often the things they write are just bullshit," I counter but without much conviction. I know he's smart enough to read between the lines.

He opens an eye and observes me without abandoning the seraphic smile he manages to impose on his person. He would be able to tell you that he killed his mother with his bare hands without ever losing that expression.

"Isn't it true that you live with a blond?" he challenges.

"Yes, but I don't sleep with her," I point out.

"Not even the newspapers say that you sleep with her but that you protect her from a stalker, but the fact that you felt the need to point out this detail makes me suspicious."

I shake my head and smile.

"I'm glad I'm not one of your political opponents. It's disturbing how you can corner people."

He opens both eyes and shows off a grin.

"Remember this when you accept my advice and decide to go into politics."

He is convinced that with my face and power, I can climb the peaks to the top, or almost. I think his goal is to become President and have me as his Vice President. It's a fantasy worthy of a script that I could buy for a movie.

"It will never happen."

"Too bad, you're pretty good at taking the conversation away from your private life. But remember that I have been in this environment for much longer. I invented this game. Why don't you sleep with her?"

I inhale deeply and tighten my lips before launching into a response that exposes me too much. Making yourself vulnerable in a place like this can have repercussions I don't want to face. Personal information here is worth more than gold.

"She's just shy of twenty-three."

He frowns and studies me for a few seconds.

"So? It's legal. She's young, but she has been a legal adult for five years now."

"She's thirteen years younger!"

"What do you care? Is she consenting? She is an adult. Or is the problem that she is not consenting? I mean, I have a lot of perversions when I'm between the sheets, but non-consenting sex is a limit that even someone like me doesn't cross." If it weren't for the fact that I've known him for years, I'd almost say he's worried about the illegality of my behavior.

"No, she is more than consenting. That's not the problem."

Raphael studies me for some time, then shakes his head as if he has come to a conclusion I don't understand and smiles.

"Do you know what you need now?" he asks with a mischievous smile.

"I'm afraid to ask," I admit with a half-laugh.

"A memorable fuck that makes you forget the girl who holds you by the balls."

"She doesn't hold me… You know what? You're right." At this point, I am willing to do anything to get Dakota—and that pouty mouth that I would like to taste again—out of my head.

***

The all-male club we slip into an hour later is one of those high-class brothels so exclusive that it is just an urban legend for ordinary mortals. Still, it is a discreet way for men in a position of power to find company where they don't shout from the roof the perversions of those who walk into this place. At the bar, in the dim light, I count a couple of well-known faces sitting with a glass of whiskey in their hands and a young woman clinging to their sides.

The perks of this place are that no one dwells enough on you to remember that you have been around here, and the women who work here are so beautiful that the men's eyes hardly wander on their occasional companions. What drives me to frequent this place is that everyone here has something to lose if they only dare to tell what happens behind these doors.

"It's been a while since we chatted." Sonia's warm sensual voice catches my attention as she approaches and lays her lips on my cheek.

Sonia is one of the escorts with whom I sometimes have the pleasure of spending some time. It has happened that when I am too busy at work to cultivate relationships, I have come to this club more often than I want to admit.

"You have to help him relax a bit. He's full of worries these days," Raphael suggests to her as a girl with flaming red hair and two-mile-long legs approaches and drags him down a corridor leading to one of the private rooms. He gives in to the woman so fast that I have no doubt that he has used her company many times since the last time I saw him. The naturalness with which they met, without the need for an exchange of words, is so evident that it leaves no doubt they know each other.

The girls who work here usually don't do it for long, but they remain just long enough to create an atmosphere of intimacy with regular customers. They are trusted people who have passed countless selections to set foot here. The discretion required by this type of clientele doesn't allow a coming and going of girls who can't be trusted.

"Would you like something to drink?" I ask Sonia, who looks at me, tilting her head slightly.

She nods but says nothing as we approach the counter and order my brand of whiskey and a glass of sparkling water for her. She is lovely, with long, dark hair sliding down her back which has been left uncovered by a black dress that wraps her like a second skin. Her large brown eyes have makeup to highlight their elongated shape. She scrutinizes me while she takes a sip from her glass.

"Are you sure you want to be here today?" she asks.

I appreciate the attention she gives me. The girls here don't want to go to the private rooms immediately and engage in the sexual act then move on to the next customer. They are paid enough that they can take their time to enjoy the moment.

"I need to take my mind off what's outside," I admit, but my answer doesn't seem to satisfy her.

"You're not someone who uses sex to vent your frustrations." She knows me well enough to know that sex has never been an outlet for me but an act of pleasure that I share with the person warming my bed at that moment.

"I need to forget a woman," I confess and smile when I see her arching a surprised eyebrow.

"Is there any woman who can resist your charm?" she asks, but it doesn't seem like a mockery. On the contrary, she looks really perplexed.

"Not exactly… it's complicated," I admit.

Sonia smiles and takes me by the hand, dragging me away from the bar.

"It's always complicated when it's worth it." Her words bounce around my chest, and when we walk into one of the private rooms, I'm no longer sure this is a good idea.

She makes me sit on the sofa leaning against one of the walls avoiding the bed, and I understand that she's sensed my hesitation. The bed immediately becomes too intimate, even for a paid sex encounter, so she takes the time to observe me and slowly strip off her dress and thong, leaving her completely naked except for her stockings and high heels. It is a vision that leaves me breathless every time.

Sonia is the object of every man's desire, perfect in every way, and when she kneels between my legs to untie my tie, I am usually ready to stretch her out on the bed and enjoy the moment with her. Not this time, not even when she unfastens my shirt one button at a time or when she pulls off my pants and boxers. That desire to get lost between her thighs doesn't come.

"Are you sure you want to continue?" she asks in a serious tone, without judgment or mockery when it is clear that the erection has no intention of awakening.

"No," I admit as I watch her get dressed.

She smiles at me when she sits on the couch.

"Do you want to talk about it?" she asks, genuinely interested.

I arrange my clothes slowly, pausing to think about what I would like to tell her, but in the end, I decide not to confide with her about Dakota. Because the truth is that there is nothing to say. What my brain tells me is the exact opposite of what my instinct tells me to do. Until I make peace with the feelings I carry within me, no one can help me solve this situation.

"It's just a stressful time, that's all." I smile at her and finish fixing my tie.

Sonia studies me for several moments before smiling.

"Put it this way, when you have clarified this 'stressful time,' as you call it, you will be happy that you have not betrayed the trust of the person you really care about."

I smile at her and nod. It's useless to contradict her on something she already understands.

***

After being out with Raphael for a round of golf and dinner, I enter my home late at night. I didn't tell him I couldn't fuck

Sonia. I paid her for the time she wasted on me and waited for my friend at the bar.

We changed at the Country Club, smiled in front of the paparazzi who photographed us, exchanged pleasantries with the other men on the golf course, and then went to dinner. He never noticed the discomfort accompanying me; or if he did, he didn't point it out.

All day, the thought of having to forget Dakota was as present as the girl herself. Not a great result for one who should put aside his obsession and return to work. I got to this point in my career precisely because I never let a woman get into my head to such an extent that she distracted me from my responsibilities.

I approach the couch and find Dakota asleep with a book held tight on her chest. She is so innocent when she sleeps that I pause to look at her for a few moments. She is not a sexy beauty like Sonia, but she is no less sensual.

I grab the book and place it on the table.

She doesn't even stir as I take her in my arms, take her upstairs, put her in bed, and tuck her in. It is a gesture that comes so naturally, I find myself surprised by my own actions. I walk to the door, and before closing it behind me, I take a few seconds to enjoy the view of her sleeping. How much evidence does my brain need to understand that "trying to get her out of my head" is no longer an option?

When I'm alone in my room, I strip off my suit and observe the massive erection my boxers can't hide, the one my body denied me this afternoon. I inhale thoroughly and lie down to stare at the ceiling. Sonia's words come back to my mind, *"Are you sure you want to go on?"* and the realization that no woman will ever be able to compete with the girl who sleeps in the next room makes its way into my chest like a pouring of concrete that prevents me from breathing.

CHAPTER 14

Dakota

Thinking of staying another Saturday night at home with Aaron when we barely talk to each other suffocates me. It's strange how the idea of living with him terrified me at first, then became a pleasant routine, and now has turned into a situation that makes me uncomfortable. Two weeks have passed since our conversation in which he told me to my face that he doesn't think of me as a woman but as the daughter of the man that died in his arms, and not a day goes by that I haven't thought of leaving.

Aaron didn't tell me to leave. Our agreement was six months, and almost four have passed, so it's not long before the day when I'll have to pack my bags and leave. There was a time when I almost wished I could stay here forever, enjoying the comforting routine we had but now I'm not so sure anymore.

I finish putting on my makeup and sandals and lean my ear to my bedroom door to hear if Aaron is out and about. He locked himself in his office this morning and never came out. He is avoiding me at least as much as I am avoiding him, and the situation has become almost ridiculous. No contract forces me to stay here, yet neither of us makes the first move to find new accommodation.

I open the door and tiptoe down the stairs, making as little noise as possible. I approach the front door, ready to go out, and when I turn to the pool, I find Aaron leaning against the doorjamb, watching me with his hands tucked into the pockets of his dark trousers and a stern look on his face.

I pause to observe him, waiting for him to say something. At this point, I would also accept a reproach, a recommendation not to get drunk, but nothing comes out of his lips. I clench my fists angrily and turn to leave. I grab the handle and stomp furiously down the three steps, slamming the door violently behind me. If he thinks I'll spend the rest of my time locked up here crying over him because he behaves worse than one of the kids I dated, he's very wrong.

"Wow! Have you eaten a toad?" Serena asks me when I step out of the Uber that took me to the front of Mystique. "You have a face…"

I didn't feel like going out with her and have been avoiding her for weeks, but the reality is that I have no one else to hang out with. Since Aaron fired Roland, no one on set has dared to ask me out for fear that the boss's wrath would fall on them. If we add all the times when I have, for some reason, declined their invitations, it isn't difficult to understand why they stopped asking me.

"I don't feel like talking about it." I stop short when she approaches the VIP entrance and expects me to come forward to help her skip the line.

It's so irritating how she assumes that everything is due to her. The bouncer smiles at us as usual and lets us slip in under the slightly bored gaze of the people who have been in the queue for a while and don't know when and if they can continue their night in this place. When we enter, the club is packed, all the tables are occupied, and we take a seat at the only two stools still free at the bar.

"Can't we get a table?" Serena looks around. "We look like losers at the counter," she adds.

I watch her swipe a bored glance around the room and then look at me. I don't know if she notices the irritation growing in me or if she's pretending that it doesn't exist, but her expression doesn't change.

"Do you think I have the power or authority to free a table?" I ask incredulously when I understand that she honestly expects me to do such a thing.

She shrugs, looks around again, lingers on a table, and points it out. "You can't tell me that those four losers are more famous than you. You're entitled to that table!"

I look at her trying to figure out if she genuinely thinks such a thing. And I regret having succumbed to the temptation to go out with her. Until some time ago, I still saw some good in her. Now, I can't stand her presence. How can a sane person think that celebrity status offers different rights? Her selfishness is so deep-rooted that she answers to no one. I don't know if it's because I'm angry with Aaron or because there's no alcohol involved to make the experience more enjoyable, but I ask myself how I managed to put up with her all this time.

"If you think that being famous gives me more rights than others, then you haven't understood anything about what it means to be a celebrity," I say, annoyed and, this time, I get a reaction.

She turns sulkily to the bartender and waves a hand to get her attention.

"I don't know why you are in a bad mood tonight, but you're unbearable. Have you argued with Aaron?" she asks, softening her gaze a little and taking me by surprise.

I take a deep breath and observe her for a few moments. I could tell her how angry I am with him, how we haven't talked in days, and how uncomfortable I feel in his house, but I'm sure she wouldn't understand. Without alcohol, I realize how fake she is. Even her fake sweetness clashes with her behavior from a few seconds ago. For the first time since we met, I know she doesn't care about me. The realization is so clear that it makes me question all of our friendship.

After running away from the restaurant without paying, she called me to apologize and offered to pay her share. I accepted her apology because she seemed sincere, but seeing her now, her behavior makes me uncomfortable. Has she always been like this, and I only noticed it tonight?

"No, we live under the same roof, but there is not much of a relationship except that of employer and employee," I lie, trying to appear as disinterested as possible.

Just thinking about him makes me smoke with anger, but I don't want her to know. From how she rolls her eyes again and arches her lips in a mischievous grin, I'm sure I don't want to tell her anything. She may be the only person I hang out with, but I'm not so desperate to tell her all my secrets.

"Sure. You're a bit frigid and don't sleep with anyone, but I don't believe you've never slept with him. Why else would he keep you locked up in that house? It's clear that he's not worried about the stalker. Otherwise, he would have put a bodyguard on you instead of letting you out and taking an Uber to join me here."

Serena is irritating but not stupid. I know that the story of the stalker no longer holds, but her question is the one I've asked myself. I don't understand why Aaron keeps letting me stay there. I have not appeared in the newspapers anymore, and it's not because I am afraid he will scold me if I drink. I realized I was wrong. If I am fired, hundreds of people will lose their jobs. Yet, I find myself walking around his house as if it were mine, no longer as a guest but as someone who has her groceries in the fridge. Aaron knows which brand of yogurt I like and always stocks the fridge with it. He also knows I love the pieces of bamboo they put in the Chinese chicken, and he leaves them to me when we order takeaway. These are things you know about the person you live with, not about a guest you temporarily host.

"You can think what you want. I don't care. Nothing has ever happened, and nothing will ever happen with him," I say, not so much because it is my choice but it's Aaron's. If it were up to me, I wouldn't be sitting at the counter of this bar tonight.

"So? Can I ask him out?" She raises an eyebrow challenging me.

The mere thought of seeing her come out of Aaron's room with his shirt on and her hair shaggy after a night of sex makes me gnaw the inside of my cheek with anger.

"If you can, go for it." I shrug, feigning indifference, but the fury grows so much that I would like to tear her hair out.

"I'll come to your house more often, then." She winks at me.

Not that I'm going to open the door, but the mere idea of finding her there makes me nauseous.

"What do you want?" The bartender catches our eye.

"A Crazy Cosmo for both," Serena orders, but I raise my hand to stop the bartender.

"For me, sparkling water, thank you. No lemon," I tell her as she nods and turns to prepare the cocktail for my friend.

"Are you serious? No alcohol?" she asks, perplexed.

I don't feel like drinking and ending up on her Instagram stories.

"Not tonight."

"How boring you have become." She rolls her eyes. Again.

I refrain from answering her because the bartender brings us our orders, and I open my purse to pull out enough cash to pay for my drink and tip. Serena looks at me as if I were an alien. When the bartender glances at her to get her money, Serena looks at me insistently, expecting me to pay her share.

I refuse to pay for her again. "Don't look at me. The last time I left the card here, I received a bill of one thousand two hundred dollars for drinks I never ordered."

The bartender reaches out her hand and takes back her glass under Serena's shocked gaze.

"Are you serious?" she snaps.

"Like death." I nod, sipping from my glass.

Serena snorts, bored and surprised by my reaction, and turns around, giving me her back and leaning on the arm of the guy next to her. The guy's girlfriend leans out, throwing a furious look at Serena, who, in response, smiles and moves away, looking at every single man most likely for a free drink. The bartender watches for a few seconds, then looks at me, and finally smiles and shakes her head, returning to focus on the cocktail she is preparing. A satisfaction that feels a lot like revenge invades my stomach making me smile.

"Are you sure you don't want your friend's cocktail? It's on the house," the bartender winks at me.

"No, thank you. But you could help me get my credit card back. I left it here some time ago, and my *friend* bought a thousand dollars' worth of drinks."

The girl frowns and looks at me suspiciously. I give her my ID, where my name matches the one on my credit card. She grabs it, walks away for a few minutes, and then comes back with both cards. I look at the bill and find a bottle of champagne worth one-thousand dollars. The receipt of payment has a signature that is not mine, but I recognize Serena's.

"Thank you for not blocking the payment with your credit card company. You'd have gotten us into trouble if you did." She smiles at me sincerely.

"Not a problem. I left here drunk while she stayed. I figured that she had ordered and that it had not been stolen."

She shakes her head again. "It's better if you lose a friend like that."

"I have every intention of doing so! By the way, she is not twenty-one. If you serve her alcohol, you could get into trouble."

She wrinkles her forehead. "She shouldn't even be in here."

I raise an eyebrow, asking her if she really thinks we got carded at the VIP entrance. She shakes her head again and walks away to prepare an order. I get up and leave the club, already tired of this place. I don't think I've ever left here sober, and not even half an hour after I've entered. All the charm that this place has always inspired in me seems a little less magical than I remembered it. I stop at the club's corner, waiting for the

Uber I called to pick me up.

A few minutes later, I hear Serena's shrill voice cursing while one of the bouncers escorts her out of the club. She is furious, perhaps because the bartender asked her for an ID and kicked her out. The people in line sneer, and I feel a little sorry for her, at least until she starts stomping her feet and insulting the guy who is just doing his job. Her arrogant attitude is so annoying that I'm glad to see that some are filming. I hope her scene goes viral, so at least she understands what it means to be pilloried and not be able to do anything to stop the humiliation.

***

I enter the house, and I am surprised to find everything is dark. It's not even ten o'clock, and I feel a little disappointed. For some stupid reason, I expected Aaron to be here feeling guilty for making me angry. The irrational part of me would have liked him to be here, basking in the desperation of letting me go when he wanted to keep me all to himself, between the reassuring walls of this place.

I realize it looks a lot like a teenager's dream at the first crush, but I can't help but think that the kiss meant something to him, too. Maybe it was just a matter of physical attraction, but I felt the possessive desire when he sank his fingers into my flesh. I didn't imagine it. Just like I didn't imagine when he threatened to tear off the guy's hands at the club.

The point is that it's Saturday night and, most likely, Aaron has gone out with friends, maybe with a woman, because he's a thirty-six-year-old man even though I haven't noticed much of his social life since I've lived here. He doesn't wait for me to return after a night out. Now he is probably smiling at someone, laughing at something she told him. He will approach and kiss her and then continue his night elsewhere, where he can undress and sleep with her.

The mere thought that he is with someone makes my blood boil in my veins. A discouraged half-laugh slips from my lips because this jealousy is stupid since Aaron is not my man, and I have no right to feel these feelings. Being aware of this, however, doesn't hurt any less.

I take off my sandals, take a bottle of water from the fridge, and open the door to the pool where I sit on the deck chair and inhale thoroughly, watching the city lights. The view is magnificent, and I will miss it when I am forced to find another place.

I look up toward Aaron's room and my heart almost comes out of my chest when I find him sitting on his balcony watching me. He wears elegant trousers and a white shirt with the first buttons unfastened. He is sitting in his usual armchair, leaning against the back with his legs apart holding a glass of some liquor.

His eyes run over my figure, burning every inch on which they rest. My heart bounces in my chest and the excitement his gaze causes me almost makes me explode with pleasure. Only he can make me come just by looking at me. The arousal is such that it makes my head lighter than alcohol could. Aaron is like a drug I can't do without. I've tasted just a pinch of what he can give me, and I'm ready to put my heart under a train if that means having a little more.

This thought makes me angry. I am the one who is willing

to get involved. It's my reputation that will be compromised if this story ends up in the newspapers, yet I am the one that wants to see where this story leads. I don't want to spend the rest of my life regretting something that might have happened. I don't want to put my heart in a box and let it die of starvation, waiting for Prince Charming to arrive. Maybe Aaron is not the stereotype of the boyfriend you show up with at your parent's house, but he doesn't have to be wrong just because the gossiper will talk.

I get up and turn to him, staring back as I begin to unfasten the buttons on the front of my dress. I do this slowly, enjoying the anticipation on his face as he watches my hands descend lower and lower until I undo it completely and slide it down my shoulders to drop at my feet.

I can't see his eyes from this distance, but when he leans forward, resting his elbows on his knees to better enjoy the show, the euphoria growing in my chest almost makes my head spin.

With a slow gesture, I bring my hands behind my back and unfasten my bra, dropping it with the dress. I don't know what he's thinking, but his gaze on my skin sets me on fire. Knowing that he doesn't look away is such a powerful feeling it arouses me more than any other man has ever done with his hands. He could get up and leave. He could tell me to stop, but he remains there, enjoying the show, following my hands that go down my hips until they slip under the edge of my panties and pulls them off without ever losing eye contact with him.

I approach the ladder to the pool, and without hesitation, dive in swimming to the far edge in front of his terrace. When I re-emerge, a smile spreads on my lips. Aaron is standing, his hands resting on the glass balustrade as if that were the only barrier that keeps him from reaching me.

I rest my head at the pool's edge and let my hands slide over my body, my breasts, then down until they slip between my legs, sinking my fingers between the folds of my pleasure. This house has always been a happy oasis where no one can reach us, stick their nose into our business, or judge what we do. Here I feel powerful, uninhibited, that woman Aaron refuses to see.

I succumb to the temptation to close my eyes, moving my fingers slowly, trying to prolong this pleasant torture I am inflicting on myself. I've never been so wet and ready for a man as I am right now.

When I open my eyes again, my heart sinks into my chest. Aaron is no longer on the balcony. The fear of crossing a line creeps into my chest, but when the patio door opens, my heart begins to pump into my chest. A mixture of fear and excitement overlaps in my stomach, leaving me breathless. I am afraid he is going to order me to cover myself. But if he tells me not to…

He approaches me, striding like a predator that chose its prey. Slow. Savoring every second of this agony. His gaze never leaves mine as he reaches and observes me from above. The heat that emanates from my lower abdomen makes my cheeks flare up. I am surprised to realize that it is not shame that I feel. I have never been so uninhibited with a man.

When our eyes meet, my whole world stops.

"Get out and lie down there," he orders, pointing to a deck chair with a voice so hoarse and full of excitement that it enters my chest until I vibrate. He doesn't move. I don't even know if he's breathing. I certainly don't.

I get out of the water and walk over to the deck chair he pointed to. He follows me with his gaze that sets me on fire. He has his hands in his pockets, and he is barefoot. I move my eyes from his face down to the erection stretching his pants. I am craving, trembling, thinking about when he will sink between my legs as I lie down as ordered and look at him as he takes in every inch of my body. Those eyes, as gray as ice, have become a storm that makes me quiver.

"Open your legs and continue what you were doing," he orders in a low, dry tone.

I watch him for a few seconds, unable to process his words, waiting, perhaps, for him to strip off his clothes. I've never dealt with someone like him. Resolved. Sexy. Dominant.

"I said," the sound comes out of his chest like a subdued roar, "open your legs and continue what you were doing."

His order comes as a wave of pleasure pours out of me, making me shudder. His gaze is hooded, his jaw contracted, and his hands are in his pockets as the erection he cannot hide stretches the thin layer of fabric. I spread my legs by sliding them to the side of the deck chair, resting my feet on the concrete and letting his gaze explore my most intimate parts.

I notice his hands moving in his pockets, his knuckles pressing against his pants. He's clenching his fists, and the knowledge that I'm causing him to lose control is such an intoxicating feeling it makes me overcome my initial hesitation. I slip one hand over my breast, easing the already hardened nipple, while with the other, I slip between my legs, caressing the most sensitive part of me, already wet with pleasure, ready to welcome the man who is here in front of me scrutinizing every single movement as if his life depends on it.

I play, moving my fingers in small slow circles, sinking into the center of my pleasure. I am so aroused, my orgasm mounts at the speed of light, making me pant, blood pumping into my veins, and groan. I close my eyes and arch my back when it explodes inside me, making my legs tremble. I feel his burning gaze on my naked skin, as if his hands were on me. He's not touching me, but I feel his arousal on me almost physically.

Blood rings in my ears and I open my mouth, panting, trying to regain control over my body. I open my eyes and meet his lust filled eyes, his mouth arched to one side in a smug smile, the erection pulling his pants, trying to free itself. The craving that has taken possession of his gaze is so evident that it almost frightens me. I feel vulnerable and exposed, but at the same time, I want him on me. His mouth, his hands over my body, and his cock buried deep inside.

Aaron moves a few steps and lowers himself next to my ear. I can't even move when his scent fills my nostrils and senses. I wait for his hands to get lost on my skin, but it doesn't happen.

"Are you still angry with me, Dakota?" he whispers before he gets up and nails me with a look and the smile of someone who reads through my bullshit.

He turns around and, with the same slow pace, goes back inside, leaving me lying, exhausted after the most intense orgasm I have ever experienced. And he didn't even touch me. He didn't lift a finger over my body.

Aaron has just succeeded in a feat no guy has managed to achieve. No one will ever be able to compete with what he has just done. I don't think I'll ever have the strength to leave this house, not after tonight. And my heart sinks when I realize that this accommodation has an expiration date that, until now, had never seemed so close.

CHAPTER 15
Aaron

"Jesus Christ, it's too early even for someone like you to be drinking." Raphael sits next to me, still wearing the sports outfit he used for the gym.

"It's sparkling water. I'm not drinking alcohol at nine on Sunday morning." I nail him with my gaze, even though the temptation to get drunk in order to forget the line I crossed last night is strong.

I watched her pleasure herself, then locked myself in my bedroom and masturbated, thinking about her. It was so out of place that I have no justification for my behavior. She is not one of the usual women I have sex with to whom I can ask even the most perverse things. She is a young woman whose only orgasms she has experienced were with a vibrator. In addition, she is the daughter of Isabella and Robert. She is untouchable from so many points of view that what I have done is unforgivable!

"What are you doing here at the Club so soon?" he asks.

"What are you doing here?" I counter, avoiding his question.

"I'm avoiding my publicist who is on a warpath because

a woman I had sex with, and I didn't call back, wants explanations. Who are you avoiding?" His sincerity is so disarming that I'm sure there's more behind the story. He has always been very good at telling the rough details in order to shift the focus from more serious aspects. I wouldn't be surprised if there was a paternity test involved.

"None."

"Not a blond with two-mile-long legs?" He sips the energizing drink he ordered.

"Is it so obvious?" At this point, there's no need to deny the problem.

As absurd as it may seem, given that the maximum of his relationships with women is with the prostitutes he pays, Raphael may be the only one who can give me a piece of disinterested advice. He's not like Tracy. He doesn't care about my well-being. He's cynical and rational and can analyze a situation I can't wrap my head around.

"You're sitting here with your face beaten. If you had fucked her last night, you would be between the sheets, receiving a blowjob to wake you up." He raises an eyebrow challenging me to contradict him.

A half-smile escapes my lips. "You are always so sensible when you speak. You always choose your word carefully. Are you sure you want to get into politics?" I make fun of him. "I swear I don't know how you convince them to not vote for you."

"It's all about what you project to the public. But I already have your vote. I don't need to convince you that I am the perfect man. And I bet it wouldn't work with you. You don't seem to be one of the perfect husbands attending church."

"You can't say that you lack self-esteem."

He smiles and sips again from his drink. He takes a look at the bartender, who is at a safe distance, considering we pay them enough to stay away from private conversations.

"Bullshit aside, can you explain why you haven't slept with her yet?"

I tell him the story. Everything from Isabella and Robert to how I watched her masturbate last night and enjoyed one of the most intense orgasms I've ever experienced. I don't leave out anything, not a single detail, and the more the words rush out of my lips, the more a weight lifts from my chest. I didn't realize how important it was for me to tell out loud my fears. As my explanation progresses, the problems and insecurities that lurk in my head scale back until they seem almost normal.

"Please tell me you left out the part where you actually fucked her," he asks after I showed him all my vulnerability.

I freeze with my glass in mid-air and cast a reproachful look at him.

"Out of everything I told you, the lack of sex is the only part you got?" I ask incredulously.

He shrugs and frowns.

"What else is there to say? You feel guilty for her father's death. Sixteen years have passed, and I would say the story is old, right? She never accused you of messing up her life. By the way, you tried to save her father. Not everyone would have climbed that scaffolding to try to help him. The point is, are you scared about what happened in the past or because you realized you really care about her?"

I don't answer because giving voice to my thoughts makes me uncomfortable. The problem is that I like Dakota. Not only physically, but also the emotional relationship I established with her. I'm afraid that if I take this relationship to a physical level, it will be harder to let her go when she leaves my house because I don't know if she will want to stay after our agreement ends.

I am at an age where living with a woman is not so strange. Indeed, it is considered normal, but she is at an age where engaging in home life is not even part of her vocabulary.

"You make it sound easy," I admit. The hope that expands in my chest is something I haven't felt in a long time. For a moment, I allow myself to imagine my future.

"Because it is easy. She stood naked in front of you, metaphorically and literally. What more do you need to convince yourself that she has already boarded that train and is waiting for you? You look like you're the twenty-three-year-old, not her." He looks at me as if I'm a kid who doesn't understand something so obvious.

I smile because, if you put it this way, my excuses for this situation seem like the whims of a child. Persisting in denying my attraction to her will not make her disappear.

"Go home and enjoy this Sunday. In every sense." He winks at me before getting up and leaving toward the corridor leading to the gym.

I look at my half-empty glass and realize how ridiculous my behavior is. I ran away this morning like a coward and when Dakota wonders what happened to me she will rightly think I am avoiding her. But after last night, I can no longer think of avoiding the subject with her, and I realize I no longer want to do that.

I enter the house, and my eyes immediately rest on a pair of feet that sprout from the back of the sofa. I pause to observe the perfection of those ankles, slender and elegant. I've never had a fetish for women's feet, but Dakota's feet show all the strength in her. The scars she got with the boots are healed but have not entirely disappeared. It will take some time before they return to being perfect like the rest of her body. They are the only visible testimony of how much she loves her job and stops at nothing, without ever complaining, without ever lacking in professionalism. If I had any doubt that she had approached this job just to get closer to me, this is tangible proof that I am wrong.

I approach and rest my hands on the back of the white sofa to watch her lower the book in her hand and look me straight in the eye. There is no embarrassment after last night, and that reassures me. I don't want to ruin this moment by bringing up the topic, so I go on to something safer.

"Do you have the second book in the series to give me? I need to know how it continues."

A smile spreads on her lips before she puts down her book and sits up. "I knew you would like it. I'll go to get it." She gets off the sofa and runs past me to go upstairs, but I grab her by the arm and stop her. To hell with my desire to avoid the subject.

She turns to me with a perplexed look that catches fire when I grab her by her waist and drag her to my chest. She rests her long fingers on my pecs, and I'm sure she can feel my heart pounding madly. I like everything about her, body and brain.

Even the naughty language when she has no problem putting me in my place.

My fingers slide through the hair on her neck and I enjoy the little moan that slips from her lips. Those lips that I dreamed of wrapped around my erection too many times for an adult man who should control his desires. Desire that has taken over and that I no longer care about. I crush her lips in a kiss as if it were the last thing I'll do before leaving this world. I take everything from her, her taste, her sighs, her groans. Everything.

I push my tongue between her lips in search of hers. Her hands run from my chest to my neck until they slide through my hair and hold my head in a pleasant grip that makes me groan. I savor her mouth, her tongue fighting restlessly against mine. It is as if she is trying to tame it, make it her own, and not let it escape. When I detach myself, her breath is as short as mine, and her eyes search my face to understand if I will disappear at any moment. It's a sight that makes me uncomfortable because I don't want to disappear, but I gave her every reason to think so. I always seduced her, and then I leave, and she believes it will be no different this time. I feel like a coward for treating her that way.

"Please, let me remove this dress," I whisper in her ear before grabbing the hem of the floral summer dress that reaches her mid-thigh.

She nods and lets me strip her. She doesn't wear a bra and those perfect breasts that make me spend sleepless nights at the mere thought of resting my lips on them welcome me as small temptations that no man can resist. I was crazy to think about staying away from her.

"Aaron," she whispers as I touch her already hardened nipples with my fingers.

"What, Dakota? Tell me what you want." I can't hold back a smile as I watch her blush.

She manages to be uninhibited, like last night by the pool, but also embarrassed if she has to express aloud what she wants. She's sexy and sweet at the same time, a mix that brings out the possessive caveman in me. I don't want any man to touch her like I'm doing now.

"You. I want you, Aaron." Her whisper is like a lava flow that pumps into my veins until I catch fire.

I lower myself and kiss her again with such a frenzy that I almost push her over the back of the sofa against which she is leaning. Her hands hurry to unfasten the buttons of my shirt, and when she finally manages to get rid of it, she detaches herself and holds her breath. She's looking at me like I'm the most handsome man she has ever seen, and my ego swells up to almost explode in my chest. There are not many people who look at me with such admiration. Fear, perhaps, lust, in some circumstances, but never the look of veneration Dakota has in her eyes now.

I lick and kiss my way down her neck, savoring her with my tongue, and bite her. I go down further to her breasts where I dwell on the perfection of those bulges, small enough to fit in the palm of my hand. Her white skin is a temptation that I can't resist. My tongue makes its way on her smooth skin to one hard nipple that invites me to take it in my mouth. And I do so, sucking hard and enjoying the almost animalistic moan from her chest. She clings to the back of the sofa with all her strength, closes her eyes, and drops her head backward. It's the most beautiful vision I've ever witnessed.

I leave her breasts, savor her belly, and when I get to her

lace panties the same pink as her dress, I pull them down until they slide to the floor. I am on my knees in front of her.

"Open your legs for me, darling. Let a man show you how to make a woman come." The mischievous smile on my lips and my words make her blush, but she carries out my command without hesitation.

"Thank you, darling." I wink at her, earning an embarrassed smile.

It's disconcerting how no one has taken the time to worship this incredible body, and the idea that she dated perfect idiots makes me angry. She is absolutely stunning when she comes, and I have every intention of seeing her quiver for me many times. I look down, and I get lost in admiring her most intimate part, and all the images that my head evoked last night don't even come close to the perfection I have in front of me.

I look up at her and find her biting her lip and looking up at the ceiling.

"Eyes on mine, darling. I want you to look at me while I make you come."

She looks down at me, and I see her cheeks are on fire. She is embarrassed but can't take her eyes off mine. With a disarming slowness, I get closer to her pale skin and sink my tongue between her folds, savoring her most sweet, intimate part. She inhales thoroughly and holds her breath. Her eyes are wild, and she stares at me with ecstasy and trepidation.

I take the time to savor her slowly, to feel her tremble while licking, sucking, and biting this softness that makes me lose my head. She is beautiful enough to take my breath away while I watch her from below bite her lips to not moan.

"You can scream my name if you want. I like to hear your

voice while you come." My voice resonates in the room as her breathing becomes more labored.

I grab her leg and rest it on my shoulder, opening her more to me and my assaults. I feel her hold her breath when I put my hands on her firm buttocks and pull her toward my mouth, feasting on her most sensitive part as a man who is starving. I lick her sweet juices, suck her clit in my mouth, and enjoy her moans. My tongue prods her opening, searching for the heat that envelopes my senses. Her legs tremble, and her fingers tighten in a grip on the cushions. She is so close to the limit that I don't even know if she will be able to stand or if she will collapse on this sofa.

"Come for me, darling," I whisper before diving back on her and sucking while she rides her pleasure, moving sinuously over my mouth.

Her orgasm fills my senses until I'm almost about to come just looking at her. She trembles in my arms as pleasure and strength leave her body. She leans on the sofa panting with a rosy complexion that colors her cheeks. I get up from the floor, holding her in my arms, trying to make her understand that, this time, I will not disappear.

"You are stunning when you come," I whisper as I skim my fingers down her arm and grab her hand. "You asked me what men feel while feasting on a woman's body." I bring her hand to my erection, evident through my pants. "Is this answer enough for you? Knowing that you are *mine*, seeing you come riding my mouth is a sight I want to enjoy every day. You are perfect, and I will never stop worshipping your body as if it were an altar in front of which to kneel and pray. And if someone thinks for a moment that he is taking what is *mine*, he has no idea what I can do to him."

Her eyes rise to mine, and the mixture of desire and veneration is something that makes my legs tremble. I have never been possessive of a woman because I have never found anyone who awakens my instincts as she is doing, looking at me as if I were the only man on earth.

"Aaron…" Her whisper is charged with a desire that burns me. "I want to be *yours*, Aaron. I want you to take everything you want from me."

Her words hit me in the chest, fueling that fire that has been raging inside me since I entered this house. I grab my wallet from my pocket, pull out a condom, and watch her as she fiddles with my pants with her long fingers, unbuttoning and dropping them mid-thigh along with my boxers.

I smile when I see her looking down at my erection, widening her eyes and holding her breath.

"Satisfied with what you see?" I tease.

"I hope you really know what you're doing because I'm afraid I'm going to die impaled on that… that…" She gesticulates without finishing the sentence.

I burst out laughing at her blatant admission and hold her in a hug. With one hand, I caress her face and circle her waist with the other.

"I swear it will be a pleasant experience." I smile and kiss her on the nose.

"I trust you, Aaron," she whispers, but it's as if she shouted those words, considering how powerful they are.

I detach myself just long enough to put on the condom, then slip back between her legs, making her sit on the edge of the sofa, and slowly sink into her, never stopping. She is so wet and ready for me that I only need a single push to get fully inside her, filling her completely and hearing her moan. We're fused in a gesture that takes my breath away. I've wanted her so much that being inside her is almost a surreal feeling. I can't figure out where she ends and where I start.

"Come for me, Dakota. Come for me, darling," I whisper as I pick up the rhythm and get lost in the warmth of her body.

Trying not to come before her is a titanic effort, sinking into her flesh, her warmth, her legs clinging to my waist, and her hips moving to suit my rhythm. My arms wrap around her to support her and also because I am afraid that if I let her go, she could take away a part of me that would leave me completely empty.

Her hands slip through my hair, clinging as if her life depends on it. Her mouth rests on my shoulder, and her teeth sink into my skin, mitigating that moan that makes her chest tremble. I feel her coming, pulsating around my erection, whispering my name like a prayer, shaking in my arms as pleasure invades her body and her strength fades.

It is impossible to resist another second. I sink inside with a couple of decisive thrusts, and I let myself be engulfed by the wave of pleasure that explodes in my body so violently it takes me by surprise and makes me almost collapse. I have never experienced an orgasm so intense that it left me empty.

Air, I need air, but my lungs don't seem to be able to contain enough of it. I'm so exhausted that I need to put my hand on the couch to support myself.

Dakota leans her forehead on my shoulder and giggles. "If I knew that doing it with an older man would be a mystical experience, I would have done it sooner."

"If another man had made you come like me now, he wouldn't have lived long enough to be able to repeat the experience. I would have flayed him alive and thrown him into the sea." I growl at the mere thought of someone sinking into her as I did.

She leans back just enough to look me in the eye. "Has anyone ever told you that you're a little possessive?" The smile that appears on her lips reassures me.

"It is you who makes me become this. I have never been jealous, never wanted to put my hands on a man because he even looks at my woman, but I imagine there is a first time for everything. I swear I never thought I could turn into a caveman. I'm sorry," I admit with a bit of shame. I am thirty-six. I should be able to control my desires and words. It's one thing is to lose myself during sex in a moment of rapture. It is different to do it during a normal conversation.

"While my feminist side is shouting at me to tear your balls off for your caveman behavior, I know you are not one of those creepy men who think their woman is just an object for their pleasure. And to be honest, I'm flattered to have this effect on someone like you."

"Someone like me?" I raise an eyebrow.

"Someone like you: elegant, self-confident, and completely out of my league," she explains, surprising me.

The women around me see me as an achievement, a challenge they don't want to lose. They are so sure of themselves, their beauty, and their charm that they have always taken for granted that I would notice and seduce them. No one has ever seen me as someone unattainable, and this knowledge settles in my chest with the weight of responsibility that comes with it.

I look at Dakota, her big sincere eyes, her genuineness, and I realize that I am not the one out of her league. She is out of my league. I am not worthy of being by her side. I am the one who must prove that he deserves her affection, and the feeling is so foreign to what I am used to that it scares me.

CHAPTER 16
Dakota

"What are you doing up this early?" I ask, surprised when I see Aaron coming down the stairs wearing only a pair of boxers and a white T-shirt.

He is sexy to die for, even when he just rolled out of bed, with his hair a little shaggy and his face sleepy. We didn't sleep much last night. I changed my mind if I thought guys my age had an enviable resistance between the sheets. Aaron, in comparison, makes them pale. Having sex with him has nothing to do with hasty fondling and the desire to get straight to the point. He takes the time to enjoy it and make me enjoy it myself. He explores my body as if he wants to brand it in his memory and discovers erogenous zones that even I didn't know I had. I think I've experienced more orgasms since yesterday afternoon than in the rest of my life.

Aaron walks next to me, rubbing his eyes, wraps his arms around my body, and gently kisses my neck. The intimacy between us is so natural that I feel both aroused and serene, as if we have been living together for years. If before it was pleasant to share the house with him because of the affinity between us, now I would like to no longer have to leave these walls since I discovered how pleasant the physical side of this relationship is.

"I knew you had to go on set early, so I thought I'd keep you company for breakfast," he explains as he grabs two cups and fills them with coffee.

"It's three in the morning."

He smiles at me while sipping his coffee. There is a sweetness in his expression that I hadn't noticed before or, perhaps, only appeared when he finally let go of what he felt. Aaron is a very controlled person. I learned this during the months I've lived with him, but since yesterday when he set free his attraction for me, it's as if I had discovered another Aaron. Passionate, sweet, and so attentive, he seems to have another personality. Outside this house, he is the usual cold and calculating professional. When he is between the sheets, he is passion personified. There are no half measures with him. When he gives you his attention, you can be sure that there is nothing else on his mind.

"I'm awake. You're not in bed with me. What's the point of staying there?" He smiles.

"I don't know, maybe bask in the idea that there are still three hours left before your alarm goes off and enjoy it?" I suggest.

"Or maybe you could help me get back to sleep," he whispers in my ear as he reaches out a hand between my legs, brushing the fabric of my pants.

If I didn't have to be on set in half an hour to get ready for makeup, I wouldn't think twice about kneeling in front of him and tiring him in all the ways that come to my mind.

"Maybe," I whisper, closing my eyes as his lips rest on my neck.

Aaron kisses me gently on the cheek, and when I open my eyes, I find him smiling at me. It's a sweet look, different from the one full of lust of the past few hours or the severe grin from a few days ago. It's an expression that I don't think many have had the opportunity to see. I feel honored to know this side of him that he seems to keep hidden.

"I know you have to be on set soon. I would never hold you back." He winks at me.

"Especially since the show is yours, and you should fire me for being late," I make fun of him.

"No, because I know you're very professional, and you've never been late even once," he says.

I am surprised by his statement. He is the boss of the bosses. He doesn't deal with micro-managing the projects he produces. He should barely know that I am the protagonist of one of his shows. Especially someone like him, who is basically a god in the Hollywood kingdom. I am glad he has been interested in me to the point of wanting to learn more about what I do. I love this job, and I'm happy he appreciates my dedication. I'm proud of it.

"It's time to take my professionalism out of here if I don't want to be really late," I tell him as I walk around him to meet the driver waiting for me in the front yard.

Aaron grabs my hand and draws me to him, giving me a kiss first on the tip of my nose, then on the lips. A sweet gesture, not sensual like those we exchanged until a few hours ago, but in some way even more intimate.

"See you tonight," he whispers.

We have been saying this every day for months, but this time it is a promise that makes my heart quiver in my chest.

***

The morning passes in a whirlwind that keeps me busy, with my thoughts far away from Aaron and the turning point that our roommate situation has taken. The shooting was long and maintaining a sad face as the script requires was more challenging than I expected. Apparently, the smile I have on my lips since yesterday is much harder to get rid of than I expected. Getting into the character who has just seen her best friend risk death is much more difficult if, in your chest, happiness overflows until it shines through your face.

For the first time since I got this job, I understand how difficult it is to be a good actress. Until now, I have never had to manage personal emotions so strong as to break through the concentration required by this work. It's hard to keep Aaron out of my mind, his kisses, his caresses, the way he possessed me with every part of his body. Sometimes the images of last night flash in my mind so vividly that I'm afraid others can see them too, and I blush.

When it is finally time for the lunch break, Emma, the actress who plays my mentor on the show, takes me by the arm.

"Who did you date this weekend that you have a smile that goes from ear to ear?" she asks conspiratorially as we walk to the catering truck to get food.

I feel my cheeks go up in flames. Emma is older than me, we are not friends or go out together, given the age difference, but she has always been a person I like to talk to on set. Her sweetness and contagious smile put you at ease immediately. She's the one who helped me understand how this world works when I arrived on set three years ago, disoriented and worried about not being able to learn fast enough. That's why I feel guilty when I lie to her.

"Nobody. I stayed at home to read a book." It is actually a half-lie because it is true that I stayed at home and it is true that I read. All while Aaron was sticking his long fingers in places I don't want to list out loud. She doesn't have to know that.

She raises an eyebrow making me understand that she doesn't believe me. "What books do you read that make you shine as if a man has given you the best orgasm of your life?"

I almost choke on the water I'm sipping. Is it so evident that I have never come so much in my life? Is it something that appears on my face? On the skin? I begin to feel anxiety rising in my chest.

"Trust that the books I read are much more interesting than the men I hang out with." This is a total lie. Until Friday, it was true, but Aaron has denied all my theories, making me think again about the fact that there is a man who can make you come as you read in the spiciest books. He took me in so many ways that I am almost sore in my private parts.

"You should read less about men and start dating more. You're gorgeous, intelligent, and sweet. I don't think you have any problem getting anyone's attention," she tells me, grabbing a salad from the refrigerated counter. I look down at my sandwich and fries and feel a little guilty. Maybe I should eat a little healthier in order to not think about diets and cellulite in a few years. Let's face it, Hollywood claims to be inclusive, but if you are an overweight woman, the only part they offer you is the one of the lonely friend.

"I've never found anyone interesting enough to get my attention." At least not until I got to know Aaron better. He intrigues me both physically and intellectually. He is the complete package.

"Speaking about interesting men," she whispers as we sit at the table. "He's someone I would sell my mother to go out with." She points to someone behind me with a slight nod.

I turn around, and my heart almost stops. Aaron is walking toward us, tucked into a dark gray suit, white shirt, and tie that makes him look even more severe. He has a serious face, but I recognize the mask he wears in public, which doesn't let feelings shine through. My heart bounces in my chest because I don't know what he is doing here. Did he come to meet me? Do I have to get up and say hello to him or stay sitting? And if he kisses me in front of everyone? The terror of not knowing what to do in this situation freezes my stomach. I have no problem behaving normally with him at home. In public, it's a whole other story.

Aaron joins and greets us, waving to the other people sitting at the table. They are all silent, with wide eyes and the meal intact on their plates. No one seems willing to eat since his presence on the set is as rare as it is worrying. Most of the time, he comes here to fire someone. He looks at everyone, and I hold my breath when he gets to me. His face is impassive, but for a moment that seems eternal, there is an emotion that I can't decipher and that he cannot hide.

"We're really in trouble if the boss of bosses takes the trouble to come to the set on his lunch break." Emma's voice is a mixture of fun and seduction that makes me look away from the man who fills my thoughts these days.

She seems to be blushing, almost with a shy smile. This is Emma's beauty. She is never brazen in showing her emotions, which also applies to the interest she feels for him. The jealousy that fills my chest is so violent that I am almost surprised. I would like to push her head in the salad bowl, and this sentiment is so new and sudden that having even thought about it disgusts me.

"Are you misbehaving? Do I have to start worrying about something?" Aaron raises an eyebrow as the shadow of an amused smile bends his lips.

"No, but if the worry makes you come to the set, maybe someone will start behaving like a rascal to have you around here." Her words include everyone, but the way she pronounces them is an apparent reference to herself. I suddenly realize that the bubble we lived in for the last twenty-four hours doesn't exist outside the house.

I have never been a person who makes a scene because of jealousy, but when Aaron looks at me for a moment and then focuses again on Emma, showing off a smirk, I get up with my tray and avoid the confused look of my colleague. That insecurity accompanies me every time I am in public, and today it is heavier than ever.

"Sorry, I have to go," I mumble and turn around, walking as fast as possible without looking crazy toward the trailer I was assigned for the breaks on set. Since I'm the star, I'm lucky I don't have to share it with anyone.

I put the tray with my sandwich almost intact on the table, lower all the shutters to prevent someone from peeking in, and sit on the sofa feeling like a perfect idiot. When I saw Aaron, my heart stuttered in my chest, but when he didn't deign to even look at me, it sank into my stomach, anchored by the harsh reality. Emma is much better suited than I am to be next to a man like Aaron.

She is a seasoned actress, knows how to behave in public without needing alcohol to relax her nerves, has never made the front pages of the newspapers for some scandal, and, above all, is almost the same age as Aaron. No one would see anything wrong with it if they were a couple, while I would be yet another scandal to be slammed on the front page.

The realization took possession of my brain for the first time since I set my eyes on him. Outside the protective walls of his mansion, the chances that he and I can function as a couple are slim. There are thousands of Emmas out there who could take my place next to him. I can only be a dirty secret for one of the most powerful men in this city, and the harsh reality hurts me. For a moment, last night, when he held me in his arms, my heart hoped that there might be other moments like these in our future. But I realized that only a naïve little girl could think such a thing.

A slight knock on the door makes me jump. I grab a tissue and dry the corners of my eyes where tears have collected, threatening to fall.

I stutter the first excuse that jumps into my mind. "I'm coming. I'm… finishing changing."

"I'm Aaron. Can I come in?" His voice is firm, raised as a question, but I suspect that if I say no, he will come in anyway.

"Come in." My voice is quite firm, even though my chest is in total turmoil.

His imposing figure enters my trailer, making it look smaller. He closes the door and pauses a few steps away, frowning and watching me carefully.

"Are you okay?"

"Yes." I bite my tongue at my insecure whisper.

"That's not true."

He is right, and I look down, trying not to meet his eyes. I'm a little ashamed to be seen like this, with tears in my eyes like a fifteen-year-old at her first breakup with her boyfriend.

"It's nothing, really. It's a stupid thing."

He walks closer and kneels in front of me, surprising me with the kindness and intimacy of this gesture as he grabs my chin with two fingers and makes me meet his gaze.

"If it were really something stupid, you wouldn't have locked yourself in here trying to hold back tears." His tone is sweet, and the smile on his lips is reassuring.

My cheeks burn from the shame. He is used to women who know exactly what they want and how to keep it. He has never had to deal with the paranoia of an insecure younger woman, and this thought makes me uncomfortable.

"It's stupid, really. It's not worth your worries," I say with a half-laugh that sounds anything but natural.

"I want to know anyway," he whispers as he caresses my cheek.

I hesitate for a few moments, but then I give in to his request. I feel ridiculous clinging behind my position like a little girl throwing a tantrum.

"I realized that maybe it's better if you go out with Emma. She is older, you can go out to dinner with her, and it certainly wouldn't be a scandal because she's not the lead."

Aaron frowns, and he studies me for a few seconds. The confusion that stands out on his face is evident. "Why should I go out with her?"

"Because she is better suited to be next to someone like you." My insecurity shines through with every word. "It was enough for me to see how you interact in public to understand that I can't compete with her. She's one of those confident people who always has the joke ready. I am… me."

The smile that appears on his face softens his features.

"The problem with all this reasoning is that I don't like her. I like *you*, Dakota. I'm not interested in dating anyone else."

"But you didn't even look at me when you came to our table earlier," I mumble, knowing I sound like a sulky little girl.

Aaron smiles and shakes his head in disbelief. "Do you really think I needed to come on this set today?" he asks.

It's my turn to look at him, confused. It's not normal for him to come here, but it has happened other times.

"I have no reason to be here today but I wanted to see you," he continues. "I can't concentrate this morning, and I found an excuse like a fifteen-year-old boy who wants to see his girlfriend." There is a bit of embarrassment on his face, and he pulls a smile from me.

"Really?"

He nods. "I didn't come straight to you because I didn't want gossip to start on set, but the truth is that I asked the director idiotic questions to have the excuse to come here," he confesses, and my heart starts hammering back into my chest.

I smile. "Are you serious?"

Aaron's face morphs into a sweet expression. It's so different from the dark mask he wears with others. He gets up and positions himself in front of me and my gaze falls on the prominent bulge of his pants. I look up and find him with a smug smile when he notices my disbelief.

"Do you understand why I can't come near you? If I flaunt my erection, the gossip will never end."

I raise an eyebrow, pleased with my effect on him. "And how do you plan to get out of here in that state? Will you clear the area so you won't have witnesses?"

He reaches out a hand and makes me stand, then grabs my pants and lets them down along with my panties to my ankles. The gesture is so sudden that a small cry escapes from my lips.

"You have to help me solve it," he tells me before kissing me with such enthusiasm that there is no doubt about his attraction for me.

His desire is such that the arousal I felt since this morning when I left him in the kitchen returns, overwhelming me. I reach out to his belt and scramble to unbuckle it, going straight for the pants next. I slide them down to mid-thigh and the boxers with it. Aaron sits on the couch I just got up from and, with a mischievous smile on his face, drags me astride his legs. His erection presses on my most sensitive parts, making me moan and rest with my hands on his chest.

He takes my hand and carries it on his face, gently kissing my palm. "This is yours, Dakota." He moves my hand over his heart as I observe his gestures. "This is also yours." He descends to his erection. "And that's yours, too," he tells me, making me blush.

I look up at him and find him as serious and determined as ever. "I'm not a man who goes out with several women at the same time, and when I decided to sleep with you, it was a conscious choice."

It's a moment so solemn I can't say anything. Any word would be trivial. He lowers himself, pulls his wallet out of his pocket, and grabs a condom. After tearing the wrapper with his teeth and slipping it on, he puts his hands between my legs and, with a decisive gesture, penetrates me with two fingers, making me groan.

"And this is *mine*, like all the rest of you," he whispers, clasping my neck and dragging me to him. "If I find another man looking at you, I'll tear his eyes out. If he touches you, I'll tear his hands off because you are *mine, Dakota*, do you understand?"

I should tell him that no one owns me, that I belong only to myself, but I understand his irrational desire not to share me with anyone. The jealousy I felt toward Emma is precisely why I don't reproach him that what he says is possessive and outdated. Aaron is *mine* in the same way I am *his*.

"I'm *yours*, Aaron. I'm only yours," I whisper as I slide on his erection and start to ride the orgasm that mounts inside me since he stepped in here.

There is no sweetness in this act. There is only the carnal desire to become one with him. I don't want a Prince Charming. I want a man who makes me feel his, who makes me feel that I belong to something that only the two of us can enjoy. I ride his cock, taking all the pleasure it can give me, making me feel dirty and alive at the same time. I ride him until I make him my own until the pleasure I pursue explodes in my core and makes me tremble. I collapse on his chest as Aaron's thrusts become more powerful and he comes in an orgasm that shakes him.

He wraps his arms around my body and holds me tight. His heart has gone as crazy as mine in his chest, and we struggle to catch our breath. I'm trying to breathe and regain control, but it's hard when his hand grabs my face and drags me to his for a kiss. His tongue makes its way between my lips in search of mine. He tastes it, possesses it, and marks it with an intensity that makes my head spin.

"If one day you decide to leave because you don't find what you're looking for with me, I won't stop you. But until that moment, every part of me is yours, Dakota. Only yours," he whispers as he caresses my hair, and my heart is lost in that bubble of happiness I didn't know I craved.

CHAPTER 17

Aaron

I watch Dakota as she untangles herself from the safety harnesses that today's filming required. She is so focused on one of the buckles that holds the safety hooks together her mouth is sulky. One of the assistants approaches her and places a hand on her belly to help her remove it. It's an innocent gesture, purely professional, but her smile to thank him when he frees her from the constraints makes my blood boil. An utterly irrational reaction but no less violent.

My first instinct is to go over there, break the boy's hands, and then fire him. My reason is lost in the fumes of possessiveness when it comes to her. I've never been such an irrational man, especially regarding women. I stifled that instinct a long time ago when I discovered women often want something professional out of a relationship. Yet, the women I dated before couldn't be more different from Dakota, both physically and in character. They expected me to chase them, well aware of their beauty, and took for granted I offered some step forward in their career in Hollywood. Dakota is the exact opposite. She doesn't let herself be influenced by my bullshit, and I like this about her. I'm tired of people kissing my feet because of my position.

Dakota looks up and crosses my gaze. First, she is surprised, then a little embarrassed, and finally, her expression turns puzzled. She walks toward me hesitantly.

"What are you doing here? Am I in trouble?" she asks seriously as if I had shown up here just to scold her.

I smile and tilt my head, studying her reaction. "Do you have a guilty conscience?"

She blushes slightly and looks around, afraid that someone could eavesdrop on this conversation. I think she is coming to terms with the implications of our relationship going public and is considering how to respond.

"I don't know. Yesterday I had sex with my boss in my trailer. I don't think that's in my job description," she whispers with a conspiratorial tone.

Her answer catches me so much by surprise that I can't hold back the laughter that rises from my chest, earning me curious glances from the technicians who wander around the set. I don't think anyone here has ever seen me smile, let alone witness my laughter.

"I think your boss would forgive you for that oversight."

"Do you think?" She raises an eyebrow and crosses her arms.

"I'm sure."

"Why are you here?" she returns to her initial question.

"To pick you up to take you out for dinner."

She stares at me for a few moments with wide-open eyes. "Seriously?"

"Dakota, I'm serious when I say I have no problem with our relationship. Why should I worry about showing up to a restaurant with you?"

"Because people will start talking, and the paparazzi won't leave you alone," she points out. She's right, it's a somewhat tricky situation, especially for her, but nothing that can't be resolved with a statement from the publicist.

"Let them talk." I wink at her and see her blush.

"Okay, give me time to change," she tells me before running to her trailer, and I watch her until she disappears behind the door. Only when I look away from her do I realize that some of the assistants are watching me curiously. I shrug and smile, and the gesture is so out of character with what they expect from me that they stare with their mouths wide open, and it amuses me. I have to look crazy in their eyes.

***

The restaurant I chose is one overlooking the ocean. The Nobu in Malibu is one of those restaurants that has the reputation of being a celebrity trap, but I actually like it because the people who dine here don't linger. I had to ask for a favor from a friend to be able to find a table with such short notice since there is a waiting list of months. Sometimes, however, dropping my last name has its perks.

The only con is that there are often paparazzi stationed here. They know that some celebrity always comes to dinner here. When I help Dakota get out of the car and leave the keys to the valet, I notice some of them stationed nearby.

"They are already in turmoil," Dakota whispers when she catches sight of them.

"Are you worried?" While there is no problem for me because I am used to managing the press and what they write about me, I didn't consider that it could be stressful for her, especially knowing her difficulty in dealing with public situations.

"No, at least now we know that this story is public." She smiles at me as I put my hand on her lower back to accompany her to the entrance. I observe her as we approach the door, and it seems she is not worried about what awaits us.

The table they give us is one on the patio overlooking the small beach. Not one of the most secluded tables but definitely suggestive with the sound of the waves crashing on the sand.

"I've always loved this place," Dakota admits as she smiles at me from across the other side of the table.

"It's a bit touristy, but the food is good, and there's a nice atmosphere," I confirm.

She smiles at me again and tilts her head, studying me when the silence lasts for several moments. For the first time since I met her, I'm running out of words. I've never gone out to dinner with a woman and worried if she feels comfortable in public with me. The women I meet usually can't wait to be photographed in my company, and it has never been a problem for me to please them. After all, it has always been good publicity for both.

"Did I say something wrong?" I ask when she is no longer speaking.

"Doesn't our conversation about this restaurant seem a bit strange to you? I mean, now that we are on a real date, we get embarrassed and start talking about the weather."

I look down and shake my head. She is right. This situation is strange. If we had been at home, we would have talked about books, the critical news of the day, and something significant about our lives, not about the atmosphere of this restaurant. I realize that, for the first time, I'm nervous about dating a woman I've been living with for months.

"It's true, but nothing in our story is normal, don't you think?"

She nods and sips from the glass of water the waitress brought us along with the menu. I notice nervousness in her gestures, and I'm happy I'm not alone.

"Yes, we certainly didn't start the traditional way." She smiles. "The real question is, how will this story continue… if it continues." Her words die on her lips as her cheeks become redder.

It's in these moments that the insecurity of her twenties comes to the surface. I thought I would be annoyed, but what I feel is tenderness. I like being older than her, guiding her in this relationship, and, in some ways, protecting her. It makes me feel important. I've never felt essential to anyone.

"Are you asking me if I'm taking this relationship seriously? If there will be a future?"

She nods. "I would like to know where we stand. I mean, we started with cohabitation, then we had sex, and now we are on our first date. I'm a bit confused, that's all. Am I your girlfriend? Do you have a girlfriend at thirty-six, or is it something you don't do anymore?" She giggles, embarrassed as she asks.

I smile and barely hold back a nervous chuckle. "Maybe at our age, we prefer the term partner because it looks less like a midlife crisis, but yes, I thought it was clear that you are my girlfriend."

She breathes a sigh of relief, and her posture relaxes. I didn't realize this label was so important to her. For me, it is obvious that when I sleep with a woman, I consider our relationship exclusive. I have never been one who dates two people at the same time, and I realize that this is not always the rule.

"I apologize. I'm young, naïve, and blond." She winks at me. "I needed to hear that."

I smile at her way of playing down her apprehension, liking her way of making fun of herself.

"Now that we have established the important details of this date, can you tell me how your day went?" I move the conversation toward the safe topics we are used to while we dine together.

Dakota throws herself into the recount of her day, and I bask in the normality of this conversation. I've never been used to these kinds of interactions, not even when I was a kid and lived with my parents. I had never seen any kind of love growing up in that house between my mother and father much less conversations sitting all around the same table. This is a novelty that immediately gets under my skin and warms my chest with a feeling of serenity.

Time in her company flies, and I don't notice anything or anyone around me. Not the table next to us whispering or the waitress bringing us the dishes we ordered. I don't even look at my phone to check work emails, which hasn't happened since I had an inbox with my name. Dakota has the power to suck me into a world of our own.

When dinner ends and we leave to retrieve my car, the paparazzi in front of the door has grown almost as large as a parade on the Fourth of July. The camera flashes that hit us are blinding. I wrap Dakota with one arm around her shoulders and pull her to my side, walking toward the valet who will bring my car. While we wait, Dakota clings to my side, perhaps intimidated by the paparazzi who, this time, have no discretion and bombard us with questions.

"Are you on a date? Or is it just a business dinner?" asks one of them.

I don't usually answer the questions they ask, leaving the floor to my publicist, but this is one of those situations in which the insinuated ambiguity gives voice to a thousand speculations that put our careers in a bad light.

"What do you think? Doesn't it seem that if this were a business dinner, it would be completely inappropriate for me to put my hands on her like this?" I nail him to the spot with my stare while the flashes go wild.

Dakota looks up at me, surprised by my answer. I smile and wink at her as questions rain down, asking me if I am confirming the relationship. When the car arrives and we finally get in, I already know I will get a call from our PRs who will want explanations.

***

The first phone call I get in the morning at breakfast is the one I avoided answering last night while we were sitting on the couch reading a book. For this reason, as I walk to Sharon's office, I already know that it will be an annoying conversation. I observe her tense face when I open the door, and she gets up before I sit on the couch in her office. I sit back and wait for her to start asking me questions.

"Did you call me into your office this morning to stare at each other?" I ask when she doesn't speak.

"I don't know. Do you have any idea why you're here?" She's furious.

"I know exactly why I'm in this office, but I don't know what you want to know."

"Maybe because you didn't tell me you were going to dinner with one of your top actresses who is thirteen years younger than you?"

I wrinkle my forehead and look to see if she is serious. I have never shared my private life with her and I am not going to start now, especially since I have never been called to her office because of the women I date. She never felt the need to give me the third degree before making a statement to the press.

"Why should I tell you such a thing? I never told you about my private life before. You've always come up with a press release that silenced the gossip. Why haven't you done it yet?"

She looks at me as if another head has grown under my shirt. She is building a scandal around our relationship, and I'm annoyed by that.

"Because we can't come up with a press release about your midlife crisis. This situation requires more exposure on your part, especially after you have confirmed that you are fucking her. How the hell did it occur to you to say it was a date?"

The anger that boils inside me makes me want to fire her. I would have done it already if it weren't for Sharon being the best in her field, and I would never fire her on a whim.

"First, be careful with your language when talking about her. And then, a midlife crisis?" My tone is so cold that Sharon pauses for a few moments to look at me. I never admonished her for her frankness. In fact, I always encouraged her.

"Aaron, you can't tell me you're serious about her. She's twenty-three years old. What can a girl like her ever give you? When the novelty has passed, you will realize how ridiculous you are to run after someone who, in two months, will have already set her eyes on someone else and will discard you like the old drool with whom she experienced the thrill of adventure. You can't seriously think that this story leads anywhere." Her tone is so condescending that it makes me shiver.

I watch her for several minutes until she begins to squirm. I need time not to open my mouth and fire her on the spot. The fact that I have been reminded of this thought twice since I sat on this couch is a clear indication of my anger levels.

"Let's make one thing clear. I pay you to keep the company's public image clean, not to give me advice on my private life. I didn't ask your opinion on my relationship status. If you can give me the results, we are fine. Otherwise, I'll have to reconsider your position in this office. I'm not the one that has to do your job," I hiss without ever leaving my gaze from hers.

"Are you firing me?" She raises an eyebrow in challenge.

"No, I'm just telling you to do your job. You are not my friend, and neither are you my therapist. My personal relationships are none of your business. I don't have to be here to explain what binds me to Dakota, and above all, you don't get to take liberty to judge my relationship with her. On what planet is it okay to tell a person that he has a midlife crisis and that his partner's intentions are not serious? You don't know anything about me, and you certainly don't know anything about Dakota. Never take the liberty to judge again. I have never told you how to do your job, and I have always appreciated your frankness, but remember that I am still your boss," I tell her, getting up from the sofa and walking out of the office.

It's the first time since she came to work for me seven years ago that we have fought like this and I can see she's torn on what to do. I can read on her face that she doesn't believe this relationship will last, and the mere sight of her lack of confidence bothers me.

"Aaron, please sit down," she pleads when she sees this situation is getting out of hand.

I freeze in the doorway to listen, but I don't sit down.

"I didn't want to disrespect you, but this news caught me off guard. You've never exposed yourself so publicly defending someone you're having fun with and you have never confirmed any of the gossip around your private life."

"This is because there has never been anything to confirm. I've never had a woman so important to me, I had to give explanations," I answer indignantly.

"So? Should I treat this like a long-term relationship?" Her voice is stern. I'm pretty sure she is offended. We have never had such a heated discussion.

"Dakota is my partner, girlfriend... call her what you want, but that doesn't change the situation." I leave the room, slamming the door behind me and letting the anger flow through my veins like a corrosive acid.

The rest of the day goes by with me growling orders to anyone in hearing range. I am so insufferable that even Tracy has decided to avoid me and only sends me emails to which I respond poorly. I know I should separate my work from my private life, but Sharon's words irritate me greatly because they dig into my insecurities. I know Dakota is young, and I know those outside our relationship won't understand why I'm attracted to her. But I know she is much more mature than many women my age. It annoys me that people around me can't see it, and they belittle this relationship.

When I finally go home, I hear noises coming from the kitchen. It's the only moment when the smile returns sincerely to my lips. I enter the living room and see Dakota leaning on the counter in the kitchen, focused on following the instructions of a recipe on her iPad. The guy's voice is telling her exactly what to do, and her mouth is frowning in concentration. Her hair is gathered in a high ponytail, and she's wearing a yellow summer dress with red spots that I think are tomatoes on the front.

When she notices my presence, she returns my smile.

"I swear this time I didn't burn anything. I prepared a salad and some croutons that I put in the toaster. Your kitchen is safe." She raises her hands and gestures to show me everything is as I left it.

Nobody ever thought of preparing dinner for me unless they were paid to do so. And that's precisely why Sharon's words slip into the background of my mind because she is not here now to see the woman in front of me preparing dinner for the two of us like a real couple.

"You know you can burn my kitchen as often as you want if you like it, don't you?" I whisper in her ear while I squeeze her from behind and slip my hands under her skirt to pull off her panties.

"I bought these too, today, while I was shopping," she tells me, showing me a box of condoms on the counter next to a box of fruit.

"I like when you think about our primary needs: food and sex," I whisper, biting her lobe.

She moves the salad bowl in front of her, pushing it against the iPad and the recipe she has forgotten before she leans against my chest, reaching out a hand to slip it into my hair. A shiver runs down my back as she rests her head on my shoulder and closes her eyes when I slide the dress's strap along her shoulder, freeing a breast. I squeeze it in my hand and tease her nipple, enjoying the moans that slip from her lips.

"Aaron," she whispers my name as a prayer, and my erection presses against the fabric of my pants.

"Tell me, Dakota, why did you stop preparing dinner?" I whisper with a smile as I unbutton my pants and let them fall down to the middle of my thigh along with my boxers.

I slide my erection against her buttocks and enjoy the sublime feeling of her smooth skin against mine, so warm and sensitive I could come without even sinking into her.

"Do you want me to prepare dinner?" she asks. The vein of seriousness in her voice comes out choked by moans as I kiss her neck.

"You could become my dinner, what do you say?" I whisper as I push her to bend over the kitchen counter with one hand. She looks at me from over her shoulder and smiles, biting her lip.

I enjoy her lusting gaze as I kneel behind her, lift her dress, and uncover her butt. The perfect shape of her buttocks is a vision that makes me stop thinking. I grab her flesh and squeeze it between my fingers, tearing a moan from her throat when my mouth moves between her folds. I lick slowly, savoring every shudder.

"Aaron," she groans when I suck her swollen clit.

"What? Do you want to say something?" I tease, biting her buttock.

Incoherent moans come from her lips when I sink my tongue into her, savoring the pleasure that wets her between her thighs. I would like to tease her, torture her a little bit until she comes, but this is torture for me too. My erection is so stiff it almost hurts.

With a slow gesture, I slip my tongue along her entire length, from the clitoris to the narrow opening of her butt. I feel her holding her breath as I linger where I have never yet entered.

"Not tonight, but sooner or later, this will also be mine," I promise her before passing my tongue one last time over her butt and descending again toward her warm folds.

I lick again on that little bundle of nerves I neglected, and a groan comes out of her chest when I begin to suck hard, sinking a couple of fingers into her. The scream that comes out of her chest when her orgasm shakes her to the tips of her toes is a sound so animalistic that it almost makes me come. I continue to fuck her with my fingers until she rides the waves of pleasure that hit her, leaving her breathless, lying on the counter.

When I get up, I find her panting, her forehead resting on the cold marble and her cheeks reddened with pleasure. She's so beautiful when she comes that my hands shake as I open the box of condoms, and I can't hold back the heat while I put one on.

I grab her hips and sink into her with a long push. A grunt of pleasure comes out of my mouth when her warm flesh envelops me. She is so perfect that I would never tire of sinking into her and enjoying her pleasure. As she looks at me from over her shoulder, her moans and lustful eyes are enough to make me lose control.

I grab her ponytail and pull her against my chest as I sink into her with thrusts that make her small, perfect breasts jump. My hand slips over her neck, and I enjoy the beating of her heart going crazy under my fingers.

"Aaron. Aaron. Aaron," she whispers like a litany as she leans on the counter with her hands to support herself as I hammer into her. With one hand around her waist and one on her neck, I hold her close as I make her mine against the kitchen counter. Her arms try to counter my thrusts, but when I am about to reach my orgasm, and my hips slam powerfully against her butt, her hand bumps into the bowl of salad causing it to fall to the floor, shattering into a thousand pieces.

The sound of shattering glass cannot cover the cry that comes out of me when my orgasm hits me. At that exact moment, Dakota also reaches the peak of her pleasure and shouts my name as she comes for the second time. It is such a violent pleasure that it shakes us to the point of making us tremble. I slump on her back, holding her tightly against my body as we try to catch our breath.

Several minutes pass before I have the strength to take her in my arms and move a few steps away from the disaster of glass and vegetables on the floor. I lean on a kitchen cabinet and slowly collapse until I sit with her on my lap, panting and with a smile planted on my face.

She curls up in my arms and kisses me on the neck between deep breaths.

"What?" I ask her when I hear her giggling.

"If we continue like this, in a month you will no longer have pots or dishes to use," she says, pointing to what remains of the salad bowl.

I smile and kiss her on the nose. "I'm willing to subscribe to a company that makes cookware if that's the case."

And I realize that my words are true. I've always been jealous of my things and spaces, but right now, I don't care about the state of my kitchen if she's in my arms. This new awareness that fills my chest almost makes me breathe easier.

CHAPTER 18

Dakota

Returning to the set after the story between Aaron and me went public was more normal than I expected. No one made comments or jokes, and not even Emma said anything or asked me for more details, a further reminder that confirms she is the sweetest person here and she doesn't need to have the seedy details. There is a cordial relationship as work colleagues between the two of us, but we have never been close friends. After I cut off my relationship with Serena, I became more lonely than ever when it comes to friendship. Like when I came to Los Angeles three years ago with a suitcase full of dreams and no one to share them with.

"Do you have plans for this weekend?" I ask Emma as we walk to the table with our lunch trays.

I'm not one who usually starts these conversations, but I'm striving to become more sociable, learning to have a decent conversation without needing alcohol to relax my nerves is a start. Emma seems surprised by my question but says nothing about it.

"Nothing special. I was supposed to go to a festival with some friends, but with our working hours, I would spend half the weekend traveling to arrive on time on Monday, so I decided to stay in the city. Do you have plans?" she asks with a sincere smile.

Maybe this is the moment, the hook I need to talk about Aaron, about how we would like to go out of town for a weekend, just the two of us. But the words die in my throat because the truth is that she is not a friend of mine. She is not a person I have ever confided with, and the relationship that binds us is not deep enough to bring out all the happiness I feel right now. I would have preferred hearing the gossip and whispers behind my back instead of this silence. It would have been easier to bring up this topic. It's strange how I want to talk to someone but have no one to do it with.

"Nothing special. I think I'll stay at home and read."

She smiles at me. "One day, you'll have to let me read one of those books. You're so engrossed in them, there must be a reason why you spend sleepless nights glued to those pages," she says as she bites into a forkful of her salad.

"Reading books? Yeah, sure."

Serena's voice makes me turn around. I hadn't noticed she had arrived and, from Emma's surprised face, I know she hadn't seen her either. Since I dumped her at Mystique and responded to her messages saying I no longer intended to go out with her, I certainly didn't expect her to show up here. The furious expression on her face makes it clear that this is not a courtesy visit.

"What are you doing here?" I ask in a low voice, as the people around us have begun to listen to our conversation.

"What am I doing here? Are you serious? First, you fuck the big boss and get the part, then you dump me at the club, telling me that you don't want to be my friend anymore." Her tone is deliberately high and her attempt to draw attention to us succeeds. My colleagues begin to stop to witness the scene, some of them puzzled.

"Serena, please, let's go to my trailer to discuss it?" I get up from the table, feeling my cheeks go up in flames with embarrassment.

My former friend, if I really can consider her as such, spits a sarcastic laugh. "Does it bother you that others know you got the part because you fucked Aaron? Do you think they don't already know?"

"These accusations are out of place. Maybe it's better if you go for a walk until you've calmed down. What do you say?" Emma comes to my rescue, and the shame makes the grip on my stomach almost unbearable.

I look around and find the faces I have been working with for three years stunned by the scene unfolding before their eyes.

"Out of place? Did you know that Aaron fired Roland because he invited Dakota out with us?" Serena replies condescendingly.

The silence that falls around us is so absolute that my voice seems like thunder on a sunny day.

"Aaron fired Roland because you both showed up at his house, uninvited, with thirty people and destroyed his pool. He fired him for disrespecting him, not because he asked me out. And if we have to say it all, I stopped going out with you because I realized that you were never a friend. You always used me to go into clubs where I always paid for you. You made me feel so guilty about having this part that I paid your rent several times. You used my credit card to pay a thousand and two hundred dollar bill at Mystique, then you and your friends ran away without paying for lunch at Venice Beach. Does it bother you that I am not your friend anymore or that you no longer have your personal ATM to ask for money?" I blurt out angrily, careless about what people may think of me. I'm tired of always having to defend myself from her.

The smile that appears on her lips makes my skin crawl. "Did you notice that you gave an explanation to everything except the fact that you had the part just because you opened your legs with Aaron?"

I feel anger boil inside me and, at the same time, shame clutch my stomach. This is what people think of me. This is the image I give when I go out with my boss. I had not realized, until now, how important people's judgment of me is. In the perfect bubble of Aaron's house, these problems don't exist. Only the two of us exist, but we can't live forever inside that house, and I have to deal with what people say about me.

"Three years ago, I didn't even know who Aaron was," I hiss between my teeth.

"Dakota was chosen because she is perfect for the part and is a great actress." The voice of the director behind me calls me back to reality.

"The *recent* personal relationship between Mr. Steel and Dakota has nothing to do with the casting decision. If I remember correctly, you didn't even make it to the shortlist of the last ten contenders for this part. Instead of coming here to spread lies among these people who have earned this job for their expertise and professionalism, you should work on your acting techniques and find your own way in some other production," he adds in the middle of the total silence.

"I'm a good actress. I don't need to work on my *techniques,*" she scoffs, mocking him.

The director looks at her tilting his head and smiling sadly. "To be honest? I don't think that after today you will have any chance of making it in Hollywood, not even for a commercial. This job is all about skills and connections. You don't have the former and you just burned to the ground the only connections you had. Did you really think your name wouldn't end up on the blacklist after this stunt?"

My gaze is fixed on my shoes while, out of the corner of my eye, I see the security guys take Serena away, who, at this point, no longer has much to say. I would like the earth to open under my feet and swallow me. I'm so ashamed I don't even dare to look around to see the reaction of my colleagues.

"Just to clarify this point, so that there is no gossip around on this set," continues the director. "The casting has *not* been influenced by anyone at any level. Who has been chosen for the part they are playing is because they deserved it by proving to be the most suitable person to represent that character. That said, the private life of colleagues is, in fact, private. I don't want gossip about it on my set," he announces before leaving.

Voices surround me again, reminding me that life goes on despite my humiliation. I feel a hand on my shoulder, and when I turn around, I find Emma's smile. I hold my breath, trying not to give in to the tears that threaten to spill.

"Don't think for a second that someone here believes that gossip," she tells me in her usual reassuring tone.

"You mean there's no gossip about my relationship?" The half-embarrassed smile on my lips is a bit pathetic, but I think

Emma is saying it just to cheer me up. She probably feels pity for me and wants me to feel better.

"Let's say there is excitement about the fact that you managed to make an unrepentant bachelor capitulate, but nothing more. Nothing bad is said, and above all, no one thinks that you have the part for a reason other than your skill."

Her words reassure me and her sincere smile makes me realize that she genuinely believes what she said.

"Capitulate? It's not like I put a ring on his finger. He's had other women in the past," I say, trying to minimize it in some way. This relationship is so new and fragile that I don't even know how much of a future it has.

"I've never seen Aaron visit a set as often as in this last period, and, trust me, it's not because the production doesn't work." She winks at me before taking her tray back to the catering truck.

***

The rest of the day is spent in a way that I can only define as surreal. Everyone avoids the topic of what happened during lunch, but at the same time, they have an extra smile for me. I don't know if it's because they're terrified of the director or because they feel compassion for me, but their continued kindness has the effect of putting me under pressure. I don't want to make a mistake when they've given me their trust, and when I finally climb into my trailer, I'm exhausted more than usual.

I had just changed and slipped into my dress when the door opens without anyone knocking. I'm ready to get angry at the lack of privacy, but the words die in my throat when I meet the icy gaze of Aaron Steel Sr. Unlike his son, his eyes lack that human warmth that makes his son as severe but not as terrifying as this man.

"I learned about your friend's little adventure." His voice is calm, but the frost that exudes on it makes a shiver run down my spine.

"I'm sorry, it won't happen again. I will ask security not to let her in anymore even if she drops my name." My voice trembles, and I can't look him in the face.

The silence that follows makes my nerves jump. Does he want to fire me because of Serena? It wouldn't be so strange since he took the trouble to come here to scold me as soon as he knew. He's not Aaron. He's not someone you can talk to. I saw him arguing with his son and heard the chilling words coming from his lips. Someone like that doesn't bother to come here just to reproach me. I wonder if anyone saw him enter this trailer before the door closed behind him. I feel terribly uncomfortable being locked in here alone with him. I look at this place with new eyes, looking for an escape route and thinking about what Aaron told me, to walk away from him.

"No, it won't happen again because I've already gone to talk to security when I heard what happened. And do you know what's not going to happen again?" he asks as he approaches the couch I'm sitting on, staying just a few feet away, making me stiffen.

I told Aaron that I knew how to handle this situation with his father, that I had been in this industry for three years now and have had to deal with my fair share of creepy men who believe they can have anything only because they have penises. The truth is that I am not ready to face his father. Never in my entire existence will I ever be able to find a way not to feel entirely in danger in his presence.

"What will never happen again is you appearing on the pages of magazines clinging to my son. And do you know why it won't happen again? Because you're going to carry your ass out of his house and out of his life. If you don't stop sleeping with him right away, I swear I'll cut the funds for the streaming division and shut down all productions. I just have to snap my fingers to take everything Aaron worked for away from him. Do you want me to take away his dream?" His wicked words hit me with a wave of ice that makes me tremble. Literally.

Aaron would die. This company is his whole life. I see the dedication he has for everything that happens here, the worries he cannot hide, and the satisfaction when some significant recognition rains on one of his projects. To take all this away from him means to kill not only his dream, but the one for which he sacrificed his whole life. I can't be the person who clips the wings of that phoenix tattooed on his skin.

"No… I…" The words die in my throat, weak and trembling.

He stares at me and I want to disappear, climb over this sofa and crawl out of the window behind me. I'm so overwhelmed I can't look him in the eye.

"Am I clear? Stay away from him if you don't want me to take everything he worked for," he states, glaring at me.

I put my hands on my lap and look down. The disgust I feel right now is overcome only by the terror that freezes me to the bones, and I hold my breath unsure of what to say. When he crosses his arms over his chest studying me, I stiffen, close my eyes, and wait for this moment to end. I have no idea if I will leave this room with my heart unscathed, but I am sure of one thing: I will not return to Aaron's house tonight if these are the consequences.

Some voices coming from outside make my heart pump into my chest. Aaron's father moves toward the door and when I open my eyes to understand what is happening, his gaze is fixed on me, icy as always.

"Don't bother to go home tonight," he adds so menacingly that it makes my skin crawl.

When he finally walks out and closes the door behind him, the breath comes out of my lips in a trembling sigh. My hands are still tight to my skirt, grasping it in a vise that can tear a hole if I let them. I'm so shaken that I can't even get up. My brain is clouded by fear and adrenaline. I can't formulate a coherent thought, but of one thing I'm sure, if I don't do what he wants, everything I care about will be destroyed.

***

The hotel room is like all those in which I have stayed in: anonymous, decorated with neutral colors, and apparently luxurious, but if you look closely, it's nothing more than bland furniture.

After leaving the studio, I didn't even go and get something from Aaron's house. I just slipped into a taxi and asked the driver to drop me off at the Hilton. I held back my tears until I closed the room's door behind me, then I slipped into the shower and stayed there until the last hiccups left my chest.

Now I linger behind the glass door that leads to the small

terrace overlooking the pool watching some people enjoy the evening at the tables that surround it. There are not many, but enough to give life to a place that would otherwise be empty and impersonal.

Aaron's father's words come to mind, the disgusting feeling of his eyes on me, his threats. I can't comprehend how the man I've lived with for the past few months could have grown up with such a nauseating human being as his father.

A slight knock on the door makes me turn around and I walk to the door wrapped in my bathrobe and open it to receive the meal I ordered. I'm surprised to find Aaron in front of me with a worried face.

"How did you find me?" I ask in a whisper, the words of his father echoing in my chest.

If he discovers that Aaron has come here, he will destroy everything he has built over the years.

"Why are you locked up in here? Is it because of what happened today?" It is enough for me to hear his voice to start crying again.

His arms wrap around me tightly, and as he closes the door, he accompanies me to the bed, where he sits and drags me onto his knees. His embrace is so full of affection that I can no longer control myself. I can't tell him about his father, and this thought scares me because I realize I've fallen in love with him, and the mere thought of letting him go kills me. But I can't let his father destroy his dreams, so I cling to him and enjoy his embrace for as long as possible.

"Dakota, please talk to me," he whispers in my ear with what sounds like terror in his voice. "I know about Serena, and some of the crew told me they saw my father get out of your trailer. Please, talk to me." His voice is broken.

His words freeze my chest. He knows about his father. He thinks he threatened me, thinks he hurt me physically. I look up at him and find terror and despair in his eyes. I saw how fervently he told me to stay away from him, and not knowing what happened today is making him run out of breath. As much as I want to save him from his father's threats, I can't leave him in doubt that he put his hands on me. So I tell him everything that happened, from Serena making a scene to his father's visit, about his threats and why I decided not to go home tonight.

I feel him tense, trembling with anger, but the words that come from his lips are the most reassuring I have ever heard.

"I swear to you on my life that my father will never approach you again. He won't hurt you, do you understand?"

He lets out a sigh of relief, perhaps because he realized that, no matter how much fear I had, no matter how much his tone made my skin crawl, his father didn't go any further. He didn't threaten me personally.

"What if he decides to hurt you? To shut down your company?" I ask between hiccups.

I feel him inhale deeply and take a few minutes before answering me. I think he also realized that his father is serious and could carry out his threats.

"He's threatened to do so many times but has never followed up on the words. He's too attached to the money to shut down the only thing that works about that company," he says, and I feel the conviction in his voice which makes me sigh in relief.

A flood of emotions stirs inside me and the fear fades, giving way to the incredible tenderness that Aaron is pouring on me as he strokes my hair and holds me in an embrace that speaks of stability and protection.

"Aaron? Do you want to make love to me?" I look up at him.

His eyes are charged with a tenderness I've never seen before, and his lips arch in an almost shy smile. He closes the distance, kisses the tip of my nose, and then rests his lips on mine.

It is a sweet kiss, different from those we have exchanged so far but no less intense. His tongue touches my lips, and the shiver that runs down my back makes me groan into his mouth. The kiss that follows is sensual and takes its time to brand every single cell of my body with the feelings that permeate this moment.

Until now, we have fucked, given vent to the carnal attraction that consumes us inside, but this goes beyond physical attraction. Our hearts are bound by an almost palpable feeling.

Aaron slides me off his lap before standing and striping off his clothes without letting his gaze lose sight of mine. He's stripped himself not only of his clothes but also all of the walls he had built around him over the years until he stands vulnerable in front of me. The power he's giving me right now almost scares me. He is giving his heart to me and it's my decision to protect it or make it bleed.

Slowly he lowers himself on me and kisses me again, savoring my every breath, every touch of my fingers on his skin. With my hands, I explore his chest and sculpted abs, then return to his shoulders and lay a hand on his neck. The vein under my fingers beats madly as if his heart can't stop its run.

He unfastens my bathrobe and lets it slip from my shoulders before kissing my lips and then down toward my neck, breasts, and belly. It is a slow, sensual descent, full of a desire he struggles to hide, but he never lets it take over. Aaron is used to taking everything he wants, doing it with determination, and dominating every situation, even when he is between the sheets. That's why he leaves me amazed when he lowers himself to take a condom from his trousers and hands it to me.

My hands tremble as I slide them over his erection. Aaron notices and grabs my hands, guiding me in my movements, accompanying me in this intimate moment but letting me dictate the pace.

He sits back down on the bed, and pulls me onto his lap, letting me wrap my legs around his hips as I slide on his erection and let him fill me to the brim, taking my breath away. His arms envelop my body, holding me tight as I move, allowing our pleasure to mount slowly. His hand slips through my hair, clenching the strands in a fist as he leaves a trail of kisses on my neck and my shoulder, and then climbs back up to my face and lingers for a long moment.

I continue my slow dance, taking the time to savor our bodies tightened in a grip that blends skins, hearts, and souls. I savor his trembling, whispered groan as he pursues his pleasure until he explodes, holding his breath. Only in this moment do I allow myself to reach my pleasure, riding the wave that overwhelms me and makes me short of breath.

Aaron and I are good at fucking, at venting those instincts that make us feel alive, but we are even better at connecting in a way that goes beyond the physical, beyond the mind. We are good at merging and becoming one person, and not even his father can take that away from us.

I never thought of killing someone. The idea is so far from my person that the mere thought of harming a human being disturbs me. Yet, I wish my father would die. I spent the night thinking about how much of a liberation it would be if I walked into his office and choked the life out of him.

My father is a bad person in every way. There is nothing that can be saved. I thought about our childhoods, mine and my brother Evan's. There is no memory of my father that is happy. Not a single day where I admired him for something. I always feared him until I learned what he wanted and followed his choices. They weren't that bad. My father never wanted to see me fail, even though he always tells me I'm a failure. I reflect his image in the eyes of the public. If I fail, he fails with me.

I enter his office without knocking, and the surprise painted on his face almost pleases me. But when it turns into a grin, the anger that has been smoldering since last night boils in my veins like magma ready to explode. I've always kept my eyes fixed on the final prize, on this company I will one day run in his place, but even that goal is clouded by a wave of anger that I can't contain.

"Stay away from her," I hiss, resting my hands on his desk.

My father crosses his arms, leans against the back of his damn throne, and looks at me with a grin I would like to tear away with my own hands. I can almost physically feel the skin of his face ripping under my nails as I tear it off. It's such a visceral feeling that it almost scares me. I have never been so violent, not even in my bloodiest fantasies, toward this man.

"Or what? What would you do?"

"I've told you this once. Stay away from her, or I swear you lose me this time, too."

I see him hesitate for a moment. A single moment in which his façade is not perfect, a single moment of indecision that appears on his face but that I see clear as day and provides me with the necessary calm for my threats.

"If you think she is worth all this trouble, you're dumber than I thought. How long do you think it will take before she leaves you?"

The fury inside me explodes and I'm unable to control it. I grab him by the tie, pull him to me, and punch him in the face. Only once, because I refuse to get my hands dirty for someone like him. When he looks at me again, anger shines through the expression he can't hide. The mask has fallen, and it will take a while before it returns to its place. The barely swollen lip is the only evidence of my assault. I don't care if someone sees I beat him. A punch is enough to make him understand how serious my threat is. I have never put my hands on anyone, and this event is serious precisely because it is isolated.

"If you dare approach her again, I swear I will not stop at one punch next time. But more importantly, if you dare do anything to her or those close to her, I will bring down your entire empire, even at the cost of dismantling it one brick at a time. I will leave you in shit so deep you can't breathe. I will work for the competition, and remember that I know many things about this company," I whisper in his ear before getting up and letting go of his tie.

He no longer has that smug smile on his lips, and although he has managed to contain his anger, his gloomy expression tells me everything there is to know about our meeting. He understands that I am serious, and I think it's the first time since I've worked with him that he's really taken what I say seriously. The irony is that it's about a woman and not the job I've been sweating over since I was eighteen.

"Is that a threat?" His tone is a mixture of severity and concern.

"It's a promise," I say before I open the door and slam it behind me. The secretary, who couldn't stop me a few moments before I walked into his office, looks at me with wide eyes as I untie my tie and walk away furiously.

When I arrive in my office and sit behind my desk, I look at my hands and notice the tremor. It's not anger that makes them so unstable, but the realization that I've just challenged my father like I've never done before, seriously jeopardizing everything I've worked for.

"Are you okay?" Tracy's worried voice gets my attention.

I look up and find her leaning against the closed door. She has an expression of concern on her face. I've never heard her so somber since I hired her, and this shakes me more than the fist I just threw, more than the threats that came out of my lips a few minutes ago.

"I don't know," I admit, looking down at my hands that show no sign of stopping their shaking.

* * *

The glass in front of me is a bit blurred like the rest of the club around me. After confessing to Tracy that I was not well, I took refuge at the Hunting Club in the middle of the working day. Never once since I was twenty years old have I missed a day of work, often also using Saturdays and Sundays to find new ideas and do what I like with all the passion I can put into it. Since Dakota came into my life, I have often found myself in this place at the most ungodly of hours, leaving my office empty.

There aren't many people around, no one I want to talk to, so glass after glass, my vision blurs, but my mind doesn't. It keeps thinking about what happened with my father and how tight he keeps my leash.

I've lived my life with blinders, focused on the ultimate goal–my father's company–ignoring everything else. I sacrificed everything for it and today felt it wobble under my feet while I was punching the one who holds the reins. It was like walking inside the mouth of a volcano, hoping not to burn.

In all these years, following the rules has never been a problem. I put a smile on my face to be able to get what I want, even if, in the meantime, I have to swallow my pride and my ideas. As long as I have to think only for myself, the situation is bearable. I tell myself that when my father retires, I will decide where to lead the company because, at that point, it will be mine, and no one can take it away from me. But Dakota barged in, turning the life I built upside down with so much effort, and I can no longer ignore the fact that what I did today undermined my relationship with my father. With him, it has always been a tug-of-war, a test of strength where I have always let him win. Today I crossed a line, and I can't go back.

"I thought you were a workaholic, but I see you are here to slack off." Dakota's sweet voice seems almost like a hallucination.

I've thought about her so often during the day that I wouldn't be surprised if she was just the figment of my foggy brain. So when I turn to her and find her next to me, I have to squint a couple of times to focus, but ultimately give it up.

"How did you get in?" It's not the first thing I should ask her. I should ask her what she's doing here, how she found me, and why she's not at work, but my brain, clouded by alcohol, seems to have decided on this path.

"They made an exception when I told them I had to pick you up. They called Gaspard while he was taking me home," she explains, and things make more sense.

The Club doesn't want problems with drunk people, so when they realized that I'd been sitting at this counter for hours, they called the emergency number I gave them when I signed up for the membership. The fact that I have my driver as an emergency contact says a lot about how lonely my life is.

"You can't stay here," I insist, and I'm not sure if it's because we're breaking the rules of this place or because I don't want other men to set their eyes on Dakota. At this point, I struggle to understand what instinct tells me since it continues to clash with my reason.

"I'll help you get home," she mutters as she helps me off the stool.

My pace is not very firm, and despite my head spinning, the alcohol has not helped me to silence my thoughts. Indeed, overthinking all day alone has done nothing but make me fall into the spiral where I am convincing myself I am self-sabotaging my career.

The drive is quiet, and Dakota helps me climb the stairs when we get home, accompanying me to my room and helping me take off my jacket, tie, shirt, shoes, and pants, leaving me with a T-shirt and boxers. I lie down, and she lies next to me.

Studying me, she reaches out a hand and skims her fingers along the side of my face. I close my eyes and enjoy her delicate touch.

"Why did you decide to get drunk today?"

"Do I have to have a reason?"

She raises an eyebrow and invites me not to tease her with my bullshit. I smile because it's Dakota's way to put me in my place instead of being intimidated. And to think that Tracy was convinced that I could intimidate her. With her, it's a bit like taming a wild horse. You can gain her trust, but you will never be able to harness her and impose your will.

"Considering you are *Mr. Perfect*, this is totally out of character."

I smile at her nickname for me. She has given me many over the past few months, but I had not yet heard this one. I open my eyes and watch her as she caresses my face with her fingers, moving my hair off my forehead and looking worried. How did I find a twenty-three-year-old who stays here to look after me during a colossal hangover instead of going out with her friends?

"Do you know that when I turned eighteen, my father made me sign a contract instead of giving me a gift? I committed to working with him for his company that day. If I hadn't I wouldn't have seen a single penny of the trust fund that is in my name."

"Really?" I don't know if she's surprised or outraged.

I nod. "My brother Evan never accepted. In fact, my father cut him off from the family money, but I like this job. I have dreamed of doing it since I was a kid and never regretted signing. When I received that money at twenty-five, it was like receiving a gift for something that doesn't weigh me down."

Dakota removes her hand from my face, slips it under her cheek, and pauses to observe me, perhaps to understand where I want to go with this speech. Maybe, I do not know either. I spent the day figuring out where the hell I did wrong in my life, but I couldn't point the finger at anything in particular.

"That was the day he tightened the collar around my neck. I was so convinced I wanted to take over the family business that signing to receive money in return was like winning the lottery. Since that day, this goal has dictated every choice I've made. As a twenty-year-old, I daydreamed about the innovations I could bring when I took my father's place. I felt almost euphoric when I came up with a brilliant idea."

I never look away from her as she listens to me in silence.

"But every time I shared them with my father, he belittled them, laughed at my naivety, made me feel like someone never good enough to do something decent in life. So I stopped telling him what I had in mind and started working with my head down, trying to become the best at this job.

"When he allowed me to open the streaming division, I thought it was the breakthrough I was looking for, that the time had finally come for him to retire and allow me to take over the company for which I sacrificed years of my life. But over time,

I realized that it was just a way to keep me quiet, a whim he granted me to appease my eagerness to get to the top. But do you know the ironic thing about this whole story?"

She shakes her head, and I continue with my confession.

"Until today, until I punched him, I never really noticed how tight the collar he put on me was. For years I've struggled to breathe, to feel happy with what I have always loved to do. Only today have I realized how much I hate my life because of him," I admit.

Dakota moves closer and holds me in a hug. I'm glad she doesn't say anything because right now, I wouldn't be able to hear anything but the echo of the regrets of all the choices I've made in my life. Never before have I felt envy for my brother, who, despite the difficulties, is living the life he has always dreamed of, being able to really enjoy it with a smile on his lips.

CHAPTER 20
Dakota

I open my eyes and find Aaron asleep next to me. His room is dim, but I see the sun is already up outside. Like every Saturday morning for a month now, we take time for ourselves to bask in pleasant idleness and live our existence without constantly thinking about work. Things changed since he confessed what he felt for his father. He started putting his personal life higher on his priority list.

It's been a while since this became my room. I don't know how it happened, but I started sleeping in the master bedroom and eventually stayed. Even though my clothes are still in the guest room, I haven't been sleeping there.

"Happy Birthday." Aaron's hoarse voice slips over me like a caress on the skin.

He reaches out and draws me to his chest in an embrace that envelops me completely, body and senses. It is beautiful how he is not afraid to express his feelings, how sweetness permeates his gestures as much as sensuality.

"Thank you," I whisper as I cling to him.

"What do you want to do today? We can invite someone here if you want," he whispers as he kisses my neck, making me shudder with pleasure.

He asked me several times this month, thinking I was reluctant to invite someone into his home and making excuses. The truth is that I don't really have anyone who would come to my birthday. When you go out and get drunk at every party, you don't have the opportunity to make many friends.

"I don't have anyone to invite, but we can go out for breakfast if you want," I say as he pushes away from me to look me in the eye.

He furrows his brow and looks too awake compared to a moment ago, studying with a worried expression.

"It's not a problem if you want to invite people here, you know?"

"It's not that I don't want to, but I've never had friends here in Los Angeles apart from Serena. I don't have anyone who would want to come on my birthday," I admit.

He holds me to himself and gently kisses my hair. "I'm sorry.".

"Don't be sorry. It doesn't bother me."

"So, where are we going out for breakfast?" he asks.

"I want pancakes."

Aaron chuckles and squeezes me tight before getting out of bed and helping me up. I never thought I would like a completely naked man so much, but I find myself admiring his perfect body every chance I get. It still seems impossible that he is attracted to someone like me.

"Are you done checking me out? I'm not your breakfast. Get up, so we can go celebrate properly," he teases, dragging me out of bed.

"Do I really have to? I like the view." I lean against him and kiss him on the shoulder.

"It's not bad for me either, but I also appreciate looking at you dressed, smiling, and talking to me about the things you like."

No one has ever told me such a thing, and my heart squirms in my chest. To think that a man like him can feel a genuine interest in a woman who is thirteen years younger is still something that in my head looks more like a fairy tale than the reality I am living. Yet he listens to me when I speak and remembers even the smallest details of our conversations.

I haven't often dealt with such attentive people, especially in Los Angeles. During the parties I attended, everyone was ready to make small talk, but no one ever got too deep into a conversation that could somehow put them in an uncomfortable position. The weight of words among these hills almost crushes you.

Getting dressed and resisting the temptation to tear our clothes off is a struggle, but in the end, we get into the car and enter the Saturday morning Los Angeles traffic. Aaron is driving, wearing a pair of light Chinos, a polo shirt, sneakers, sunglasses, and hair a bit messy.

"Why are you staring at me?" he asks as he reaches out a hand and intertwines our fingers.

"I like you when you're not dressed in elegant suits. You have a more relaxed face, and you look almost younger."

He glances at me before looking back at the road, smiling. "Are you saying I'm an old man?"

I bring his hand to my lips and kiss the back.

"No, I'm saying you look relaxed."

He nods and seems to think about it for a few seconds before answering. It is his nature to weigh the words, to pause to think if something is worth saying or if it is better to keep quiet. I have always appreciated his way of never speaking inappropriately, of using words in the right measure.

"Isn't this age difference a problem for you?" From his tone, he almost seems to need to be reassured.

I know how much he's fought against himself for what he feels for me.

"Why should it be? You are sexy to die for, have abs to drool over, are fantastic in bed, listen to what I say, and have much more interesting topics than the latest game just released. I'd be crazy to have issues with the age difference."

He bursts out laughing, amused. "You sure know how to pump a man's ego."

"If you're worried about what people say, you don't have to be. I've never felt compelled to have sex with you because you are my boss or for fear of losing my job. I know people often don't understand, but I grew up among adults and always found their conversations much more inspiring than those of kids my age."

"I don't care about people's gossip, but I want to be more than certain that they don't have a foundation."

"You can sleep soundly." I smile and shake his hand as he parks in front of a small Beverly Hills bakery that, from the outside, almost goes unnoticed.

I have the impression this is one of those celebrity places that tourists cannot find because you'd only know about it if you are famous and through word of mouth. When we enter, we see some familiar faces that are having breakfast and don't go beyond the initial glance. No one stares at us or starts whispering with the person who sits next to them pointing, something that often happens when I visit Rodeo Drive, where tourists walk with wide eyes and sweat dripping on their foreheads.

Aaron puts his hand on my back and leads me to one of the tables near the wall with a bench covered with fluffy pastel-colored pillows. He sits next to me, instead of sitting in the chair on the other side of the table, and wraps his arm around my shoulders, dragging me for a hug and gently kissing my hair. I like how it is not a problem for him to prove himself tender in public.

"How do you know this place? Do you always bring your conquests here?" I ask, looking up from the menu and watching his expression get slightly darker.

"Actually, no. A person I know called me one day and told me that my mother was in here, drunk, making a scene with the waitresses. I ran here to pick her up, and since I couldn't convince her to leave without loading her on my shoulders and forcing her into the car, I stopped with her for breakfast until she calmed down. I discovered that here you can eat delicious pastry." He smiles at me, but I notice a veil of sadness in his eyes.

Of all the explanations he could give me, this one didn't even cross my mind. I have always seen his mother in public next to his father, elegant and perfect in dresses sewn on her. Not even a hair out of place, let alone drunk enough to make a scene, always with a smile, but her eyes, perhaps, a little sad. He's never told me about her, and it seems a bit strange since we exchanged several anecdotes about our childhood, but now that I think about it, his memories are never tied to his parents.

"How is your relationship with her?"

Aaron shrugs and shakes his head slightly.

"Nonexistent." He inhales deeply and stares at the table in front of us as if looking for words. "My brother and I were raised by nannies. Our parents never took care of us, as happens in ordinary families. We never received any gesture of affection from them. When we were old enough to understand how much my mother was always stuffed with antidepressants and alcohol, Evan and I began to keep an eye on her to prevent her from making headlines with a scandal."

"I'm sorry," I whisper, resting my lips on the back of his hand.

The smile he gives me is tender, sincere, almost melancholic. I get lost in his eyes that at first seemed the color of ice but now warm my heart. Boiling ice, that's what I would call Aaron. A man who can set you on fire with just a glance.

"You don't have to be sorry. In all honesty, I don't miss my family. Evan is the only affection I care about, and he is present, even if we don't see each other often. He squeezes me to his chest, letting slip away some of the melancholy of this moment. "But can we talk about happy things like your birthday? What do you want to do to celebrate?"

I understand that he doesn't want to continue on the subject, but I appreciate that he decided to share something so personal with me. This little glimpse of his life is the most beautiful gift he could give me for my birthday.

"This cherry cake looks great."

"But weren't you the one who wanted pancakes?" He chuckles amusedly.

"After seeing the cake, they took a back seat."

He holds me to himself and doesn't let me go even when the waitress comes to take our orders.

"Sorry to interrupt you. I wanted to hug the birthday girl." A voice I don't recognize catches my attention.

I look up and see a younger version of Aaron, same ice-gray eyes, dark hair, and tailored suit.

"Oh my God, there are two of you!" I squeal surprised making them laugh.

The guy in his early thirties lowers himself and hugs me. "Happy birthday," he whispers to my ear.

"Dakota, this is my brother Evan," Aaron introduces.

"Nice to meet you" A smile spreads on my face. It's sweet Aaron wants to introduce me to his family, or at least the part that is more attached to him.

"I didn't want to crush your birthday breakfast, but I'm in town for a few more hours and wanted to meet the girl my brother can't stop talking about," he explains, sitting in front of us grinning and looking at his brother.

I look at Aaron and find him hiding an embarrassed smile. I didn't know he talked about me with Evan. He seems almost shy in front of this confession.

"It's not like we had a lecture about the topic. You asked me about the gossip magazines, and I answered you." It's clear he's trying to downplay the conversation they had.

"You definitely bragged about it," his brother laughs while I smile seeing Aaron embarrassed.

"So, are you both born with those suits? Is it something branded in your DNA?" I joke, focusing my attention on Evan and giving Aaron some respite.

They both chuckle and nod.

"You can say that. The Jailbirds give me shit about it all the time." His eyes soften when he talks about his clients, and from what Aaron told me, best friends.

They are the most famous rock band in the world, and I can imagine them making fun of his un-rock attire.

"But I can see you have some influence on my brother," he continues. "Why are you wearing Chinos in public? You look like an old dude. What is the next step? Cargo shorts and New Balance? Are you trying to pull off the dad outfit?" He gives Aaron a hard time, but I can see the amusement on their faces.

"Shut up, you idiot!" Aaron pushes him by his shoulder.

I love this interaction between those two. From what Aaron told me during our endless conversations, they weren't on good terms until a short while ago, but they are fixing their relationship and becoming closer by the day.

"I'm happy you succeeded in the hard task of getting him out of that office. It's time for him to enjoy his life," Evan says, returning his attention to me.

"From what I've heard you are a workaholic, too." I raise my eyebrow daring him to contradict me.

His smile is genuine. "I like you, girl. Now I understand why my brother is so crazy about you."

I blush and feel Aaron's arms squeeze me in a reassuring hug. I like the light atmosphere at this table, and I loved to discover that Aaron talked about me to Evan. It's further confirmation that he is invested in this relationship more than I thought, and the mere thought makes my stomach squirm with butterflies.

We sit at the table for almost two hours, eating sweets, drinking good coffee, and talking about the most trivial things, such as our favorite color and our most hidden dreams–such as winning the Oscar. Two hours where the world around us disappears and only the three of us remain, with our fears and hopes.

***

I was wrong if I thought breakfast was the only way to celebrate my birthday. Aaron made it almost a mission to take me out and pamper me all day. After breakfast, he took me to a spa for a couple's massage, then to eat at one of the hottest restaurants in Los Angeles. In the evening, he took me to the cinema after buying me a dress, shoes, and a bag from one of my favorite designers, spending a disproportionate amount despite my protests. When we finally get home, I'm tired but shining inside my new clothing.

We park in front of the house, and I am amazed to see that every light inside is turned off. Usually, there is always some light that turns on automatically when it starts to get dark. Aaron puts his hand on my back and invites me in after opening the door. I don't have time to reach for the light switch when a chorus of voices shout "Surprise," and the lights turn on in the living room, leaving me stunned in front of about twenty smiling people, most of who are my colleagues and people who work with me on the set and with whom I am in contact with during the day. There are several technicians, some extras, and even Sarah, the girl who has been doing my makeup for three years.

Emma, who is in the front row, runs toward me with a smile from ear to ear and holds me in an embrace. "Happy Birthday."

"Thank you… but…" I don't even have the words to describe the surprise that overwhelms me right now.

"When Aaron asked us if we wanted to attend your birthday party, we were blown away because we didn't even know it was your birthday!" Emma scolds me good-naturedly, putting her hands on my shoulders and forcing me to look at her again.

I turn to Aaron, who stands one step behind me smirking. He arranged all this for me, and I almost can't contain the heart pumping crazily in my chest.

"Is that why you kept me out of the house all day? To organize such a thing?"

"No, I did that because I wanted to have you just to myself before tonight. I wanted this birthday to be special." He kisses the tip of my nose.

"Enough the two of you! You are so sweet that you make me want to find a guy!" Emma scolds us, laughing before leaving and chatting with the people who crowd the living room and move to the pool where catering has been set up.

I turn to Aaron and smile at him, raising an eyebrow. "Did you force the people in the production to have a surprise party for my birthday?"

He watches me frowning, resting his hand on my cheek and gently stroking my skin. He is so handsome even when he worries about me. Especially when he does, when his eyes suck me into his world and never let me go.

"I didn't force anyone. When I asked Emma, she was thrilled, and when the word spread, the others joined in. Do you think I can force people to do something like this?"

"Really?"

He smiles at me with tenderness. "Dakota, the people around you are genuinely interested in you. You always focused on Serena, thinking she was your best friend, the *only* friend you had, but the truth is that many people take pleasure in being in your company."

I blush because I have always felt like a fish out of water in this industry, and when we walk out by the pool, I realize that people greet me and wish me well, despite being off set. They are genuinely happy to be here and come up to talk to me.

Andrew, one of the camera operators who has been working on the show since the beginning, brings me a plate with the salmon canapés that are on some tables set up on one side of the pool. "Here, for you. I saw that you always take a double portion when there is salmon at lunch. I thought I'd bring some to you before they are gone." He smiles at me, and I realize it's the first time we've spoken without being part of a conversation in which Emma is also present.

"I love salmon. I didn't think anyone had noticed this passion of mine," I answer, embarrassed.

I feel Aaron's hand resting on my back, a comforting gesture that calms me from the anxiety slowly rising to my stomach. It is a presence that helps me not to fall into the spiral of catastrophic thoughts during this conversation.

"Rita, the girl who runs the catering for the production, is a friend of mine. She knows the tastes of more or less everyone who eats regularly on set because she has to manage the grocery shopping. She told me when I asked her for the recipe, and since that day, I have noticed that you always take two portions," he admits.

"I love how she cooks it! Did she really give you the recipe?"

"Seriously. It's super simple but has a secret ingredient that makes it special."

"Really? You have to tell me, you can't keep me on my toes like this," I laugh at his smug smile.

I realize for the first time I'm having a normal conversation with another person at a party without Serena making me feel inadequate or laughing at my attempts. The weight that lifts from my stomach almost makes me breathe better.

"Okay, on Monday I'll bring the recipe and explain it to you, so you can prepare it whenever you want."

"No, you can't leave me like that without telling me the secret ingredient," I exclaim, making him laugh.

I'm making him laugh. I, the most inadequate person to have a conversation with at a party, am making a guy laugh. The sense of gratification and victory that expands in my stomach is almost incredible. Next to me, Aaron watches the conversation as if I were the center of his world, and my head begins to spin because of the euphoria and not because alcohol is involved.

"Dill," Andrew whispers to me, amused.

"I don't believe it!"

"I swear."

"Wait, in this recipe, there is nothing to simmer with alcohol that could set the house on fire, right? I wouldn't want to repeat that experience." I glance at Aaron, who smiles amusedly.

"Did she set your house on fire?" Emma questions Aaron after she joins our conversation.

"The situation was not so serious. She just set off the alarm and blackened the furniture above the stove," he tries to downplay.

Andrew and Emma listen to us open-mouthed.

"Don't forget the vegetables on the floor. Those were also

part of that dinner." I laugh and then launch into an explanation of what happened.

No alcohol to help me relax, just my voice, Aaron's comforting presence, and a story that keeps them entertained. I've never been so comfortable as this night by the pool.

One of the waiters approaches and offers me a glass of champagne, but I decline.

"If you want to drink it, it's okay. It's your birthday. Nothing will happen if you drink a glass to celebrate, I'm here to stop you if the situation gets out of hand," Aaron reassures me, whispering in my ear.

I look up and smile at him. "In all honesty, I don't feel the need. I've never done it because I like it, but because it gives me courage when I'm among other people. But if you're here with me, I feel less insecure."

Aaron lowers himself and kisses me gently. "I'm proud of you, you know?" he says before taking me by the hand and dragging me to a table where a cake with twenty-four lit candles is waiting for me.

I blow on them, among the applause of those present, and for the first time since I can remember, I don't really know what wish to make because at this moment I feel I have everything I want from life. Perhaps this happiness never ends. Maybe that's the only thing I really want right now.

***

When the last guest finally leaves, Aaron and I find ourselves in the kitchen putting dirty dishes in the sink and leftovers in the fridge. It takes us a while to finish, but it is pleasant to do it in silence next to him. When the last dish is stored in the dishwasher, I sit at the counter and bite into a forkful of the delicious cake Aaron brought in from one of the best pastry shops in town.

I inhale deeply and enjoy this moment, still incredulous at how much things have changed in these five months and how much they are still about to change. I didn't talk about it with Aaron today so as not to spoil the atmosphere, but in one month, we will have to deal with this accommodation which, according to the press office, is temporary. A thought I tried to stifle all day, but never completely disappeared.

When he gets closer, he gives me a small box that, for a moment, makes my heart skip a beat. The logo of a famous jewelry store makes me go into fibrillation.

"Open it. It's your gift."

"But wasn't the dress my gift?"

"Those were to keep you busy while the caterers set up the pool." He winks at me.

I grab the box and remove the paper. Inside, a small velvet box makes me widen my eyes. "It's not a ring, is it?"

He chuckles, amused. "Open it"

My trembling fingers struggle to open the box, but a smile appears on my lips when I do. Inside is a keychain with a small dragonfly with diamonds covering its body and a padlock with a heart-shaped keyhole. It is so beautiful and elegant that I barely touch it for fear of ruining it. I look up at Aaron, who is watching me carefully.

"Thank you, it's beautiful," I whisper as I stroke his face with one hand.

"I know our agreement ends in one month, and you are free to find yourself a new apartment if you like. But I would like you to consider staying here and putting your copy of the keys permanently on that keychain." He seems almost nervous as he speaks, a reaction that is difficult to associate with someone like him.

"Are you asking me to move in with you?" I ask.

"It's not been that bad in the last five months, has it?" he asks, perhaps worried that my answer is no.

"It was perfect, and I would love to stay," I answer, standing on tiptoe and kissing him as if my life depended on this kiss.

He squeezes me in a hug, then, with a sudden gesture, takes me in his arms, making me squeak in surprise.

"Aaron!" I laugh as he walks through the living room and climbs the stairs. "Have you gone crazy?"

"Now I can finally give you your birthday present." His smile is a call to the lust that makes me melt to the tips of my toes. "It's been all day that I dreamed of worshiping your perfect body and making you come until you beg me to stop."

"What if I'm never tired of coming?" I raise an eyebrow.

"Is that a challenge?" he asks while, with a kick, he opens the door of the master bedroom and throws me on the bed, making me laugh.

"Are you able to keep up? Because you know, given your age…" I tease, enjoying as his gaze catches fire.

"Take off your clothes," he orders in a firm tone, and my whole body reacts to his voice.

It's incredible how his commanding tone alone can ignite every single cell and send shivers of pleasure down my body. I never thought such a thing could turn me on, I always felt uncomfortable in front of people who imposed their will on me, but this is different. The way Aaron worships my body and brain makes me trust him, turning this moment into something exciting.

I grab the zipper on the side of my dress and slide it slowly off while I enjoy Aaron's gaze following my every little movement. It almost makes me breathless to see him lose control over his body, with his erection waking up and straining against his pants. I drop the dress at the foot of the bed and enjoy his eyes burning for me.

"Naked." His tone is so low that it sounds more like a growl than an order, and as I take off my bra, I surrender to his will.

Aaron knows what I like, he guides me to discover my pleasure, and I let myself be carried away by his voice, his gaze, and the anticipation of feeling his hands on my body. When I pull off my panties, I don't feel naked or vulnerable but the most beautiful woman that ever walked on earth. Aaron is the one who makes me feel this way, who makes me love every part of myself as if it were perfect. Even my battered feet or my ears sticking out a bit or my slightly cracked teeth in the front seem unique and inimitable to his eyes.

I watch him slowly undress as he lets me admire his sculpted body and worship his erection. That dark trail of hair that descends from his navel to the base of his cock is a path I have walked many times with my imagination but to which I have never done justice. Reality is more perfect than I can imagine.

I look at him as he slowly crawls onto the bed, lies on top of it, and looks at me with a half-smile on his lips.

"Sit on my face," he orders, and I freeze, watching him as if he had told me to get out of this room dancing the tango.

"What?" I whisper uncertainly, sure I didn't understand correctly what he said.

His smile widens, and he reaches out his hand, grabbing mine.

"Put your hands against the wall, straddle my head, and sit on my face," he repeats.

I feel my cheeks burn with embarrassment. I've experienced so many first times with Aaron, but this is something that makes me shy.

"I'll guide you," he whispers with a sweet look when he sees me hesitating.

I do as he tells me, and I bite my lip with shame because of the intimate and exposed position. Can there be something too intimate in the requests of a man in the bedroom?

"You are perfect," he whispers, and a shiver runs down my spine.

"Eyes on me," he orders, and when I look down, I see all his lust as he grabs my hips and drags me toward his mouth, taking me by surprise.

"When I tell you to sit on my face, I mean sit on my face," he orders before sinking into me with his tongue.

My whole world turns upside down when, with the same vigor as a hungry man, he devours my innermost part, licking, sucking, biting. His eyes never leave mine as he sticks his tongue deep into my folds, alternating small bites on the bundle of nerves at the apex of my opening that sends shocks of pleasure down my spine.

I watch him the entire time while his hands anchor my hips and guide my movements, seeking my pleasure riding his face, and I don't miss for a moment the satisfied smile in his eyes as he sucks until I explode in an orgasm that makes my legs tremble.

With one hand, he grabs my hair behind the nape of my neck and drags me to him for a kiss that takes away what little breath I have left. I savor myself on his lips, on his tongue, in a dirty, greedy kiss, full of a desire that has not dissipated with my orgasm.

I move far enough back to observe his perfect body lying next to me, his tan, those sculpted abs that descend to the taut erection, and the small drop of pre-cum inviting me to dive with my lips on his cock. I slip between his legs and watch him hold his breath while I savor with my tongue that salty drop, and I envelop his warm erection with my lips.

"Dakota." My name escapes from his lips in a moan while his hand sinks into my hair and guides me as I slide him down my throat.

It's a feeling I've never felt before, the one of having a man in the palm of my hand. I watch him close his eyes and bite his lips. He is tense and holding back, thrusting his hips with powerful blows I'm familiar with.

Deciding to reciprocate my orgasm with the same fervor, I grasp with one hand the base of his erection and squeeze, accompanying the movement of my lips with those of my hand. The roar that comes out of his lips is animalistic. I'm soaked between my legs when he lays his eyes on mine, and I read the desire to take me and make me his own. I squeeze my lips to his flesh and savor its length from the base to the tip with my tongue. I suck, lick, and taste the silky warm skin while, with the other hand, I slip between his legs, gently squeezing his testicles until he groans.

I never take my gaze away from his while he pulls my hair slightly, silently telling me to move away because he is about to come. But I don't want to, so I stretch my lips and sink his cock deeper into my throat, sucking vigorously until I feel him coming with a growl piercing his chest.

I swallow as waves of his pleasure invade my mouth, but some of it drips down my chin. It's a dirty orgasm loaded with a pleasure that is almost animalistic. Aaron drags me to him for a frantic kiss as soon as my lips leave his erection, his tongue invading my mouth, the taste of our pleasures mixes, sending a shiver down my spine. His hand slips between my legs, and when two of his fingers make their way inside me, they find no obstacle to stop them. I'm so wet that Aaron slips up to his knuckles, and when he starts fucking me with his hand, he swallows the moan that comes out of my lips.

I ride his hand, chasing a second orgasm that comes as soon as his fingers bend, touching that sensitive part of me that no other man has ever been able to find. I thought it was an urban legend, that that famous G-spot didn't really exist, but Aaron proved to me several times that I was wrong and that he memorized my body to the point that he could find it on the first try.

I reach the peak of my pleasure and arch my back while Aaron puts a hand around my waist to prevent me from falling back. His lips on my hardened nipples amplifies the pleasure that explodes from my lower abdomen and expands under my skin to every part of my body.

Aaron kisses me before he slips his fingers out and leaves me empty, but I know it won't be for long. I see him reaching out toward the bedside table, grabbing a condom from the first drawer, and sliding it on the erection that has awakened again.

With a decisive gesture, he makes me turn, hands and knees resting on the mattress while he sinks into me from behind, filling me up until I catch my breath.

His thrusts are powerful, his fingers sink into my hips, and the dirty noise of our sweaty skins colliding is the only sound in the room. It's such an overwhelming feeling that another orgasm starts to mount. I chase it, pushing my hips against his but never being able to reach it. A frustrated sigh escapes my lips when Aaron grabs my hair and lures me against his chest.

"Come for me, Dakota." he orders, sliding one hand around my neck, squeezing slightly, while the other rests on my clit, playing with it while he fucks me with firm blows until I reach that pleasure that escaped me.

His thrusts get faster, like my breathing, and when my third orgasm explodes, I feel him throbbing inside me, coming with a roar that is lost when he bites my shoulder. The silence that follows is broken only by our labored breaths.

We slump onto the bed and I snuggle up on his chest as he strokes my hair. I have never felt as much pleasure as tonight.

"Happy birthday to me," I whisper and feel his chest shake with a low laugh.

He squeezes me even closer to him while he grabs the sheets with one hand and wraps us in a cocoon that tastes of stability and home. Before I fall asleep, exhausted after this day, I realize that the wish I made blowing out the candles has just come true.

CHAPTER 21

Aaron

"You're gorgeous" The words choke in my throat when I look up and see Dakota walking down the stairs wrapped in a silver evening dress that enhances her curves without appearing vulgar.

I always thought she was a unique beauty, the girl next door, but dressed for a red carpet, she is breathtaking.

"You're not bad in this tuxedo either." She puts her hands on my chest and raises her face to leave me a light kiss on the lips.

I would like to hold her to me and deepen this kiss, but I know it took her hours to get ready, and I don't want to ruin the perfect work of the makeup artist. I've been in this industry long enough to know that the red carpet spotlights are merciless with imperfections. I don't want Dakota's face to be slammed on the front page tomorrow because she looks like I just fucked her. We will already have to face the newspapers because we walked together on that red carpet.

"The limousine is out here waiting for us. Are you ready?" I reach out an arm to which she leans against with an almost regal bearing.

"I've never been so ready," she says with a smile as we walk out, and I help her get into the car.

We arrive in front of the cinema where the film premiere to which we were invited is held. Or rather, where I was invited because it's one of those with a big budget my father's company produced, and Dakota is my "plus one." We wait for our turn on the limousine line to get out and face the red carpet.

"Are you nervous?"

When we left home, the conversation was light, we laughed and joked, but as we approached the destination, Dakota began to look out the window and remain silent. I know that in these moments, she needs to focus on finding the tranquility to face fans and the paparazzi, but I am worried she regrets being seen with me. In Hollywood, walking the red carpet with someone is almost a wedding.

"Not so much. I'm not here as a protagonist, and my presence will go quite unnoticed apart from the gossip of being here with you. I don't have performance anxiety." She smiles at me serenely, and I relax a bit too.

"Better this way because they will ask us questions we must answer." I study her expression, trying to understand if she has changed her mind about this first official appearance together. It's baffling how she deals with the array of photographers and journalists.

"And we will answer with a smile," she reassures me when the limousine stops and the door opens onto the red carpet lined with photographers.

I'm the first to get out, and the flashes are so dazzling that I have to squint for a moment. I reach out my hand to help Dakota, and the photographers seem crazy as I put my hand on her back and guide her along the carpet that extends to the cinema entrance. The photographers are irrepressible, calling us, asking us to pose for them.

We arrive in front of the board with the movie title and stop for the official photos of this event. I wrap an arm around Dakota's waist and she looks up at me and smiles, then puts a hand on my chest. If anyone still doubts the nature of this relationship, how we look at each other erases any uncertainty. I could spend my evening watching her instead of the movie. We go back to looking at the photographers and smiling with that perfect and often insincere expression that we have tried in the mirror hundreds of times for these occasions.

"Aaron, are you confirming your relationship with Dakota?" one of the photographers asks.

I feel Dakota's head leaning against my chest, and when I look down on her, I find her eyes full of sweetness and a sincere smile to welcome me. I don't need to answer the photographer's question. I just lower myself a few inches and lay my lips on hers to unleash the flashes that make this relationship official in the eyes of the world.

I've never done such a thing in public, mainly because I've never had a serious relationship to let go this way in front of everyone. Dakota, however, brings out the part of me that makes me feel like a kid at the first crush.

"Do you think that's enough as confirmation?" I whisper in her ear when I separate from her lips. With a finger, I try to clean my lips from the veil of lipstick that the kiss left on me, but Dakota raises a hand and helps me make myself presentable.

"Are you used to kissing people who walk the red carpet with you?" she asks, raising an eyebrow.

I chuckle. "No"

"Then I think it's enough of a confirmation." She winks at me before returning to pose for the photographers.

Every form of nervousness leaves my body, leaving only the pleasant feeling of being out for this evening with a woman who has turned my life upside down in the most delightful way.

***

The film is one of those where action and explosions are not lacking. It's a good film, suitable for making huge grosses in the first few weeks right after launch. Those who took care of the launch managed to do a great job creating hype, and the public will certainly not be disappointed, amplifying the word of mouth that has already been made. But I had no doubt about this. My father didn't reach this success leaving things to chance.

At the bar during the after-party where we are, while waiting for the bartender to prepare me two glasses of soda before returning to Dakota, I had the opportunity to eavesdrop on the conversation of two prominent bloggers who were pleasantly surprised by the quality of the film. When it comes to movies released to make money, rather than to move the conscience of the public, the journalists always are a little biased, but this time my father managed to bring out a good product that entertains the masses.

I watch Dakota converse with one of the protagonists and she seems at ease. I'm glad to see that she doesn't need alcohol to feel a part of this evening. It's nice to see how, after dumping her friend, she's slowly coming out of her shell and growing as a person. She never needed my help to become a pleasant person to converse with, but she needed to convince herself of it. The birthday at our house was just the catalyst for something she already had inside. *Our house.* It's strange how I can no longer think of that villa as mine alone, and a smile appears on my lips.

"You chose the young and sexy girl," a voice that I recognize all too well makes me turn to Jeremiah, one of my father's oldest partners. An old fox who changed more wives than underwear in his lifetime. His latest conquest is a twenty-five-year-old he will bring to the altar next month. I think she's wife number seven if I'm counting right.

The smile that appears on my face is taut and fake. "I chose a woman I feel good with and like to live with."

In all honesty, I am annoyed by his way of dismissing my relationship with Dakota. He has always been looking for younger and younger women, despite his seventy years, and the fact that he insinuates that this thing links us makes me shudder. I have the same respect for this man as I have for my father, which says a lot about my irritation at having a conversation with him right now.

"Of course. We will talk about it again in a few years when she has cellulite and begins to talk about children," he laughs, amused.

The blood boils in my veins, and the disgust I feel for him almost makes me vomit. I've always kept my mouth shut because annoying people like him make my job in this industry more challenging. Still, until now, I had never had anyone I really cared about to be outraged by these statements. I realize only now how wrong my behavior has been in front of certain remarks. I should have put them back in their place years ago when they began to involve me in their sexist and misogynistic jokes.

"I wouldn't be so much of a braggart if I were you. We all know that the women you marry just want one thing, and I'm sure it's not your prostate or halitosis problems." I put a hand on his shoulder while I see him get serious and tighten his jaw in a vice. "What? Do you really think you're the only one who speaks ill of your exes? Trust that everyone in the industry clearly knows how you are between the sheets." I wink at him and leave him there with his anger bubbling inside.

I reach Dakota just when she turns around and looks for me.

"I'm starving. How about going for something to eat?" I ask, resting my hands on her hips and dragging her to me. Her hands rise and rest on my shoulders. The man next to me glances at Dakota's butt, and it annoys me so much that I slip my hands in the direction of his gaze and cover her. The man looks up at me with an embarrassed smile for being caught, shrugs his shoulders almost to apologize, and then turns to talk to the woman he ignored. I have surrounded myself for years with certain people, and only now do I realize how much annoyance their arrogance gives me.

"We've just arrived. We can't leave now" There's not much conviction in her voice.

"They saw our faces. In a while, they will all be drunk enough to forget about us." And I don't want to meet my father. I avoided him all night, but I don't want him to approach me while I'm with Dakota. He could start making jokes with his ass-kisser that always surround him on these occasions and would end up with a public scene, which I prefer to avoid.

"Ok, let's go. I'm famished, and in these places, they don't serve food." She grabs me by the hand and drags me to the exit.

"I'm glad it wasn't hard to convince you." I smile, amused as I avoid meeting the eyes of people who might stop me to exchange a few words. It's quite a difficult task, as I know pretty much everyone in this room.

"You know I came here for you. If you say we can leave, I will always agree with you. Have you seen the microscopic canapés they serve?"

I laugh, amused, as we exit the main entrance and call Gaspard to pick us up.

***

We enter the small place near Santa Monica that seems to be deserted. Apparently, not many people want a sandwich at one in the morning on a Wednesday, and I don't mind it since, with our clothing, we certainly don't go unnoticed.

"I have to say you're the most elegant couple I've ever served." The waitress' cheerful voice makes us smile as we sit at one of the many empty tables.

The woman in her fifties approaches to fill the cups on the table with coffee. It's one of those places open day and night, serving breakfast at any time, with vinyl benches and stools screwed to the floor in front of the counter. Not a place that often sees Hollywood celebrities, but certainly has a more relaxed and genuine atmosphere than the places we are used to, starting with the smile of the woman standing next to our table.

"When we go out to dinner, we like to dress up." Dakota smiles at her as she arranges her evening dress, and I unfasten the buttons of my tuxedo jacket.

"Surely you have dedicated time for this outing," she laughs, accentuating the wrinkles surrounding her eyes. "What can I bring you?" she asks while pouring the coffee.

"A double cheeseburger with bacon and a mountain of fries." Dakota's face as she orders looks like that of a person who hasn't touched food in weeks.

The woman laughs, amused. "Don't they feed Hollywood celebrities at parties?"

"There are only bars to get drunk but not even the shadow of something edible. The canapés are so small that they look like confetti," confirms my partner.

I watch her grab her cup and squint as she sips the hot liquid. A small moan slips from her lips, and I am lost imagining her in the bedroom while she comes. A thought that awakens parts of my body in these pants that are too tight to hide an erection. I look down at my cup of coffee and try to take my thoughts elsewhere before dragging her into the bathroom of this place and making her moan for entirely different reasons.

"What do I bring to you?" the waitress asks me, and I am happy that, for once, there is someone who doesn't strip me with her eyes or hits on me while completely ignoring the person who accompanies me. I like this place more and more.

"The same that she ordered." I smile at her as I bring the cup of hot liquid to my mouth.

She nods as she writes down our orders on the pad of paper to take to the kitchen and then walks away with the coffee jug in her hand, humming "These Boots Are Made For Walkin'" by Nancy Sinatra that they are playing on the radio. Everything in this place has been frozen in the fifties, making the atmosphere almost surreal.

"Am I the only one that feels like we stepped into a time machine and went back seventy years?" Dakota asks as she looks at me from behind her cup of coffee.

"I was thinking the same thing."

"I liked the movie. What do you think?" she then asks, changing the topic.

"I think it's a great product. They have worked very well on the promotion. It will be successful," I confirm.

Dakota tilts her head and studies me carefully. I look at her curious expression and know she is thinking about something.

"But it's not something you would produce for the streaming division." This is not a question, more of an observation.

"That kind of film is suitable for cinemas. You need large investments, and the economic return is in gross income on the weekends following the release. Producing something for a streaming company is different. You need to retain the audience on the platform, make them pay the subscription month after month, and find a way to ensure that sponsors are constantly enticed to invest. A movie like that is a product of its own. You have to grab the viewer's attention for those few hours. A show on our platform must keep the viewer glued to the screen even after it ends. It has to make the viewer loyal to the platform." I like her concentrated expression as I explain how it works.

"That's why you prefer to opt for famous books and then adapt them for TV. Because this brings you to the platform and all the readers who are already passionate are already faithful to that series," she reasons while biting into a potato chip that the waitress has brought us along with our food.

"It's one of the ways to do it, yes. It's easier to create hype around something that people already know," I say before biting into my sandwich and hearing my stomach growl. I hadn't realized until this moment how hungry I was.

Dakota seems to be thinking about it while chewing on her dinner. Her furrowed brows and sulky lips are the most beautiful sight I have seen tonight. The film, in comparison, becomes banal.

"Is that why you don't want to opt for the series I suggested? Isn't she famous enough to take advantage of her fan base?"

I shake my head while wiping my mouth with a paper towel and swallow the bite I was chewing.

"No. We can invest a budget to make a blast with the book and reach other readers besides her avid fans. The problem is that we can't find the author of the book. She has no contacts, not even social. We're still working on it."

Dakota wrinkles her nose, and a grimace appears on her face. "I know. The comments against her were so bad that she decided to completely eclipse herself from social media. Sometimes people don't have a limit when it comes to crucifying someone online."

I nod and start with the fries. "I saw. For certain comments, I would have hired a lawyer and dumped a lawsuit on them."

"Me too!" she agrees with me.

Between a potato chip and a bite of the sandwich, we fall into the comforting routine that has accompanied us for months. We talk for hours, and I will never stop enjoying her expressions when she tells me about the things that fascinate her. It is a bottomless pit of stimulating conversations, never banal, that touch on topics that link us with a disarming naturalness.

That's what I like most about her, not her perfect physique, her sensual lips, or the chemistry we have in bed. It's her brain that makes me her slave. I am totally enraptured by this woman who, on paper, should be too young but who is actually more adult than many of my peers with whom I usually interact.

***

"It's dawn," Dakota says with a yawn as I put my jacket on her shoulders and we leave the diner.

"Would you like it if we let Gaspard sleep for a few more hours before he picks us up?" I ask, unable to let go of this night that turned out to be perfect.

She turns and looks at me, raising an eyebrow. "What do you have in mind?"

I shrug and smile. "Something I've never done in my life."

I wink at her and lower myself, signaling her to jump on my shoulders. She doesn't think twice before she slides the slit of her dress up to the thigh and jumps to cling to my back. I grab her legs and wait for her to hold firmly to my neck before walking down the road with a few cars passing us at this hour.

We must look like a circus for those who see us, dressed in elegant clothes as we walk to our destination. I notice some cars slowing down and looking at us strangely before resuming their drive toward their destination.

"You have never been to the beach?" she asks, perplexed as I let her descend on the slightly cold and damp sand of Santa Monica's beach.

I support her as she unfastens the high heels she wore all evening.

"I've been to the beach many times, but I've never spent a night out with a woman watching the ocean as the sun rises, sitting on the sand," I explain as we walk to the shore.

"Really? Not even when you were in college?" she asks as she snuggles between my legs, and I squeeze her against my chest.

"When I was in college, I was already working with my father. I never had time to enjoy these little things when I was younger," I admit.

"Do you ever regret not having a normal life?"

I shrug and think about it for several moments. "It's not just sacrificing what I've made. I have reached several goals I had set for myself. I would never have achieved these results if I hadn't done that. And then I'm living these moments with you, now. I may not have the euphoria of my twenties, but I appreciate the nuances of these moments much more because I don't take them for granted."

She grabs my hands and intertwines our fingers.

"So I'm kind of your first time." I notice a smile on her face.

I smile too, thinking about what she said. "You are so many of my first times."

Dakota is my first time on the beach, the first time I publicly announced a relationship, the first time I've lived with a woman, and the first time I've fallen in love. Because the time has come to admit that the feeling that is growing in my chest has nothing to do with lust and desire. With her, I could think of giving up this life if she asked me.

CHAPTER 22
Dakota

My grandparents' house, where I lived all my life with my mother, hasn't changed in the three years I've been living in Los Angeles. The light-colored veranda is shaded by the giant oak tree in the garden in front of the entrance. The only thing you notice is that my grandmother has changed, again, the rocking cushions on the porch since the last time I was here to visit them. I imagine my grandfather grumbling because he doesn't understand my grandmother's mania to change their color every six months. I smile as I pull out my copy of the keys to enter.

"Anyone at home?" The silence that welcomes me is a bit strange.

You usually hear the television at full volume with my grandfather sleeping in the armchair in the living room. And if my grandmother tries to turn it off, he wakes up shouting that he was watching and just resting his eyes. For this reason, the empty living room leaves me a little perplexed.

"In the kitchen!" my mother's voice calls out, bringing a smile to my face.

"Where did Grandpa and Grandma go?" I wrinkle my forehead as I place my travel bag on the floor next to the stool then enter the kitchen. I watch my mother finish washing the vegetables she picked from the garden this morning.

"They went on a day trip with a group from the Country Club. Can you believe it?" She smiles at me, lifting a corner of her mouth. It is a genuine gesture, but I don't miss the bit of tension that permeates her features.

"On a trip? We are talking about the same people who put a fence six feet high because they don't want to talk to the neighbors, right? Did they go on a hike with other people? Did you threaten them?" I ask, stunned by the news.

My mother laughs and shakes her head. "I suppose it's senile dementia," she teases.

"Wait, what do you mean they went with a group from the Country Club? Since when have they been members of the Country Club?" This is the most surreal conversation I've ever had with my mother.

"Since you became a famous actress, they say they must keep your name high. They love to brag to the rich about your success. I told you. Senile dementia." She laughs again, and I join her because I know that my grandparents are in excellent shape.

It's the most absurd news I've ever received. My grandfather is the one who drives five hours to go watch the pig race. I can't imagine him in a polo shirt playing golf with other old men of his age.

"If you visited us more often, you would be aware of the news. I thought you had forgotten about this place."

"Mom, I came back less than a year ago. I have not disappeared from the face of the earth." I hug and hold her tightly as she wipes her hands after washing the vegetables.

We often quarrel, but the truth is that I love her. She is not happy that I live in Los Angeles and doesn't miss an opportunity to remind me of it, but she has never prevented me from leaving or chasing my dreams. Except that every now and then, she insists on suggesting that I pursue other interests that she thinks will lead to a better future.

"Is one meeting a year what you give to your mother? Inmates have more visits to prison than I do." She raises an eyebrow in reproach as she grabs a tea kettle, fills it with water, and puts it on the stove. She doesn't need to ask me if I want tea with cookies. She knows I would never give up this afternoon ritual we have had for as long as I can remember.

"You know I'm busy with work. And then, you can always come to Los Angeles. You know that money is not a problem, I just need to know the day and the time, and I'll buy that damn ticket for you." I sit at the kitchen counter as I watch her prepare a dish with homemade cookies and place it in front of me.

She watches me for a few moments, crossing her arms and studying me, tilting her head. I have no physical resemblance to my mother. Where I am blond, she is raven black, while she has generous shapes, I am skin and bones. But there is one thing I took from her. We're both skilled at nailing someone with our gaze when we want to emphasize an issue close to our heart. Before she even opens her mouth, I already know what she will say.

"Where should I sleep? In the bed between you and Aaron?" she asks seriously, bringing up the topic I flew here to discuss.

After I learned from Aaron about their past, I didn't want to address this topic with her on the phone. It's delicate, and, since she has been accepting checks from the man I live with for years, the least I could do was take a plane and know what she thinks about it.

"What the heck, Mom! Make as many jokes as you want, but not this one, please. It's…weird. Just weird," I blurt out, shivering.

The idea of a bed populated by me, Aaron, and my mother is the most disgusting image I can think of. And from her expression, I understand it's the same for her.

"He told you about everything," she says, as if afraid of what he might have told me.

"More or less. What did you think? When he found out whose daughter I am, he got angry. He thought I had approached him for some kind of revenge. He told me you went there when Dad died to sue them, and then he convinced you not to file the lawsuit," I say, not knowing where to start this conversation.

Sixteen years have passed. It is something so far away that it could have happened in another life, but it still happened, and I cannot ignore it.

"Broadly speaking, that's how it went," she mumbles as she pours the herbal tea into the cups.

"And are you upset because we are dating? Can we finally talk about it without you getting angry or sad?" I implore her.

It's a conversation I've been waiting to have since I was a teenager. She cannot refuse to communicate with me on the subject, even if she feels sad about reminiscing about those days. Because considering how my mother raised me, I'm sure she's dying to get this burden off her chest. She always tried to protect me from the aching pain of my father's death, but I'm an adult now. I can deal with my emotions.

"No, I'm not sad. And I'm not angry, either. We survived just fine without the money we could have gotten with that lawsuit. But that doesn't change the fact that I'm worried about you."

I observe her for several moments, trying to understand what is going through her head. She first saw something good in Aaron because otherwise she wouldn't have dropped that lawsuit. She is more stubborn than me, that's something I got from her, so I don't understand all this concern.

"Because of the age difference?" It's a reasonable apprehension for a mother, but she shakes her head.

"That's not what worries me. I mean, it's not the main reason. It's his job, his family. I saw him when I got there. I saw how that job meant everything to him. He did everything to keep his father happy, even convince a widow to go home and suck it up. I don't want you with a man that will put his career before you," she admits, fishing a cookie from the plate and coming to sit next to me.

"Actually, we're both very busy with our careers, but we manage to carve out time for ourselves. We often stay at home to read or watch TV, even if it is only for a few hours. Living under the same roof it's easier to meet, even if it's just while brushing our teeth before going to sleep. His career is now more than solid. He doesn't need to elbow anyone to make his way. He's already the biggest fish in the tank," I explain, seeing her frowning.

She shakes her head and inhales thoroughly. I see that concern that makes those little wrinkles appear between her eyes. Her eyebrows furrow, and she looks worried.

"Didn't you rush a little moving in with him? Isn't it better if you go out and have fun with your friends instead of being a good housewife? You live with a man, Dakota. You're only twenty-four!" The plea in her voice makes me uncomfortable.

"Friends? What friends, Mom? You know that I have always been terrible at making friends with my peers. I was the one who had lunch locked in a bathroom because all the tables in the cafeteria were occupied, and I didn't dare ask my classmates if the seat next to them was free. Living in Hollywood doesn't help you find friends and in all honesty, I feel good with Aaron. Better than with guys my age. I know it sounds absurd, but I have more in common with Aaron than with much younger people. And then you, at my age, already had a daughter. You more than anyone else should know that sometimes 'having fun with friends' is not all you want in your twenties."

She inhales deeply and shakes her head. "I suppose this is my fault. I had to push you harder to play with kids your age instead of indulging you and letting you around us adults. Do you really have no friends in Los Angeles?"

"I don't mind how I grew up. I don't feel the lack of having frivolous fun. I like the stability I've had since living with Aaron. It makes me feel safe and alive at the same time. And for the friends part, I'm working on it. I'm trying to talk more with my colleagues and not hold back when they invite me out. It's not easy, and I feel very insecure, but I'm trying. Aaron helps me a lot in this, to open up to others," I confess, thinking back to my birthday and how he was by my side all evening. He always understood where I wanted to go with my conversations and helped me navigate them without the help of alcohol.

"Are you in love with him?" she asks with a sweetness in

her eyes that I recognize. It's the one she has when she is afraid for me but lets me live my life, make mistakes, and try again until I get what I want. She suffers from seeing me fall, but she is always ready to reach out her hand when I have trouble getting up.

"I think so…" I think about it for a moment, and the feeling that expands in my chest reassures me. "Yes, I'm in love with Aaron."

"Are you happy?" The smile on her lips is that of a mother who hopes for the best for her daughter.

"Yes." I reciprocate her smile because I really am.

We sip our tea in silence then while munching on my mother's homemade cookies. If there's one thing I didn't take from her, it's how to cook. Despite her trying to teach me hundreds of times how to juggle the stove, I never manage to pull off anything decent.

"I hope you are right about him. He was very convincing and he used the right words. I'm scared he is convincing you that everything is fine when it's not," she mumbles, worried after a long silence.

I study her, her serious face and her mouth set in a stubborn line.

"Did you know he held Dad on that scaffold until the firefighter came? He climbed it risking his life trying to save Dad."

She looks at me surprised and a bit sad.

"Are you serious? He never told me something like that."

I wrinkle my forehead and observe her, hoping she will be ready for this kind of conversation.

"Maybe because you were a young widow grieving her husband and he didn't want to give you a graphic visual of

Dad's last breath, but this is what he did. He tried to save him. I asked about the insurance thing. From what he told me, it was Dad's company who did the wrong paperwork. You would have lost that lawsuit, but he felt guilty, and he started to send us those checks. Those are literally part of his paycheck in the beginning of his career," I explain and she seems to soften.

"I knew it wasn't their fault with the insurance, but I was hurting, scared to raise you alone, and I wanted to find someone to blame. They seemed rich enough to not sink if they had to pay," she admits.

"This is not going to bring Dad back, but I want you to know that he is a good person," I whisper softly.

"I'm happy to hear that," she says, finally smiling a bit.

"I didn't ask him, but I'm sure he will talk to you about that day, when you are ready. Maybe it will help to talk about it," I suggest cautiously. I don't want to push this argument and shut her down again.

"I will think about it. Thank you." She kisses me on the crown of my head and hugs me fiercely.

I'm happy with this answer. I never came this far in a conversation about Aaron like the one we are having now. She always avoided the conversation about my father and I always thought it was because she didn't want to traumatize me when I was younger, but I think she did it also to protect herself.

I was seven when my father died. I remember him but I was still young enough to not feel the melancholia when I think about him. He is all my favorite memories, and I can understand my mother not wanting to contaminate them with tears and suffering. She did a great job protecting me, but I always had this lingering feeling of wanting closure. There's always been a lot of mystery around his death and talking about that day with Aaron helped me to make peace with his absence.

"Is he angry with me for what I did?" she asks after a long silence.

"No. He never once thought you were in the wrong there. On the contrary, he felt guilty for not being able to help you more. To save Dad, even. But he understood you were desperate. And I can understand that, too. I would probably react the same way if something happened to him. You are human, Mom. You were allowed to grieve and hurt. You were young and a widow, nobody expected you to be strong and carry on like nothing happened. But you were able to make this tragedy more bearable for me. I survived Dad's death because you made it easier, and it's time for me to be strong for you. When you decide to talk about it, I will be there every step of the way," I tell her, and I see a smile appear on her face.

"How old you are? Twenty-four or forty?" She smiles and caresses my cheek.

I laugh, amused. "So many of you ask me that, I'm starting to ask myself."

The atmosphere lightens the weight I carried with me when I left Los Angeles this morning. As much as I know that I am not doing anything wrong with Aaron, I needed to clarify things with her.

"Do you promise me that you will tell me if you are not happy?"

"I'm happy, Mom. You don't have to worry about me. And I would really like it if you would come to Los Angeles to visit me sometime. If you want to stay in a hotel there is no problem, but there are plenty of rooms at Aaron's house, and I bet he would like it, too."

"I promise I'll try to take a few days off and join you, okay?"

At the moment, this promise is enough for me. We will not be able to magically change our relationship with a conversation. It will take some more time to accept that this is my life, that it is not something temporary. But I'm sure that if she comes to Los Angeles and sees how much I love my job, that I've found stability and a future, she'll be convinced that this is not just a little girl's dream but a career I can really pursue.

CHAPTER 23
Aaron

"Can I post the photo of you wearing your floral shirt on social media? You're cute!" Dakota has been teasing me since last night when she returned from visiting her mother's house, and surprised me with an old photo she found in a folder I completely forgot I had in my home office.

I don't know how to take this new step in our relationship. While I'm happy that she clarified our relationship with her mother and found the answers she was looking for, I know it's time for me to have a chat with Isabella, if only to reassure her of my relationship with Dakota.

"If you want me to shut down all your social media accounts, post it," I threaten, grabbing her by the waist and throwing her on the couch before slipping between her legs and lowering myself to kiss her.

Dakota squeaks and bursts out laughing when I start tickling her. We just finished having breakfast, and the idea of going to the office hasn't crossed my mind once. The absurd thing is that I wouldn't have thought of skipping a day's work until a few months ago unless I had been hospitalized. Yet now, I don't feel even the slightest sense of guilt.

"Stop, please! I'm about to vomit breakfast," she begs amid the laughter that fills this house.

The bell rings, catching our attention. "Are you waiting for someone?" I furrow my forehead and study her expression which is as disoriented as mine. The fear of opening the door and finding myself in front of her mother crosses my mind, and I shudder. I want to have this conversation on my terms, not through an ambush.

She shakes her head, and when I get up to open the door, she follows me in silence. I find myself in front of my father's lawyer, who greets me courteously with a severe face.

My perplexity soon turns into irritation. It's not my pleasure to deal with my father's lawyers, especially at eight in the morning when I decided to spend my day home with Dakota.

"Can I enter?" he asks when he sees that I show no sign of moving from the threshold.

I step aside and let him enter the landing without continuing further. I've never enjoyed surprise visits, and I don't want to make him more comfortable than necessary. The less he stays here, the more my day improves.

"Is there a reason why you came here?" I ask through gritted teeth.

He lowers his gaze slightly and swallows nervously, turning my discomfort into apprehension. I've never seen him struggle as he is doing right now, and I'm starting to think there's something to really worry about.

"Can we speak in private?" he asks, nodding to Dakota.

"No, we can't. If there's something important to say, have the courage to do it in front of her. Don't ask me to give her shitty messages," I reply, furious when I'm pretty sure my dad concocted some of his bullshit against Dakota. There is no other explanation for the presence of this man in my house.

"There is no easy way to say it…this morning, your father was in an accident on his way to the airport. A garbage truck had a problem with its brakes and hit his car at the intersection. He was taken to the hospital, but unfortunately, his injuries were too serious, and he didn't make it. They couldn't even get him to the operating room. Aaron… your father died less than an hour ago."

His words wash over me, making me waver. My chest empties of any emotion I have felt so far, and I have no words to say. There is so much confusion in my head that when Dakota puts her hand on my arm, I turn to look at her, completely disoriented.

It's such huge news that I don't even know how to process it. I lean against the wall to get some support and inhale thoroughly.

"My father is dead," I repeat to ensure I understood right.

"I'm sorry. I offer you my condolences. If you need anything, don't hesitate to call me. I'll be with your mother when I give her the news," he tries to reassure me, but the only thing I can think of is his words.

An annoying buzz fills my ears, and I realize it's my heart pumping wildly.

"He was killed by a garbage truck." My words come out more like a statement than a question.

The lawyer nods and studies me as if to understand my reaction. Surely it is not what he expects, given his surprised face when I start laughing. I try to hold back a laugh that rises from my chest and burns in my throat, but I explode in a desecrating grunt.

"My father was killed by a garbage truck." I keep laughing in front of Dakota's bewildered face and the lawyer, who seems worried. Maybe he thinks I'm crazy.

I'm so out of control that I slide down the wall until I sit on the floor, laying my hands on my face to hide my entirely misplaced reaction. But I can't help but think of the irony of this story. The man I have always considered a disgusting scumbag was killed by a garbage truck. How many chances were there that he would leave this earth in such an indecorous manner?

"How is my father's driver?" I ask when I can compose myself enough to formulate a decent sentence.

"He died on the spot. They couldn't even take him to the hospital," the man tells me, a little disoriented.

This news makes me stop laughing and brings a pain to my chest that makes me run out of breath, not my father's death, but that of the driver who, when we were kids, took my brother and me to polo training when my parents did not even know what sport we had chosen.

This is how I realize how much death doesn't wait for anyone. It doesn't matter if you're laughing and joking with your partner or in the middle of a speech, a movie, or dinner. It doesn't matter if you're reading a book or taking a shower. Death doesn't wait, and when it comes, it puts a stop to your life, whether you are ready or not. Whether you planned it or not.

CHAPTER 24
Dakota

I stare at the black dress on top of the bed and wonder what to do. When Aaron received the news of his father's death two days ago, he started to bark orders to lawyers to organize the funeral and ensure that his mother didn't get carried away with pills and alcohol. After the initial hysterical crisis in which he couldn't stop laughing, he started to get silent and open up less and less with me.

When we went to visit his mother the night of the accident, after being in the hospital to deal with the papers that the death of a parent entails, we found her in her room, stuffed to the brim with drugs and alcohol. She didn't recognize her son. I don't think she even knew where she was.

I had never met her before, but compared to what I'd seen on TV, the person I encountered was a shell emptied of any feeling or willpower. I don't know what my mother was like when my father died, I was too young to remember properly and she always hid from me when she wasn't brave enough to not cry, but I know she held me during the funeral and wanted me with her all the time. She's always told me I was her life-line. Perhaps, never having established a relationship with her children is what is dragging Aaron's mother to the bottom.

I saw the coldness with which her son treated her, saw the disgust in his eyes when he found her unable to recognize him. I can't even imagine what it could be like to live a childhood in which your parents don't give you even the slightest sign of affection or deny you a hug, but I know what the consequences of this choice are: indifference.

For this same reason, Aaron's brother Evan didn't take a flight from New York for the funeral. His father cut him off from his life years ago, so everything falls on Aaron's shoulders and his lawyers.

Aaron has switched to the "organization mode" I have seen him in so many times for work and is directing everyone with maximum efficiency. Not a bit of emotion transpires from everything he does, so I'm not sure if he wants me next to him at his father's funeral. It seems more like a work event than a moment for the family to grieve. A family that I don't think ever existed.

I turn to the door when I hear him enter the room. He is already fully dressed in a black suit, always perfect in his elegance, while I am still tucked into a bathrobe.

"Are you undecided about what to wear? You don't have to dress in black if you don't want to," he tells me with a smile that never reaches his eyes.

It is strange to see him like this, closed in on himself and detached from his emotions. I think the only gut reaction he's had since he got the news is the initial laugh he couldn't hold back. He is light years away from the attentive and caring Aaron I have known in recent months, and I don't know how to approach him and make him understand that he can count on me.

I sit on the bed, and he sits next to me. "It's not a problem of what to wear. Do you want me with you at the funeral? It looks like you're organizing a movie premiere, and I can't figure out if you want me with you or not," I admit without beating around the bush. He has always appreciated my sincerity, and I don't want to start to be shy now when he needs me the most.

Aaron grabs my hand and brings it to his lips to kiss my fingers. It's the only gesture from which sincere feeling shines through and raises a little of the concern that grips my chest.

"Of course, I want you there. I haven't been particularly attentive to you these days, but I need to focus on this. I'm the only one who has taken over the reins, and I need to focus my attention on what I'm doing."

He can't even pronounce the word funeral. He is so detached that, for him, this is an event like any other. My heart bleeds to see him like this. I can be close to him, but as much as he is an adult, he needs a family with whom to mourn a father who has passed away.

"How are you?" My voice comes out in a whisper as I study the tense features of his face.

For days I have been trying to understand his feelings through the small signals he cannot hide on his face, but years spent controlling his emotions don't help me to see beyond the walls he's built these days.

"Good. I wasn't emotionally attached to my father. I'm fine, really."

I have the impression that he really believes what he is saying and hasn't realized how much deeper his bond with him goes. Maybe it's not love that he feels but resentment, anger, even disgust, but he was never indifferent to his father. He stayed by his side all his adult life, got angry with him, and even punched him; these are not signs of indifference.

For this reason, I am afraid that sooner or later, he will explode into a tangle of feelings from which he cannot extricate himself. Sooner or later, that spark will ignite in his chest and blow up all the emotions that, over the years, he has crushed and compressed in the corner of his heart to not feel.

"Give me a couple of minutes to change, okay?" I tell him and watch him walk toward the door, hesitate on the threshold, as if he wants to add something to our conversation, and then disappear downstairs.

The feeling of discomfort that squeezes my stomach is powerful, almost breathtaking.

***

The funeral is a parade of Hollywood bigwigs who seem to walk a red carpet rather than witnessing the burial of a friend. No one is shedding a tear, all are perfect in their thousand dollar suits, no one's face is marked by the pain that death causes. Not even his secretary, sitting in the second row, who has lived next to the man every damn day for years, seems troubled by what has happened. She's been staring at her fingernails since we entered the cemetery as if her main concern right now is a manicure.

I look at Aaron staring at the coffin, his lips clenched in a thin line. His back is straight, resting on the back of the chair, one leg crossed on the other, fingers intertwined in his lap. He is the portrayal of composure. He almost looks like he is sitting in the middle of an important meeting rather than in front of his father's coffin.

When the priest asks him to say something, he gets up, buttons his jacket, approaches the man in the black tunic who makes room for him, and lays his eyes on the coffin again. His speech is one of those that praises the deceased without exaggerating. He lists all his achievements and seems more like praise for his career rather than the desperation of a son who lost his father. There is no reference to a personal anecdote. It was written this morning and learned by heart. I don't even know if he or Tracy wrote it, considering how impersonal it turns out.

When he returns to sit next to me, I notice the embarrassment of the priest, who struggles a few moments before resuming the service, but no one around me seems scandalized by what just happened. Perhaps because none of them have any feelings for the deceased.

I reach out my hand and intertwine my fingers with Aaron's. The firm squeeze is the only indication that something in him is alive and rattling in his chest.

***

"Condolences." Jacob Lautner, one of the writers of Aaron's show, extends his hand and shakes it.

He is just one in a long line of Hollywood bigwigs who stopped after the funeral to offer condolences to Aaron, all with a word of comfort and all determined to be on top of his list, to be noticed, because from this moment on, Aaron is the most significant piece on the Hollywood chessboard, the one whom everyone must kiss his feet before climbing a step higher on the social ladder. Because while everyone has always called Aaron "the producer," the truth is that he is much more. He is the owner of the streaming division and will soon become the owner of the entire broadcasting company.

"Thank you."

"I hope our relationship will not change now that your father has passed away." The half-smile accompanying his words makes me cringe as he tries to juggle this situation.

I don't know how he managed to get so high in this industry, but he doesn't seem to be someone who has the communication skills to be a writer. Especially when he is surrounded by sharks and is talking to the biggest of them.

Aaron tilts his head and studies him for a few seconds, certainly as intrigued as I am by his choice of words. "Jacob, you should hope that our relationship will change now that you no longer have my father saving your ass." He coldly dismisses him as his gaze rests on the man behind him in line, who struggles to hold back an amused smile as he reaches out his hand and squeezes Aaron's.

I see Jacob pale and lower his head as he reaches a small group of other writers waiting for him a few feet away from us, mumbling something to them as they walk away. Some of them glance at us and then return to talk, shaking their heads. I don't know what just happened between Aaron and that man, but I'm sure the tension between the two isn't pleasant.

"My deepest condolences." A man's voice makes me turn around, too close to be addressed to Aaron, who is a step ahead of me.

When I look in front of me, I find a hand stretched out in my direction. The mourner is a man in his seventies, with gray hair, few wrinkles on his face, and tucked into a black expensive tailored suit. On his arm is a woman only a few years older than me, wearing a little black dress that shows her curves without making her look vulgar, with raven hair that descends her shoulders in perfect waves, and red lipstick that accentuates her fleshy mouth.

The man studies me for a few moments with a look full of curiosity, which gives me the impression of a fox, cunning and waiting to see what my next move will be. Only after long interminable seconds of embarrassment do I realize that those words are addressed to me, not Aaron. He is the first person who has offered condolences to me, no one before him has deigned me more than a look passing by.

"Thank you." My voice comes out without hesitation, and my grip on his hand is firm.

His grip lasts for a few seconds longer than expected. It seems like he is almost trying to evaluate how much power I have in this circumstance, why I am next to the most important man in this cemetery instead of waiting for him in the black limousine parked behind us. I feel like a token in a chess game. Only in this game, he is the king, while I am one of the simple expendable pawns.

"I'm sorry we're meeting under these circumstances, but I'm sure there will be other opportunities in the future." The phrase seems innocent, but the way he says it almost seems like he is trying to understand if I am a permanent figure in Aaron's future or if I will be forgotten like the previous flames of my partner.

"I'm sure there will be other more joyous occasions to meet." My voice comes out firmer, accompanied by a discreet smile that I learned to show on the set.

I feel my heart hammer in my chest and buzz in my ears. This is one of those moments when my inability to relate to people in a social context is what can determine my inadequacy next to the man I have chosen. Being able to stand up to this man is essential to project an image of strength, or I'll soon become Aaron's weakness, the one they use as a lever to manipulate him.

The flash of surprise he can't hide makes me realize that I earned my first victory in this game I discovered too late I was playing, and Aaron's hand on my back is the warmth that comforts me and helps me calm my crazy heart.

"We should go." My partner's voice is calm, and when I look up at him, I find him studying our faces.

"It was a pleasure," I say more strongly toward the man, then turn around and walk next to Aaron toward the limousine that awaits us.

I glance at him one last time and find him with the ghost of a smile on his face.

***

We arrive in front of a house in Burbank in a limousine that stands out among the other cars parked along the road. They are regular cars, without too many luxuries, some have seen better times, but all polished, almost as a sign of respect for the family that mourns his deceased between the walls of the blue house, the same color as all the others on the street. It's not a luxurious neighborhood like the one I've gotten used to, but it has something that makes it more homely, unlike the impersonal mega villas in the Hollywood Hills.

I was surprised when Aaron asked Gaspard to take us here instead of his mother's house for the funeral vigil. When I asked him why he told me that there would only be bigwigs talking about work but that the people who were really crying over the tragedy of that accident were here. I never knew his father's driver, but from how Aaron hesitates in front of the entrance, I realize that the emotion of being here is stronger even than at his father's funeral.

"Are you okay?" I grab his hand and squeeze it as I watch him stare at the house as if he can't go any further.

He looks at me with a sad smile, the first semblance of emotion that I've glimpsed in days. He inhales deeply, then, one decisive step after another, we enter a house whose living room is full of people whispering with sadness in their eyes and defeat curving their shoulders.

More than one is surprised to see the imposing figure of Aaron on the doorstep, but, apart from the initial shock, he is greeted with smiles of compassion and pats on the back. It's the first time since the accident that I've seen sincere pain on the faces of those around me, including Aaron. A man about Aaron's age approaches and embraces him tight.

"My deepest condolences," he whispers in a voice broken by emotion.

"Thank you. My deepest condolences to you, too," Aaron replies, and I understand that the man must be one of the sons of the driver who drove his father's car.

It is a gesture that brings tears to my eyes that I struggle to hold, especially when he wraps his arms around me as if I were the one who needs comfort right now.

"Condolences," I mutter as he holds me tight and a small hiccup escapes from his throat.

"Please, come in, don't stay at the door," he invites us in as two children who are just over five or six, with the same raven hair as his own, cling to his legs and peek in our direction.

Aaron reaches out his hand over the baby's head and ruffles his hair, a slight smile on his lips, the first since we entered here.

"Is your mother here? I'd love to see her." Aaron's voice is low, almost a whisper not to disturb the guests.

The man nods and beckons us to follow while a woman a little younger than him with chocolate hair and eyes smiles tiredly at us while grabbing the hands of the two boys and dragging them into a room that, from what I see, must be the kitchen.

"She's sitting on the back porch. She needed a breath of air," he explains as he opens a back door and lets us out.

There is no one out here apart from a woman in her early sixties, with her hair gathered in a low chignon and a black dress, sitting on a small sofa. She is staring at the small garden in front of her, but when we approach, her gaze rests on Aaron's, and a sad smile paints her lips.

"Oh, Aaron, I am so sorry for your father." The whisper is almost imperceptible, but I hear it despite the door closing behind me when the son leaves us alone with her. It's a moment of such intimacy that I almost feel one too many, at least until Aaron beckons me to sit in an armchair next to the door, and he sits next to the woman.

"I'm so sorry. I'm so, so sorry." Aaron's voice comes out hoarse, charged with an emotion he struggles to contain as he embraces the woman.

I hear her sigh, then detach herself from him and put her hand on his cheek. There's the sweetness of a mother in her gaze, and it's the first time I've seen Aaron struggle to hold back his emotions.

"How is your mother?" she asks him in a loving tone.

Aaron shrugs. "Nothing a good dose of antidepressants and alcohol can't solve."

I am surprised to hear him confess such a thing. There is a confidence that I didn't expect.

The woman shakes her head and studies him gently. "Stay with her. Maybe she doesn't give it to see, but she will need you. When the house empties and everyone returns to their lives, she will need comfort," she whispers.

Aaron smiles and nods. "Will you have someone here with you when these people leave?" There is concern in his voice.

The woman nods, and a sad smile appears as she grabs Aaron's hands and holds them tight.

"My children don't leave me for a moment. And then I have my grandchildren who keep me distracted. Don't worry about me. I have so many people around. Do you have someone holding your hand when you are sad?"

Aaron looks in my direction, and I feel my cheeks go up in flame when the woman looks at me and smiles.

"Yes, I think I've found someone who will hold my hand," he whispers and never stops looking at me.

My heart hammers into my chest at the speed of light, and I struggle to resist the temptation to get up and hug him.

"Is there anything I can do for you?" he then asks her.

"I'll be fine, Aaron," she tries to reassure him.

"I know…but I also know that his paycheck was your only income. I know it's not polite to talk about money in these situations, but I'm worried about you."

The woman smiles at him and puts her hand on his cheek. "Don't worry about me. I have always found a solution. This time will be no different."

"You are not reassuring me, you know?" he whispers.

The woman smiles and kisses him on the forehead.

"Everything will be fine, Aaron. Have faith."

And for the first time, I see my partner's eyes veiled in tears.

An hour later, we are sitting on the leather seats of the limousine after talking to the driver's son and discovering that their economic situation is not great. A few years earlier, their father took a second mortgage on the house to solve the foundation problems that were added to the purchase. Losing the only source of livelihood, they risk losing their home.

I grab Aaron's hand, but he never moves his gaze from the road that runs beyond the window. Only when I hear the hiccup shaking his chest, do I realize that his cheeks are wet with tears.

"Aaron." My voice is like a cry in the silence of this car, and my heart breaks for him.

He rubs a hand over his face, wiping away the only traces of his vulnerability, takes deep breaths, then grabs the phone and starts calling his lawyers, giving orders to pay off the debts of the family we have just left. I remain silent to observe this man who seems invincible but who sheds tears for the only affection he ever received as a child, that of a driver who was more family than the one in which he grew up.

CHAPTER 25
Aaron

My parents' butler opens the door for me in his impeccable dark livery. Ten days have passed since my father's funeral, and I find it ridiculous to continue to dress in black. To tell the truth, I find it ridiculous that the employees who work in this house were forced to do it as if it were the eighteenth century and were servants. My mother probably sees them that way.

"Please go back to the gray suit and drop this funeral uniform."

He smiles at me and tilts his head slightly in greeting.

"Your mother prefers black these days," he justifies with a cordial expression on his face.

He would never dare to tell me anything different. My family has employed him for as long as I can remember. Never once have I heard him comment with something disrespectful or even inadequate for the context of the conversation. He must be born with this inclination to count to ten before verbally expressing his opinion.

"My mother is stuffed with antidepressants and alcohol. I don't think she would notice if I walked around the house in a rainbow dress." I don't have the same inclination to bite my tongue, especially when I talk to someone who has lived here day and night for years and knows exactly what's happening. My mother is not depressed. She is just a high-class junkie that gets high on prescription drugs and alcohol.

"These days, she's a bit… it's hard to find the right mental attitude," he confirms, accompanying me to my father's studio.

It has never been easy for my mother, but I avoid pointing it out and thank him before closing the study door. I look around at the room that reflects my father's office at the company: all too much decorated with dark and tacky furniture that shows his desire to flaunt his wealth. I've always hated this studio, always found it too decorated and stuffy. It's so dark that in the middle of the afternoon you have to turn on the lights even during summer.

I sit on one of the two sofas and wait for the others to join me for the reading of the will. I don't even bother to go upstairs to my mother's room. She didn't recognize me on the day of my father's death. I don't think she's in better condition now. A sense of discomfort squeezes my stomach. The natural thing to do would be to go to her and hug her to console her about her husband's death, but our family has such toxic relationships that my brother didn't even come to the funeral. I never really reasoned about this fact until I found myself managing all the papers on my own. And even in that case, the feeling that hit me was annoyance.

I look at the door when I hear it open, and I'm surprised to find Alan, my brother Evan's lawyer.

"They called you here, too?" I can't hold back a half-laugh in disbelief.

The man shakes his head laughing, unfastens the buttons of his blue suit jacket, and sits next to me, leaving the leather messenger bag at his feet. He leans on the backrest, crosses his legs, and pulls his mobile phone out of his pocket.

"Pure formality. We don't expect Evan to be included in the will, but being a rightful heir, I slipped this appointment in among the various that I have this morning," he explains as he reads emails on his cell phone.

"Legitimate because he did not have time to disown him as a son. A few years of success with his agency, and he would have burned him at the stake. No one can outclass my father in terms of power," I tease, and Alan bursts out laughing.

The door opens again, and my mother's lawyer enters, followed by my father's. The small talk they were making dies on their lips as soon as they see us. I am not surprised that my mother is not here in person to read the will. I don't think she would even be able to stay awake, sitting on this couch, for the time it takes to make a list of all the possessions my father has accumulated during his lifetime.

"Good morning. I'm happy we're all here already. We can get started," my father's lawyer announces, sitting on the couch in front of us and pulling out from his leather briefcase the sealed envelope with my father's will. He drafted it, he knows precisely what is written inside, but the formality of sitting here and opening that envelope is what it takes to make that document legal.

As soon as he breaks the seal and pulls out the papers, Alan leans forward, grabbing his briefcase. "My presence here is superfluous, isn't it?" he questions with a half-smile.

My father's lawyer shakes his head. "Evan is not included in the will."

"Surprise, surprise!" I mumble, pulling a smile from the rest of those present.

Alan gets up from the couch. "Gentlemen, it was a pleasure," he announces.

"Say hello to my brother when you see him and tell him to call me. I know he has an agency that grinds millions of dollars, but he could answer my calls every now and then." I wink at him as he grabs the door handle, ready to get out.

"I'll tell him when I bring him the bill for these five minutes of work," he answers, laughing before exiting the room and leaving us again occupied with my father's last wishes.

A vice tightens my stomach. Few times in my life have I felt so nervous that I physically perceived it on my body, but this time the reason is one of those that cannot be ignored. I have dedicated sixteen years of my life to this moment. I've sacrificed holidays, weekends, evenings to devote myself to my passions. I gave up my private life, bowing my head on the desk and working to prove to my father that I am the worthy heir to his empire. I supported him in his decisions, created an entire division of this company from scratch, and made sure to rejuvenate it to keep up with the times. I took what my grandfather started and took it to the next level.

I would have preferred this step to happen with my father, who decides to retire rather than with his death, but the result doesn't change. This morning I will walk out of this room as the head of my father's empire, with seventy percent of a company for which I sweated, shed tears, loved, and hated at the same time. It has been a sixteen-year-long ordeal, but it will finally be mine.

The first half hour is spent rattling off the list of his possessions. My mother takes the houses, and I have the art pieces and his investments. The yacht goes to my mother, the private planes to me. It's a long list of luxuries I've always been immersed in since birth but only now do I realize how much they're worth. There are pages and pages of goods that, if sold, could feed an entire third-world nation.

I wait calmly until the part that interests me most, and when the lawyer gets to the Steel Broadcasting Company, my back straightens, and my attention returns to him.

"The streaming division of the company remains separate from the company itself and goes to Aaron Steel Jr.," he announces, and I expected that. Although everyone knows it as a part of the parent company, legally, the two companies have always been separate. Now that piece is one hundred percent mine and not shared with my father. I smile because it's the first victory.

"Forty percent of the company's Class A shares go to Sharon Rachel Lee Steel, while thirty percent of the Class B shares go to Aaron Steel Jr.," the lawyer's voice punctuates the words as he looks me in the eye.

I'm focused on his impassive face as I record the words he just uttered. It takes me a few seconds before I realize what he said, and my stomach freezes in a feeling of disbelief and terror that I didn't think I could feel. I observe my mother's lawyer, who seems uncomfortable on that couch.

"I beg your pardon?" My voice comes out still but a few octaves lower than usual.

The lawyer clears his throat, and for the first time since we sat here, he drops the mask and seems nervous.

"Your mother has forty percent of the Class A shares that

give her the right to vote at the board meetings. You have thirty percent of the company but no voting rights. The Class B shares have no right to vote, but you have dividends at the end of the year," he explains to me as if I were a kid who has no idea what he's talking about.

"I know what Class A and Class B shares are. Class B shares are those you give to your wife when you sign the prenup to prevent her from ruining the company if you divorce. They have zero value as far as control of the company is concerned!" I shout.

"Aaron, I know it's a surprise, but you still have thirty percent of the company. At the end of the year, you will take home a nice nest egg with dividends." He tries to convince me that this situation is a good deal for me.

The anger that boils inside me almost makes me spit the rancid taste I have in my mouth on the carpet. My mother's lawyer doesn't dare to breathe, focused on studying the situation to understand if it's better to run before a fight breaks out. I can't blame him since I could punch the man with the will in his hand right now.

"Surprise? Do you really think it's a surprise? I sacrificed my whole life for this company to be able to run it when my father retired. I've been spitting blood for sixteen years, and he gives the majority of control to a woman who is upstairs right now so stuffed with drugs and alcohol that she's drooling over her pillow. A woman who can't even get out of bed in the morning, let alone decide where to lead one of the biggest broadcasting companies in this country. I worked my entire life for a company I can't lead." I'm so furious that I feel the blood pumping into my ears.

The two men in front of me have the decency to look down and say nothing. There is perhaps some pity for me in their silence. Everyone in this industry knows I would have taken the company's reins once my father was out of the game. I had the confirmation at his funeral when everyone came to kiss my ass and prostrate themselves at my feet, aware that it was my turn to be the largest shark in the tank.

If my father were here right now, I would punch him in the face; this thought reminds me that I have already done it. I dared only once to challenge him. Perhaps this is his way of taking revenge for my insubordination. Once. Just once, and it cost me everything I've built in sixteen years. The icy chill that runs down my spine makes me short of breath.

"When was this will last amended?" My voice comes out almost in a muffled whisper as if my body refuses to deal with my father again.

"Four years ago." He looks me in the eye for the first time after giving me the news.

"So he didn't do it after I punched him." It's not because of Dakota.

While this news cheers me because it means I haven't blown up a lifetime of work for not keeping my anger at bay, I feel hollowed out when I realize that my father never intended to leave me his company, no matter how much I sweated to get it.

"The new version was drafted when the streaming division was opened to add its fifty percent to the list of its assets," he confirms.

The feeling of emptiness inside is so immense that my head is spinning. I get up under the perplexed gazes of the two lawyers and walk to the door.

"Where are you going? It's not over yet," my father's lawyer tries to protest, but his lips tighten as soon as he crosses my gaze.

"For me, there is nothing left in here that is worth staying for," I say before opening the door and leaving at a slow pace.

The sense of stillness that permeates my chest is strange. There is no more anger, disappointment, disbelief, or that desire to destroy something. There is only a sense of emptiness that anesthetizes my every feeling. I spent years controlling my emotions, but only at this moment do I turn them off completely. This will was my father's last *fuck you* that he sent me from the grave. He managed to make me feel small and useless like he did all my life. But this time, the insult is so evil, violent, and definitive that it no longer hurts.

As soon as I see Tracy, Aaron's assistant, near the chair on the set with my name written on it, my heart stops for a beat. Since he was at his mother's house last week for his father's will, he has become another person. He has closed in on himself and spent the nights in his home office, rarely coming out. Some nights he doesn't even come to bed, and I wake up in the dark looking for him in the large house that seems uninhabited. Then I see the light filtering through from under his studio door, and my heart sinks into my chest.

When the director stops the scene, I approach her with my heart hammering in my chest. Her half-smile almost makes me want to run away to not receive bad news that I don't know if I could bear.

"Do you have any idea where Aaron is?" she asks without even bothering to say hello.

The heart that tried to escape from my chest since I laid eyes on her stops in my throat, almost choking me.

"Didn't he come to the office this morning?" I ask, worried because I don't know where he may be.

She shakes her head. "For days, he hasn't shown up. He

skips meetings without an explanation. I'm trying to stall with people who ask me about him, saying he's busy with the papers after his father's death, but I can't do it for much longer. I need him to tell me something," she whispers to prevent prying ears from turning this conversation into gossip.

I turn to the director and sign that I need to take five minutes and make my way with Tracy toward my trailer, and when we close the door behind us, I flop on the couch.

"He hasn't come to the office all this week?" I ask worriedly.

"Since the reading of the will," she confirms.

I inhale deeply and try to calm the nerves that stir under my skin. The squeeze on my stomach is overwhelming, and the worry that makes my heart hammer is rooted and shows no sign of slowing it down.

"When I leave the house, I know he is locked up in his home office, but I thought he had come out and come to work at some point," I admit.

But to what job? Everything he worked for was shattered with the death of his father.

"Can you tell me what the hell happened?" Tracy asks as she sits next to me. On her face, there is all the worry that has accompanied her for days.

"From what I understand, from the few things he told me, his father must have left the company to his mother and not to him." I summarize briefly what I sensed from the few words we exchanged.

"Holy shit." The breath comes out of Tracy's chest and seems not to want to return. Her eyes and mouth are wide open in surprise. I think that of all the explanations I could give her, she hadn't even considered this one. Everyone in the industry knew that the company would go to him. Even I, the newbie, had no doubt about this.

"I've been trying to talk to him for days, but he always shuts me out of every conversation. I don't know how to help him," I admit.

If there's one thing Aaron and I have always done, it's talk. About everything, even the most complicated and thorny topics. It's as if after that meeting, he has turned off all his feelings and is surviving on autopilot, cutting off anyone from his life. I was hoping at least that during the day, he would talk to someone who is not me, but now I only realize that I was too optimistic.

"This explains why the other members of the board of the company are asking for a meeting with him," she pauses to think about the implications of this situation.

"I thought you knew. I mean, such news is huge, and I don't know how anyone is not talking about it yet." I try to reason with her and come to terms with the questions I asked Aaron but didn't get answered.

Tracy looks at me and smiles, but the worry never leaves her gaze. "Maybe because before his mother can take over the company, they first want to know who will take care of the decisions. His father's death has already shaken investors, and the stock tumbled on the stock market. Announcing that a woman who doesn't even know how to take care of herself will be at the head of an empire would collapse the stock to the point that I don't know if the company would survive," she explains, with the knowledge of someone who is not a simple assistant but has been working shoulder to shoulder with Aaron for years.

I inhale deeply, put my hands on my eyes, and then remind myself that I am wearing makeup and should get out of here to do my job. As much as I feel pain for Aaron, I can't leave the set without a valid reason.

"Do you have the keys to our house? Can you text me if you find him in his office? Can you let me know if he's okay?" I plead, getting up and walking her to the door.

"Of course. And Dakota, don't worry. Aaron is someone who has always been reborn from every defeat. He will get up again in time." She smiles at me, but her words don't reassure me.

I think of the phoenix tattoo on Aaron's shoulders and wonder if he will be reborn from his ashes this time.

***

It's ten at night when I get home, and when I enter, I am surprised to not see the light filtering under the door of Aaron's studio. When Tracy texted me today that she found him here at home and that he was fine, I breathed a sigh of relief, but now my heart pumps into my chest. The house is completely dark.

I walk to the kitchen and catch a glimpse of Aaron in elegant trousers, barefoot, and with a shirt with the first buttons unfastened, sipping from a glass and staring at the horizon, sitting on one of the deck chairs. His expression is severe but doesn't reveal anything more. Not anger, disappointment, or any other feeling that would normally stir in his chest after the news he received.

This is what scares me the most about this situation, he is

keeping everything inside, and this apathy is not his normal reaction. Aaron doesn't let himself be knocked down. He is one of those who sets the terms in this industry. He doesn't stand still sitting on a deck chair. Not in a situation like this.

"Can I sit?" I ask as I approach him.

He beckons me, so I sit next to him, and I stop to study his face, hoping he will tell me something. But he doesn't even look at me. He keeps staring at the city beyond his pool, holding his glass tightly. The dark circles around his eyes are deep, the wrinkles next to them and on his forehead are accentuated, and the tiredness is visible on his tense features.

"Aaron, please talk to me. I don't know how to help you, and it's wearing me down," I plead when the silence between us continues until my throat is tightened by despair.

He looks down at his glass and shakes his head. "There's nothing you can do. Get over it."

His words are like a lash in my chest. I have never heard such resignation in his voice.

"Aaron, you can try to challenge the will, convince your mother to sell you the company, do something. You can't sit here drinking all the time." My voice comes out more convinced than I feel.

"What do you know?" he asks, raising his eyes to mine and dropping the mask of indifference. The anger that runs over his face is shocking.

"I don't understand much about wills, but there will be something you can do." This time, I can feel all the insecurity gripping my stomach.

Aaron bursts into a half-laugh and shakes his head.

"You don't know anything about it. And do you know why?

Because you've been working in this industry for barely three years and have no idea what it's like to sacrifice half of your life to have nothing when it's your turn. You don't know what it's like to swallow shit to have your place on the throne and then have it taken away from you when you're about to sit on it," he hisses angrily as he nails me to this chair.

For the first time since I entered this house, I am intimidated by Aaron. Not because I'm afraid he'll hurt me physically, but because there's nothing I can do to appease his anger. There is not the slightest glimmer of hope of finding a way out.

"Aaron, I understand you're angry, but you can't stay here and do nothing," I raise my voice too.

"Are you serious right now? You know nothing. You're just a little girl. We'll talk about it again in a few years when you have real problems on your plate," he hisses, taking his gaze in the direction of the city.

Anger boils in me. I understand his position, but he can't leverage my age only when it suits him.

"You know what? I'll behave like a little girl throwing a tantrum and leave," I hiss as I get up.

"Leave the keys on the table when you walk out."

His words freeze me on the spot. My intention was to go to my room, but it's clear that he wants me out of his house. Tears run down my face as I pack a bag and call an Uber to pick me up.

***

When I arrive on set the next morning, I immediately realize something is wrong. Despite my dark glasses to cover swollen eyes before dawn, it's hard not to notice the line of my colleagues in front of a still-closed set. When I get next to Emma, she turns around and grabs me by the shoulders.

"Did you know anything about it?" she asks me, shaken.

"I have no idea what you're talking about," I whisper as other people turn to me, expecting answers.

"Aaron didn't tell you anything? He shut down the streaming division, canceled all productions, and said we have to go to the HR office to get our checks," she explains, pointing to a piece of paper hanging on the door.

I make my way forward to see. All eyes are on me when I read the paper that Emma has just summarized to me. I feel my blood freeze when I realize that not only has he thrown in the towel, but he is destroying, piece by piece, all the good things he has built in his life. Despite being angry with him, the fear that grips my chest makes me short of breath. This time the phoenix will not rise from its ashes.

CHAPTER 27

Aaron

"What the hell are you doing here?" I ask my brother Evan when I open the front door.

The grin on his face as he takes off his sunglasses and slips them into the pocket of his elegant suit tells me he is happy to be the one to surprise me for once. Of course, I didn't expect to find him in front of me when he didn't even come to our father's funeral. But it is also true that if he had come for my father, I would have been more surprised than now.

If there's one thing my brother and I are similar in, apart from eye color and dark hair, it's the fact that we always dress impeccably. It has been branded on us since childhood. In fact, he is here with his tailored suit looking concernedly at my sweatpants and crumpled T-shirt that I have been wearing for a couple of days.

"When Tracy and Dakota call me to tell me they're worried about you, I guess the situation is serious. And I was right since I find you trashed like a frat guy after a hangover."

What strikes me most about what he told me, though, is that Dakota called him because she's worried about me. When I kicked her out, I immediately regretted it, as I regretted what

I said. But the anger at what my father did was too intense and the humiliation so strong that I got defensive when she confronted me with her determination. Dakota has the power to lay bare all my insecurities, my vulnerability, and sometimes I can't cope with what I feel.

"Did you know what Dad did?" I ask him while I offer him a beer, and we sit on the couch.

He nods with an indecipherable expression on his face. "I got a copy of the will."

"And what do you think?" I urge when he doesn't add another word.

"What do you want to hear? Were you expecting something different? He has always been a piece of shit. He confirmed it even from the grave."

I remain silent and look at him. I don't know what answer I expected from him, but then I don't even know how to get out of bed these days, so no surprise here. Everything I've worked for in the last sixteen years has gone up in smoke. I never had a plan B because I always gave it all for what was my dream. Now that it is wasted with no chance of saving it, I find myself lost.

"I could try to buy Mom's shares, but I doubt the other investors will let me do it. They were never thrilled that our father had seventy percent of the company. Maybe they let me buy nineteen percent, but they will never give me the majority, even if I have no full control over the right to vote."

My brother's furrowed brows make me feel naïve. Can he really not understand what I want to do, or is it me who can't reason lucidly and I am missing some critical detail?

"Why the hell would you buy Mom's shares?" he asks incredulously as if he can't really get it.

I watch him carefully, sure he's making fun of me. He must have the same thought about this situation. It's the basic strategy to acquire the company's control.

"Because I can regain possession of the company. It will cost me a lot, I will have to deal with my financial advisors, but I can come out of it with my head held high." The hope that is in my voice is extinguished as my brother's face turns into a mask of disappointment as he shakes his head.

"Are you really sure that's what you want?" he asks.

"Why shouldn't I? I sacrificed my whole life for it. I don't want to throw away everything." My tone is petulant.

"Really? Because you closed the streaming division the same week you discovered about the will and didn't even look back. Those were the last four years of your life when you spat blood and didn't even bat an eye before you did. It was a company with a positive balance sheet, healthy, without debts, and that alone dragged a good part of an old and obsolete company that is struggling and will close if it doesn't change direction. But you really want to buy that dinosaur instead of the jewel you created?" he asks incredulously.

I say nothing. Shutting down the streaming division was a retaliation against my father. He always threatened to close it, but he never did because he knew very well that it brought the company's coffers a good part of the proceeds, a percentage that's been increasing every year. When I read the will, the anger was so violent that I acted on impulse.

"I can bring my experience to the other side and rejuvenate it. But without the right to vote on the board of directors, I can't do anything about it."

"Or you could take that experience elsewhere," he proposes, raising an eyebrow.

"Where, to work for the competition?" I spat indignantly.

Evan rubs his hand over his face, exasperated. "I've always considered you the smartest brother, but sometimes you reason like an idiot," he mumbles, making me feel like the younger brother.

"Thank you for your trust." I half-smile at him.

Evan shakes his head. "You finally have the motivation to take off that leash that our father put on you since you were eighteen. Sell the shares he left you. Even better if you sell them to the competition, use that money to build something of your own. You worked and sacrificed your life for something that wasn't even yours. I have no doubt that you will be able to do great things with something with your name on it. He always treated you like a mere producer, but the truth is that you have always been the CEO of the streaming division and have always taken responsibility like the boss you are. You have a woman who cares so much about you that she calls me in the middle of the night to tell me what is happening to you. Don't you think the time has come to take your life into your own hands and start living it for real?"

His words hit me like an icy wave that I didn't expect. I never considered that I could have something of my own. I always thought of earning that part of the company that I would inherit. I never thought I was entitled to that share just because of my last name, so I sweated blood to deserve it. Starting from scratch scares me. It was Evan who gave up everything, who was brave enough to give up the family fortune to build a life from scratch.

I am terrified at the idea of failing, but my brother's words have awakened a part of me that in recent times went dormant, crushed by the continuous fights with my father that made me give up: the desire to innovate and get involved in a new project. I've always thought about new productions, new shows for an old and struggling broadcasting company. But the idea of bringing this enthusiasm into something bigger, like my own company, scares and excites me at the same time.

"You've always been obsessed with this idea of inheriting the family business, but you've never considered building something of your own," he continues when I don't say anything.

"You have always been the brave one of the family. I would never have had the balls to give up everything at nineteen and start from scratch," I admit.

Evan seems surprised by my remark. He sips his beer and shakes his head.

"And to think that I have always considered you the brave one to be able to stand up to our father. It's easy to pack your bags and start a life elsewhere. Apart from the initial uncertainty, you can do what you want without accounting for anyone. If I made a mistake, the only person involved would have been me. If you made a mistake, you would drag down dozens of families who depended on your work. It takes much more courage to stay and fight for what you believe than run away when things get rough."

His words reach the center of my chest as a hug that warms me. Until this moment, until I heard them spoken out loud, I didn't realize how much I needed to hear them.

"They will never let me sell to anyone other than the board members at the price they want. They have the right of preemption and also the right to vote," I point out.

But it's a great idea, the one my brother suggested, especially since it sends a big fuck you to my father, who spat on my sacrifices even from the grave. But the reality is far from being so straightforward. The other board members will never miss the opportunity to get their hands on thirty percent of the company.

"Not if Mom can't vote." My brother's smug smile makes me realize he already has a plan.

I sit comfortably on the couch and invite him to continue.

**

It took me five days after my brother's visit to be able to put together all the pieces I needed to free myself from the leash that my father continues to hold tight. When the secretary tries to stop me before entering the conference room where the board members are gathered, I don't even stop to look at her.

"Aaron, I don't know if you understand how your shares in the company work, but you can't sit on boards," Warren, the oldest of the board members and the one with the most shares in the company after my mother and me, reminds me with a sly smile on his face.

He has consistently pushed for a bigger slice of the cake and has never been shy about voicing his idea that the company should not go from father to son like a throne but that a person should earn the right to run it. He's never kept it secret that he considers my streaming division havoc against traditions.

I smile and shake my head as I sit in one of the free chairs while the other ten board members look at me as if I have gone mad. In fact, I must look like someone who just escaped from the asylum, but I can't get the smile off my face.

"I know very well. In fact, I'm here to get rid of that annoying thirty percent that I don't want anymore," I say, pulling out one of the sheets my lawyer has drafted.

The murmur of approval that rises around the table fills my chest. Everyone wants a bigger slice of the cake, especially Warren, who has crossed his arms as grin spreads over his face.

"Are you here to get an offer? Of course, after closing the streaming division, your percentage will not be worth much since the company is worth less. Still, we can certainly make you a good price." His condescending tone makes me taste the victory I have at hand.

With a feeling of calm in my chest that makes me feel almost light, I say, "No, I'm here to get you to sign the waiver of your right of preemption on selling my shares so I can sell them to whoever I want."

The silence that falls in the room is almost absolute, at least until Warren bursts out laughing, and the others follow him with perplexed smiles.

"The girl must have fried your brain if you think you're coming here thinking that we will accept such a thing," he says amusedly. "Who do you think you are dealing with? Inexperienced idiots you can command to do what you want? Your father was right not to leave the company in your hands. You would have sent it into bankruptcy."

Once his words would have hurt me, but now the conviction that I can do something great on my own gives me the push to launch the counterattack.

"I imagined you would have said that. After all, you are not stupid. That's why I had a psychiatric evaluation done on my mother, which determined that she is not even able to take care of the most basic needs for her survival, much less make decisions for a billion-dollar company," I say, giving everyone a copy of the papers the doctors gave me.

Their eyes focus on the words in front of them, and their expressions become severe as the reading goes on.

"You had a psychiatric evaluation done on your mother without me being present? I'm her lawyer. It's not legal what you did," her lawyer yells at me from the other side of the table.

I turn to him with a smile that fills my face as I hand him the papers my lawyer has drawn up together with those the judge has provided me.

"Unfortunately for you, you have no power in this matter. This is the order from a judge who declares that you took advantage of a disabled person. There is evidence that you got prescriptions for drugs through your doctor friend, who will be banned from working in this country. There is also the testimony of my brother Evan who was present when my father ordered you to make sure my mother never contacted him. You helped him to isolate her from family members who want nothing but the best for her, aggravating her condition. A lawyer has already been appointed by the judge who will replace you in managing her life and assets with my and Evan's advice."

I see him bleaching in front of me without being able to give voice to anything that could change his situation. He has been doing whatever he wanted for years because he has always been first in my father's service rather than my mother's. Now that he no longer has anyone to protect his dirty business, he has to come to terms with the reality of his twenty years of crimes.

The silence is total. None of those present dares to argue because they realize that they didn't consider someone who has really worked for the good of this company a threat. They always thought I was just a pawn of my father's, a rich son who finds his job served on a silver platter. They have consistently underestimated me and treated me as a privileged person who doesn't deserve the place he occupies. They've never seen the efforts and passion I put into bringing forward something I believe in.

"We will have our lawyers on your back. We will appeal this ruling and drag you to the bottom," Warren threatens. Gone are the bold smiles and his arrogance.

"Of course, go ahead. Meanwhile, my brother and I have full control of forty percent of our mother's shares and will challenge every single decision you put to the vote. We will oppose every proposal until you can no longer lead this company where you want. The stocks will sink before you even get to court for a lawsuit."

I see the concern making its way into the expressions on their faces as they cast glances at Warren. He has always influenced their decisions. Everyone has always lowered themselves to kiss his feet; even now, they are subdued.

"Who to say that if we sign you will not do everything possible to put a spanner in the works?" he hisses between his teeth.

I shrug. "No one can guarantee it, but if you don't sign, you are certain I will do it. You are old enough to assess the risk."

I lean back and watch them fry in their chairs inside their

thousands of dollars suits. They are torn, but they don't need to contact their lawyers to understand that this matter could quickly become a bloodbath in which everyone loses money.

Warren is the first to take the papers and sign them, followed by all the others. I send a message to my lawyer waiting for me outside the door to formalize all the steps, and when Warren sees him, he shakes his head.

"I see that you have prepared for this ambush. You are your father's son."

I raise my shoulder and smile though the comparison hurts. "It is you who have always underestimated me."

***

Tim Harold's mansion is one of those tacky ones that dot the Hollywood Hills. He was never one who had good taste when furnishing his properties, but on the other hand, he was always one of my father's fiercest competitors. His broadcasting company has always been the one we have to compete with for any award. That's why when he comes to open the door, he is surprised to see me.

"Do you need a job now that your old man is dead?" he asks without even thinking of giving me his condolences. He's not one of Hollywood's ass-kissers. He's one of those used to having his kissed.

I laugh and shake my head. "No, I have other plans. But it's true. I came here on business."

I see the interest making its way across his face, but he shows no sign of letting me in.

"What do you think of owning thirty percent of the Steel

Broadcasting Company? Class B shares, no voting rights, but still a good chunk of the cake when it comes to dividends." I don't mince my words.

He studies me for a few moments with his impassive face.

"I heard the rumor that your old man hadn't left you the company, but I didn't want to believe that he had done such a thing. Do you want to take revenge on him?"

"I have other plans for my future. If I can also make him turn in the grave, why not have fun?"

As I say this, I realize I don't care about the company anymore. What for a lifetime was my goal soon became irrelevant, devoid of any meaning, and that doesn't give me any emotion.

"Tell your lawyer to talk to mine. I will make myself heard." He smiles at me.

The way Tim works, this is as good as a signature on the paper. He wouldn't have bothered if he hadn't already tasted the idea of getting his hands on my father's company.

"Right now, they are both already in his office discussing the proposal," I say with a smug smile at his surprise.

"You are a son of a bitch. Are you sure you don't want to come and work for me?" he asks with a smile on his face.

I shake my head as I turn around. "As I have already told you, I have other plans."

***

Dakota looks at me with her arms crossed and an eyebrow raised when I show up at her hotel room door. She's breathtakingly beautiful and reminds me of how stupid it was to let her go.

"I came here to apologize, but not to beg you to take me back," I begin, earning a furrowing of her eyebrows.

"It's not a good start." She nails me with her gaze.

I smile. "What I mean is that you will decide whether to forgive me or not. No forcing and no epic gestures. Just a sincere apology."

"Okay, go ahead."

I smile at her determination and her pout.

"I was wrong. There are no excuses or justifications. I behaved like an immature kid when I should have just talked to you and tell you how things were. It is not true that you can't understand. You are intelligent and mature, and you would have understood if I had told you that I felt humiliated and robbed of sixteen years of career." I feel a weight that I had been carrying for quite a while lift from my chest.

Dakota looks at me, less sulky than before, but says nothing.

"I struggled to put up with everything that happened. I still struggle to get clarity on where my future will go, but that doesn't justify the horrible way I treated you. If you decide to give me a second chance, I will be the happiest man on earth, but if you decide that you no longer want to deal with me, I can understand. I'm not going to sit here and tell you what I feel for you because a person my age would have come to terms with his feelings sooner and told you when it was time, not at the end of an apology. You deserve to hear it for real when there are no grudges or quarrels. You deserve to smile when I tell you what I feel for you, not hear it in front of a hotel door with a pout on your face."

I look into her eyes and see the tears shining. I would like to hug her and tell her I am sorry, but this would mean dragging her to me in a moment she is weak. I want her to think about it and evaluate the idea of forgiving me because she trusts me and not on a moment's impulse. So I leave the keys to the house in her hand, turn around, and retrace the corridor, hoping that sooner or later she will decide to use them.

***

"Are you sure you want it? It has been closed for years, and there is a lot of work to do. If you want, I have new ones in Burbank where you would spend a third to fix them as you want," says the owner of the warehouse in front of me.

I observe it, noticing the peeling walls and the graffiti that can be glimpsed on the innermost parts.

"I'm sure."

The man shakes his head and smiles.

"Your father asked me for years, but he wanted to have them for a cheap price, and I always refused to sell them to him," he confesses.

I smile. I know that my father wanted this complex of warehouses because it borders the studios of his company, and he wanted to double the area on which to expand. He had to give in and take another complex in Burbank. That's why I want it.

"I'll pay you the market price if you give it to me quickly."

The man studies me for a few more seconds. "You know your offices will face your old office, don't you?"

I turn around and smile at him. "That's why I want it."

I want my father, from the hell he is in, to see my empire grow and become bigger and more prosperous than his. I want them to be close so that he always has a clear comparison from down here and can gnaw in the knowledge that I, too, can do something great. Perhaps even bigger and more important than what he built.

CHAPTER 28

Dakota

"So you decided to forgive him?" Tracy asks as she sips a Frappuccino while we walk along Venice Beach.

It's been a month since Aaron came to my hotel to apologize, and as much as his words touched me, he was right about one thing, I had to be the one to decide, and doing it in the rush of the moment was not a wise decision. Too many times, I forgave Serena because the apologies seemed sincere, but then I found myself in front of the same behavior. I needed to be sure of the step I was taking.

The relationship between Aaron and me was born from a forced cohabitation and inside the bubble of his home that protected us from everything. As soon as reality crashed our lives, our relationship began to falter. Deciding to use the keys and go live with a man I am in love with requires more than beautiful words and a repentant look. It requires that I am sure of taking this step. And I needed to reflect on whether I'm ready to commit to him for what seems to be a long, very long time. Strong feelings and phenomenal sex shouldn't cloud my judgment. For this reason, I needed time to detach myself and think about it.

"Why? Shouldn't I?" My question is a bit hesitant because, although I've made a thousand reasons about what I want to do with Aaron, maybe she knows some reason why I shouldn't live with him.

"No, I was wondering why it took you so long. I mean, you are both very invested in this relationship, and, although I admit that he behaved like an asshole, there are extenuating circumstances that make me cheer for him." She smiles at me.

The squeeze in my stomach her first question caused dissipates, leaving room for a feeling of butterflies when I think of Aaron.

"Because I'm not forced to live with him this time, and I want him to be the right choice. There will always be someone who will say that I don't deserve the success I have because of my relationship with him. I don't want to make this decision lightly."

Tracy smiles at me and shakes her head.

"Are you sure you're only twenty-four?"

"Trust me that sometimes I feel as old as Aaron."

Tracy laughs leaning against the back of the bench on which we sit, then observes me carefully.

"Are you really determined to help him? Many of those who worked in the division have already found another job."

"I know. But you are still without a new boss. This gives me hope that the bests are waiting for his return."

I know Tracy is waiting for Aaron to call her to work for him again, but if I've come to know him at least a little over the last year, I don't think he's going to involve anyone at least until he's gotten back on his feet and has something to offer the people who work for him. Rumors circulating in the industry say they saw him in jeans and a T-shirt at the warehouse he bought for the company he found, throwing garbage in the bins. As much as I made fun of him because he never takes off his jacket and tie, I can't believe he is doing it.

"Now, don't be the know-it-all with me, but you're right. I know some are waiting for the right job," she confirms.

"Can you see if they're interested in a new streaming service?"

"I already contacted them when I received your phone call. They are calling other people. As much as Aaron has a reputation as a person who terrorizes his employees, everyone knows that he is the best in this industry."

"I knew you were waiting for him!" I laugh amusedly.

"Why, aren't you? I know you've received at least three offers, but you've turned them all down." She winks at me, and I blush.

My agent is having panic attacks because I'm refusing offers that are nothing short of amazing. Two of these are as the protagonist in two films next to Hollywood stars who I didn't even know were aware of my existence.

"I'm waiting for the right job." I wink at her while sipping from my Frappuccino.

"Okay, since you are sure about it, I will send you a list of people you need to call to explain the situation. You have to tell them to spread the word. I'll take care of the other half of the list," she tells me before a group of teenagers approaches us, squeaking.

"Dakota, can we take a selfie with you?" a blond asks, the bravest one, perhaps thirteen or fourteen years old.

"Yes, of course," I say as Tracy gets up from the bench and walks away, saying goodbye with a wave of her hand.

"We're so sorry that your show has been canceled," says another who sits next to me for the photo.

"I'm sorry, too, but there will be other shows you'll love, I'm sure." I smile.

"Really? Do you already know which one?" she asks with eyes that shine with emotion.

This is why I love being an actress. Not the selfies with fans or the number of followers on Instagram or TikTok. But because I can give a face to characters that kids love and want to see on screen. These girls cry, laugh, despair, and rejoice together with those characters who, week after week, appear on the screen. It is as if, little by little, they become their friends, part of a family and a community that unites them beyond the geographical area in which they live. They feel they belong to something, whether it's the fandom of a show, a book, or their favorite band. The sense of belonging is so strong that the feelings that bind them become sincere, powerful, and sometimes more than family ties.

"I still can't tell you anything, but if it goes as I hope, you'll soon hear from my Instagram account." I wink at her as I get up and get ready to go and make those phone calls that Tracy has instructed me to make.

"Really?" the blond asks, almost jumping on the spot with excitement.

"Of course!" I smile at her, and an idea comes to mind seeing their excitement. It could be a total fiasco or the reason why we soar. "Actually, you know what? We will need a street team to promote this project. If you give me your emails, I will contact you as soon as we have news. What do you say? Would you like to be the first official participants of the street team?" I ask them and the excited screams from their lips are almost deafening.

"Are you kidding? It would be an honor to be part of it," another girl who has remained on the sidelines until now tells me.

When I leave Venice Beach, I have seven email addresses of enthusiastic girls and an idea in mind that I don't know will ever work. Still, if Aaron is brave enough to clean garbage from his warehouses, I can think of setting up something that could help us launch this company.

***

When we arrive in front of the address that Tracy sent us, we find the gates closed by a chain that doesn't have a padlock. The woman next to me looks up and lingers on the shining entrance of the Steel Broadcasting Company, then on the graffiti-covered plywood panels of Aaron's new company just a few meters away.

"Of course, if he wanted to send a big middle finger to his father, it is loud and clear," she chuckles in amusement.

I smile because it's true. There was a never-before-seen uproar when Aaron sold his shares in the company to the competition. They almost cried scandal. Many have said it was his way of taking revenge on his father for not giving him the company, but those who know him know this is not the case. Selling the shares for an exorbitant amount of money was just a way to get the money to buy an entire neighborhood next to his old company and build a new one with his name on it. This is his revenge against his father. The middle finger Tracy talks about.

"Shall we enter? Let's see if inside he has a neon sign with his name that he will place right next to their immaculate gates," I suggest, and some of those who accompany us behind me chuckle.

It doesn't take long to find Aaron in front of the only warehouse with the doors open and hear him swear. When we enter, we watch him kneeling on a pile of rubble in jeans and without a shirt, sweaty, with his hair undone and dirty with dust. I think no one has ever seen him like this, given the shocked faces of those present.

"You know you have enough money to hire labor, don't you?" Tracy's voice makes him turn around, startled.

"What the hell are you doing here?" he asks, getting up and wiping the sweat from his forehead. I can't look away from his perfect body. Tracy notices that I'm staring and elbows me.

"We heard that a new streaming company in the city will start with new productions, and we thought we'd bring our resumes." I wink at him as he approaches.

"And maybe even a desk where we can put them," adds one of the technicians behind me, pulling a laugh from everyone.

Aaron looks at the fifty-six faces in front of him, all people who worked in the streaming division he built and carried on from scratch. People who believed in him from the beginning and now continue to support him. His eyes are veiled with gratitude and tears. It's the first time I've seen him so vulnerable in public.

"You know there's nothing, don't you? What you see is all that exists of this company," he points out, making sure that the people here have understood that there is still a lot to do.

"You think about finding the movies. We'll take care of setting up this place," says one of the guys who wanders around with his nose in the air to evaluate the situation.

"Also, if you thought you could get this place back on its feet alone, either you went crazy, or you overestimated your skills as a carpenter," adds another, and, this time, Aaron bursts out laughing too.

"I didn't go crazy. I wanted to get an idea of what is in here to give clear instructions to the workers. Physical work helps me think."

The people who have followed us so far begin to look around and evaluate the situation, especially the technicians. At the same time, some of the writers and production assistants are simply curious to see the wagon they are jumping on.

"It's better if you really find a desk because we can't work in these conditions," adds Sarah Webber, one of the executive producers of Aaron's shows, a big name who could have gone to work for anyone but chose to stay by his side.

"Weren't you the one who can work anywhere, even in a trailer next to the explosions of a war movie?" he teases her.

"I do, but the little boy, the intern you told me to hire as a writer, needs a quiet place to create magic. By the way, you were right. He's brilliant. He has fresh ideas that can interest people of the age group we are aiming for." She nods to one of the guys who is more or less my age.

Aaron smiles. "Did you have any doubts about my ability to understand the potential of people or projects?"

"Do you think I would be here if I thought of such a thing?" She raises an eyebrow to challenge him.

Aaron again lays his eyes on our faces and pauses for a long time as if to understand what we really think.

"Are you sure you want to embark on something like this? There are no guarantees. Christ, I have no idea what to start producing."

I smile at him. "For that, I have some ideas. But if we are here, it is because we are all convinced. When Tracy and I called them, we explained the situation, and they accepted the challenge."

The sweet smile that he gives me almost melts me on the spot. I missed him, and I only realized now how good I was at resisting a month without seeing him. His fingers reach out toward me and touch my hand.

"Have you decided to give up the actress career?" he asks me, perplexed.

"No, but no one forbids me to give you suggestions." I wink at him and see him smiling again.

"Now go take a shower. You stink. I have already rented a conference room at the Hilton so we can get everyone together and make a plan on how to get started. As romantic as it is to have the first meeting here, we need a place to sit, power outlets for our computers, and a table to place notebooks." Tracy begins to give orders with her usual efficiency.

"Are you going to come with me?" Aaron whispers to me when Tracy and Sarah walk away to call the others and tell them the plan.

His voice is insecure, almost uncertain whether or not I have decided to return to live with him.

"Yes. Let's go home," I whisper before kissing him.

I don't know if this company will ever take off or if there will be a future for me as an actress after the show's cancellation, but I'm happy to find it out next to a man like Aaron.

CHAPTER 29
Aaron

I watch Dakota's long legs lie on the deck chair next to me in the pool. She's focused on her computer, researching something she didn't want to tell me. She's beautiful as always, and I still don't believe I almost lost her because I can't handle my feelings when my father is involved.

If there's one thing that this whole ordeal has taught me, it's that I want to enjoy life more. I will certainly not give up my job, but I will devote more time to being with the woman next to me who has decided to embark on this adventure with me. Because despite having received several proposals for auditions, she believes so much in this project that she decided to wait for the right opportunity with my company. She said she is sure that sooner or later, the right job will come, and in the meantime, she has started to work hard to set up a street team of girls who can spread the word online for our new projects. I don't know how she came up with such a thing, but the fact that she believes in me to the point of pausing her career to work on it is something I never considered I could want in life.

"If you keep staring at my legs like that, you'll never be able to finish your work. Didn't you have to go and check on the progress at the new offices?"

I smile as I look away from her legs. She has one of those serene expressions I enjoyed over the last three months since she returned to live with me.

"Are you going to tell my boss if I don't do my job? Wait, I'm the boss," I tease, reaching out my hand and pinching her side lightly.

She sticks out her tongue and laughs, amused. "You're never going to stop pointing this out, are you?"

I am the owner of a neighborhood with seven semi-destroyed warehouses, and I have never felt so rich and powerful as right now.

"No. I will keep repeating it until I am a decrepit old man and someone is doing my job for me."

"Good, because you must never forget how far you have come and how successful you have been," she tells me before returning to the laptop.

"You know I love you, don't you?" I tell her as her head snaps in my direction.

I've never told her this. I promised her that when I did, it would be at a time when we were not driven by a quarrel or an irrepressible joy. Because it is easy to love someone in a rush of emotions, but when routine creeps into your relationship, you see if that love remains. It is easy to say *I love you* when violent emotions stir in your chest, but in the tranquility of silence, you really understand the value of that feeling.

Dakota gets up from her deck chair and slips between my legs, kissing me before sitting down and leaning her back to my chest. I put her laptop on the table and hold her to me.

"I suspected you loved me, but it's nice to have verbal confirmation." She laughs, and I laugh with her.

"Well, I want you to be sure I have no doubt."

"I can't tell you now. Because it would appear that I only tell you in response to yours. Because I feel obligated," she says, and I smile. I cannot contradict her logic.

I hold her tighter and enjoy her warmth on me.

"But I have one thing that will make you fall in love with me more," she continues, stretching out her arm and grabbing her laptop.

I look at the screen where there is a girl with blue hair and arms covered with tattoos.

"Do you remember that you couldn't find the author of the fantasy saga I shared with you? I did some research and went back from her pen name to her real name. You won't believe it, but she lives here in Los Angeles, and every day, she goes to have coffee and write a few chapters here." She smiles at me as she points out a spot in the Westwood area.

I lean over and look at her in disbelief. "How the hell did you do it? Tracy searched for her for days, and not even my lawyers could find anything."

She shrugs and smiles at me. "I remembered an old post on Reddit where they talked about her. I discovered another pen name of hers, and I found out that she opened an LLC to publish her books. The company's data are public, so I found her real name, searched for her online, and found out that she lives around UCLA."

"You are incredible. Really. Are you sure you want to be an actress in life? Because you would have a future as a private investigator." I laugh amusedly.

We tried for weeks without results to find this woman, and

she managed to find her name and address in half a day of research.

"No, I'm not so good. I couldn't find you an address. She uses a PO Box." She shrugs as if not to believe that what she has done is really a miracle.

"What do you think we should do now?" I ask, curious to know how she would deal with this situation.

"I think you should go to her. Writing her a letter or even sending her the contract would be completely impersonal, and there is no way to see her reaction when she receives it. But you can't show up alone as one of those chilling stalkers. You should bring a woman, like Tracy, who can reassure her that you are not a maniac who wants to kill her," she explains, and I am fascinated.

"Come with me," I suggest.

She turns to look at me, puzzled.

"Seriously? Tracy has more experience than me. She could help you convince her."

"You're a fan of the series. You are the one who adores her books. You managed to get me to read a fantasy romance. I'm sure you'll be able to get her to read the contract."

She watches me for a few seconds, as if trying to understand if I'm making fun of her.

"Prepare the contract. We are going to visit her today."

***

Two hours later, we are sitting at a café in front of a woman with blue hair and a bewildered look named Linda.

"You two have completely gone crazy."

Dakota just explained that she's a fan of hers, that we'd like to use her books for a series, and that we have a contract ready for her to sign. I must say that I would have the same reaction if someone came to the table where I am drinking coffee and told me that they have a contract that could change my life.

"We are very serious. We want your saga to be the first series produced by Aaron's company." The smile that Dakota has on her face is something to frame. I have never seen her so enthusiastic about proposing her idea to someone. Because, in the end, I have to admit that this was her idea, I just followed it.

"Tell me if I understood correctly. You would like to offer me a contract to sell you the rights for a TV show when you don't even have an office for your new company? Do you have at least a budget for the series? Or to pay me? I understand that you have experience, given what you did for your father's company, but you have no financial guarantee. By the way, congratulations for having the courage to leave what you worked for all those years. It takes balls to make such a decision. I still have to find the courage to give up my job as a lawyer despite being a seven-figure author," she says with a firmness that tells me she knows what she is talking about.

I nod and hand her another document the company's lawyer and financial advisor have prepared for me. I expected doubts from her.

"Here you can find the financial situation of the company, the names of the lenders who have already agreed to finance the project, and the business plan that will allow us to produce the first season and, assuming it is successful and renewed, also the second and third. I didn't plan for other seasons because it would have been just speculation with numbers impossible to predict." I offer her the sheets, and I find her pleasantly surprised by my preparation.

"Did you manage to prepare all this in two hours?" Dakota asks me with wide eyes.

I smile at her and shake my head. "No, I've been working on it for months in the hope of being able to put her under contract one day. I just couldn't find her."

The smile that spreads across her lips is priceless.

"And you give me all this documentation without making me sign a confidentiality agreement on this meeting?" Linda rightfully questions me.

I raise an eyebrow. "Would you have signed it at the beginning when two crazy people sat in front of you to interrupt your afternoon?"

"No, I would have you kicked out of this place and called the police." She grins.

"Do you want to sign it now?" I ask her hopefully. If my lawyer knew what I just did, he would kill me, but I had to win her trust first.

"Yes, give me that piece of paper." She raises her lips in a half-smile aware of the game I played.

I don't know what kind of lawyer she is, but I'm sure she knows this is not the standard procedure to option a book. She also understands that I came here playing all the cards I had in my hand, hoping she would sign. She could take this transparency of mine as a weakness because I am desperate or as my way of making her understand that I am so confident this series will be successful that I exposed myself personally. I just hope she doesn't use my proposal to raise the price and sell the rights to the competition.

"I'll take the contract home and the documents you gave me and read them. That is the best I can promise you. I exposed myself publicly once by publishing these books and almost found myself on drugs because of the threats I received. As much as I like to see my stories on screen, I don't trade my mental health for success."

This is enough for me. It is an outstanding achievement that we have already managed to convince her to give us a chance.

"We know what happened to you, and I'm already moving to build a street team of teenagers who will help me keep negative comments away. Our social media team can filter out bad comments. Still, I'm convinced that by giving the right people a voice, we can create a positive environment where people who like to stir up controversy won't find fertile ground," Dakota says with a fervor that makes me smile.

I like how she uses *us* to describe this project. Linda also smiles in front of her fervor.

"Have you decided not to pursue an acting career anymore? It's a shame because you would be perfect as the protagonist." Hers is a genuine regret of not being able to see her on-screen as the character she described so accurately in her books.

The smile that appears on Dakota's face is priceless.

"No, have you gone crazy? I'm already preparing for the part because I intend to participate in the auditions."

Linda laughs and nods, then gets up, grabs her stuff, and leaves.

"I'm happy." She winks at her. "I'll let you know what I think, okay?"

"Take as much time as you need," I say as I greet her with

my hand and watch her walk out of the coffee.

Dakota is practically quivering in the chair as she drinks from her coffee.

"Don't expect her to call us soon. It will take days to read the contract. Probably she will get help from some colleague who deals with this type of contract. Don't have too many expectations, okay? We are only at the beginning of the negotiation," I explain.

Dakota nods, but I see from how her eyes shine that she has high expectations from this meeting, and I am afraid she will be disappointed.

***

We arrive home a few hours later with the dinner we bought at the Chinese restaurant, returning from our appointment with Linda. While Dakota rests the containers on the table, I set it up. That's why I answer without thinking when the phone rings with a number I don't recognize.

"Aaron Steel."

"Aaron, it's Linda," she replies on the other side.

I am so petrified by her answer that I freeze in the middle of the kitchen with Dakota watching me, worried.

"I didn't expect to hear from you so soon." I try to probe the ground. Usually, when they call after so few hours, it is because they have looked at the figure and want to raise the stakes, refusing to sign the contract.

"Yes, it's not that there's much to think about with the amount you propose," she admits. I feel a little uncomfortable because I already know that it will be a rejection, and I will have to explain it to Dakota, who looks at me with hopeful eyes when she understands who it is.

"Have you read the entire contract? Including the part of the royalties for merchandising?" I try to bring the topic to other forms of payments. Sometimes people dwell only on the amount they collect upfront but gloss over the percentage of merchandise that can bring a continuous flow of money when the series is well underway.

"Yes, of course. That's why I decided to sign. It's a good proposal. I talked about it with my husband. I added some small clauses to the contract, nothing too disrupting. If you like, send it to me modified, and I'll let you have it signed through a courier," she replies efficiently, like someone who is used to doing this for work every day.

"That's fine. I am on it tonight and asking my lawyer to make the changes. I think I can send it to you in the morning." I try not to let the excitement I feel at this moment shine through too much.

I've signed hundreds of contracts, but this one tastes different. The excitement I feel in my chest is difficult to contain, and I must remember that she has not yet signed. I have yet to look at the changes she has requested, but it is difficult not to feel overwhelmed by this news that tastes of victory. I didn't realize how worried I was about receiving a rejection until I got this news.

"Perfect, I'm waiting for your email then. And write down my number. Not many of you have the private one," she adds with a smile that I can perceive from her tone of voice.

"Definitely. So I can brag to Dakota that I have the number of her favorite author."

Linda laughs as Dakota squeaks and jumps on the spot like a little girl.

"Speaking of Dakota, you don't need to do a casting for the protagonist, is it? You're not so crazy that you think she is not perfect," she asks me with a certain seriousness in her voice.

"I didn't even think about it, but I don't tell her because that way, she prepares better for the part." I wink at my partner, who is blushing, while Linda laughs again.

"Well, we'll hear from you tomorrow then."

"See you tomorrow," I confirm before closing the call.

Dakota throws her arms around my neck as soon as I put the phone down. I hold her tightly as she laughs and cries at the same time.

"Don't get caught up in the euphoria. She hasn't signed yet," I tell her, trying to protect her from any last-minute unforeseen events.

"Details. I would say that, at this point, it's just a formality," she tells me, giving me a light kiss on the lips.

"I have to look at the changes she asked me to make to the contract," I insist.

"Unless she asks you to sacrifice your firstborn, I don't see what she could ever ask, so out of mind, you can't sign." she kisses me again.

The tone of the phone call leaned toward a yes, and I can't help but share Dakota's optimism.

"Are you happy?" she whispers, looking at me with happiness in her eyes.

"Yes," I answer without having to think about it because I understand what happiness really is for the first time in my life. Sharing this success with the person I love is what I have always missed. This is what makes me happy, not the signing of a contract or the beginning of the first production of my company. It's Dakota's arms around my neck as she looks at me and rejoices with me in our success. A success that took two to achieve.

EPILOGUE
Dakota

"I've found a new movie for you!" I rush into Aaron's office with the book I just finished in my hand.

He looks up from his computer and shows off a smile that, like every time for two years now, makes my legs tremble. He leans against his chair and crosses his arms to his chest. His muscles stand out under the white shirt, and I'm happy to admire them since he doesn't wear a jacket.

Many things have changed since *Steel and Anderson Entertainment* took off to become one of the most dynamic and successful realities in the Los Angeles entertainment industry. The first thing is that Aaron no longer dresses in elegant suits but wears his shirt out of his pants, like the fake-young people he calls those his age who don't dress appropriately for the office.

The second is that he spends his lunch break in the common room furnished with sofas, armchairs, and tables, where most of those who work here stop for a quick lunch break. He never used to do something like that but decided he didn't want to be labeled *The Butcher* again, so he started trying to have some relationship with his employees. He found that during these moments is where the best ideas to bring to life come out. At least two new productions for two tv shows were born between a salad and a sandwich sitting on the sofas of that room.

The third is that he takes a lot of time for his private life. He learned to delegate some of his work, and on weekends, when neither of us is busy, we like to explore the city or sometimes spend the nights reading books.

"Really?" he says, reaching out a hand and inviting me to sit on his legs.

"Really. She is an independent author who has a lot of success on TikTok with a retelling of Peter Pan." I enjoy his arms around my waist and his lips on my neck.

He laughs, amused.

"I don't even want to know what Peter Pan could do to Wendy. The books you read are usually interesting."

"It may not be suitable for minors, but you would definitely attract the attention of many women," I admit.

"Is there something in there I don't know? Something we can try on this desk?" he whispers as he puts his hand under my shirt.

I really wish I could stay here and enjoy his attention, but I don't want to keep my colleagues waiting.

"We are on a break because they have to dry a part of the set that flooded after the stunts in the pool. If I don't come back, they'll kill me," I tell him getting up from his knees, earning a grunt of protest from him.

"By the way. Linda called me this morning and told me to compliment you on your interpretation of last night's episode finale. She said she cried all the time." He smiles at me sweetly, with that proud look that I often see on his face when he talks to me about my work.

"So all the tears I shed and the nightmares of the following days were useful!" I smile as I place the book on the table. "I'll leave you the novel if you want to read a few pages during your lunch break. I really like the gloomy atmosphere. I think it is suitable for an adult audience that loves the slightly less romantic version of fairy tales."

"I'll definitely take a look," he confirms, pausing to study my face.

"Why do you look at me like that?"

"Because I don't know if you're sexier when you pull out an Oscar-winning performance on set or when you turn into a producer." His words are sincere as if they were a reason more than a compliment.

"I'm sexy when I use my brain, Aaron. That's how I won you over." I smile at him before winking and leaving the room.

I look at him through the glass wall, and I see him smiling with that mixture of sweetness and desire that made me capitulate almost three years ago, and that will never stop making me feel butterflies in my stomach. They told me I was crazy when I decided to live with him at twenty-three, but no one ever understands how difficult it is to find two brains traveling on the same wavelength. When you find someone with whom you just need an exchange of glances to understand his thoughts, you don't stop in front of the age difference or social status. Because in a world of chaos and distractions, when you find the person who brings the silence around you every time you look into his eyes, you don't let him escape.

I arrived in Los Angeles alone with a suitcase full of dreams. I never imagined that the best part of making them become true was to find someone to share them with.

***

As an indie author, I sincerely appreciate you reading and helping spread the word!

If you loved The Producer: Aaron, please consider leaving a quick review. Reviews help readers like you find books they'll love.

***

Sign up for Erika Vanzin's newsletter to get free short stories, exclusive deals, and more:

https://www.erikavanzin.com/newsletter.html

BOOKS BY ERIKA VANZIN

ROADIES SERIES (Complete)

THE HUNTING CLUB

About the author

Erika Vanzin is the Italian Amazon bestselling author of the rock star romance Roadies Series.

After traveling around the world with her husband, she settled down in Seattle, enjoying the marvelous Pacific Northwest. She brought from Italy a couple of suitcases, fifteen boxes full of books, and her most successful novels translated into English.

While she is not writing, she enjoys reading books, watching the Kraken hockey games, and working on DIY projects.

Keep in touch with Erika via the web:

Website: https://www.erikavanzin.com/

BookBub: https://www.bookbub.com/authors/erika-vanzin

Goodreads: https://www.goodreads.com/author/show/14437720.Erika_Vanzin

Facebook: https://www.facebook.com/erikavanzinauthor

Instagram: https://www.instagram.com/clumsyeki/

TikTok: https://www.tiktok.com/@authorerikavanzin

Twitter: https://twitter.com/ErikaVanzin

Newsletter: https://www.erikavanzin.com/newsletter.html

Acknowledgements

I could not have written this book without the support of my husband. Thank you so much for always being there for me and also for embarrassing me by telling your colleagues, "My wife writes very spicy books. You should read them!" They will never look at me the same, but I love the enthusiasm you put into pushing my novels. I would like to be brave as you are when you talk about my books.

To my beta readers and best friends, Chiara and Annalisa, thank you for your friendship, support, wisdom, and, most importantly, the laughs. I wouldn't be doing this without your endless cheering.

To my editor, Cameron, thank you for saving me when I thought I would have never published this book. Thank you for the encouraging words and the enthusiasm you put into helping me to give Aaron and Dakota the story they deserved.

To my TikTok mastermind, Chelsea, I have no idea how you do it, but you are the miracle I was praying for. Thank you for always putting a smile on my face.

To my ARC team, what can I say? Your enthusiasm for my books astounds me, and I can't believe the amount of interest you had in Aaron and Dakota. Thank you from the bottom of my heart for reading this book and providing your honest review.

To all the Bookstagrammers, Bloggers, and Booktokers who have supported me and reviewed my books, thank you from the bottom of my heart. You are a vital part of this journey. Thank you for always having my back. I'm so grateful to be part of this wonderful book community.

Last but certainly not least, to all my readers. Thank you for sticking around with this one. I know it was difficult to let the Roadies Series go. Thank you for reading Aaron and Dakota story and waiting for them with the same trepidation you had for Damian, Thomas, Michael, Simon, and Evan. Thank you for your support! I hope you will continue this journey with me.